Better Daddy

Dad Coms

Book 2

Brittanée Nicole

Jenni Bara

First Edition October 2025

Cover Art: elenbushe_art

Cover Design: Mel D Designs

Formatting by Sara of Sara PA's Services

Editing by Beth at VB Edits

Dedication

To the moms who feel forgotten. You all deserve a British Daddy who calls you sweetheart and whispers dirty things in your ears. We'll lend you Sully.

PLAYLIST

Wild Thing - The Troggs
Pour Some Sugar On Me - Def Leppard
Someone Like You - Van Morrison
(I Can't Get No) Satisfaction - The Rolling Stones
Don't Stop Believin' - Journey
Have Yourself a Merry Little Christmas - Michael Bublé
Bye Bye Bye - *NSYNC
Before You Leave Me - Alex Warren
Us - James Bay

<u>Jersey Boys:</u>
All The Way - Frank Sinatra
One Call Away - Charlie Puth

Contents

CHAPTER 1
Sloane

No, no, no. Not this one too.

I blow out a breath, sending the curly wisps from my fancy updo fluttering, and growl. I styled my hair this morning, and now I'm regretting my choice, wishing I'd pulled it back in a simple ponytail to keep it out of my face. Maybe then these stray hairs wouldn't be sticking to my sweaty cheeks. Because yeah, now I'm sweaty on top of everything else.

Today, for the first time in seven long years, I'm *supposed* to be in court. For seven years I've been deprived of doing the one thing I love most about law. Arguing. God, I was good at it. For the last few years the only practice I've had arguing is with a pint-sized opponent.

We've argued over time limits on his tablet: he wanted seventeen hours; I gave him thirty minutes a night.

We've battled over sock colors: white seemed perfectly reasonable to me, but last week, bright blue was the only color he'd wear.

For years we've gone rounds when it comes to what he eats. Nothing but chicken nuggets, and only a certain brand. Oh, and slushies, thanks to his Uncle Cal. Maybe I should be annoyed by the slushy part, but honestly, a little variation, even if it's one hundred percent processed sugar, feels like a win.

Yes, I celebrate the tiny wins against my six-year-old son. What mom doesn't?

In the last seven years, I've also become really good at losing fights. Every single one of them with my ex. Though, can I really call him my ex if we're still married?

If asked, he'd probably say I was the one picking the fights. He'd also swear I won the majority of them. Of course, he'd be wrong. No one wins in a marriage like ours. Where both people are miserable, barely talking to one another, and almost divorced.

But I've been working hard to start over. My life now is supposed to look different. *I need it to be different.*

"Julius, I need you," I call from the bathroom suite. It's possibly the fanciest one I've ever been in, and I've been in plenty over the years. Especially early on in my marriage, when I often traveled with Sully.

Sully, with his charming English accent, a smirk that, for years, he reserved only for me, and his expensive taste. He only ever wanted the best of the best, and his love for me made me feel as if I was the best. For a while, it was my reality. We were *the* couple. The ones on Instagram who look like they have hot sex all the time and live amazing lives.

We did too. The sex was truly amazing. God, I miss sex.

I didn't fake it for social media. Hell, I didn't have social media. Our life really was perfect.

I glare down at the next test. "You will not be positive." I twist both of my fingers, willing my wish to come true, then yell, "*Julius.*"

My overzealous and slightly sarcastic assistant peeks in, his brown eyes scouring the space like he's worried he'll find me standing naked in the freaking lounge.

"Get in here," I hiss.

He steps in slowly, his shoulders practically at his ears. "Are you feeling okay?"

"Has Will left yet?"

My boss, and my former law school colleague, is a partner in this firm, *his father's firm,* and he and I were supposed to be in court in—I glance down at my Movado watch—ten minutes ago.

Julius winces. "Yes, about thirty minutes ago."

I sigh, my body slumping. This is my case, and I stayed up late to prep every night for the last week. I figured that explained the exhaustion. The dizziness this morning? My body's reaction to missing dinner last night because I was too busy reading the wife's deposition and the Bergen family's best interest reports.

"Look at that and tell me what you see." I point to the counter, then turn around and pace the luxury cushioned floor.

Is it heated? Is that why I'm drenched in sweat? I slip off a heel and plant a foot on it. *Motherfucker.* It is heated. I toss the other one off, accidentally sending it flying through the air. It hits the wall with a loud thud, then clatters to the floor.

There's no point in wearing Louboutins when all I'm doing is occupying the women's restroom at the firm. My celebratory heels mock me from where they're tipped on their sides. Looks like it was premature of me to wear them before my first day back in court.

But they're rose gold! How could I not buy the rose gold heels?

Julius steps up to the counter, his reflection clear in the gold-etched mirror, his eyes darting every which way. He's probably worried that I was aiming for him when I kicked off the shoe.

"Stop being so dramatic and tell me what you see."

He takes a deep breath, his chest rising and falling, and looks down. Immediately, he lets out a loud screech. "Is that a pregnancy test?"

"Shh," I hiss, seriously contemplating picking up that shoe and lobbing it at him. "Could you *not* tell the entire office what we're doing in here?"

"We aren't doing anything in here," Julius says, backing away from the stick.

"Oh, for fuck's sake. Can you just tell me what you see?" I pluck the stick off the marble counter and thrust it into his face. "Is that a plus sign?"

He stumbles back, almost falling on his ass this time. "Did you pee on that?"

Annoyance courses through my veins, bringing my body temperature up to molten levels. "It's got the cover on it. Stop being so dramatic and *read.*"

I flick it with my wrist, and this time, he really does trip and fall. Now that he's on the ground, I crouch and hold it close to his face. Can't get away from me now. "So?"

He squeezes his lips shut and winces like he's worried he'll get splashed with pee. Men are so freaking dramatic.

I wait him out, knowing he'll give in eventually. Like clockwork, thirty seconds later, he sighs and says, "Yes, it's a plus sign."

"Shit." I shoot up and stride to the line of other tests. "Check these."

"Mrs. Murphy," he says, standing, "when I said I'd do anything for you, I meant in the capacity of an assistant. Not *this.*"

"And I told you not to call me Mrs. Murphy. It's Sloane. Mrs. Murphy is married to Mr. Murphy, and I am *not.*"

He shrugs, backing toward the door. "Pretty sure Mr. Murphy's going to be very surprised to learn that Mrs. Murphy is having his baby."

I dart around him, arms out, feet planted wide, blocking him from exiting. "We don't even know if that's true. Get over here and look."

Finally realizing he's not getting out of here, he dusts off the lapels of his very fancy Tom Ford and shuffles over to the tests. "Positive, positive, positive. This one says *plus three weeks.*" He glances back at me. "Did you buy out the pharmacy or what?"

I roll my eyes. "Uh, yeah. Law school 101: always be prepared."

"If you really lived by that rule, I'm guessing you wouldn't be pregnant." He turns around, and when he locks eyes with me, he cringes, hands held up in defense. "Sorry. You've got me all out of sorts with your pee sticks."

I shake my head. "I need to see a doctor."

"Yes, I think you do."

"Now." Stepping aside, I throw out an arm, motioning to the door.

He points to his chest. "You want me to make an appointment for you?"

I don't deign to respond. I only glare.

"Right, of course," he mumbles, likely giving in so easily because it means he can leave the women's room.

"And make sure they can see me this morning."

He shakes his head. "You want me to come hold your hand too?"

For a single second, I feel relieved. The idea of doing this alone scares the shit out of me. The relief quickly evaporates when I take in his flat expression and realize he was being sarcastic. I don't reply, instead turning toward the mirror and absentmindedly fixing my hair.

The second the door closes, the first tear falls. I really am on my own. I have no one to hold my hand. That's the only thing I ever loved about these appointments. Having my husband at my side, his attention fixed on me. With his hand in mine, I felt like I could do anything.

Two hours later, as I sit in the exam room by myself, I feel lost, without the first clue what to do.

"You're sure that's not like a cancerous mass?"

The tech throws me a scowl. Yeah, I'm guessing most people wouldn't prefer cancer over a baby.

For the record, I don't either. But lately, everything has gone wrong, so it would be par for the course. Can't blame me for being thorough.

"No. Cancerous masses don't have heartbeats. And this is a strong one."

I nod as I stare at the little gummy bear on the screen. That's what we called T.J. the first time we saw him. A little gummy bear. Sully brought home a whole bag of them the next day. Of course, I didn't eat a single one. He laughed his ass off at me, but I thought it'd be weird to eat something that looked like our child.

"Hi, little bear," I say to our baby.

My heart thuds painfully. Looks like I have to call my future ex-husband to tell him we're having a baby.

CHAPTER 2
Sully

"Hellooo!"

I wince at the sound of Madame Esmeralda's voice. The high-pitched greeting instantly sends my blood pressure rising. The psychic who lives above our shithole of a law office is always dropping in unannounced. Her gold bracelets jingle as she peeks in, her head tilted, her curly black hair—and that haunting white streak—bouncing.

Cal, my brother and law partner, constantly talks about a ring this woman supposedly wears. He swears he can never look away from it. I, on the other hand, am always caught off guard by her haunted hair and violet eyes. They *have* to be contacts.

"Callahan." Just his name sounds like a song as it leaves her lips. The woman is a walking psychic stereotype, from the layers of flowing floor-length dresses from the 1970s to her big hoop earrings, to the airy, sometimes chilling voice. "We will need to reschedule our session."

My brother's shoulders slump. Why he's disappointed that she isn't going to babble at him for thirty minutes is ridiculous to me, but he's bought into her so-called predictions, hook, line, and sinker.

"I know it's disappointing, but it's for the best. Your path is stable."

Successful scam artists tend to focus on telling people what they want to hear and talking in riddles. Madame E is good at both.

With a shake of my head, I drown out their discussion. My workload is unmanageable now that we've moved into my dad's old office in Jersey. The three partners—Cal, Brian and I—are required to be here, and by some miracle, we convinced Lo, our paralegal, to come too. She's the only reason we're keeping our heads above water.

Until recently, we ran one of the biggest family law firms in New York City, with over one hundred support staff and associates. I suppose technically, we still do. But thanks to my father's idiotic trust provisions, the four of us are stuck working in a rat-infested office building in Jersey for the next year.

Fuck, we have so much work to do, yet Madame E has once again distracted Cal and Lo with stories of the ghost she swears lives in this building.

"Enough," I bark before they can fall deeper into her nonsense.

Instantly, I'm hit in the side of the head with a small orange ball. It falls to Lo's desk and bounces along the edge until it falls to the floor. My arsehole brother has such good aim he hardly needs to look at me to nail me with that bloody basketball.

"Wanker." I snatch it off the floor before Cal can. "No more balls."

He smirks. "It seems Mr. Grumpypants hasn't had his happy-nappy today."

While Madame E chuckles, Lo groans. "No. That one doesn't work."

Cal shrugs. "I like it."

Of course he does. He's thoroughly annoyed us all with his little rhymes since he decided walkie-talkie was such a fun word.

It's baffling to me that we share DNA.

"I'm done." I'm not sure why I'm even standing here anymore. I came into Lo's office to ask her about a complaint we need served, and she confirmed it's done, so it's time to get back to my office and the peace and quiet it'll give me. As I turn for the door, Madame E steps into my path.

She tips her head, that single white streak of hair catching my eye. Lips pursed, she narrows her purple eyes on me.

I try not to squirm under her gaze.

"Sullivan," she says, her tone serious. "You need to get ready. The incubator is on the way."

See? Riddles.

"Incubator?" Cal's face lights up. "Are we getting chickens next?"

"No." Lo is the one who practically shouts the single word, but it might as well have been me. Over the last few months, my brother has brought home forty-odd plants, at least half a dozen fish, and an oversized cat, all because of this damn woman's riddles. "You promised no more things."

"This is for Sullivan. Nothing to concern you." Madame E turns and sashays out.

For me? There is no bloody way I'm bringing home a chicken or any other type of feathered creature. Especially since Cal's enormous cat, one of Madame E's more outlandish suggestions, would probably eat it.

"Wait." Cal rushes after the old woman, with Lo on his heels.

"For fuck's sake, let the woman go. We need to work." I stalk to my office and slam the door. They won't listen to me, but that's no longer my problem. Inside my quiet office, I can get back to work so that when T.J. gets out of school, I can focus on him.

Since I'm forced to live in Jersey while my wife and son remain in the flat we once shared in New York City, I don't get nearly as much time with him as I want. If I have it my way, that'll change soon.

This move was forced upon me by my father's will. Even in death, the man is a force to be reckoned with. Maybe it should have come as a surprise that he was in bed with a woman not even half his age—hell, she's practically half my age—when he died, but alas, it was completely on brand for Terrance Murphy. The will is what truly shocked us all.

Before the reading, we were all under the impression that it would be straight forward. He'd leave the firm to his two sons and our best friend Brian, who's always been like another son to our father. The firm he spent his entire life building, elevating it from a two-person operation in Jersey to the current massive office in New York.

Technically, he did all of those things. He just put the firm into a trust first and included a bunch of ridiculous stipulations for us to keep it. Brian, Cal, and I can eventually take over, but in order to do so, we have to spend a year in New Jersey, working and living in the building where he long ago started out.

If that wasn't enough, our spouses and children are required to live here with us as well. And getting my wife, who filed for divorce just months before my father's death, to agree to leave her beautiful New York penthouse for a run-down mouse-infested flat in Jersey hasn't been easy. She'd rather finalize the divorce than ever set foot in this building.

But I have hope that I can change her mind. Hell, all I have is hope. I cannot lose everything. For months, I've been haunted by the idea that I drove away the one person who has always been there for me because I focused too much on providing for my family and too little on actually being with them. I've made it my mission to show Sloane that isn't true anymore, that I can be better. But with this bloody trust issue thrown into the mix, it's become exponentially harder. If I abandon the idea of living in Jersey, if I stay in New York, where Sloane and T.J. live, I'll lose the firm, and won't be able to provide the life they deserve.

Eyes closed, I run a hand over my face. I've spent enough time berating myself. There's no point in doing it again. I need to focus all my energy on doing better.

On the other side of the flimsy hollow door, the bell chimes. Then the sound of my favorite voice floats down the hall.

"Where is he?"

"Sloaney," Cal calls.

"*Where is he?*"

The angry tone should probably worry me, but any fear is drowned out by the knowledge that Sloane made the forty-minute drive from the city to see me. If Madame E had said Sloane was coming, then maybe I would have stuck around and listened to her. That's the kind of foresight I'd prefer. Not the nonsense she was spouting about an incubator.

I'm standing, ready to round my desk so I can greet her, when she storms in, blue eyes spitting fire.

She stomps—impressive in five-inch heels—across the room, straight to me. "*You,*" she accuses, poking me in the chest.

I have no idea what I've done this time, but it got her here, so I can't be too upset about it.

My lips twitch, but I know better than to smile when she's this angry. "Hi."

"Come." She clutches my burgundy tie and yanks me toward the door. The glare on her face says she's upset, but fuck if I'm not a little turned on. There was a time when she'd drag me out of my office by the tie for sex. It still baffles me, how we got from that to divorce papers, but I'll do anything to get that kind of passion back.

Sloane has always inspired me to be my best. From the moment I met her, she blew me away. Her brains and her fierce attitude drew me in and quickly led me to obsession. The first time I saw her argue in torts class, I knew I'd met my match. For more than a decade, she challenged me to be better. A better attorney. A better man.

But for the last few years, I've been failing her.

"We have to talk." She drags me down the hall and into the supply cupboard.

As the door shuts behind us, dousing almost all the light, she tosses her purse onto the counter. Even in the darkened space, I can make out every detail of her expression. Probably because I've been obsessed with this woman for half my life.

Her dark hair is a bit of a mess, but the contrast between it and her light skin tone and stunning blue eyes literally steals my breath every time I look at her. My beautiful Irish wife captures the attention in every room she enters.

I'm still dumbstruck by the sight of her when she crosses her arms over her chest and huffs a hard breath out of her nose. Bollocks. Whatever I did must really be something.

Her nostrils flare as she inhales and exhales, like she's trying to calm herself. "Do you remember that night back in September?"

I nod but keep my mouth shut, afraid that if I speak, I'll wax poetically about it, and that'll only send her storming out.

"The night I brought T.J. over for his first sleepover in this shithole? When we took the boys to dinner?"

I nod again. Hell yes, I remember that night. Vividly. Although dinner with T.J. and Murphy isn't the part that's replayed in my mind constantly since.

"The dinner where you ordered Irish whiskeys and insisted I drink with you?"

I almost stop her, because that's not precisely how I remember it, but this conversation—and the way the night ended—makes me think that my hope that she dragged me out of my office for sex might not be that far off, and I don't want to mess that up. I'd bloody kill to be allowed to touch my wife again.

"Where we ended up in bed."

"Our anniversary," I remind her.

She scowls and hisses a *yes.*

She's giving off a peevish vibe, yet she's pulled me into the supply cupboard and she's bringing up the last time we had sex? Color me confused.

She's no longer speaking. Instead, she's breathing heavily, bloody staring at me like she's waiting for me to respond.

So I take a stab in the dark. "Did you bring me in here hoping for a repeat?"

She stomps her foot, and I swear smoke pours out of her ears.

"No," she snaps. "I brought you into this damn closet to say *I'm pregnant.*"

The words rattle around my head, loosening cobwebs as thick as the ones in this dark, dusty space.

Utter elation hits me first. This may be the solution I've been searching for. If Sloane is pregnant, maybe she'll want to be a family again. She'll call off the divorce. We'll have our second chance.

I still remember the first time we found out we were pregnant. It was seven years ago, and after almost a year of trying, my wife flew out of the master bathroom of our penthouse, a little pink stick in her hand and a smile on her face, shouting the words I'd been waiting to hear.

Everything is different this time around, though, because while Sloane is technically my wife, the *ex* part is there, floating in the periphery.

Could a baby be the answer? Honestly, another child has been the farthest thing from my mind since she asked me to move out. Then again, the night she stayed over wasn't in our plan, and look how that turned out. Every day since our anniversary, I've been desperate to have her again. And again. I want to keep her forever.

But that's not in her plans.

Now, though, those plans will have to be altered.

I take her in, scanning her fitted black dress, appreciating the way it clings to her luscious hips. I drink in the long legs that have always been my obsession, stopping only when I get to the sky-high rose gold heels. The ones with red souls. *Her* obsession.

She must have come from the office. She looks dressed for a day at the fancy firm where she works with the man who tried his best to steal her from me during law school.

Frustration flares like it always does when thoughts of her going to work for the enemy hit me. They dissipate quickly, though, when I notice the tiniest of bumps pressing against her suit jacket. It's practically imperceptible. In fact, I'm probably imagining it. It's more likely the leftover C-section bump. That doesn't detract from the fact that this woman, the woman I still love more than words could express, is growing my child.

I blink at the idea. "Oh shit. You're *the incubator.*"

Sloane's mouth falls open, and she gasps.

My stomach instantly plummets. What a fucking terrible response. Anyone with half a brain would know not to say something that fucking stupid to a woman who's just announced that she's with child. Especially when said child is theirs. Apparently my brain shut down at *pregnant.*

Despite the faux pas, I can't help but smile. This might be exactly what we need. My wife is carrying my child. A heady sensation rushes over me. There is nothing I want more in this world than my wife and son. To put my family back together. And now, not only do I have the opportunity to pick up the pieces, but our family is growing.

"Incubator?" The word is rightfully shrill. While I've been skipping along, mentally healing our wounds, she's been stuck on that. Can't exactly blame her. That wasn't my best moment.

Before I can respond, the door flies open and two people fall into a heap on the ugly gold carpet.

"Cal!" Lo, one of said people, yells at my brother, who is standing in the doorway.

Naturally, Cal would be the idiot who opened the door.

"Sloaney, you're pregnant?" The sod breaks into a blinding smile. "Wait, if you're pregnant, that means you have to move in."

"Oh shit," Brian says from where he's still tangled up with Lo on the floor. "He's right."

"You've got to be kidding me," Sloane hisses, her blue eyes blazing with fury. "Sully, tell them this is ridiculous."

Despite my best efforts, my lips wobble into a smile. The sensation is unfamiliar, like my facial muscles have forgotten how to do this. But they're right. This is perfect. "Of course you're moving in. You're the incubator." The moment the words leave my mouth, I wish I could inhale them, take them back, and rearrange them into something far more tactful. I've never been known to speak out of turn, but with Sloane, I lose my head.

And technically—according to Madame E, at least—I'm not wrong.

Lo's eyes are wide. "Shh, Sully. You'll ruin it."

"You called her an *incubator?*" Brian glares at me as he heaves himself to his feet.

"This closet is for private conversations," Sloane hisses before I can defend myself.

Lo gets to her feet with help from Cal, and when she's steady, she shakes her head. She and my wife are incredibly close. Until two minutes ago, their friendship was my only hope. If it meant moving in with her best friend, then there was a minuscule chance that Sloane would give in and come to Jersey. Now that she's pregnant? Fuck, my lips twitch again. My wife is pregnant. This is bloody brilliant.

"I don't know why you think that. The walls are paper thin and everyone can hear everything."

Lo's right. Also, the cupboard is dark and dirty, and I have to duck to pass through the doorway. We should have stayed in my office, but the honest truth is that where Sloane leads, I follow. It's been that way for about twenty years.

"We're having a baby!" Cal shouts to the dingy ceiling.

My brother is a handful, always full of life and joy. Most days, it makes me want to clobber him. But at this moment, I'm struggling not to join in on the celebration. Because yes, we're having a baby.

My wife turns her silent ire on my brother. If he's not careful, he'll go up in flames. This kind of fierceness is only one of the hundreds of things I miss about her.

I reach for her. "Sloane."

She jerks back before I can touch her. "Maybe incubator is better. You should call me that from now on." She glances past me to her purse. In a quick motion, she clutches it and storms out of the cupboard.

"*Sloane,*" I call after her.

She doesn't stop. Of course she doesn't. My wife has a temper like no other, and I set her off.

Rushing past the idiots I work with, I stalk after her. "Sweetheart, wait." I catch her arm before she makes it to the front door and force her to look at me. "You are not an incubator. That was bad timing. It wasn't even my first thought. But Madame Esmeralda was just here telling us we were waiting for the incubator."

Her brow wrinkles. "Who?"

"The woman upstairs." I shake my head. Bugger. Suddenly her predictions seem a lot more accurate. When she convinced Cal to get forty plants, a fish, and a cat the size of a small tiger, I thought she was out of her mind or fucking with the tosser. But she told me in a roundabout way that Sloane was pregnant. And if she knew that, then what else might she know?

Sloane lifts her chin in defiance. "The psychic lady told you I was an incubator?"

I nod. It's eerie, really, but we have more important things to discuss than Madame E.

Like how far along my wife is or when she found out. Though I suppose I know the answer to the first question. In the last half a year or so, we've only been together once. That was six weeks ago.

"Did you take a test?" I ask instead.

"No," she deadpans, hand on her hip. "The first thing I did when I realized my period was late was come over here and announce that I'm pregnant." She jerks her purse open and digs around in it, then thrusts a photo at me.

My chest pinches at the sight of the black and white image.

"You've been to the doctor." The words slip out in a tone more accusatory than I mean. Fuck, I'm a giant arse.

She steps away, putting space that I don't want between us, and crosses her arms. "Of course I have. I tested. Then I went to the doctor and confirmed before I dropped this bomb on you."

I sigh, my whole being sinking. This child doesn't even have fully formed limbs, yet I'm already missing the important things. God dammit. Just like with T.J., who I only see every other weekend and the occasional weekday now that Sloane and I are separated.

But complaining won't help at this moment. No, in this moment, my wife and children are all that matter.

"It's not a bomb, sweetheart."

"Don't call me that," she growls.

Right. I'm not allowed to do that anymore. She made that clear.

"This isn't a bomb," I correct. "It's incredible."

She blinks, her blue eyes going a little glassy, and sucks in a breath. "You don't want more kids."

That isn't entirely true, but this is not the time to get into that. "I will always love our family, no matter the size, because it's ours."

She scowls. "There is no ours."

Pain ricochets through me. She's wrong. This pregnancy is giving us another chance at an ours, and I won't be the arsehole who messes up this gift.

"That's not true," I say, keeping my voice gentle. "There will be an ours again." Instinctively, I tuck her dark hair behind one ear, and for a moment, she almost leans into it. Smiling, I duck closer. "Because you're carrying my heir, so now you have to move in with me."

Her eyes narrow to slits and she steps away. Maybe her reaction should discourage me, but nothing could take away from the hope that's pumping through my veins. My wife is pregnant. Everything is going to be perfect.

CHAPTER 3
Sloane

"**B**ecause you're carrying my heir." The words play on repeat in my head. Of course his main concern is the damn company. I learned a long time ago to expect nothing less. I just forgot for a moment this afternoon.

We're getting divorced, I remind myself. That night—the night I've thought about more than I'll ever admit—meant nothing to him. It was *just* sex. Amazing sex, really, but just sex. Because even though my husband and I might not know how to have a civil conversation anymore, our sexual chemistry is as strong as it's ever been.

I blink at the man who's owned my body for the last two decades, and it's like I'm seeing him for the first time. His light brown hair is slicked back perfectly, while when we were younger, it was always just a little messy. And the hints of gray are new. He's wearing a crisp white shirt beneath a blue Tom Ford suit that emphasizes the wide shoulders and strong chest I used to love resting my head against when we'd stay up late talking and fucking and planning for the future. A dusting of stubble covers his chin, the gray making an appearance there too. And his eyes? They've always done me in. A silvery blue that turns glacial when his emotions run high, whether it was because we were fucking or fighting.

His eyes were the same color either way, as was his tone.

I always liked the way he talked to me in the bedroom. Still do, if our night a few weeks ago is anything to go by. I don't mind his single-minded focus when we're in a lust-filled haze. How he doesn't mince words. It's nice to shut off my mind and allow him to control my pleasure since I spend so much of my life in my damn head, ensuring I keep my weaknesses from showing. From a young age, I was taught never to let an opponent see my vulnerabilities. Being raised by serious, dedicated lawyers—one of whom went on to become one of the first female judges in our district—will do that to a kid.

No, I don't actually have to appear in front of my mother, but when I started practicing law, she'd sit in when I was in front of her colleagues and later point out all the ways she could tell I was rattled. She'd focus on the instances when I showed *weakness*, as she put it.

It took time, but eventually, I mastered the mask that my husband has told me a time or two makes me seem like a shrill bitch.

Okay, he's never actually used those words, but it's implied.

"Sloane, *breathe*." It's Lo who has me sliding out of ice mode and softening.

I turn away from Sully and nod at my best friend. For as long as I've known her, Lo has worn her red hair in a tight braid down her back. Today, though, it hangs loose like a curtain around her freckled face as she studies me like I'm deranged.

"Do you want Cal to go grab coffees for us?" She winces immediately, probably realizing it at the same time I do. I can't *have* coffee.

Dammit, if I'd known this morning's cup would be my last, I would have savored it. You never know when it will be your last sip.

I glance around the disaster of an office the Murphy brothers have moved into and have to hold back a snort. It's so like Terry to pull something like this. The man always had to have the last word.

And he's certainly gotten it. This is the last place I'd ever picture any of the posh Murphy men in. Sully and his brother Cal grew up in England with their mother but came here after high school, and for as long as I've known them, they've had this crisp, put-together air about them.

Their late father was the same way, though he was American.

It's still hard to believe he's gone.

Terry and I always got along. I was never bothered by his interest in women less than half his age. It was amusing. Odd, yes, but he wasn't a sleazy old man by any means. He was funny. Charming.

He was the epitome of a Murphy.

Rather than the slight British accent my husband and his brother have, he had a thick New York accent.

My parents made comments about it here and there, but only to me and each other. They weren't the type to gossip, and my mother respected Terry as a lawyer. He built a legacy and a very successful firm. A firm that looks absolutely nothing like this dump.

The New York office houses almost one hundred employees, both lawyers and support staff, just like my firm.

Okay, not *my* firm. I'm just an associate. But Will promised that if I came to work for him, he'd put me on the fast track to partner. It's a better gig than I had here with the Murphys. I was never a partner. There was a time where I thought it was possible that I'd become a partner here but after T.J. was born I said goodbye to the courtroom and worked in the office handling trusts and estates around T.J. and Sully's schedules.

After seven years away from the courtroom I'm lucky the new firm is giving me a chance. I'm sure part of the reason Will hired me is because he despises my husband and knew this would irk him in a way nothing else would.

But as my mother always says, one should take the opportunities that are given. A person can't control someone else's motivation, only their own.

My only motivation is to create a life for myself. A name set apart from my husband's. Because soon he'll simply be my ex.

And my baby daddy.

I drop my head into my hands at the thought.

Lo cups my shoulders and shakes me. "It's going to be okay." Despite the words, her tone is full of panic. "Sully, *do* something."

I'm spiraling, a myriad of emotions churning through me. Every single thing about this is ridiculous. My soon-to-be ex-husband just referred to me as an incubator because of the absurd trust provision Terry wielded, which left his sons living and working *here*. The man died while in the midst of a tryst with a twenty-four-year-old, for god's sake.

To top if, off, Lo, my best friend, the most uptight boss bitch I know, has fallen head-over-heels in love with my dopey brother-in-law—whom I actually adore. And now at forty fucking years old I'm pregnant with my almost ex-husband's baby.

A shrill laugh leaves me, echoing off the yellowed ceiling. I double over, practically panting as I try to catch a breath.

The giggles won't stop. This is absurd.

"I think she's losing it," Lo mutters.

I nod, my hand covering my mouth, and straighten, the laughter now joined by tears. The situation I found myself in couldn't be more ridiculous. The world is crumbling around me, and here I am, *incubating* this new, precious life. I splay my hand over my stomach, already protective of my child. A child who will be brought into the world under less-than-ideal circumstances.

Finally I blow out a breath. "I'm good. I promise."

My husband stares at me, slack-jawed.

I can't blame him. I don't think I've ever acted so irrationally in my life.

Except the day we got married on a whim. Just the two of us at city hall, followed by a drunken lunch in Central Park.

Not a soul knew about it but us. He proposed, and I suggested we do it that day. I didn't think he'd go along with it, and I still have no idea how he got a marriage license approved so quickly. But when Sully uses those charming blue eyes and that British lilt, he could talk a nun out of her panties.

He certainly talked me out of mine.

Over and over through the years. Even when I hated myself for it. Like the night we made our little bear.

Our little bear. The thought brings a smile to my face.

Unfortunately, I'm still looking at Sully when that happens, and his eyes widen in shock.

Dammit. I doubt I've looked at him that way in years. Normally I'm better at hiding how desperately in love with my husband I am.

"I'm going to go," I say, searching the room to make sure I haven't left anything other than my dignity behind. "The incubator needs to be plugged in."

Lo snorts and Sully sighs like I've exhausted him again.

Good. It's better when he looks at me like that. Like I'm an issue to deal with rather than the love of his life.

Before I can make my escape, though, he takes a step closer, his eyes narrowing, piercing me in a way that makes it impossible to flee. "You can't leave."

I glare at him. "Well, I certainly can't stay here. I've got a job, Sully, remember? It's in New York City. Miles and miles from here. How the hell would I live here and work there?"

Sully straightens, his chin lifting, as if he has all the answers. "You won't. You'll come back and work for us. Or not work at all. It's not like you need the money."

My jaw hits the disgusting floor. *Did he really just...*

Sully holds his hands out. "What?" he asks, his tone challenging. "You know I always pay for you. Hell, I probably paid for that new car. So if you're set on working in the city, you can use that to get back and forth."

I don't respond. I can't. The gall of this man has rendered me speechless.

He huffs, like I'm the ridiculous one. "Why are you looking at me like that?" He turns to Lo. "Why is she looking at me like that?"

I'm going to kill him.

Tamping down on the rage burning inside me, gathering figurative ammunition, I take a deep breath. Then, as evenly as I can, I explain, "This is my career, Sully. A career I'm proud of."

A career he never took seriously. But it's always the same with him. We've been having this argument for years. Why would today be any different?

His shoulders rise and fall. "Wonderful. Be proud *here*. Will only hired you to piss me off anyway."

That rage is back with a vengeance, my vision going red. "Are you serious right now?"

"It's also because he's always wanted to get into your trousers, and now he thinks he has a shot..." The man just keeps going, digging himself a deeper grave.

Is he for fucking real?

"Sully, shut up," Lo hisses.

He runs his hands through his hair like he's losing his patience.

Me too, buddy. Me freaking too.

"I'm getting this all wrong. But please, Sloane, you can't leave. You must stay. It's—"

"If you tell me I have to stay here because I'm the vessel for your progeny one more time, I'm going to strangle you, and then Cal will be T.J.'s only male role model. Is that what you want?"

As my husband's eyes fall shut, I take the opportunity to dart for the door. The bitter fall air has just stolen my breath when I hear the footsteps chasing after me.

"I can't do this," I say, my entire being defeated. I don't want to battle with my husband any longer. I don't have it in me. I need to wrap my head around this before I talk to him again.

"Are you okay?"

My shoulders sag in relief at the sound of Lo's voice. I turn around and shake my head. "I don't freaking know. This isn't how I thought my day would go."

This isn't how I thought *my life* would go. I never would have pictured myself like this: a *pregnant* almost-single forty-year-old.

Lo glances back at the building. "Why don't you come up to the apartment? We can talk alone."

I shake my head. There's no way I'm going back in there.

She sighs and loops her arm through mine. "Fine, let's walk, then."

I glance down at Lo's impossibly high black heels and then at my rose-gold Louboutins. Neither are walking shoes. Especially in this neighborhood. The inside of the office building is bad enough, but the outside? On either side of the three-story brick building are almost identical structures. Some have windows, and some *don't*. A plastic bag sways in the wind of one of the open doors and garbage liters the street.

Across the street, is no better. The façade of the bar across the way has seen better days, the sign tilted to the side. It's the place Sully and I took Murphy, Cal's son, and T.J. the night we got into this whole mess, so I know, despite its outward appearance, that the food is incredible.

I point there. "The Grasshopper?"

Lo looks both ways, then guides me across the street.

Inside, we settle at the long oak bar. It's smoother and glossier than it was a few weeks ago, like it's got a fresh coat of lacquer. The man on the other side is wearing an Irish cap and a friendly smile. "What can I get you ladies?"

God, what I would do for a martini right now. Or a shot. A shot would definitely help. A little Irish whiskey, maybe.

On second thought, that's a terrible idea. Irish whiskey is what got me here in the first place. It's what we drank twenty minutes before we walked into city hall and got married. We had it again the night we created this baby. While the boys played on the old Pac-Man machine, Sully settled beside me at the bar and ordered two Irish whiskeys. When he slid mine toward me, his blue eyes held mine as he repeated the words he said to me on our wedding day. "A thousand todays with you will never be enough, sweetheart."

The words were achingly sweet. They hit the same that night as they did all those years ago. When we were young and so carefree. They're words he used to murmur when he was feeling extra romantic. Sometimes, right before he slid inside me, he'd whisper them between kisses. They hit just right every time. They never felt cliché because he meant them wholeheartedly. And I felt the same way. When we were good, there wasn't another person in the world who could catch my attention. He couldn't be lured away either. At least not by another person. In the end, what stole him from me was his job.

His dedication to the firm.

"I'll take an iced tea," I say to the bartender, trying to forget Sully's words and all the emotions they drag to the surface.

Lo settles on the stool beside me. "Make that two."

"I know what you're going to say," I murmur as the bartender saunters toward the stack of clean glasses.

It's obvious where her allegiance lies. Yes, she's my friend, but she loves the firm. It's her home, and she's working her ass off to save it. Plus, she's in love with Cal. I'm not naïve enough to think our friendship could trump all that.

Everyone has always put that firm first.

She turns on her stool and faces me. Despite the stress radiating off her, she's glowing. I'm happy for her. It's tempting to fall in line and do what I know she'll ask just to keep her this happy.

But I can't keep putting myself last. It's time to choose me. To live my own life. It's why I asked for the divorce. And if I can break my own heart to chase my dreams, then I can figure out a way to let Lo down easy.

"I'm not going to say anything. I just wanted to sit with you."

"You're not here to talk me into moving in to that dump now that I'm carrying a Murphy heir in my womb?"

Lo's lips twitch. "If you'd heard Madame E going on about the incubator, you would be laughing too. She's eerily accurate."

I sigh.

Lo puts her hand on mine. "Seriously, she told Terry to be careful of Ginger. Wanna know the name of the woman he was with when he died?"

I shrug.

Her eyes dance. "Ginger."

My mouth falls open.

"She told Cal he needed fins, hence the fish. Then she told me I'd need ten to replace all of them. It's been two weeks since the sixth died, but Bubbles the Seventh is holding on strong."

I snort. Okay, that is funny.

"My point is, I know that Sully sounded like an ass—"

I glare at her.

Her green eyes flash with humor. "Okay, he absolutely is an ass most of the time."

My muscles relax a fraction. It's good to know I'm not the only one who sees it.

"But he was probably just thrown off because he hasn't believed a single of Madame E's predictions. He thinks she's ridiculous. Yet today, you showed up and proved her right."

"I can't live there," I tell her as the bartender slides our drinks in front of us. "I know you're happy. I get that you're swept up in this blissful haze where you don't see how bad it really is—"

She snorts. "No amount of bliss can hide how awful that place is."

Relief washes over me. Thank god she's not as delusionally in love as I thought.

"But we're doing what's necessary to save the business," she continues. "Your reasons for hating the firm are valid, but you're about to have a baby, and your six-year-old attends an extremely expensive school."

With a slow sip of iced tea, I narrow my eyes at her. "Yeah, and?"

"Sully needs this job. If he loses the firm, how will he pay tuition and child support?"

I wince. Being reliant on Sully's money is another sore point, but there's no sense pressing on it right now. I've already aggravated too many tender spots today. "I can't live with him, Lo."

What I don't say, what I can't admit to anyone, is that I'm scared as hell. I've just begun adjusting to life on my own, and now it's all gone topsy-turvy. The idea of having a baby on my own is terrifying, but I don't know how to be around the man who still makes my heart skip a beat, because the last time I gave it to him, he was reckless with it.

CHAPTER 4

Sully

"**D**o you need help, Mr. Murphy?"

Shite. I was two steps from freedom. Two steps from the door that leads to the parking lot, where I could have slipped safely into my Beemer. I've already loaded up everything I need, including the basket of stuff I spent the last eighteen hours tracking down. If only I'd remembered to slip my mobile into my pocket before I snuck Sloane's stuff out.

Because of my distraction—all my wife's fault; it's hard to think about anything but her—I'm forced to deal with Amy, our intern, before I can make my escape.

It was Cal's brilliant idea to bring on the twenty-two-year-old intern, and though she's terrible at just about everything she does, having her here frees Lo up a bit.

And we're unlikely to find a better alternative, since the trust, a.k.a. the bane of our existence, made it clear we could only bring one paid member of our staff with us. Lo is incredible at what she does. The best paralegal the firm has. But even she doesn't have the time to deal with all the work Brian, Cal *and* I need from her.

I understand my arsehole brother's reasoning for bringing in the space cadet, and I admire him for doing what he can to help the love of his life. However, Lo hates Amy with a passion. So he missed the mark completely with that gesture.

Lo can barely interact with our intern without losing her shite. I have very little patience for incompetence, but Lo? Hers is practically nonexistent. And Amy's incompetence knows no bounds. If she were really trying, maybe I'd have a little sympathy. But she's not. And every time she fucks something up, she just shrugs and says *that's so weird.*

The phrase is like nails on a chalkboard.

"I'm heading out." I point out the obvious.

With her head cocked to the side, she flashes me a smile. I fight the sigh working its way up my chest. She's beautiful, with long dark hair, and two months ago, the tight outfits and flirty smiles made Lo jealous as hell. But my brother and I can agree on one thing: young and dumb is not our type.

I have one type. Sloane Murphy. And I'm wasting time I could be spending with my wife while I stand here waiting for Amy to explain why she stopped me.

Instead, she looks at me expectantly, as if she's the one waiting for a response.

"Do you need something?" I ask, trying to keep my tone subdued.

"I mean." She shrugs. "I think you should call them back."

I blink. "Who?"

"Oh." Giggling, she holds up a Post-it. "I can never remember what I've said aloud."

For fuck's sake. Whoever it is will be getting a call from the car.

For the next thirty seconds, she continues the bloody giggling. And when my blood pressure rises enough to send smoke billowing from my ears, I finally growl her name.

"Here." She thrusts the Post-it at me. "He called earlier, but I couldn't find you."

"He who?" I squint at the mobile number on the yellow square. She's scribbled ten numbers on it, and that's it.

"Hmm." She tips her head again. "Kevin...Keith...Ken, maybe? It started with the *K* sound."

Right. Names aren't her thing. She can't keep them straight. Rather than waste my time trying to get accurate information from her, I flip through a mental list of clients and then my adversaries. Maybe Ken White. But he doesn't have a 551 area code. The man is in Manhattan. I can't think of another person with a *K* name who would be calling me. Though I suppose it could be a Chris or a Chuck. Hell, I wouldn't be shocked if it was a woman. I'll figure it out when I call.

"Is this a five?" I point to the fourth number.

She peers at the Post-it and shakes her head. "How would I know?"

"Because you wrote it," I grit out. "I can't tell what it says."

"I hate it when that happens." With a sigh, she spins and sashays back into the conference room. No apology, no attempt to help me. And I'm once again cursing my sod of a brother for bringing her in to *help.*

Crumpling the Post-it in my hand, I stomp for the door. Whoever called to speak to me will just have to do it again. And I'll have to bring up terminating Amy at our next partner meeting.

"Sully," Cal calls from the doorway where Amy just disappeared.

Annoyance zaps through me. Once again, I was so close.

"Yes," I snap without turning.

"We need to talk about Sloaney and the plan to get her to move in. I have an idea—"

"No." I have a plan. I do not need help. I will win my wife back.

"No?" Cal's tone is full of confusion.

I refuse to turn around. I don't need to see him to know exactly what expression he's wearing. Part of me wants to be a wanker and remind him about the forehead lines he's always warning me about, but that would just lead to more talking. That's the last thing I want.

"No talking." I push the door open, bracing myself to be pelted with the bloody orange ball he's always armed with. By some miracle, I make it out to the parking lot unscathed. I pick up my pace, heading straight for my black 7 Series.

The door to the building clunks open again, and I risk a glance over my shoulder, ready to curse at Cal. Instead, I find a pair of purple eyes watching me.

I whip around completely, smiling now. "Madame E." Even to my own ears, my voice comes out like a song, bright and cheerful. I might not want my brother's help, but this woman might have answers.

"Sullivan." She nods, adjusting her bags.

I stride toward her, chewing up the distance in a heartbeat, and hold out my hands. "Let me."

She cocks her head and that thick gray shock of hair catches my eye. It always stands out against the jet-black, but today, she's dressed in flowing dark purple layers, making it even harder to ignore.

Forcing my focus back to her face, I flash her my most charming smile. "I insist."

"Well, aren't you the gentleman?" She passes over the three reusable bags.

As she releases them, gravity takes over, and my arm drops. Bloody hell, they're heavy.

She waves a hand at the empty air beside her. "Sebastian and I are heading to a friend's for a seance. Can't lead one properly without my candles and these books."

Yes, this woman spends a good part of her time with a ghost, and yes, I'm going to ask her for help. Don't judge me, I'm desperate.

"Have you seen any more about Sloane?" I ask.

She narrows her eyes, her lips pursed like maybe she's concentrating. Or annoyed. Hell, maybe she has gas.

After a moment, she straightens and breaks into a bright smile. "A bubbly dance."

A bubbly what? Dance? My unhappy pregnant wife, who

stomped out of here practically cursing my name, is doing a happy, bubbly dance today? What the fuck happened? Was it something at work?

Hurt and envy surge up inside me. I want the best for her, to celebrate every one of her successes, but I don't want Will *Bloody* Higgins to be the one making her happy.

The wanker was in our class at Columbia, and he had his eye on my girl from day one. Sloane never gave me a reason to worry back then, but now? So much has fucking changed. She kicked me out, is moving on, and went to work for the tosser. Is there a chance she wants to be with him now?

In the last several years, she's drifted away from me. Our struggles with T.J.'s excessive energy and horrible ideas, and her desire for—and my apprehension about—another baby, put a wedge between us. Not to mention all the time I had to put in to get where I am in my career. Sometimes I'd fall asleep thinking I didn't even know the person next to me anymore. And in those moments, I missed Sloane desperately.

But I never knew how to explain any of it to her.

Maybe I should have just given in when she told me she wanted another child. But at the time, we were barely hanging on with just T.J. I didn't see how we could handle another little one. Especially after the scare we suffered during her first pregnancy. Even now, when I think about how her placenta ruptured and I almost lost both her and T.J., that overwhelming grief threatens to take hold of me.

I fight the shudder.

We discussed it multiple times, and each time I was adamant that the timing wasn't right. I never imagined that asking her to wait would mean losing her.

I should have paid more attention. I don't know how to be *me* without her.

When we met, I was the get-by guy. My father owned a successful firm. My position was all but guaranteed. All I had to do was make it through law school. There was no pressure to live up to potential, because no one ever saw more in me. Not my mother, who was too busy with her own life to remember I existed half the time, nor my father, who was building his empire. As long as I wasn't a problem, I was left to my own devices. Until Sloane came along. She saw a kind of potential in me I didn't know existed. She pushed me to be better.

I worked hard to prove I was worthy of her. She blew me away with her brains and her beauty and her excitement for all things in life.

Now that she doesn't want me anymore, the world has lost its color.

I'm miserable without her. My life is nothing. But is it possible that she's flourishing without me?

"Why is she happy?" I demand, my already demolished heart aching.

Madame E floats past me and opens the back of her green Mini Cooper. "Like I told your father and your brother, I only see what I see."

I drop the bags into the cargo area with a bit more force than I intend, but I don't apologize for it. I'm too frustrated to do anything but back away, hands balled into fists at my sides.

"Have a good night, Sullivan, and remember to smile." She hops into her car with an exuberance a seventy-year-old should not possess.

She peels out, and I'm once again alone. I scrub a hand down my face. Bubbly dances and smiles. Sounds like a load of gobshite. But then again, so did the prediction about the incubator. So as I drive into Manhattan, I remind myself over and over that I'm happy, even bubbly.

When I reach the high-rise not far from Rockefeller Center, I pull into the underground parking garage, trying not to agonize over how fucking nice it is compared to my office building in Jersey.

It's bloody absurd to be jealous. Will's father's firm is rubbish. Bunch of nutters overcharging clients and winning less than half their cases. Murphy and Machon, the New York Office, is still running six blocks away, even if Cal, Brian, and I are stuck in Jersey for the time being. The atmosphere my father created far surpasses that of Higgins's firm. And in nine months, Sloane and I will be back there together. As long as I can convince her to move in with me now.

And I will. We can't lose the firm. So, I take Madame E's advice. With a forced smile on my face, I step through the doors and ride up the enemy's elevator to my wife. As the numbers lit up above the door creep higher, I double-check the basket I brought. It's full of all of Sloane's favorite pregnancy items. Belly butter, Earth Mama heartburn and anti-nausea teas, ginger candies, and a picture of the body pillow I purchased and left on the bed for her. I even tossed in a box set of *Grey's Anatomy*, the show she binged while she was pregnant with T.J.

My smile becomes easier as I remember how many of those episodes ended up with Sloane naked and crying out my name. The happiness is joined with longing the more I think about it. What I'd give to have those days back. If only I could go back in time and tell that young, dumb sod just how good he had it. Warn him not to mess it all up.

The elevator dings and I shake myself out of my melancholy. Right now, I'm the only one who can fix my marriage. And the only way to do that is to convince Sloane to give us a chance.

I breeze past the reception area with a quick greeting. It pays to have the reputation I've curated over the years. No one even bats an eye. Though the man sitting at the desk outside Sloane's office seems less than pleased to see me. He's maybe twenty-five, with the kind of preppy look that says he uses summer as a verb. I can picture him talking about how he summers on the Cape and winters in Aspen.

His immediate smirk when he spots me has me rattled. "Well, if it isn't the baby daddy."

"Husband," I snap, forgetting that I'm supposed to be smiling.

"Hmm." He chuckles. "Not sure about that." His brown eyes cut to the basket in my hands.

I pull it closer to my side, like it needs protecting. I spent hours finding Sloane's favorites because I want her to know that I remember. That I care. But I don't want this arsehole judging me.

He arches a brow. "The baby daddy is a sure thing, though."

Jaw tightening, I turn toward my wife's office. The move only ratchets up the tension that's worked its way back into me. Because Will Freaking Higgins is there, leaning over my wife's desk. They aren't touching, and his hands are firmly planted on the wooden surface, but my body rebels at the idea. Without giving the preppy boy behind the desk another glance, I storm into Sloane's office.

"For my wife." I drop the basket in front of her, though my attention is fixed on the man with beady green eyes who's standing too close.

He looks down at the basket, and his brow pinches slightly as he takes it all in. When he zeroes in on me, his expression turns pensive. "Sully," he says as he steps away from the desk.

"Will." I frown, stepping closer.

"*Sully*," Sloane hisses. "What are you doing here?"

My attention shifts instantly, disappointment sinking like a stone in my stomach. I'm not surprised by the frustration in her tone. Not after yesterday. But it hurts all the same. She's my wife and the mother of my son and my future child. She's the center of my universe.

The urge to round the desk and splay my hand over her belly is strong.

I couldn't feel T.J. move for months, but the action made me feel connected to her and to the baby growing inside her, regardless.

She watches me, the emotion in her eyes unreadable. There was a time when a look like this was enough to tell me exactly what she was thinking. Clearly, that's no longer true. Her blue irises are stormy, but I don't know why.

Will clears his throat, reminding us of his presence. "We'll finish this later, Sloane." He dips his chin my way. "Sully."

I frown as he leaves the room.

"I can't believe you did this," she hisses.

Fucking hell. The gesture was supposed to be sweet. It took hours to track down all the brands she loved during her first pregnancy, including a pillow with the exact medium firmness she preferred. Is it so wrong of me to hope for a reaction that included something like *Aw, I can't believe you did this; it's so sweet*, rather than *I can't believe you did this, arsehole?*

I cross my arms and spin back to her. "I wanted to do something nice for you," I growl. "To show you how happy I am. So you know I want to support you."

Only now do I remember to smile. So I force my lips up into something that should be a grin.

Sloane's expression pinches. "What is wrong with your face?"

Oh for fuck's sake. I can't even smile right.

"Sully." She pushes the basket to the far edge of her desk. "No one here knows about the baby."

"Mr. Puffy Hair does." I lift my chin, signaling to her assistant.

"Julius was the only one until you basically told my boss."

Panic hits me. I'm fucking it up already. "Well," I hear myself say, the words coming out without my permission, "if I have anything to say about it, it won't just be Caesar for long. Everyone will know."

Sloane drops her elbows to her desk and cradles her face in her hands.

And suddenly I feel like a dick.

"Sweetheart." I stride to her side and drop to a knee, rubbing her back. She relaxes at my touch, as if the response is ingrained in her, but after a heartbeat, her entire body tightens and she pulls away.

"Don't." She sighs.

I put both hands up. "I just want to be there for you and the baby. Your first pregnancy wasn't easy, and I don't want you to go through that alone. You haven't responded to my texts, but please tell me you're at least considering moving in."

She opens her mouth, and I'm hit with the overwhelming certainty that she'll say no, so I continue before she can speak.

"Not for the firm, or Cal or Brian, or even me. But because you and the baby deserve the support system we can give you. I want to be near so I can take care of you."

She slumps, the fight leaving her. "I'm considering it."

CHAPTER 5
Sloane

My vision goes hazy and my thoughts drift as I wait for the teakettle to whistle.

I know the rule, but I can't look away. Eventually, this watched pot *will* boil. It's ironic how slow the process is, considering every other aspect of my life is moving at lightning speed. I'm ten weeks along already. I don't know yet whether it's a perk that comes with finding out one is unexpectedly pregnant two months in or whether it's a curse. I'm a planner. An over-planner, really. So losing those first few weeks, when I could have been making preparations, means it feels like the clock is really ticking. It's counting down quickly to the day I have to move out of the penthouse. The home I've only started to redecorate.

My gaze flits to the little sign I put on the window ledge.

In this kitchen, we dance.

We don't. I wanted to. Before work became all Sully cared about, we fucked in this kitchen. We could never keep our hands off one another. We'd come home from a night out with friends, a little tipsy and ravenous. I'd reach for the ice cream, and he'd reach for me. He'd set me on the counter, and we'd eat the desert straight from the carton between kisses. Eventually, he'd be licking it from between my legs.

The teakettle sounds, and I jolt. I wasn't even watching it.

I shake my head, trying and failing to rid myself of the vivid memories. Of the phantom sensation of my husband's thick cock sliding inside me and his fingers toying with my nipples.

Without my permission, my core clenches. Shit, this pregnancy is going to test my restraint. At least I was allowed to be this horny during my last pregnancy. Yes, Sully was pretty invested in work then, but even after twelve-hour days at the office, he'd let me ravage him, and if the days were longer than that, I found time to sneak into his office, lock the door, and convince him to be reckless with me.

When was the last time we did something like that?

Other than the night in September.

I can't remember a single time after T.J. was born that my husband showed that kind of interest in me. The kind that gave me the courage to be so bold.

That's why we're getting divorced. With or without this baby, I refuse to live like that again.

How can I be with a man who no longer makes me feel comfortable enough to ask for sex?

I never had trouble initiating. I'm a woman who goes after what she wants. Equal opportunist and all that. Mama didn't raise no wilting flower.

But I know when I'm not wanted and I'll never live like *that* again.

I grab the tin of tea Sully gifted me and pop it open. It's the kind that always quelled my nausea. Though my stomach is fine this morning, I have a big day in court, and I'll do anything to ensure nothing goes wrong. The last thing I need is for a random bout of nausea to hit me mid-argument.

I drop one of the teabags in the steaming mug and look around my apartment while I wait for it to steep. In two days, I have to leave this little haven of mine.

Little. I snort. The penthouse Sully and I bought when we turned thirty isn't little by any stretch of the imagination.

The day we toured it, I wandered from room to room, eyes wide, shocked that we could afford it. But with the proceeds from the condo my parents had gifted us when we got married, as well as the bonus Terry insisted on giving us when we'd been at his firm for five years, it wasn't much of a stretch. And that was before we factored in the money we'd been saving on our own.

And when we celebrated our birthdays here that year—together, because somehow, we were born on the same damn day—it felt like we'd finally made it.

On my twenty-second birthday, Sully started a tradition. Every year, he'd find me—at school, at work, at home—carrying a cupcake and two candles. Then he'd sing. His voice was rich and charming. His damn deep baritone always made me weak in the knees. He never got up on stage and sang during karaoke nights. He did something so much better. He'd tug my chair close, wrap his arm around me, and sing in my ear. Because of course Sully knew every word. He had a ridiculously good memory.

That only made it all the more heartbreaking when, years later, he forgot date nights and anniversaries.

I take a sip of the tea and wince. Yuck. I'd forgotten how terrible it tastes. I only suffered through it during my first pregnancy because it worked so well. As I choke it down, the alarm on my phone blares, reminding me that if I don't go now, I'll be late for court.

It's annoying, having to resort to alarms to make sure I don't forget simple things like going to work, but my brain isn't cooperating with me lately. I set an alarm to keep me on track because now that I'm at a new law firm, starting over at forty, I have to prove myself. *Again.*

I check the stove to make sure it's off, snag my purse from the counter, and head downstairs with my teacup.

Until recently, I didn't own a car. Typically, having a car in New York makes little sense. Parking is a bitch, so Ubering would be a hell of a lot easier, but now that Sully—who lives in *Jersey*—and I share custody of T.J., I don't have a choice.

Something else Sully doesn't understand.

He scoffed when I bought a car, like I was spending his money frivolously. *His* money—as if I wanted to live off him. God, what I would have done to go back to work after a standard maternity leave, but it took two years for me to get back to the office.

T. J. was colicky. He never let me put him down, and he didn't sleep. There was no way I could be up with him all night, then fight effectively for my clients during the day. That first year was a damn blur, and Sully acted like I was at home lounging around.

He'd come home and wonder why the dishes weren't done, yet he never listened long enough for me to explain that I hadn't found time to even eat or shower, let alone clean up the dishes *he* left in the sink the night before.

Laundry? I hadn't worn clothes without baby vomit on them for months, but God forbid I forget to drop off his suits at the cleaner.

We went from being so in sync that it seemed impossible that anything could come between us to two strangers living parallel lives. And year after year, it got worse. When I went back to work, I was the one who always took off for T.J.'s needs. Not to mention everything around the house fell on me too.

By the time I asked for a divorce, I resented Sully so much that I pictured murdering him at least once a day.

Can't spell marriage without murder. Is that a saying? It should be.

As I get situated in the driver's seat, I giggle at my little joke. When I catch sight of myself in the rearview mirror, I jolt, because I haven't seen that kind of smile in a long, long time.

It shouldn't be weird to see my own smile. *That's* why we're getting a divorce.

And this is exactly how I'll combat falling for Sully again. Every time a good memory floats through my mind, I'll remind myself of the reasons I asked for the divorce in the first place. I'll force myself to think of any given day over the last six years. I have to, because living with Sully—this new version of him, where he's actually trying—will make it hard to remember all the bullshit I've put up with.

He's incredibly charming, hence the baby in my belly right now. But I can't forget. I can't gloss over the years where I was nothing but an afterthought, another line item on his long, long to-do list.

Meet with clients. Check. Review complaint and service. Check. Have dinner with wife. *Check.*

I won't do it again. I *can't.*

I'm busy repeating that mantra when the light ahead turns yellow, then, too quickly, red. Reflexively, I slam on my brakes. My tea sloshes over the top of the cup, and in an effort to save my baby and the sensitive skin of my belly from being scalded, I holy my hand away from my body.

Of course, that move ensures the entirety of the mug spills all over the center console.

Dammit.

With a ragged sigh, I toss the mug on the passenger seat since the handle won't allow it to fit in the cupholder. The phrase etched onto it, the one telling me I'm the best mama, taunts me as I search the console for napkins. It doesn't feel like I'm the best at anything lately. Not being a mother, certainly not a wife, and definitely not as a lawyer. No matter what I do, I'm failing at something. It's only eight a.m. and I'm already exhausted.

The tea seeps through my suit, confirming my fear. I didn't make it unscathed. Fortunately, the liquid isn't hot enough to burn like I worried it would be. A quick glance down, though, confirms that my white silk top is tinted a light greenish brown. Dammit. I don't have time to go back home and I don't have anything else to put on.

A car beeps behind me, and I look up to see the light has turned green.

I hold up a hand to apologize and accelerate slowly. By the time I've parked in the garage attached to the building that houses Higgins, Smith, and Dodge, I've resigned myself to running to the bathroom and blotting at the spot. It's the best option I have. It'll have time to air dry before court.

I think.

Fuck.

Once I've collected my things, I scurry to the elevator and head up to our floor. When the doors open to the office, Will is standing five feet away, waiting.

He hasn't changed since law school. While Sully hair is threaded with gray, Will's is just as dark as it was twenty years ago. I'm sure Sully would say it's because Will's never had a wife or kids to stress him out.

He wears it slicked back, and today, there isn't a hair out of place. His bespoke charcoal gray suit complements a body far more toned than it was during our days at Columbia. That's one thing that has changed since law school; Will somehow got better-looking.

He smirks at me now. Or smolders, maybe, his eyes eating me up. With my purse in front of me, he can't see the stain on my shirt, but with the way he's checking out my legs, I'm not sure he would have noticed anyway. I've always had nice legs. Though my middle never returned to normal after my pregnancy, my legs give me an edge. They make me feel sexy.

It's empowering, knowing I can affect a man like this. I have no interest in Will, and I never have. Even so, I like his eyes on me. When I'm the object of attention like this, I don't feel like a single mom who's failing at life. I feel like a desirable woman.

I drop my purse and nod. "Let me grab the file from my office and then we can head to court."

Will's eyes narrow on my breasts.

Okay, I may have liked the look of appreciation a minute ago, but his scrutiny is a bit too intense. Shoulders rounding, I curl in on myself a fraction, hoping that'll deter him from staring.

"Why are you wet?" He drags his focus up to my face.

My stomach sinks. "Um, spilled tea in the car. I'll get cleaned up quickly, and then we'll go."

With a sigh, he checks his watch. "There's no time for that. As it is, you're late."

The words are matter-of-fact. If I were a twenty-five-year-old male associate who'd just started at the firm, he'd be berating me. And I'd deserve it, to be honest. But we have a history, and because of that, he rarely treats me like the lowly associate I am.

Thank God for that, because if he yelled, I'd probably cry. And then I'd hate myself. Damn pregnancy hormones.

With a nod, I say, "I'm sorry about this."

He shakes his head. "Not a problem. Get cleaned up. When I get back, we can grab lunch and I'll fill you in."

I force a smile and watch as he strides into the elevator, headed out to do my job for me.

Dammit. I was really looking forward to arguing this case this morning. I spent all last night prepping.

This is all Sully's fault. If I hadn't been drinking his damn tea, this wouldn't have happened. If I didn't have to drive to Jersey so T.J. could see his dad, I wouldn't have been in my own car to begin with. And if he hadn't been such an ass for those last several years of marriage, I wouldn't have been distracted by thoughts of what could have been.

I stalk past Julius, who gives me a once-over, a phone pressed to his ear, and shakes his head.

Yeah, I know I look ridiculous, but does he have to be so obvious about it?

The moment my office door slams shut behind me, I pull out my phone and call Sully. No one but him deserves to deal with this version of me.

"Is everything all right?"

No *hello*, no *hi, sweetheart; how are you?* Nope, this man's only concern is that the incubator is adequately taking care of his heir.

"Everything is not, in fact, all right," I grit out.

Sully sighs. It's loud and gruff and, ridiculously, makes me want to cry.

He's annoyed with me. I'm interrupting his day. It's like déjà vu. I can't count how many times I've found myself in this situation. Maybe I should hang up. If I never felt this way again, it'd be too soon. I don't want to be a bother.

I just want someone to fucking care.

I swipe away a lone tear.

"What happened?"

Annoyance flares to life inside me, choking out the self-pity that's been trickling through my veins. "What happened is I spilled the disgusting tea you bought all over me while driving to work. Now I don't get to go to court, and it's all your fault."

"Are you okay? Did you burn yourself?" he asks, his tone slightly elevated.

Oh, now I have his attention.

"I'm fine, and don't worry, the incubator protected your baby. The car bore the brunt of the spillage. I basically dumped it on the center console to keep from injuring myself or your progeny," I grumble, wiggling my mouse to wake my computer.

He makes a choked sound. "Did you make sure the car wasn't smoking?"

The frustration that's become a constant when I see, hear, or even think about this man mixes with confusion. "Why would it be smoking? I've never smoked, and now you think I'd pick up the habit while I'm pregnant?" I may hate my soon-to-be ex-husband, but I love our child. I would never put him or her at risk.

"No, Sloane," he says, his tone patient. "The car. Where did you spill the tea exactly?"

I shrug. "I don't know. Below the radio area, where I plug my phone in." Sully's responding sigh has me pushing back from my computer with a grunt. "The freaking car is not smoking."

"Maybe not, but it's worth checking. Otherwise, you're liable to burn the entire building down."

My vision goes red as I absentmindedly click on folders on my computer screen. I hate him. God, I freaking hate him. If he were here, I'd run him over with my car. Back it right over his stupidly good-looking face. Then he wouldn't sound so smug.

"Why don't we go check, then?" I say in a high, placating voice.

Chin lifted, I disconnect the call. I'm too annoyed to listen to him any longer. Then, phone in hand, I stalk back out of my office, heading toward the elevator.

Julius pushes back from his desk and scurries after me. "Where are you going? Shouldn't you be in court?"

"Should be, yeah," I call over my shoulder without slowing.

He follows me to the elevator, and as we pass one glass wall after another, each one leading into another associate's office, no one spares us a glance.

Every one of them is absorbed in their work. Meanwhile, I'm acting like an incompetent fool. All these twenty-somethings have their lives together. They show up at the crack of dawn and don't leave until late into the night.

I, on the other hand, stroll in here late and leave early. This is just one more reminder that I don't belong.

I hit the elevator button aggressively as Julius steps up beside me, fixing his jacket.

"What is happening? And why were you running through the office?"

I grin. "Couldn't keep up with me?"

"People should never run in Louboutins or Tom Ford, darling. Now tell me why you broke the rule."

I glance down at my rose-gold shoes, cursing myself for putting them on this morning. Every time I wear them, something absurd like this happens. First the pregnancy test, now the tea incident and the car on fire.

I snort. The car is definitely not on fire. My husband is so dramatic.

"Because I spilled my tea and my ex thinks my car could be on fire. I'm rushing so I can prove to him how dumb he is." I sound like a petulant child, but I don't care.

Julius raises a styled blond brow. "Is it on fire?"

My expression flattens out. Is he fucking serious? "Of course it's not."

He shrugs as we step onto the elevator. "I hate when they mansplain."

Validated by that response, I relax against the back wall of the stainless-steel box. "Exactly."

"But what if it is on fire?" Julius muses.

"It's not." I stab at the button for the garage.

With his hands in his pockets, he leans against the wall beside me. We're silent as we descend, and we remain that way until we make it to my car. The one that clearly hasn't burst into flames. "Ha." I point at the SUV and hold up my phone.

The screen is filled with missed call notifications. It buzzed in my hand the whole way down here, but I ignored it. Now, I navigate to Sully's contact and tap the FaceTime icon. While I wait for him to accept the request, I climb into the driver's seat, grinning. See? It's perfectly fine.

When Sully's face finally appears, I stab the icon that activates the camera on the back side of the phone so he can see that everything is as it should be.

"Jesus, Sloane," he says. "I've been calling you nonstop."

With a roll of my eyes, I grasp the charging cord plugged into the console. I must have forgotten to plug my phone in last night; the battery is dangerously low. "What was the point of arguing before I could show you that the car is fine?"

"Uh, Sloane," Julius says from the other side of the open driver's door. He points past me, his eyes wide.

From the phone, Sully curses. "The console is sparking! Where the mobile is plugged in. It's smoking. Get out of the goddamn car."

Instantly a cloud of smoke engulfs me, making my eyes water. Shit.

"Sloane, get the fuck out of the car," Sully booms.

"Right. Uh, sorry. I'm just so confused." Coughing, I step out of the car.

Unsure of how to handle the situation, I leave the door open. I keep a firm grip on my phone, but I can't back too far away since it's still plugged in.

"Are you okay?" Sully asks, his tone still elevated. If I didn't know my husband so well, I'd think it was panic rather than just anger.

Julius yanks the cord from my phone and lets it fall to the ground.

Realizing all Sully can see is the concrete beneath me, I flip the camera again. My heart pounds wildly in my chest, but the alarm is quickly edged out by frustration when I notice that he's not even on screen. No, where his image should be, all I find is a black screen.

It shouldn't surprise me. The man is an expert multitasker. Why would that change when he's on the phone with his wife, whose fucking car is on fire?

"I don't understand," I mutter.

"You shorted the circuit and now it's overheating," he explains, clueless to my true concern here. The man really doesn't give a shit, does he?

"It's a new car." I keep my tone even, hoping that'll keep me from getting emotional. I can rely only on myself. I know this.

"Brand-new cars can still be wrecked," Sully grunts out.

"But how will I get back and forth to New Jersey?" Fuck, I hate my life.

He's silent for a beat, then, "You're moving in?"

"God, Sully, focus."

"I am focusing. I'll buy you a new fucking car," he grouses.

"Right, because that's how you handle every problem. Throw money at it and hope it goes away." I hang up, wondering why I bothered to call him to begin with.

"I think we should shut the door," Julius says, pacing.

He stops at my side again, and we both peer into the car. The interior is still smoky, but it's hard to tell whether the console is still short-circuiting. It could be what's left from that initial spark.

"Step back," he says, turning in a circle, like he's looking for help.

My phone chimes, and on instinct, I lift it to check the display. *Sully*. Of course.

Sighing, I accept the FaceTime request, but when I'm met with a black screen again, I grit my teeth. "Sully, I'm busy dealing with this car. I don't have time for your dramatics, and clearly you don't have time for them either."

"What are you talking about?"

"You're busy. The damn phone is obviously facedown on your desk while you work and try to deal with me. Well, I'm not your problem anymore. Don't worry about me, I've got this covered."

The dark screen is replaced by a blurry image I can't make out. After a second, Sully's crazed face appears. "I had the mobile on the seat because I'm driving."

"Where?"

"To you," he mutters, the lines on his face deepening.

"Why?"

"Because, sweetheart, you *are* my problem. Nothing matters more than your safety, so before I get into an accident because I'm preoccupied with worry, would you please get away from the fucking car? And stay away until I get there to deal with it."

My mouth hangs open. Forget the car; I've short-circuited.

"Sloane, *please*," he begs in a tone that pulls at my heartstrings despite how badly I don't want it to.

"Oh, baby daddy is having a meltdown." Julius breaks into a smile and snatches the phone from my hand. "I'll take care of her. Should we leave the door open or closed?"

"Caesar," Sully grits out. "Just turn the bloody car off and get her out of there. I don't care what you do with the door."

"Right."

The screen goes dark, the line disconnected, but his words echo in my head. Nothing matters more. I blink once, then again. Is that really true?

Another tear slides down my cheek as the words settle in my heart. Shit. This is so not my day.

CHAPTER 6
Sully

I fly into the parking garage with my heart in my throat. All the way here, I told myself to remain calm. That Julius would keep Sloane away from the car. But until I see her with my own eyes —far away from the car and perfectly fine—I won't relax.

When her white Mercedes comes into view, I slam on the brakes and haul myself out of the driver's seat.

Sixty feet away, Sloane stands, arms crossed, staring off into space like she's lost. All I want is to make her feel better.

"Sloane," I call as I sprint to her.

I want to wrap her up in my arms and hold her close, but as I get closer, she steps back. Her expression shutters, locking me out. Fucking hell. Every time I remember I'm not allowed those moments anymore, it's like a bullet to the heart.

I pull to a stop and keep my hands to myself while I inspect her from head to toe to ensure she's not injured. Because even though I'm standing here next to her, my heart still doesn't believe it. "Are you okay?"

"I'm fine," she assures me, though she shakes her head, contradicting herself. "Great. Just wonderful. So what if the car is on fire?" She waves a hand at the vehicle, which is not currently on fire. But...

"As long as you aren't near it, I agree."

She assesses me, a storm of emotions brewing in her eyes.

"What are we going to do with it?" she asks, averting her gaze.

"I called for a tow. Should be here in"—I pull back the cuff of my suit jacket to check the time—"thirty minutes."

She nods. "So I have no car."

My chest tightens at the defeat in her tone. "I'll buy you a new car. Bullocks, I'll buy two. But please, I'm begging you, move in with me so I can be around to help with shite like this."

Instead of looking at me or answering my plea, she eyes Julius.

He cocks a brow, and her body slumps. "Fine. I'll move in with you."

My facial muscles, so used to frowning, twitch awkwardly as a smile takes over. Her agreement might be a begrudging one, but it's a step in the right direction.

"Don't get too excited. I'm not coming today. I have to pack."

"Okay." My heart feels lighter than it has in years. "Tomorrow."

"Tomorrow" seems like a fantastic idea until I make it home that night and assess our shitty flat.

I spend fifteen minutes rearranging Cal's forty-three plants, relegating them to a few areas to free up a little space in the lounge, but it's useless. The buggers are invasive as hell.

"Greenery makes people happy," Cal says as he picks up a small white ball from the pool-slash-Ping-Pong table he purchased when we moved in.

I shoot him a glare. "If you throw that at me, you plonker, you won't like what happens next."

Cal chuckles as his enormous Maine coon cat darts out of the room and lunges for the kitchen counter, where Brian is busy making a sandwhich. "Relax. You're scaring Fuzzy Wuzzy."

"Dammit," Brian barks from the kitchen. "Get down. You're too big to be on the counter. I said down, Dammit."

"Don't call him that." Cal spins and stomps away to deal with Brian and his cat.

Normally, I'd chuckle at the little tiff the two are always engaged in over the animal's name, but I'm too bloody stressed about bringing Sloane into this shithole to find any satisfaction in it.

"I still don't know how you did it," Lo says from the couch. "I was sure she couldn't be convinced to move in."

Roughing a hand over my jaw, I turn her way. "I—" I snap my mouth shut when I notice the fishbowl that should be in Cal's room.

"Why is that thing out here?"

"He needed a walk." Lo rolls her eyes. That's code for Cal killed another fish. Seven down, and according to Madame E, three to go.

"Again?" I step closer to the bowl and examine the blue beta fish. This one is much more bug-eyed than the last. How in the bloody hell does my sod of a brother not notice how often Lo changes them out?

She nods and mouths, "We're almost to lucky number ten."

Straightening, I put my hands on my hips. "So how do I fix this?"

She chuckles, scanning the dreary room. "There is nothing you can do to fix this place. Absolutely nothing."

"Yet you stay," I point out.

With a shrug, she sits back. "Because your brother is here."

That simple phrase is like a knife to the chest. Sloane and I used to feel that way too. Once upon a time, we were happy just because we were together.

From the beginning, we were inseparable. That's how I went from just getting by to really putting in an effort at school. Sloane didn't love the library, so when I suggested she could study with Brian and me at our place, she was more than willing.

Very quickly, she created a study schedule for the three of us, building in time not only to get our work done but to enjoy a few beers and watch movies. My GPA jumped almost a full point when impressing her became my motivation. The best part of our nightly study sessions was curling up with her on the sofa after. It took three movie nights and a whole lot of shite from Brian before I worked up the nerve to wrap my arm around her and tuck her against me. The small smile she sent me that evening will be forever locked in my heart.

Another *Dammit* from the kitchen pulls me from my revery. I swallow past the lump in my throat, my heart sinking. These days, experiencing a simple night like that with Sloane again feels implausible.

Lo stands, head tilted, like she's waiting for me to speak. I can't find the words. Sometimes I think it'd be easier to stop breathing than to live another day like this.

"Brian," Cal complains. "Stop with the Dammit."

With a chuckle, Lo skirts around me and follows the sound of the guys.

A massive cat, dozens of plants, and a bug-eyed fish. At least we've eradicated the mice and most of the bugs. And the place is clean. *Ish.*

Hands on my hips again, I take in the peeling paint. Lo is right. There's no fixing this.

A loud thud downstairs startles me, and I pinch the bridge of my nose.

Murphy, my nephew, pokes his head out of his bedroom. "Guess Sebastian is messing around with the law books again, huh?"

I wince. Make that an oversized cat, forty plants too many, the fish, and a ghost with a heavy foot.

I scrub my hand over my face. This can't be a disaster. I have to have hope.

CHAPTER 7
Sloane

I turn in a slow circle in the middle of my bedroom, rethinking every decision I've ever made. Today is move-in day, and I still haven't broken the news to T.J.

I'm afraid of getting his hopes up. What happens if he thinks this means we'll be one happy family again?

Do I tell him that I'm moving into the apartment so his dad can save the business? Should I prepare him now for the inevitable? That we'll eventually go our separate ways?

What I won't mention for now is the baby. I'm still in the first trimester, and because of my age, as well as the complications I experienced during my first pregnancy, I can't help but worry.

With a deep breath in, I shake the thoughts from my head. Instead, I remind myself of how fortunate I am to have T.J.

As the only child of two career-driven people, I was often forgotten about. An afterthought. And I vowed from an early age that I would never treat my child that way. It's why I wanted another baby so badly. So he'd never experience the loneliness that was my reality as a child. I wanted him to have the kind of sibling bond that Cal and Sully have.

Sully was uninterested, not only because T.J. was a difficult baby, but because my pregnancy was almost as hard on him as it was on me. He missed a lot of work while I was on bed rest, and when he was working to make partner not long after T.J. was born, that kind of time off could have been detrimental to his career.

Through it all, my longing for another child never waned.

And now here we are.

Maybe the circumstances aren't the greatest, but I can't help but be thrilled to add to my little family.

And though I have to move into the disgusting apartment in Jersey, at least I'll be living with my best friend. Lo will help me get through this.

One of the most difficult parts of separating from Sully was losing her, Cal, and Brian. Sure, they're still my friends, but because they work with Sully, by default, he got custody of them.

I was a lonely child, though it wasn't until law school that I realized just how isolated I'd been my whole life. The bond Brian and Sully shared opened my eyes to what I'd been missing out on. And when I went home with Sully that first holiday and met Cal? My mind was blown. I'd never been part of a boisterous family event. I'd never heard such laughter and teasing.

My parents, Roger and Beverly O'Malley, are the definition of serious. Dinners were quiet affairs, the silence interrupted only by the clinking of silverware and the subdued conversation of the adults. Because in our home, children were meant to be seen, not heard. Once I was old enough to hold a conversation that interested them, they used family meals as a way to foster debates. My parents would give me a topic, and I'd have to argue both sides.

It was riveting, as one can imagine.

But I'd prefer that kind of interaction at dinner over the nights I spent waiting for Sully. Night after night, I'd make dinner, set the table, get myself dressed, and wait for him to get home. On the days that I didn't go to the office, it was the only adult interaction I'd have, and I longed for it.

But after months of blowing out the candles and going to bed without my husband, I stopped trying.

Experiencing one of those nights was heartbreaking enough. Suffering through it for months on end killed something inside me.

Sully feels like the divorce came out of left field, and in truth, I can't connect my decision to ask him to move out with one specific moment. There was no knockdown, drag-out fight. Instead, it was one tiny moment built on top of another and another that led to a resentment I could no longer push down and a loneliness that swallowed me whole.

Last April, he made it home for dinner, which hadn't happened in months. The entire time, we sat across from one another in silence. It wasn't until we were almost finished that T.J. piped up and asked why everyone was so quiet.

Sully was reading over a case file and I'd probably been staring into space. It hit me then that my child was living my childhood. A childhood I wouldn't wish on even my worst enemy.

I panicked. And I realized I didn't even recognize myself anymore. I couldn't live like that for another second.

"Ready?" T.J. asks, pulling me from my thoughts.

Not really, but it's now or never.

So I turn around and assess my son. He's dressed for school, with his backpack secured over his shoulders. His big blue eyes, the same shade as his dad's, see more than we give him credit for.

"Yeah, I wanted to talk to you for a second before we go."

The moment the words leave my mouth, he bounces on his toes. T.J. is a doer. He's always moving. Standing in one place and listening can be a challenge. So when he shakes his hips back and forth and giggles, all I can do is smile. "Sure."

"Remember when you asked about moving in with Uncle Cal, Uncle Brian and Dad while they live in Jersey?"

T. J. nods, his hair falling across his forehead.

"Is that something you'd still like?"

"Yes," he practically screeches, bouncing around in a circle.

My heart aches in the best and worst way. He's so excited, yet the idea of leaving this place is painful.

I clear my throat and wait for him to settle again. "Would it be okay if I came too? I think I'll miss you too much if you go without me."

T.J. scans the room rather than looking at me. "Sure."

I close my eyes and shake my head at his indifference. My feelings aren't actually hurt, because come bedtime, he'll be thankful I'm there. Bedtime has always been special for us, and since Sully moved out and T.J. has spent weekends with him, it's been hard on us both.

"Hey," I say, snagging his attention. "Do you have any questions for me?"

Head tilted, he presses his lips together, like he's really thinking hard. I worry constantly about the damage we're doing to him by splitting up. It was the right thing to do. I have no doubt. I was miserable and I couldn't stand the idea that T.J. could pick up on the tension and resentment.

With any luck, he hasn't sensed the underlying turmoil. I'm heartbroken enough for the both of us as it is. I just want good things for my son.

"Is cat poop poisonous?" he finally asks, catching me off guard. "Because Simon at school said it is, but Fuzzy's poop isn't poisonous, right?"

Poop. That's what he was contemplating all that time.

I bite back a laugh and shake my head. "Let's just stay away from poop in general, bud." I brush his hair back from his face. "Is there anything else you want to bring to your dad's?"

Before I've finished the sentence, he's darting out the door, yelling a *no* over his shoulder.

I wince. I *think* that conversation went okay.

Hopefully, the move goes as smoothly.

—

. . .

"Thanks, guys," I say as Sully, Brian, and Cal appear in the doorway, each carrying a suitcase.

Sully ordered me to sit here on the couch while they collected my things from the car Sully ordered.

My reply? *Right, because the incubator has one job. You guys can handle the rest.*

Cal winced, Sully sighed, and Brian shook his head. Lo just smiled at me knowingly. Thankfully, she gets my sarcastic sense of humor. If not, she'd surely think I was a bitch. Maybe I am a bitch. I don't like myself very much lately, but once again, I blame my husband for that.

"This is all you have?" Sully glares down at the three suitcases.

I nod.

He drags a hand down his face. "You used to travel to Florida with more than this."

My death glare is strong this afternoon. I went into the office for a bit this morning, but I wanted to get our stuff situated here before Cal picks T.J. and Murphy up from school, so I took the afternoon off.

"I traveled with three suitcases because I was packing for our family, Sully. The Sully and Mike monsters T.J. couldn't go anywhere without took up an entire bag. Snacks from his approved list, bottles, diapers, extra changes of clothes. And don't forget that I packed all of *your* things too."

The room goes deathly silent.

Shoulders slumping, Sully gives me a sheepish frown. "I just mean you have more stuff than this. A penthouse full."

Why must this man insist on having this conversation in front of our friends? I don't want to fight, but he never stops pushing.

"Listen, I've agreed to this little arrangement because it's what's best for T.J. You need this firm and he needs a father who isn't miserable. But make no mistake: I'm not here for you. My stuff is in New York because T.J. and the baby and I will return to the penthouse when you complete this insane trust provision. Then we can all move on."

"It's also what's best for you," he says, like the man can't help but pick a fight. I arch a brow, allowing him to dig himself a little deeper. It's more fun this way. "You're pregnant—"

I slap my cheeks and widen my eyes. "I am?"

His face reddens, a sure sign that he's lost hold of any vestige of patience. "For fuck's sake, Sloane. Could we have one rational conversation?"

Beside me, Lo sucks in a breath. Brian subtly turns, surveying the room rather than looking at either of us. Cal grimaces, but he keeps his mouth shut.

I'm not surprised by Sully's outburst. It's par for the course, honestly. If he doesn't get his way, he loses it.

And I don't have the bandwidth to put up with it. We have a child who acts the same way, who's too young to have a handle on his emotions and reactions. *That* I can handle. But I refuse to let a grown man who should know better behave that way.

"Yes, I'm pregnant. And yes, my last pregnancy was difficult, so I may need help." I glance down at my hands, hating to admit that kind of weakness. Yes, I'm a stubborn ass sometimes, but I won't ever allow my pride to get in the way of the well-being of my child. I want this baby so badly, and I won't do anything to risk this pregnancy. My hands tremble in my lap at the mere thought of things going wrong. "So I'm moving in here to be with Lo. I *need* Lo. She's here, so I'm here."

Lo squeezes my forearm, making it difficult to maintain my tough-bitch façade. If I'm not careful, I'll end up in tears.

Sully lowers his head and gives it a shake. Then he hefts the suit-case he carried up again and heads for *his* room. "You're moving in with *me*," he says without looking back. "I'm helping you with this pregnancy because you're carrying *my* child and you're *my wife*."

"I am *not* sleeping with you." Annoyed again, I haul myself to my feet and follow him.

Not a single one of our friends follows. Not that I blame them. If I could, I'd run and hide too. Between my blood boiling and the steam coming from Sully's ears it's clear this fight could go nuclear.

He sets the suitcase by the door and motions to the queen-size bed pushed against one wall. "You can have the bed."

I inhale a steadying breath but immediately regret it when I'm assaulted by a scent that is one hundred percent Sully. Nostalgia washes over me, and memory after memory pummels me. He still wears the cologne I bought him for our first anniversary. For nearly twenty years, the familiar smell has grounded and comforted me.

Mask, Sloane. Put on your damn mask. You will not cry.

I swallow back the melancholy threatening to cause tears and pull my shoulders back. "Obviously. You can sleep in the bunk with T. J." I nod at the beds. Both are made up, as if this was his plan all along. I hate him for knowing that I'd force him into the bunk and not even attempting to argue about it. For knowing I'd put a grown man— a six-foot-four man, with broad shoulders and, well, broad everything —in a bed designed for a child.

Just the thought of him on the top bunk, since T. J.'s afraid of heights, is ridiculous.

Sully steps aside, giving me a better view of the queen mattress and the oversized pregnancy pillow on top of it. "That's the plan. I have your bed all set. If you need anything else—"

I shake my head and press my lips together. I want to tell him to get rid of the damn pregnancy pillow. I hated the one I had seven years ago, and I hate this one just as much. But seven years ago I had my husband to cuddle with. My husband's body was my pillow.

So I'll keep the dreaded thing. It's all I have now. I guess Sully knew that was the case. That or he's so oblivious to my preferences that he never noticed how, night after night, I'd kick that pillow to the floor, then turn over and snuggle up to him.

"I'll grab the rest of your things and then leave you to unpack." His voice is quiet, the tone defeated, like maybe he doesn't actually want that.

I wish I knew how to move on from this stalemate. How to navigate us into the kind of rational conversation he asked for.

But there's nothing rational about divorcing the love of my life. The person who broke me time and again while I waited, day after day, to see if the man I once adored would reappear. Eventually, I stopped waiting. I stopped hoping. This man in front of me is nothing but a mirage. It's too hard to stand so close physically, yet be so, so far away emotionally. It's easier to pick fights than it is to work through how we got here. When he sighs like I've annoyed or exasperated him, just by existing, it's easier to remind myself that he's not my Sully anymore.

Finally, I find my voice, keeping my focus averted. "Sounds good."

He disappears, and I slump down on the bed, giving myself a moment to fall apart. Not a single thing about this situation sounds good, but for T. J.'s sake and the sake of this new life we've created, I have to try.

"Lo," I call.

I took my time unpacking in peace, leaving my toiletries for last. I wander past what can only be described as a locker room in search of a second bathroom, but all I find are three additional bedrooms. Makeup bag pressed to my chest, I shuffle back into the tiled room I used on that fateful night several weeks ago.

Slowly, I turn in a circle, surveying the space. This can't actually be the *only* bathroom. God, I'm a terrible mother. How did I not investigate every inch of this apartment when I left T. J. here the first time?

The plastic curtain with pretty flowers on it looks new. No doubt because of Lo. I remember the curtain being very masculine. Navy blue, maybe?

There are seven of us now. And there's only one shower? There's no way we can all use it without coming up with a detailed schedule.

I stick my head out the door and call for my best friend again.

Lo rushes in, her eyes wide. "What? Did you see a mouse? I was sure Fuzzy would scare them all away."

Mouse? Heart rate picking up, I back myself up against the wall and search the floor for rodents.

"Cal!" Lo shouts. "There's a mouse."

My brother-in-law charges in, wielding a broom *and* a mop like swords, nearly hitting the both of us. "Where is it?" he demands. "Lola, get on my back. I'll protect you."

My best friend jumps on her boyfriend's back and clings to him like a baby monkey as he scours the floor.

"Where did you see it, Sloaney?" With the mop, Cal pokes at the trash can beside the toilet. "Point me in the right direction and then run. Save yourself."

My momentary panic is quickly replaced by annoyance. This man is so damn dramatic. I step away from the wall and edge away from Cal's weapons. "I didn't say there were rodents."

Lo, who's got her legs wrapped around Cal's waist while she clutches his shirt, squeaks. "There aren't any mice? You're sure?"

I inhale deeply. I can't take her seriously when she looks like this. "No mice. Can you get down?"

With a quick kiss to Cal's neck, she thanks him for rushing in, then slides down his body. It's oddly endearing how adorable they are. Though it's equally nauseating.

I blame it on the pregnancy hormones.

Cal props the broom and the mop up in the corner and holds up his hands. "I was specifically warned not to enter the bathroom when you're in here," he whispers. "So I'm going to back out slowly, and we'll pretend you never saw me. Okay?" He takes an exaggerated step back, then another, and at the threshold, he shoots me a wink, then spins and disappears.

Lo wears a dreamy smile as she gazes out into the hall. "So," she finally says when she snaps back to the present. "Why were you screaming for me?"

"There aren't really mice, right?" I ask at the same time.

With a roll of her eyes, she puts her hands on her hips. "You just told me there weren't."

"I literally just moved in. How would I know? What the hell is this place? And tell me this isn't the only bathroom."

Lo bites her bottom lip. "Yeah, it's less than ideal."

"Less than ideal?" I hiss, my blood pressure spiking in a way that probably isn't good for a pregnant woman. "Warts are less than ideal. Mice, less than ideal. Hell, the commute to Jersey is less than fucking ideal. This, Lo"—I motion to the space around us—"This is ludicrous."

She sighs, her shoulders lowering. "I don't understand how Terry lived here, and I'm not sure I'll ever figure out why he insisted that the guys move in."

"Nothing about this makes sense. Why are we here?" I whine. Yes, I'm being difficult, but I'm not sure how much more I can take. "I have to share a room with my ex-husband. And my kid. And before you say that second part isn't a problem, let me promise you, it really, really is. I have a naked-sleeping problem, and the last thing I need is to scar my six-year-old by stripping down in our shared room in the middle of the night."

Lo scrunches her nose. "A naked-what now?"

"I—uh..." I grimace. "I tend to undress while I'm sleeping." I peer out the open door to make sure we're alone.

My secret should still be safe. I can't imagine Sully mentioning this to his law partner or his brother. Hell, he probably doesn't even remember. The man has barely spared me a glance in the last few years.

"Like you kick off your pants?" she asks. "That's normal. We've all done it when we get overheated."

"No, Lo." I shake my head. "Like completely naked. Half the time I can't find my clothes the next day. I am apparently very neat when I sleep. I fold my pajamas like clean laundry and put them away. One time, I found them in the fridge the next morning." I wave a hand. "The point is, I wake up naked, and I can't be naked in a room with Sully and T.J."

Lo claps a hand to her mouth, but not before a snort escapes her. "Sorry." She winces. "I know all of this is less than ideal, but can't you put on a few more layers or something? It's only a few months."

"It's nine months, Lo. Nine freaking months. Not to mention I'll be hotter than normal because I'm freaking pregnant."

She hums, her focus drifting up and to the side like she's thinking. "What if—"

I hold up a hand, cutting her off. It's not up to her to come up with a solution. And it's not fair of me to put the responsibility on her. Everything seems even more dire since I walked in here, but that isn't her problem. "Forget it. You're right. I'm just emotional. Extra layers make sense."

"Are you sure?" she asks, frowning. "What if you and I share a room? Cal could bunk with Sully and T. J. If that's what you need to feel comfortable here, he'd understand."

My heart sinks. I'm being selfish, and here she is, willing to kick her boyfriend out of bed to accommodate me. "No. You and Cal are just starting out. You deserve this time. It's special."

Her green eyes brighten and her cheeks go pink. She's so damn happy, and I'm happy for her. She deserves it. So does Cal. Just because Sully and I are miserable doesn't mean everyone else should be.

I pad over to the sink and unzip my toiletry bag. "I'm going to take a shower and get ready for bed."

"It's six." Lo holds up her phone like I might not believe her.

I nod. Yeah, it's early, but I'm ready for this day to end. Tomorrow will be better. It has to be.

CHAPTER 8

Sully

At the sound of a clunk on the hardwood floor, I bolt upright. I regret it instantly. *Fuck.* I haven't even opened my eyes when I slam against the low ceiling above me. *Again.*

I bite back a string of curses as I rub my forehead. Men over six feet should not sleep in bunk beds. The pain ebbs as I lie back again, but as I shift, my lower back twinges, sending a bolt of pain down my leg. The bloody leg that's hanging off the end of this cursedly tiny bed. Fuck my height. Sleeping arrangements like this are a nightmare for men over forty.

Teeth gritted, I straighten my leg and flex my foot to ease the locked muscle. Two knee bends later, the pain subsides. Damn, getting old sucks.

By now, my eyes have adjusted to the dark, and from here, I can see two Columbia Law sweatshirts folded neatly on the floor.

My lips twitch. Sloane climbed into bed wearing both of them, looking like the cutest marshmallow man I'd ever seen.

I didn't think I'd see the pregnancy waddle for a few more months, but it was almost there tonight when she wandered in wearing at least three pairs of trousers.

Movement on the bed catches my attention, so I turn on my side.

Sloane slowly rolls to sitting in a way that would probably be eerie if I hadn't seen her do this hundreds of times.

She's self-conscious about her tendency to strip-sleep.

Is that what it would be called? Strip-sleepwalking, maybe?

Regardless of how it would be labeled by a professional, I've always enjoyed watching her do this.

Standing now, she looks ten pounds lighter than she did when she went to bed, which means the two sweatshirts on the floor probably aren't the only things she's shed so far tonight.

With bated breath, I lean closer to the edge. As much as I want this to be the last layer so I can get a peek at the flawless skin beneath, skin I haven't seen in months, I know if it is, I'll have to look away. She would hate me for looking without her permission. It hurts to admit, but it's the truth. There was a time when I got this show every night.

Damn do I miss those days.

She slips her hands into the waistband of her gray sweats and lowers them slowly. I prepare to look away, my heart thudding heavily, but when the black fabric beneath is visible, I let out a long breath.

My bloody wife is the most put-together person I know in the light of day. But this quirk, this imperfection, is one of my favorite things about her.

She folds the gray material, but instead of putting the sweats in the pile of clothes on the floor, she moves efficiently to the dresser and slides them into a drawer. While she stands there, she drags her long-sleeve shirt over her head.

This time, the pale skin of her back comes into view, interrupted only by the strap of her bra.

Groaning, I lean back and stare at the ceiling.

Her footsteps are nearly imperceptible as she moves back to bed.

If I look down now, I'll get a peek of her full breasts covered in nothing but a thin layer of lace. I want to. Fuck, am I desperate to see more of her. But I shouldn't. No. I'll keep my eyes to myself until she gives me the go-ahead.

That's what I'm trying to convince myself of when, without my permission, my attention drifts down to my wife and I catch the swell of the most perfect breasts in the world.

I only allow myself to look for the space of one breath. Then I'm flat on my back again, my eyes screwed shut. I am a bloody creeper.

The bed creaks, signaling that she's snuggled under the blankets again. My girl is a burrower. I sit up, allowing myself to look at her again, knowing she's covered.

It's a mistake. Karma, maybe, for peeking at Sloane. Because I smack my head on the ceiling again, and stars dance in my vision.

But when they clear, I can't help but take in my wife, who's now buried beneath three massive comforters and surrounded by a mountain of pillows.

Fuck, she's beautiful. Yes, we're sleeping in separate beds, and yes, every word she says to me is laced with derision, but this is a start. For now, we're in the same room, and that gives me hope that we're heading in the right direction.

I'm only slightly disappointed to discover Sloane hasn't removed any more clothes when I quietly slip out of bed to get ready for the day.

I'm up earlier than usual, determined to shower and dress early, then wake T.J. and get him ready, allowing Sloane time to focus on herself. With any luck, I can talk her into stopping for breakfast after we drop T.J. off.

Unfortunately, my wanker of a brother throws a wrench into my plan.

"I always take Murphy to school. Tell him, Lola." My overdramatic brother spins toward his girlfriend, his brows hitting his hairline. "Tell him," he huffs. "I. Take. Murphy."

Yeah, he typically drops Murphy at school in the city, and even T.J. on the days he's with me. But I figured he'd be thankful for a break from carpooling.

Lo rubs her hand up and down Cal's back, her eyes shifting from my brother to me to Sloane and back. "Of course you do, baby."

I want to tell him to fuck off, but my conscience stops me, reminding me that he only discovered his son existed a matter of months ago, and the transition wasn't easy on either of them. And as much as my brother irritates me, for as over-the-top as he is, his love for Murphy is pure. His plunge into fatherhood wasn't all that graceful, but he proves to his little lad every day that he can be counted on.

"Okay," I say with a sigh. "You take Murphy and I'll take T.J."

"No." Sloane narrows her eyes, her expression shifting into a scowl I've become very, very familiar with these last several months. Actually, years now that I think about it. "Taking two cars to the city is ridiculous."

"No, it's not."

"Why are you arguing this? Is it because you don't think I'm capable of taking our son to school?" she almost growls.

"Of course not," I rush out.

Fuck. I walked right into a trap.

"Because I'm pregnant, I'm no longer capable?" she asks, her face flushing an angry red. "Or have you always found me so incapable?"

"You are more than capable," I choke out. "That's what I meant." When her expression doesn't relax, panic overtakes me. "Of course I think you're capable," I go on. "Of course I don't think you're not capable."

Lo and Cal watch us with matching expressions of confusion.

My wife still looks like she's gearing up to send laser beams shooting from her eyes.

Cal clears his throat, forcing his expression from that of *What the fuck did he just say?* to one of confidence. "I'll take them in the mornings. You can pick Sloaney up after work."

I know a losing fight when I see one. "Fine."

Better Daddy

Since I only get one ride from the city with Sloane, I make the most of it. I show up fifteen minutes early with my wife's favorite decaf caramel macchiato and take the elevator up to the twenty-second floor.

The stainless-steel box creeps up so slowly, I begin to think I could have made it there faster if I'd taken the stairs. By the time the doors open, my body is buzzing with anxious energy. All I want is to lay eyes on Sloane. Back in law school, there were days I could hardly make it through a class because every cell in my body was desperate to be in her presence.

Though it seems impossible now, that sensation subsided over the years. Somewhere along the way, I allowed myself to believe that I'd always have her. I took our time together for granted, so sure that I'd always start and end my day with her.

Living without her for the last several months has brought that anxious need to be caught in her orbit back in full force.

I nod at the people I pass as I stride toward Sloane's office. Each one greets me with a friendly look. All except the good-looking wanker behind the desk outside her door.

"Look." He smirks, his white teeth practically glinting in the fluorescent light. "It's baby daddy. She might kill you for drinking coffee in front of her."

Irritation rips up my spine. "I'm the husband, Caesar."

He chuckles, unfazed. "We'll see."

There is no world in which I'll allow any outcome that doesn't involve Sloane and me together forever. Even if it means chaining her to me.

I scowl and loom over his desk, satisfied when my shadow falls over him. "Want to bet on it? Because I will win my wife back, and I won't let anyone get in my way."

The fucker doesn't even bother to look intimidated. No, he straightens, grinning, and claps. "Ooh, baby daddy's got grit. Didn't see that coming."

With a step back, I huff. "How does Sloane put up with you?"

"Sloane adores me. You, on the other hand." He shakes his head. "I've heard some not-so-nice rumors."

"I very much doubt that." I sneer. "My wife has never liked an assistant." Sloane went through more than a few while she worked for our firm. She may be my perfect match, but that doesn't mean she doesn't have a flaw or two. And she's never gotten along well with any of her assistants at Murphy and Machon all the years she worked for us.

"That's because she never worked with me before. I am a magical unicorn of an assistant."

I bark out a laugh, but the sound cuts off when I hear my wife's voice.

"We need to push for Cartwright or Sauter. Both tend to be more pro-father."

Straightening, I turn toward her door, my body once again eager to be near hers.

As she turns the corner, her eyes widen, and she breaks into a look I know without a doubt means she's pleasantly surprised to see me.

My chest swells. It's been forever since I've had this kind of effect on her. This is officially the greatest moment of my day.

That is until I take her in and discover that Will fucking Higgins is touching her.

The sense of elation that hit me at the sight of her is quickly stomped out as I zero in on her lower back, where Will's hand rests just above her ass.

Any lower and I'd have to kill him.

It takes superhuman strength not to lose my fucking mind when he looks up and breaks into a taunting smirk. "Sully, what brings you out of your shithole office and back to New York?"

Lo complains about our place in Jersey constantly. That I can handle. But as the words leave Will's mouth, my hands tighten into fists. I want to snap back, but I have absolutely no legitimate argument. He's right. The place is a shithole.

"You're early," Sloane says.

Those two words are enough to wash away the urge to punch the motherfucker beside her in the nose. This woman is what matters. Her and our children.

And the delighted surprise on her face. Because dammit, she still looks happy to see me.

"It's not your job to wait for me," I tell her, taking a step closer. "It's my job to wait for you." I give Will a pointed look, and the arsehole has enough sense to step back.

With a huff, Sloane rolls her eyes. "Because I'm the incubator."

Fuck.

"No." I hold out the decaf caramel macchiato. "Because being with you is the best part of my day."

To my utter shock, for what feels like the first time in a millennium, my wife smiles at me.

CHAPTER 9
Sloane

I don't know what to do with my hands as Sully eases into traffic. Do I put them in my lap? Is that how I normally sit when I'm the passenger in someone's car?

I actually have no idea because I'm rarely a passenger sitting in the front. Normally, if I'm driving with anyone other than Sully, it's a hired car, so I sit in the back. Before Sully and I were separated, I think we'd hold hands. Or I wouldn't focus so much on my damn hands because we'd be talking. Or maybe T.J. would be in the back, screaming, and I'd be working to entertain him so he wouldn't drive Sully nuts.

I reach for the coffee he picked up for me and take a sip, settling my nerves. The gesture was sweet. A surprise. Just like how he showed up early to pick me up.

I'd even go so far as to say I liked it. For a singular moment in time, I forgot all of our baggage, and when his eyes met mine, I couldn't help but feel the tiniest flutter in my stomach.

But now it's back to awkwardness, because I'm not sure what to do with my fucking hands.

It's one thing to spend time with him in the apartment. At least we're not alone there, and I can wander into another room if I'm feeling uncomfortable.

Even in our bedroom, T.J. is with us, and I ensure all conversations stay centered around him.

Now that it's just the two of us, I don't have the first clue what to talk about. I used to tell this man my every thought. He, on the other hand, has never been a big talker, even when we were at our happiest. When we didn't have a lot to say, the silence was comfortable. Or we'd turn up the music—normally sixties rock—and he'd rest a hand on my thigh while he drove.

That's what I'd do with my hands. I'd settle mine on top of his. The memory leaves my thigh feeling unbearably cold.

I glance over at Sully, wishing I could somehow say how much I'd love his hands on me again. How much I miss his hands.

Now he keeps both on the steering wheel, in a grip like he's strangling it. Rather than music, the only sounds come from the traffic around us. And there are no smiles to be found.

"How was—"

"Can I turn on the music?" I say, inadvertently cutting him off.

He clears his throat and nods. "Sure, put on whatever you want."

I wince, kicking myself for interrupting him. "You were going to ask a question."

"I was just making conversation. Thought I'd ask how your day was. That kind of thing." He blows out a breath, keeping his focus on the road. "Music is probably better, though."

"Right." I nod woodenly. Dammit. When did we become a pair of robots who don't know how to make conversation? Rather than turn the music on, though, I take a steadying breath and say, "My day was fine. Did the school call you too?"

He glances my way, his forehead creased. "Call me for what? Is T.J. okay?"

His response melts the ice around my heart further. Because while our hellion of a child is more likely to be in trouble at school than hurt, Sully's first instinct is to check on his well-being.

T.J. is always getting into mischief, and we're always getting calls from the principal. I am, at least. Maybe they don't call Sully as well. Maybe I should be relaying these incidents to him so he's in the know. "He's fine. Luckily, the fire department was already at the school doing a demonstration—"

"Oh fuck," Sully mutters, tipping his head back.

I snort. "Yeah, T.J. climbed up the side of the building and then refused to get down."

The corner of his lips twitch. "He does hate heights."

I let out a breath of a laugh. "Yup. The lovely men of the NYFD had to get him down. I stopped by, got a talking-to from the principal, and promised we'd deal with it tonight."

"I'll take care of it," he says with a sigh.

My heart clenches at the pain in his tone. "You don't have to."

Sully hates being the bad guy. He gets so little time with T. J., so I get it. Though I suppose that's changed now that I've moved in.

Hands at ten and two, he sits straighter, his attention still on the road. "I will. You dealt with the principal. Seems only fair I deal with the discipline."

"You won't yell at him, right?"

I'm more sensitive to yelling than most, I think. It seems strange for an attorney, but my whole childhood, my parents functioned in one of two modes: anger or indifference. Long before T.J. was even a possibility, I made a vow not to raise my child that way. Yes, T.J. needs discipline, but parenting is like walking a tightrope. It's ensuring I don't take my anger out on him while also holding him accountable. And it's only made more difficult when one's child would be considered naughty by some standards and high needs by professionals.

Without turning, Sully eyes me, offering me a small smile. "I promise I won't raise my voice."

With a sigh, I settle back in my seat, and as silence descends, Sully hits the button for the radio. When "Wild Thing" by the Troggs filters through the speakers, I have to hold back a smile. At times, I may feel like I don't know this man anymore, but at least his taste in music hasn't changed.

When a commercial comes on, I turn the volume down. "How was your day?"

His eyes widen, like my question surprises him. "It was fine." Then he shakes his head. "Actually, it was awful."

I cough out a laugh. "Really? Not loving your new office?"

He rolls his eyes, though he's smirking. "What is there to love?"

"You've got a psychic, a ghost, and a magical closet." I shift in my seat so I'm facing him. "Sounds a lot more exciting than New York."

Sully nods. "At least Amy didn't mail any motions to the deli this week."

"Amy?" It's embarrassing the way my tone rises a full octave. Last year, he had an intern who seemed a bit too comfortable with him. She was everywhere. I didn't work in the office too often, mostly I drafted the trusts or wills from home, but every time I came in to meet with a client, there she was. Young and perky and beautiful and far too familiar with my husband. But she was in New York. Only Lo works in the Jersey office.

Unaware of my inner turmoil, Sully continues. "Yeah, you remember her. She's in her third year of law school, so she's interning for us again."

"In New Jersey?" This time I couldn't hide my annoyance if I tried.

He frowns at me. "Yeah. Lo hates her, but she's gotten better over the last month. Like I said, no certified mail to the deli." He chuckles like I should find this funny.

"Right." I fake a smile. "Small wins." As an old pain flares to life in my chest, I turn toward the passenger window.

Dammit, Sloane.

I need to get a handle on these thoughts of mine. Why do I care if Amy works in Sully's office? We're getting divorced. His personal life is no longer my concern. And for the first time in months, we're getting along. I should be thankful we've made it to this point.

My stomach does this weird twisty thing, though, when I imagine Sully signing the papers. And when I think of how Amy is probably waiting for that to happen, I have to fight the urge to double over. She'll probably be the one who files them for Brian, and she'll wear a big smile when she does. Then she'll stalk into my husband's office, wearing a low-cut dress, and ask him out to dinner. He'd have no reason to say no. By then, he'd owe me nothing. Meanwhile I'll be pregnant and at home, likely on bed rest.

"Sloane?" Sully's voice pulls me from my inner ramblings. When I turn to look at him, his face is etched in concern. "Are you okay?"

I dip my chin. It's a lie. And pretending is becoming harder every day. I nod once more but follow it up with a shake of my head. "No."

He grips the steering wheel tighter, his knuckles whitening, and inspects me between glances at the road. "What's wrong?"

"I never liked the way Amy looked at you."

His lips tug down as he glances in his rearview mirror. "Intern Amy? That's what this is about?"

My cheeks heat with shame, but I'm tired of hiding my every thought. We're having another child. We live together, even if it's temporary and under duress and with far too many roommates. We'll spend the next eighteen years co-parenting, and if we're going to be successful, then we need to learn to communicate better.

"Yes." I blow out a breath as we inch forward in traffic. "Be honest with me, please. You said you never cheated—"

Sully growls, the steering wheel creaking as he grips it tighter. "I haven't so much as looked at another woman since I met you." Though he keeps his eyes on the road, the pain radiating from him pummels into me.

I ignore the sensation, pulling my shoulders back. "Until we separated."

With a grunt, he turns the wheel, maneuvering the car to the shoulder, and slams the gearshift into park. When he turns to face me, his slate blue eyes are molten and his breaths are ragged. "Never. Not since the day you walked into torts wearing that black and red plaid skirt and a turtleneck. I heard you laugh. You were talking to your friend—" He closes his eyes like he's trying to conjure her name.

"Samantha," I supply.

His eyes fly open and he gives a jerky nod. "Yes. Her. I heard you laugh and my heart went up my goddamn throat. I knew in that moment I would marry you. I knew I'd spend the rest of my life chasing that sound." He shakes his head, frustration rolling off him. "Sweetheart, I know I've fucked up. You haven't made that sound in far too long, and that's *my fault*. But I swear on everything I have, those feelings have never gone away. They've never even dimmed. There isn't a woman who holds a fucking match, let alone a candle to you."

My heart races in my chest not only at his words but at his delivery. At the way he's staring at me, like he's trying to imprint what he's saying onto my brain. Into my heart.

And dammit, it's working. I trust him. Fuck, do I hate myself for it. He's being honest. He feels all those things. I just don't think we can find our way back to being the people we were back then.

I close my eyes, unable to handle his intense gaze. "I believe you. We should, uh, get back on the road."

When I find the courage to look at him, he's checking his mirrors and merging back into traffic. I steal glances every minute or so as we make our way toward the tunnel, and with each passing mile, he relaxes a little. By the time we're out of the Lincoln Tunnel, he's smiling.

Only now does it hit me that I can't remember the last time he smiled. Genuinely smiled, not the forced expression that makes him look like he's snarling. I study the way his lips lift, the curve of his shoulder when it's no longer tense. I focus on his fingers as he taps to the beat of the music still playing quietly.

"Why do you seem happier?" I worry I'll start an argument, but I have to know.

My husband turns to me, wearing a full on grin. "Because you, sweetheart, just gave me hope."

"Hope?" A huff of a laugh escapes me.

"Yes," he says, one side of his mouth hitching up higher. "You were jealous." His eyes dance, the once stormy irises now a brighter blue. "And if you're jealous, I've still got a shot."

I blow out a breath, my brain short-circuiting. Damn this man. He's right. I was jealous. And yeah, after this conversation, I, too, am feeling a hint of that wistfully scary emotion.

For the rest of the drive, we stick to humming along to familiar songs. It's better this way. Safer. It ensures we don't ruin the tentative truce we unwittingly agreed to.

When we step into the apartment, dinner is already on the table. The rest of the night moves at lightning speed, full of chatter and homework and table tennis. The kids con the guys into three rounds while Lo and I clean the kitchen.

While the boys take showers and the guys play pool, I change into five layers of clothes in preparation for bed. I'll start the night sweltering, but it's necessary, and five seemed to work well last night. This morning I woke up to a pile of sweatshirts on the floor, but I was still dressed, so I'll take that as a win. Though overnight, I managed to leave the bedroom and hang a pair of pants in the coat closet without waking anyone. It's wild.

After T.J. is showered and in pajamas, Sully sits on the end of his bed. Though we found a little slice of normalcy today, I don't think I can share this bedtime routine with him, so I duck out to brush my teeth, promising to come back and say good night after.

As I pad back to the bedroom, T.J. is speaking just loud enough to be heard in the hallway, so I stop and give them another minute alone. "They told us we couldn't climb *the monkey bars*," he says. "No one said anything about the wall."

I creep a little closer and peer into the room, finding them snuggled together in the bottom bunk. T.J. is beneath the covers, but Sully is on top of them, now dressed in a pair of black sweats and a white t-shirt. The sight melts my heart, and for a moment, all I want is to climb in with them.

"The teachers probably assumed that you knew not to climb walls," Sully says, his tone patient.

"You always tell me not to assume. And they're teachers. They know so, so much, so they should know not to assume." T.J.'s thought process is always astounding. "I wish they didn't assume, though, because I didn't like it when I got to the top."

Sully hums.

"But then the firefighter saved me. Now I want to be a firefighter."

"Probably gotta work on that fear of heights, then," my husband says, a hint of laughter in his tone.

"I can work on it on the monkey bars at recess tomorrow. Because firefighters have cool outfits. I don't want to be a lawyer. You don't have cool outfits."

Sully lets out a huff, though there's no heat behind it. "How do you know I'm not like Superman? Maybe my cool outfit is under my suit. Ever think of that?"

T.J. grasps the hem of Sully's T-shirt and yanks.

Sully, who's got to be the most ticklish person I know, squeals like a girl and tugs the cotton back into place while gently grasping T.J.'s arm to stop him.

When T.J. goes for him with his other hand, homing in on the spot that only he and I know about, I can't hide my giggle. Both of my boys crane their necks to look at me, and T.J. brightens. "We're having a sleepover, Mom. Come snuggle with us."

I step into the room but stay near the door. "I don't think I'll fit, bud." The mattress on the bottom bunk is a full, but Sully's a big guy. I have no idea how he sleeps on the top bunk.

"I can give you two some time alone," Sully offers, shifting like he's going to sit up. "This is how we end our nights when T.J. is here."

"Yup." T.J. loops his arms around Sully's neck, pulling him back down. "Dad and I talk until he falls asleep, and then I move to the big bed because he steals all my covers."

Sully's mouth falls open, and he gives our little guy a look of feigned shock.

In this moment, I don't even recognize him. This teasing, joking man disappeared years ago. Yet here he is, resurfacing in Jersey, making T.J. smile.

My icy shield melts just a little more. My son deserves this.

"No," I say. "You two enjoy your tradition. It's sweet."

"Mom," T.J. whines. "I need my good-night kiss."

Right. He'd never let me forget about *our* good-night routine. I don't let T.J. sleep in my bed because of the whole naked sleeping thing, of course. I never even lie down with him because he's never been big on cuddles. Yet here he is, snuggled up close to his dad like it's the most natural thing in the world.

Without thinking, I lean over Sully to plant a kiss on my little guy's forehead.

Sully sucks in a breath and goes completely still beneath me.

I freeze too. We haven't been this close since the night he knocked me up. And before that? I can't remember the last time we touched, let alone brushed up against one another. The familiarity of not only his scent but the warmth of him makes my stomach swoop.

"Now kiss Dad good night," T.J. instructs.

The swoop turns into a bit of a drop. If I didn't know better, I'd think the two of them planned this.

Though Sully's lips twitch, I'm like a deer in headlights. But I don't want to ruin this perfect moment with our son, so I peck the scruff of his cheek, the move quick and meaningless.

Or so I try to tell myself. Because nothing is meaningless when it comes to us.

And if the way Sully is looking at me is any indication, my husband feels the effects of that simple touch as well.

CHAPTER 10
Sully

Sloane slips off the bed and moves over to her own. It creaks as she slips under the covers, though the sound is barely audible over the way my heart is pounding in my chest.

My wife just kissed me.

Willingly.

Yes, it was on the cheek, and yes, it was quick. But her lips were soft, and as she pulled away, I swear she sighed. Not a sigh of frustration but more like longing. Like she wished for more.

Hope once again races through me. Just like when I picked her up from work. When I told her she was the best part of my day and she teared up. And just like the moment I realized she was jealous of our intern.

Do I love that she was jealous? No. Does it kill me to know that she ever believed she *wasn't* the best part of my day? Yes. But both instances prove that somewhere, maybe buried under all the hurt I've caused, her feelings for me still exist.

I might be crammed into a small bed with my six-year-old in a room half the size of his at the penthouse, but tonight feels so much better than any night I spent there over the last year. Maybe more.

Because now I appreciate how amazing simple interactions like this are. Because I see now that what's important is that I'm lying here *with* my son.

In my flat.

And my wife just kissed me.

She's here too. Just a few feet away. Close enough that I can hear her breathing.

My life may be a mess, but I've got the people I need here with me, and that makes it the best.

I refuse to let go of what we have again. It may take a lot of work and some patience, but I have faith that I can convince her that this life is what she wants. That *I'm* what she wants.

CHAPTER 11

Sloane

"Why at are you doing?"

I jackknife up from the floor, bleary-eyed and sore. Blinking, I pat my chest and arm. Shit. Am I naked? When my fingers brush against cotton, I sigh in relief. Nope. Still fully covered.

"Um, sleeping?"

"Yeah, I see that," Lo says, looming over me. "But why are you on the bathroom floor?"

Oh. Right. I suppose it seems strange that I'd be curled up beneath a mountain of blankets on the floor of the handicap stall, using my new maternity pillow as a mattress. Honestly, it wasn't the most uncomfortable night of sleep I've ever had.

I give her a sheepish smile. "Didn't want to risk being naked."

Lo's shoulders sag. "Oh, I thought that was getting better. You know, because of all the layers." She waves a hand.

I look down. Sure enough, I'm still wearing two sets of pajamas. That's good news. The bad news is that there are three sets somewhere in this apartment.

Once I've brushed my teeth, I'll search for them. Honestly, the naked thing isn't really the reason I'm hiding in here. I've yet to strip all the way down since I moved in, so I think five really is my lucky number.

No, I crashed in here because of the kiss. The pathetic peck to my husband's cheek. The brush of my lips against his stubble that, even the next morning, makes the butterflies in my stomach flutter.

I peer up at Lo. Did she feel this way when Cal kissed her on the cheek before they became official?

Not that Sully and I are heading toward anything official.

Other than officially divorced.

The moment the D-word crosses my mind, the butterflies revolt and bile works its way up my throat. With a gasp, I slap my hand over my mouth and focus on breathing through my nose.

"You okay?" Lo drops to her knees in front of me, disregarding the gross bathroom floor.

I shudder. At least I laid a few blankets out before making my little nest down here.

"I kissed Sully last night," I blurt out.

Lo's eyes go wide. "What? Does that mean you're back together?"

Holding tight to the resentment I've felt for so long, I snort. "I'm hiding in the bathroom after kissing my husband. What part of that makes you think we're back together?"

She grins ruefully. "You called him your husband."

I roll my eyes and slump against the wall.

She settles on her butt next to me and hugs her knees. "How was the kiss?"

Just the thought makes my cheeks burn again. I bring my cool fingers to them to soothe the heat.

Lo gasps. "That good, huh?"

I roll my eyes. At me. At her. At the feelings swirling inside me. The damn things are liable to bubble over and escape like a fantastical giggle if I don't bottle them up. "It was on the cheek." I press my hand to my own face and smile at the memory. "He was laughing."

Lo gives me a confused look. "Sully doesn't laugh."

That pulls me back to reality. "Exactly."

I explain how I found Sully in bed with T.J., discussing the incident at school rather than reprimanding him. How it made me feel warm all over seeing the two of them together. "He's a good dad." I shake my head. "Maybe he always was, but I couldn't see it beyond my resentment."

Lo squeezes my hand. "Sully was absent a lot. That's not your imagination. And yes, he's trying now. He's good *now*."

The words sober me. I needed to hear them. I needed the outside perspective to remind me that I didn't throw away a good marriage with a good man on a whim. Sully is a good man, yes, but for the last few years we were together, he was a shitty husband and an absent father.

I'm glad he's finally making the changes necessary to be there for our son, but I can't allow myself to get swept away by a few gestures. Those gestures only go so far when life gets as complicated as ours.

T.J. is more than a handful on a good day, and I've just gone back to work. It's no secret that Sully is a workaholic, and now we're adding a new baby to the mix. That's what I should be focusing on: how to do it all as co-parents. Building a friendship with this man so that we can do it better. Be better.

I can't go back to where I was six months ago. I can't fall back into the pit of resentment I wallowed in for years. And I couldn't handle it if he resented me. I want to like the father of my children. Whether we're married or not.

My heart thuds heavily against my breastbone, like it's unhappy with that decision. But I fear it's the only way we can come out of this without hating one another. And I have Lo and her astute observation to thank for the reminder.

"Thank you," I say softly.

"All I did was remind you that your memory hasn't failed you, but you're welcome. Now, back to the more pressing issue. What are you going to do about this sleeping situation? You and I both know that when Sully figures out that you're sleeping on the floor in here, he's going to lose his mind."

I sigh. "He won't find out."

She drops her head into her hand. "This is absurd. You cannot sleep in a bathroom to avoid your husband because he's giving you butterflies."

"This isn't a bathroom." I motion around the stall. "This is Sloane's."

She scowls. "What?"

"You know how the place across the street is called the Grasshopper? This is *Sloane's*."

Lo's lips twitch in amusement. "So this is a bar?"

I slap a hand to my abdomen. "No. I can't drink. But this is my personal space. My place to decompress." I wave at the stall door. "It's crazy out there. Too many Y chromosomes."

She snorts. "I'll give you that."

I drag my hand in a circle over my nonexistent bump. "I hope this baby is a girl."

Lo grins. "God, me too. How fun would that be?"

I smile back at her. This is the first time I've felt as though I can be excited about this pregnancy. So far my thoughts have revolved around how we're going to do it and what it means for our future.

It's time to allow myself to focus on the possibilities. Though I told Lo I hope the baby is a girl, I'll be thrilled either way. And I really feel like it will be another boy. But it would be nice to live with one other person who doesn't pee all over the bathroom.

"Just so you know, I noticed how you didn't deny the butterflies."

I scan the space, ignoring her. "I was thinking I might put a lava lamp in here. Maybe some pretty curtains."

Snorting, Lo pats my leg. "Okay, Sloaney. We'll get you curtains."

CHAPTER 12

Sully

"**B**aby daddy!"

My instinct is to growl at Julius, but his pleasant tone stops me. It's as if, rather than wishing I didn't exist, he's happy to see me.

"Pretty boy." I dip my chin.

His eyes light up in response to my greeting, instantly making me wish I could take it back.

He rests an elbow on the desk and leans in closer. "Baby daddy thinks I'm pretty."

"No, I think my wife is pretty," I correct. "*You* are a pain in my ass."

He chuckles. "Good. Someone should be a pain in your ass." His focus drifts over my shoulder and his smile falls, his eyes hardening slightly.

Frowning, I spin.

"Sully." Will greets me with his signature *my shite doesn't stink* smile.

Despite his air of self-importance, the man's nothing special. He's just under six foot, with an *I don't work out but I was blessed with good genes* build. He's not the kind of good-looking that makes women flock to him, but he's not unfortunate-looking either.

If I look close enough, it's clear the way he styles his hair that it's thinning at his crown. With any luck, he'll be sporting a smooth, shiny head in a few years.

"Will." I attempt not to scowl. It's a challenge, but it's warranted, since, for once, he's not touching my wife. "What brings you here?"

"I work here." He blinks at me.

Right, I'm the one out of place. In my own wife's office. It's wrong, but it's my reality. For now.

I'm saved from having to respond when the man who's usually giving me shite throws in a snarky comment.

"Considering how much time you spend trying to get past me, one would think you worked in this office specifically." Julius thumbs over his shoulder, giving Will a fake smile.

Hmm, the assistant doesn't like Will. Maybe the enemy of my enemy really could be my friend.

Julius stands and smooths out his suit jacket. "What do you need this time?"

"Just dropping off the official invite for the Christmas party." He passes the younger man a large tube.

Julius immediately goes for the cap on one end, but Will holds out a hand, stopping him.

"It's for Sloane."

"Right." Pretty boy scowls.

Slipping his hands into his pockets, Will turns back to me. "Too bad you won't be coming this year."

The fuck? I've gone to the Higgins, Smith, and Dodge party every December for the last fifteen years.

"New York attorneys only," the wanker reminds me with a smirk.

"Julius." Sloane pops her head out of her office, her expression morphing into a confused frown as she takes in Will and me. "Will?"

My confidence swells when she doesn't question my presence along with his.

"I brought that for you." Will's eyes brighten, making him look like a puppy begging for attention. If he weren't focusing that energy on my wife, I might find it funny. "Open it."

Sloane takes the tube from Julius and slides out a rolled-up piece of literal parchment. "Hear ye, hear ye." Her lips flatten. "Is the theme *A Christmas Carol?*"

I bite back a laugh. These fuckers throw an over-the-top Christmas party every year, and every year, they waste entirely too much of their firm's money to create a *magical adventure*—their words, not mine.

"Yes, and we've booked the best place in the city."

Sloane tips her head to the side.

"It's going to be the event of the holiday season." He eyes me, reminding me that it's for New York attorneys only.

Over his shite, I pull myself up to my full height and smooth my tie. "It's a good thing my wife works for a New York firm and is allowed a plus-one, then." The words rumble out of me like a growl. I might as well have pissed a circle around her, claiming her. And it feels fucking good to remind him of exactly who she is to me.

Until the uncertainty in her expression registers and my stomach drops.

Bloody hell. What if she already has a date, and it's not me?

CHAPTER 13
Sloane

"What do you think of this one?" I hold up the shower curtain and peer around the package at my phone, which I've propped up against a soap canister on a shelf at HomeGoods.

"I think," Lo says, "that you're dragging your feet rather than heading home because your husband asked you on a date."

I pick up a second option. One with light blue waves. "Oh, I could do a beach theme."

"Sloane's is so not beach vibes."

My shoulders sink. She's right. My bathroom turned personal space is not beachy at all. So I pick up a pink one accented with black bows. "French? I always wanted to go to Paris. Sully promised we'd go for our ten-year anniversary."

"Wasn't that like a decade ago?" Lo teases.

Five years ago, but who's counting? Certainly not Sully. He was too busy working his ass off to even remember.

"Ha ha. Laugh at me because I'm old," I deadpan. I regretted mentioning Paris the second the words were out of my mouth. "Be careful. One day you'll be old like me, and when you find yourself standing in the middle of HomeGoods, pregnant and wondering what you're doing with your life, I hope you remember this moment."

"Wow," Lo says, cringing. "That is oddly specific."

I groan. "You're right. That won't happen to you because Cal is obsessed with you. You'll never be at a HomeGoods trying to avoid him because he asked you on a date."

"Ah-ha!" Lo says. "I knew you were being cagey."

I snag my phone and lean against the shower display, hoping I don't go down with it. "I'm not being cagey. I'm avoiding. I'm very good at it."

She snorts. "Yeah, you are. But why are you avoiding?"

Hmm, let's see. Because I liked the way my husband looked at me yesterday when he picked me up from work. And I like that he always comes inside to get me. That rather than just calling to tell me he's in the garage, he parks and takes the elevator up, even knowing he'll have to deal with not only the receptionist but Julius, who gives him constant shit, just so he can walk me down to the car. It's...*sweet*.

Which is pathetic.

Such a simple gesture shouldn't make me weak in the damn knees. But God, does it ever. Even now, just thinking about it makes my legs wobbly. So I drop to the scuffed beige floor and sit crisscross, ignoring the silk flower debris and glitter I know will stick to my pants when I find the energy to get up again.

"The anniversary was five years ago, by the way."

Lo's eyes soften. "You had a one-year-old. Sully had just made partner."

I nod. Yes. While I spent my days changing diapers, Sully made partner. He chased all his dreams, while mine became more like distant thoughts. That's about the time I realized I was no longer even a part of his dreams anymore. I was on the sidelines and he was out living his life.

At least that's how it felt.

"There will always be something, Lo. Another big case, another milestone to work toward. That's the problem. When our tenth anniversary hit, we didn't even have a conversation about it. There was no *oh, we'll go eventually*. Our plans turned into yet another discarded dream. Tossed aside, forgotten." I sigh. "Kind of like me."

Lo shakes her head. "Nope. We're not doing this. Yes, Sully sucked. But that's not why you're hiding." She brings the phone closer to her face, glaring. "You're hiding because you *want* to go on this date with him, and that scares you."

I sniff and look away, surveying the shower curtain options again. She's right, but no one likes a braggart.

The growly voice he used when Will insinuated that he wouldn't be coming to the Christmas party almost did me in. The deep, commanding way he said *my wife*.

As I replay the moment, my pussy flutters to life like she's hearing it again for the first time, and I clamp my slutty legs together.

"Actually, I don't. It's the opposite, really. Everyone at my firm knows we're separated. Hell, half the legal community does, I'm sure. The last thing I want is to show up at the event with my ex and deal with all the staring."

"Oh," she huffs, "so you'd rather deal with being stared at while everyone you encounter wonders whose baby is in your belly?"

A shocked gasp escapes me. "Are you telling me I'm showing? Oh my god." I tuck my chin and assess my stomach. Sure, I've got a little pooch, but I figured it looked more like I'd had a big lunch than anything. Although really, what's worse? Rumors that I've gained weight because I can't stop snacking or rumors that I'm pregnant with my ex's child?

Honestly, I don't know.

"You're pregnant, Sloane. Eventually, the truth will come out. And you'll be what, twelve weeks by the time the party rolls around?"

I groan. She's right. "I don't think I should go."

"No, you are definitely going."

"Why?"

"Because you're determined to choose yourself for once, remember? You are no longer letting a man—*any* man—control you. You're in charge of creating your own happiness, and you get to choose what you go after."

When she puts it like that—

"You've wanted to return to litigation, not just desk work, for years," she continues before I can respond to her. "And this Christmas party is a big deal. It's where you can finally show your peers just how great you're doing. You are a professional, and being pregnant doesn't mean you aren't just as competent as your colleagues. You can do it all. You can have it all. Because you are amazing."

"I am amazing," I whisper-hiss, bringing my phone closer.

"Though maybe you'd be more amazing if you weren't sitting on the floor in HomeGoods."

I shrug. "Maybe."

"Pick yourself up, *dust yourself off*, and go to Neiman Marcus. Buy yourself a gorgeous dress—using your husband's black card, of course—and enjoy what you've worked your ass off for. Stun the shit out of that man the night of the party. Remind him of just how incredible you are."

"Or," I say, my heart thumping, "I can buy the dress and walk into that party with my head held high *without* Sully."

Her face falls. "What?"

I set my phone on the floor and tilt to one side awkwardly, forcing my legs to shift in the same direction so I don't accidentally flash anyone my underwear. I so shouldn't have dropped to the floor while wearing a skirt. With my hands on the filthy floor, I ease myself onto my knees. Then I use a shelf to maintain my balance while I climb to my feet.

Finally upright, I snatch my phone and my purse from the floor, and the pink Parisian shower curtain from where it hangs on the shelf, and head for the checkout. "I could go with someone else."

"Pretty sure you've lost the plot, my friend."

I shrug. "It'll make me happy. And that's my goal. To find happiness again, *right?*"

She narrows her gaze at me. "It's annoying being lawyered by everyone in my life."

I giggle. "I'll see you at home."

CHAPTER 14
Sully

"**G**et down, Dammit." Brian uses the back of his hand to push the massive cat off his desk. Except Fuzzy Wuzzy, now lovingly known as Dammit, thanks to my best friend, has other ideas. He turns in a slow circle, unbothered by Brian's cursing and his efforts to force him to the floor, then lies down, his body taking up half of the oversized desk.

Brian lets a slow breath out of his nose and looks up at me. "What?"

I shake my head. "Better you than me."

The growling sound he makes is typically the kind reserved for Cal, but I stand by my statement. I have enough going on without having to care for a cat the size of a donkey.

"Did you come in here just to mock me?"

"No." I nod down at the bright blue box in my hand.

Brian frowns at the illustrations of deformed animals on the top.

I pluck out a bright blue rabbit, then a pink sheep, and a red mouse.

"I don't want those things," he says, rolling his chair back.

Ignoring him, I set each one on his desk and press down, ensuring the suction cups keep them firmly in place. When I glance back up, he's glowering at me.

"They aren't for you." He's not the one who needs a distraction.

"Then why are you putting them on my desk?" He swipes at the blue one, causing it to make a satisfying set of pops as the suction cups release from the wood.

"T.J.'s therapist suggested that we try fidget toys to help curb his impulsive behaviors."

And that word, impulsive, immediately made me think of another person whose impulsive behavior I've dealt with my whole life.

"I thought that maybe if we leave these around the office, Cal will play with them instead of throwing shite at me."

The laugh starts deep in Brian's chest. "You bought these for your brother? I can see the appeal for kids, but for an adult? Good luck with that." Yet even as he says the words, he continues popping the bubbles on the front and back of the bunny.

The cat recoils at the sound and swipes the cup of pens off the desk.

"Dammit." Brian growls.

I swing into Lo's office next, because my brother spends more time there than anywhere else. Can't blame him for that. If Sloane worked in this office, I'd want to be in her presence every chance I got.

"So what?" she's saying as I approach. "Pregnant or not, you'll look hot in that dress."

I freeze, taking in Lo's profile. She's looking out the window, her mobile pressed to her ear, obviously talking to my wife. I inch closer, eager to hear more of the conversation, but before she can say more, there is another crash from Brian's office.

"Dammit." He growls again.

Lo startles, her attention darting to the door, and upon seeing me, she says, "Got to go."

Bugger. Would have been nice to know what she was wearing without having to outright ask Lo and put her in the middle.

"Sloane?" I ask innocently as I step into the room.

She nods as she watches me line up a yellow elephant and a green giraffe on the edge of her desk. "Cal or T. J.?"

"Both," I admit.

She chuckles. "T. J. will love the noises they make when he rips them off, but you may regret giving Cal more things to throw at you."

I wince. I hadn't considered that he'd use them as ammo. But I'm too distracted to care about these damn fidget toys now.

"What's Sloane up to?"

Lo glances away, not meeting my eye. "You know. Shopping. Her favorite."

I hum a nonresponse and wait. Lo babbles when she's nervous, so all I have to do is be patient, and I'll get the information I need.

"She's worried because her clothes are getting tight, and she wants to look good for the Higgins, Smith, and Dodge Christmas party." She swallows, still not looking at me. "She'll look great in anything. She always does. But you know how she gets."

"That I do." I could let this go, but Sloane and I have a tradition that I have no intention of breaking. "What's she wearing?"

She taps her desk, her bottom lip caught between her teeth, then snags the green giraffe. Instead of playing with the bubbles like Brian, she sticks it to the desk and pulls it away again, then again.

"Lo?"

Attention still fixed on the toy, she mumbles, "You know she's going with someone else..."

My heart lurches. I've been afraid to even mention the Christmas party since the day she received the invite. That night, just before we stepped into the flat, I risked her wrath and gently grabbed her by the elbow.

"Sweetheart," I said.

She hummed but didn't meet my eye.

"I'd love to take you to the Christmas party. If you'd like." I tacked on the last few words as if I wasn't dying to go with her, trying my damnedest to be nonchalant.

Sloane nodded quickly, though she wouldn't make eye contact. "I'll, um, I'll let you know." Then she rushed inside. I stayed out in the parking lot for a few minutes, composing myself. I'd seen her lack of interest. And I'd felt in my bones that she might already have a date. That or an interest in going with someone else.

Every inch of me rebels at the idea of my wife dating another man. Not this weekend. Not ever. But I keep my mouth shut. Yelling at Lo won't get me what I want.

Yelling and growling have become my default over the last couple of years, but I've promised myself that I'll do better.

I clear my throat, willing the ache in my chest to subside. "Since the first event Sloane and I attended together, I've made it a habit to rent a necklace to match her dress."

Sloane should always feel like the most treasured woman in the room, and I've always loved spoiling her with jewelry from the finest designers. Almost as much as I love watching her expression when I slip the necklace around her neck.

Lo finally looks up at me. "You'll do that even though she's going with someone else?"

The pain in my chest flares. "There is nothing I wouldn't do for her."

Lo's eyes widen like she's surprised by the intensity of my statement.

Good, because I mean every damn word. And if I thought it'd do me any good, I'd crash the damn party to win her back from the jackass she shows up with.

"I see you will be taking matters into your own hands. What a lovely plan," a husky voice says from behind me.

I whip around, startled, and find Madame E beaming at me.

"What does that mean?" I ask.

She leans against the doorframe and smirks. Today, rather than wearing layers and layers of flowy fabric, she's dressed in a one-piece...uh, unitard? I think that's the appropriate term for the skintight pink-and-white-striped garment.

"Oh, Sullivan." Her violet eyes dance. "I think you know exactly what that means."

Do I? I blink, rehashing my idea. Which parts did I say out loud? Because I'm pretty sure I didn't verbalize the party-crashing option. *Does that mean she can read my thoughts?* No. That's absurd.

She gives me a nod, as if she knows exactly what I'm thinking.

Lungs seizing, I step back. Bloody hell. Maybe she can hear the inner workings of my brain.

But Madame E shifts her attention to Lo. "Don't just sit there gaping at me. You and Callahan are accompanying me to yoga. Get moving."

"We are?" Lo asks, standing from her desk.

"Spit-spot," she commands.

Without hesitation, Lo hurries out of the room.

Madame E follows, calling to me over her shoulder. "Into your hands, Sullivan. Into your hands."

There's no stopping my smile. Yeah, I'm going to crash a party. How very unlike me.

CHAPTER 15
Sloane

I am feeling myself right now.

My hair is having a day, and this dress? Damn, this dress makes my boobs look incredible. I sway my hips to the beat of the Def Leppard song and turn my brush into a microphone. As the chorus ramps up, I sing along to the lyrics about sugar and sex.

Two of my favorite things.

God, I haven't had sex in so long.

Just as I arch back, hitting a high note, the curtain swishes, and I spot Sully in the mirror, watching me with an amused smirk on his face.

Cheeks burning, I straighten and silence the music.

"I always loved sneaking in and catching you doing this while you got ready." His tone is warm, soft even. Like he's talking to himself.

I bite my cheek. "Haven't done it in a while."

He moves his arm, pulling the curtain back another inch. "May I?"

"Oh, yes. Welcome to Sloane's," I tease, holding one arm out as if showcasing the oversized stall.

I planned to get ready at the penthouse, and I still plan to stay in the city overnight, but then T.J. had a meltdown about not seeing me, so I promised I'd get ready here.

Sully slides his hands into the pockets of his pants and surveys the new décor. "Like what you did with the place."

In addition to my Paris curtain, I moved Cal's ficus in and put up a neon sign that says *My Happy Place*. It's pink, though it provides the right amount of additional light for doing makeup.

"Thanks." Nodding, I turn back to the sink and toss my makeup back into its pouch.

At the sound of shoes on the tile floor, I snap up straight and meet Sully's eye in the mirror. He stands so close now that his warmth engulfs me, but he's far enough away that we're not touching. His blue eyes blaze as he takes me in, like he's familiarizing himself with every curve all over again.

"Fucking beautiful," he murmurs, like he's once again speaking to himself.

Feeling awkward, I spin quickly and grab the edge of the sink for balance. "Do I look pregnant?"

His attention drifts down, getting caught on my breasts for half a second before settling on my stomach. Lips lifting slightly, he says, "Yes."

"Shit." My heart races. "I was hoping I could get away with hiding it for a little longer." I smooth my hand over the emerald green fabric covering my abdomen. The hem of the crushed velvet dress falls to the toes of my favorite rose gold Louboutins and fits me perfectly, making me feel sexier than I have in years.

Sully narrows his eyes. "Your date knows you're pregnant with my child."

I don't correct him. I don't tell him that I don't have a date. He's got it in his head that I'm going with Will, and I'm too keyed up over the possibility that my mother could be at this thing to dive into an explanation.

I really don't want my mom to know that I'm pregnant just yet. I'll have to make sure Will knows not to say anything. Other than

Julius, he's the only one at the firm who knows. As long as the two of them keep quiet, I'm sure I can pass off my bump as the result of eating too many tacos this week.

My alarm sounds, letting me know it's time to leave. "Shoot," I say as I tap the screen. "I forgot to schedule an Uber."

Dammit. I forget everything lately. I'm going to be so late.

Sully takes half a step closer, catching my attention. His eyes are soft and warm, making me foolishly want to sink into them. To lean against his chest, press my skin to his, share a singular breath.

He brushes a bit of hair behind my ear, and his touch burrows beneath my skin, sending shockwaves through my system. It's the simplest of gestures, yet it's the most decadent sensation I've experienced in months.

"Your car should be here in a few minutes."

He might as well have murmured filthy words against my mouth with the way he's looking at me.

"What?"

"I got you a car, sweetheart." He grazes his thumb down my cheek and gently pinches my chin, tilting my mouth up so he truly is only a breath away. "If you won't let me take you, then I want to make sure you're taken care of."

With him so close, I can barely think. Still, I recognize that despite him believing that I'm going with someone else, he hasn't expressed his frustration, and he's still ensured I have a ride. Shit, I should put him out of his misery. "I'm—"

"*Mom.*" T.J. barrels into the bathroom, interrupting my confession.

Sully holds my chin another second, as if hoping he can pluck my thoughts from my mind. T.J.'s presence though is just the reminder that I needed. It's better we co-parent and I keep the secret of my non-existent date to myself. As if he can read the warning in my expression, he releases my chin and steps back.

A heartbeat later, T.J. pushes open the curtain and stumbles into the stall.

"What have we discussed about knocking?" Sully asks, his tone firm but gentle.

"That I should knock." Our son straightens, head tipped back, like he's proud that he got this right.

"Right. And then?"

Our little boy shrugs. "I think that's it."

Sully shakes his head. "Try again."

Full of energy, as always, T.J. bounces on his toes. It's a challenge for him to remain still in any situation. And like this, when we're watching him, when he feels the pressure that comes with being under the scrutiny of another person, it's nearly impossible. The teachers are working on it with him in school, as is the therapist we've hired for him, but it's been a process. I take a step toward him, ready to put him at ease, but Sully beats me to it.

He crouches so he and our little boy are eye to eye. For a moment, he doesn't speak. He simply watches T.J. with an even, open look on his face. After a moment, our little guy settles. It's a tactic I've read about, though I haven't mentioned it to Sully. Is this a fluke, or has he heard about it too?

T.J. clasps his hands, his head tilted. "That I should wait to be told to come in."

"Can you do me a favor and go try that again?"

With a nod, T.J. takes a step back. But before he can turn, he zeroes in on me and his mouth drops open. "Oh, Mommy, you look so pretty."

A light laugh escapes me. I can always rely on T.J. to notice me. Even in moments when I felt invisible to my husband, I always felt love because of my little boy. "Thanks, bud. Now go do what your dad asked."

"But I'm already in here, and all I wanted to say was can I go with Murphy to walk Dammit?"

Sully growls. "I'm going to kill Brian."

T.J. tilts his head. "Why?"

Sully tries to keep his voice even. "You can't use that word, pal."

"Why?"

"Because it's a bad word."

His little lips turn down in a puzzled frown. "*Why* is a bad word?"

Sully stands and roughs a hand down his face. "Dammit."

T.J. steps back, cringing. "That's a bad word, Dad."

Before this can go off the rails, I step between them and guide T.J. out of the bathroom by his hand. "No, the word *dammit* is a bad word. Your father wasn't cursing at you."

"But that's the cat's name." The innocence in his tone makes it impossible not to smile.

"I know, baby." I press a kiss to his cheek. "Be good tonight, okay? And yes, you can walk the cat so long as Cal or Brian is going with you."

My brother-in-law appears out of nowhere with his mammoth cat on a leash. I try to stay far away from the animal. I get the sense that he only likes Brian and his paws are freakishly long.

"Looks like your car is here. Want to walk down with us?" Cal asks.

I glance over my shoulder at Sully, who's stepping out of the bathroom wearing a frustrated scowl.

My heart aches at the sight. He handled the situation with T.J. well, even if he didn't have the success I'm sure he hoped for.

That's the thing with kids, though. They're great at throwing wrenches into even the best-laid plans.

Assuming he'll brood for the rest of the night, I drop my phone into my clutch, preparing to walk out with T.J. and Cal.

Sully skirts around me, surprising me by ruffling T.J.'s hair easily, and says, "Give me a second, and I'll join you."

Remembering just how cold it is today, I scurry to our bedroom to find my jacket. In the doorway, Sully stands, already holding it out for me. Hesitantly, I turn and slip my arms into it, and when he lifts my hair so that it doesn't get caught and brings his cheek to mine, I shiver.

"Have a wonderful time tonight, sweetheart," he whispers.

"Thank you," I say, voice caught in my throat. As I step into the stairway, I can't help but wish that I allowed Sully to take me after all.

On the way into the city, Julius texts, informing me that several junior partners are meeting for drinks at a bar a block or so from the party, so I give the driver the address and ask him to drop me there. When I arrive, everyone is tipsy, including Julius.

"Oh, Mommy cleans up nice," he teases when he spots me.

I hit him with my purse. "Shush, you."

Secretly, I revel in his compliment. Because though he was teasing, I know him well enough to know he meant it. After the way Sully looked at me, then T.J., and now Julius, I feel like I'm floating. I haven't dressed up like this in so long, and it feels good to be noticed.

Forty-five minutes later, we walk into the restaurant where the party is being held. In New York, Christmas parties are more about showing off than they are about celebrating the holiday season. This is how firms boast about how well they're doing. Judges and clients are invited. Colleagues from other firms are often on the guest list as well.

I scan the elaborately decorated room, relaxing a bit when I don't spot my parents. I'm not out of the woods yet, since they typically show up at functions like this. But they're punctual people, and they don't hang out at the bar, so their absence means it's possible they won't be here at all.

It hurts, feeling this way. I hate that my instinct is to hide from them. But I'm not ready for my mother's judgmental response when she discovers I'm pregnant or the demands she'll make. She'll most surely tell me the divorce is off. That if I have any hope of having a career, it's imperative we raise our children in a two-parent home.

Millions of single parents make it work, so the second thing isn't even a consideration for me. And the divorce? That's definitely not off.

Even if my husband's heated gazes are making my stomach do that swoopy thing again, and he's clearly making an effort with T.J.

It's not enough to erase the pain he caused each and every time he forgot about me.

As impressed as I was by his calm attitude tonight, I can't help but wish he'd thrown a fit. That he'd gotten angry about my "date." Maybe growled that I was his wife again.

I snort at myself. Because if he'd done any of those things, I'd be complaining. Maybe I'm the problem here. Maybe I don't trust that he's really in this for me. I don't want to be the kind of couple that stays together for the children. I want to be enough on my own. I want my husband to lose his mind over me. I want him to—

"Damn. I thought Mommy looked good, but Daddy is looking *mighty* fine," Julius singsongs.

Like a record scratching, my heart stops the moment I spin and follow his gaze to the bar where I find the most unusual suspects.

Will and *Sully*.

Sully, whom I left at home two hours ago.

Sully, who arranged for a car to bring me to the city.

Sully, who told me to have a great night.

Freaking Sully, who is wearing the hell out of a black suit with an emerald tie that, from here, looks like it matches my dress perfectly.

Lo. That tie has Lo written all over it.

Have my roommates been plotting to derail my night?

And what the hell is Sully doing talking to Will? He *hates* Will.

When Will notices me watching, his eyes flare and he licks his lips.

"Shit." I elbow Julius. "Pretend you're my date."

He grimaces. "What?"

I snap my fingers, struggling for words. "You. I need you to pretend you're my date. I told Will I had one, assuming he'd think it was Sully. And I let Sully believe I had one too. I figured he thought I was coming with Will. But I didn't actually tell either who I was coming with. So if you are my date, then it's not really a lie."

He frowns like I've lost my damn mind. "Uh. That's not how lies work. And you're not really my type."

"Oh my god, shut up," I hiss as Sully holds up a hand to the bartender. "I don't actually want to date you. I just want you to be my date."

"I struggle to see the difference in those statements," he muses as Will and Sully step away from the bar.

"You are a terrible wingman," I whine, my armpits suddenly sweaty.

He huffs. "I'm not trying to be a wingman. I'm your assistant, remember."

Shit. He's right. This is completely unprofessional. "I'm sorry." I hold up a hand. "I shouldn't have propositioned you. I'm in a position of power over you, and it was—"

He snorts. "I'm kidding. Would you stop it with the whole serious vibe right now?"

"I thought *you* were serious," I screech.

The guys are headed our way, both looking at me.

I spin and focus on breathing evenly. Shit, Sully is totally going to know I fibbed about having a date. He'll think I was trying to make him jealous.

I so wasn't trying to make him jealous.

Oh god. Was I?

Here he is, doing exactly what I was just wishing he'd do, and my stomach is in knots because, oh my god, my husband is here to crash my date. "So will you play along or not?" I grit out from behind a fake smile.

"Yes, Mommy. Your date awaits." He holds out his elbow. "Let's go make baby daddy jealous."

A smile slips free before I can catch it. "I'm not trying to make anyone jealous."

Julius chuckles. "Right, and I'm not attracted to Pedro Pascal."

"Oh, he is hot, but I don't know. Chris Evans might be hotter. No —Ugh. I can't decide," I whine.

Julius winks at me. "Why choose, baby, why choose?"

"Because she's my wife," Sully growls, as if Julius was speaking to him. He wraps an arm around my waist and presses a kiss to my cheek. "There is no choice."

And dammit, my panties are wet, and now I know precisely how I wanted tonight to go.

CHAPTER 16
Sully

"What are you doing here?" The words may escape my wife in a hiss, but the way her body arches against me tells me the annoyance is an act.

I won't call her on it. My plan tonight is to thaw the ice lingering between us, not add fuel to her anger.

"I forgot to give you this." I slip my hand into my pocket, brushing my fingers against the sharp edges of the gemstones. As I pull the necklace out, I ensure the thick string of diamonds and emeralds rests on my palm so she can get a good look at it. So Will, the prat, can get a good look too.

Sloane's breath catches as she stares at the jewelry. "Sully...I..." She shakes her head slowly and runs a finger along the line of jewels. "It's stunning, but..." She looks up at me, her eyes full of questions.

"Just because you're not here with me, sweetheart, doesn't mean I don't still want you to feel like a queen."

Her eyes flash and her throat bobs. I've memorized all of my wife's looks. Everything from *you're in deep shite* to *I'm having the time of my life*. And right now, her expression tells me that my simple words touched her in a way nothing I've said in months has been able to.

"May I?" The words are rough, full of uncertainty.

With her teeth pressed into her bottom lip, she spins.

Carefully, I shift her hair over her shoulder, and as I drag my fingers along the silky skin, she shudders. For a heartbeat, I freeze, taking in the way she feels. Warm and soft. She's always had such flawless pale skin. For years, it's tempted me to mark it. To leave behind proof that she's mine. Even though she's not at the moment, I can't help but rub a slow circle against her spine with my thumb.

What I wouldn't give to pull Sloane into a dark corner and drag her zipper down her spine. Drop the dress to the floor so she's naked in front of me. Because I know by the way her breath has picked up and her shoulders have tightened that if I did, I'd find her wet and wanting.

Will clears his throat, breaking through the tension.

"Sully," Sloane whispers. Although her tone is laced with a longing I wish she would unleash, there's an underlying question there too.

She probably wants to know what the fuck I'm doing. Especially in front of Will. Her *date*.

He doesn't deserve the title. Not after he let her out of his sight like he did. Sloane and I have attended dozens of events together over the years, and the only time she wasn't within arm's reach was when she excused herself to the bathroom.

Tonight, I'll be forced to watch Will fail to treat her even half as well as she deserves.

Though I suppose if I'd treated her as well as I should have, she wouldn't be on a date with someone else right now.

Bloody hell, I'd been such a wanker.

Gritting my teeth, I focus on getting the rope of emeralds and diamonds secured around her neck. Once the clasp is fastened, I reluctantly step back.

Turning, she fingers the jewels, her eyes wide and her expression open. "Thank you."

Quickly, that look disappears, and she eyes her assistant, then Will.

As much as I hate it, that's my cue. I refuse to make this hard for her. I won't make a scene. I won't demand she come with me. I want to. In my mind, I've already tossed her over my shoulder and stormed out. But she's her own person. She makes the choices. And if we're going to repair our relationship, she needs to choose me.

So I give her a small smile and take half a step back. "I'd better go. I'm sitting with Judge Masters." I tip my chin to the far side of the room. "Enjoy the night and save me a dance." Angling in, I press my lips to her cheek. The hitch in her breath will haunt me for the next two hours.

Though nothing haunts me quite as painfully as Will's flirting does. All night, he works hard for her attention. He sits beside her, his arm on the back of her chair, a sleazy grin on his lips.

Instead, I try to focus on the conversations happening around me. On the music. On the food. Every year, Higgins, Smith, and Dodge throws an elaborate themed party, and this year's is just as extravagant. The entire floor looks like it's been transported to nineteenth-century London. The walls of the large ballroom are decorated to look like 1800s storefronts and homes. Just outside the double doors are cobblestone streets, complete with carolers and live horses. There are at least twenty lit Christmas trees and even gas streetlights set up between building façades.

The cost of this kind of party is staggering, and they're not the only firm in town vying for the best holiday event.

My father never saw fit to waste resources on such frivolity, instead giving his employees large holiday bonuses and making charitable donations.

It's a tradition Brian, Cal, and I have continued.

Despite my efforts to distract myself, I once again end up zeroed in on the meaty paw of the man who's now touching my wife's hair. It takes all my willpower to stay in my seat when my insides are roiling, telling me to stomp over there and break Will's arm.

"What do you think about the proposed law changes?"

At the sound of Judge Masters's voice, I inhale deeply and force my attention to her.

"Bloody ridiculous to say the court can't order reconciliation therapy between a parent and a child," I grumble.

Although the proposed law is utter rubbish, my mood has more to do with Will's proximity to Sloane than anything related to work.

"The AAML needs to do something about it." The man across from me postures. The American Academy of Matrimonial Lawyers has had an email chain going for days, with dozens of attorneys ranting about the law. Unfortunately, more than one senator has backed it.

"I don't know. It seems to be getting legs."

Davis leans my way. "Couldn't you put some pressure on the New York bar? You've got clout."

I frown at him. "I work in New Jersey now."

He winces, like he expects me to be upset by the reminder.

I'm not. At first, I was sure Jersey would be a nightmare. And yeah, maybe it was for a couple of weeks. Now, I like being stuck in a single room with my son and Sloane. The rest of our flat is so small and crowded that it's hard to find even a moment alone. It's a huge change from the way we rambled around our penthouse in the city. But shockingly, we all seem to be happier.

And at this exact moment, I'd give just about anything to be locked in that shitty room with my family.

Without my permission, my focus drifts back to Sloane, who is leaning so far away from her dickhead of a boss she's practically in her assistant's lap.

As if he can feel my glare, Julius turns and locks eyes with me. He arches a brow, and I swear I can hear the mocking words he wants to say. *What are you going to do about this, baby daddy?*

I'll show him exactly what I intend to do.

"Excuse me." Without waiting for a response from my table-mates, I stand and stroll to the bar.

When she was pregnant with T.J., my wife had a favorite mocktail. I might not know whether she'll crave the orange juice, cranberry, and soda like she did then, but at least she'll know I remembered.

With the drink in hand, I wander to Higgins's table.

I come up behind them, causing Will to drop his arm so he can crane his neck.

His face falls when he sees me. I get it. I don't want him near her either. But he can piss off. I'm done watching him flirt with my wife.

Especially because while he's been all over her, he's oblivious to her body language and has yet to notice that she finished her drink at least a half hour ago.

The wanker isn't even a good date. Probably shitty in bed too.

My jaw locks at that thought. He will never touch my wife.

"Sloane." I step into the small space between them. She looks up at me, and her eyes brighten at the sight of the drink in my hand. "For you." I hold the stemmed glass, and when our fingers brush, a thrill shoots through me.

"I can't believe you remembered," she murmurs as she brings it to her lips.

"How could I ever forget?" That's the problem though, she believes I did. Sloane's eyes flicker with surprise at my comment and I don't look away. I hold eye contact, and that surprise melts to warmth. To desire. So I take a chance. "How about that dance?"

Her lips twitch almost imperceptibly, and my heart rate kicks up. Se sets her glass down and holds out a hand to me. The second I take it, my body electrifies because in a moment, my wife's body will be pressed up against mine. Finally.

I allow her to slip past me, to head to the dance floor, and when her back is to me, I shift and give a quick snap of my heel against the leg of Will's chair, causing the chair to give out and fly backwards. As he tumbles, falling onto the floor, I can't hide my smirk.

Dumbass didn't even brace himself.

With long strides, I'm behind Sloane before she even spins to face me. "What's so funny?"

I shake my head, not wanting to ruin the moment with talk of Will. Focusing instead on her, I tell her exactly how I feel. "I'm just happy to be here with you." When her cheeks flush in response, that kernel of happiness grows. "Come here, sweetheart," I murmur as the live band breaks into a slow ballad.

Hesitantly, she steps toward me, and I wrap my arms around her waist, pulling her close in the way my body has been craving. I expect her to be rigid beneath my touch. Instead, she melts against me like she's been wanting this as much as I have. Feeling bold, I tuck her against my chest. She rewards me by resting her head on my shoulder and letting out the softest sigh. The almost inaudible breath, a sign of her finally relaxing with me, settles something in my chest, and then inflates like a balloon. Nothing could be better than this.

We need more of these moments. I have to find a way to make them happen. To create time for the two of us. If we have the opportunity to reconnect, to really be all-in with one another, I'm certain we can fix the brokenness between us. We have to because nothing has ever felt as right as having Sloane in my arms. She was made to be mine. And I'm most certainly only hers.

As the song plays, we sway without speaking, my finger making slow circles on her lower back. I want the song to go on forever so we can stay here in this moment until the end of time.

Unfortunately, the music fades all too soon, and Sloane pulls back.

She peers up at me. "Walk me to the ladies' room?"

I want to pull her back in and stay right where we are, but I release her easily. She could have used the restroom as a way to escape me. Instead, she isn't quite ready to let me go either. So I take her hand in mine and hold out an arm, gesturing for her to lead the way.

She looks from our hands to my face, her throat bobbing, but she doesn't pull away. It's another small victory. One I'll gladly take. Though she doesn't say anything as we make our way out the doors, her eyes light up as we meander down the cobblestone streets toward the loo, and when the carolers start an a cappella version of "Oh Christmas Tree," she breaks into a smile.

With each step we take, I'm lighter on my feet. I'm full of an ease I haven't experienced in years.

"You'll wait?" she asks when we finally make it to the bathroom.

"Forever." I duck my chin and meet her eyes, hoping like hell she sees how sincere I am. If I have it my way, I'll be standing in front of her with open arms until my last breath.

Her chin wobbles, but she dips it quickly in a nod and then disappears inside.

"Kicking his chair was *a little* childish, baby daddy," Julius teases as he approaches.

I shrug. Maybe, but damn did it feel good. "A man shouldn't take another man's wife out if he's not willing to pay the price, Caesar."

Julius chuckles. "She's here with me."

My heart thumps against my sternum as he rocks back on his heels, a smile on his lips. It's not a cocky one. It's friendly.

Bollocks, the bloke is giving me an olive branch.

Sloane is not the kind of woman who'd date her assistant. Ever. Though I wouldn't put it past her to make me jealous. Hell, I'm not even the slightest bit upset about the white lie. It shows she cares.

"My wife wanted to make me jealous," I mutter, almost to myself. My lips twitch as a smile breaks through.

Julius nods and holds out a hand. "It's possible you don't deserve it, but I'll help you anyway."

I eye it skeptically. "Help me?"

He lifts one manicured brow. "If you're going to win baby mama back, you'll need all kinds of help."

I frown at the insinuation. I've got a plan. I just have to stick to it.

"Julius?" Sloane steps up next to us.

"I feel awful abandoning you," he says, "but if we want to get the Lexan hearing date moved up, I need to go use my masculine wiles on Judge Wilcox's law clerk." He waggles his brows. "But I have a feeling I'm leaving you in good hands." He tips his head my way. "I told Sully to take my seat."

Hmm, dammit. That's actually the kind of help I could use. Now I owe the kid.

He smirks like he can read my thoughts, then wanders down the cobblestone street.

I splay a hand over the small of my wife's back and steer her toward the ballroom. "Come on. Let's get you off your feet."

"How about we get a drink and sit out here?" She nods at a bench along the fake street.

Even better. I'd never say no to time alone with my wife.

I leave her on a bench while I fetch her a drink, and when I return, I slide in next to her, a smile on my face. "So, you and Little Caesar?"

Sloane's eyes widen and her mouth falls open on a laugh. "Oh my god. You can't call him that."

I grin. "Why not? He's younger than us both."

She rolls her eyes and sips from her straw.

I nudge her. "He was your date?"

She shrugs, and then with her lip caught between her teeth, her hesitant blue eyes find mine. "Who'd you think I would come with?"

I hold her gaze, waiting her out, because she knows bloody well who I thought she came with.

Those cheeks of hers go pink and she drops her eyes. "I was just afraid to tell you that I wanted to come with you."

Her statement takes me out at the knees, and I'm sitting on my damn arse already. Bloody hell, the woman was nervous? My pulse quickens. On the one hand, she's just told me she wanted me to be her date. That should leave me ecstatic. But I'm gutted knowing how much I've failed her. Knowing that my wife doesn't have a clue how crazy I am for her. That she would be afraid to tell me anything is a problem. But to be afraid to tell me she wants to spend time with me? That she wants my attention? That won't bloody do.

"Sweetheart." My voice is firm. I want her to hear these next words. I wait for her to raise her eyes so she's looking at me. I won't grab her chin and force it. I won't even squeeze her hand to get her attention. I don't deserve to touch her until she understands precisely how wrong I was for ever making her feel that she not only deserves my attention, but that I want to give it to her. That I ache to give her every bit of me.

When she finally lifts those blue eyes, there's hesitation there—there's bloody longing—and fucking hope. I won't let her down again.

"I know I have failed you, again and again, and I can't fix this all overnight. But if you believe only one thing I ever tell you, believe this: there is not a moment when I would rather be anywhere other than by your side. So if you ever want a date or a friend or even an escort to the bathroom, let it be me. Know that I want it to be me. *Always.*"

Sloane's blue eyes turn iridescent as they fill with tears, but she gives me a quick nod and swipes them away quickly. My heart is in my throat as I try to figure out the right thing to do next. Do I touch her? Comfort here? Bring her into my chest and stroke her back until she knows with certainty that I want to be nowhere in this world but by her side?

Before I can decide, three carolers step up in front of us, and one pulls out a harmonica, blowing loudly. Then they break into "Have Yourself A Merry Little Christmas."

My wife's posture straightens, and she catches my eye, smiling. She loves Christmas. She always has. And because of that, I do too.

My life before Sloane was gray. I don't say that to be dramatic. It's the simple truth. She brought a brightness to everything. My favorite thing by far, though, has always been the way she communicates with me through her eyes. If she finds something funny, she searches me out to see if I'm smiling too. If she's pissed off, she looks to me for assurance that she isn't being overdramatic. If she's happy, like right now, she looks to me, not because my presence is vital to her happiness, but because she wants me to experience the joy as well.

My wife has been a giver throughout our entire marriage. Hell, our entire relationship. And I'm only now realizing it.

I grin right back at her and then slide an arm around her shoulders, swaying to the song that brings her such joy. When the carolers finish their tune, they turn to leave, and I call after them. "One more?"

Sloane settles against me even further at the request, and the singers brighten as they launch into "It's the Most Wonderful Time of the Year."

We garner a bit of a crowd with this one, and requests are shouted, one after another. As the minutes tick on, Sloane remains pinned to my side. The next hour flies by, and before I know it, Sloane is yawning and the crowd is dispersing.

"It's probably time to head back to the penthouse," she says. "Otherwise, I'm at risk of falling asleep on this bench."

Surprised, I blink at her. Did my wife just ask me to come back to our bed? "Sloane, I—"

Her eyes widen. "No, I wasn't—" She shakes her head. "I wasn't inviting you back with me. I was just saying I should get to bed. I know we're—"

I stop her there. "I'd love nothing more than to come back to our bed, sweetheart. And one day, when you're ready, I will."

Her lips part, just the slightest bit, and she sucks in a breath. "But not tonight?" The words are whispered, and damn does the hope in them make my chest tighten.

"I promised to take T. J. for donuts in the morning."

She nods almost robotically. Like she hasn't quite caught up to our conversation. That's okay. I know she's not ready for all of this yet. I know I haven't earned her yet. But I will. I tilt her way and brush the back of my hand against her cheek. "Come home with me, sweetheart. I don't want to spend another night away from you."

The smile she gives me is the best response I could have hoped for. "I guess I could go for a honey-glazed donut."

I chuckle and press a kiss to her crown. "Then that's what you'll get."

CHAPTER 17
Sloane

There's nothing quite like Christmas in New York. It's the one time of the year when New Yorkers don't mind each other. We all slow down—marginally—and every day there's something new to discover. The light show in front of Macy's. The windows at Saks. The Christmas tree at Rockefeller.

The air is crisp but not yet bitterly cold. Here and there, when the buildings block the wind, the warm scent of roasting peanuts replaces the chill.

The sounds don't change much—car horns and the engines of the vehicles stuck in gridlock—but the atmosphere is overtaken by a sense of possibility. A sense of wonder.

This afternoon, I duck out of work early for my twelve-week appointment with my ob-gyn and wander down the sidewalk, soaking it all in.

My mood brightened, I take the elevator up to the doctor's office, excited to see our little bear again. The instant the elevator opens into the lobby of my doctor's office, I get a whiff of Sully's cologne. Maybe I'm so attuned to it because pregnancy has heightened my sense of smell. Or maybe it's because the man has burrowed himself beneath my skin. Either way, it's like I'm trained to seek him out.

I kind of despise it. Being so aware of him makes it very hard to keep my wits about me. And hard to remember that we're co-parenting only. Dancing with Sully the other night, laying my head against his chest and allowing him to press his lips to my forehead, had me keyed up all night.

It must be the pregnancy. Add how starved for human affection I am, that even a brush of his lips sets me off.

That's a lie. I can't blame my hormonal state for everything. In reality, it's Sully. It's always been Sully.

The hour we spent on the bench might have been one of my favorite hours of the last year. And I've replayed the words he uttered with such complete devotion in his eyes again and again.

There is not a moment when I would rather be anywhere other than by your side.

The craziest thing about that night is that I believe him. Sully wanted to be there with me. He wants to be here for me. My heart races as I acknowledge that fact.

Now, he strides toward me, eating up the distance between us quickly, his lips kicking up on one side. "I wish you had let me pick you up at the office." He holds his arms out like it's second nature to sweep me into them. But before he makes contact, he pulls up short. "You must be freezing from the walk."

I wave my gloved hands. "The fresh air felt good. And it seemed silly to have you drive past this building to get me, only to turn around and come right back."

A low growl rumbles between us as he shakes his head. "When will you realize that there is nothing I wouldn't do for you?"

In the past, I would have pushed back. I would have lamented the last few years and how little he was there for me.

After the other night, though, I trust that what he's saying is true.

I have to trust that this isn't just a phase for him. That he's making changes to be a better parent.

So instead of my usual snark, I simply smile. "Thanks."

His eyes, more blue than gray today, widen in surprise, but he quickly schools his expression and nods. "Shall we check in?"

After I've confirmed that the office has my new insurance on file —not the policy Murphy and Machon offers—we sit in the waiting room side by side.

"I don't like that they're paying for this," he grumbles, his forearms resting on his knees.

Amused, I eye him. "You act as if Will himself is paying for my pregnancy."

His scowl deepens. Yup, hit the nail on the head with that one. "It's unnecessary. We're married and this is *our* child, and my firm provides family insurance. Why would you need your own?"

I don't even acknowledge the question. He knows why. Because we were getting divorced. And yes, the settlement Brian drew up for us includes medical insurance unless I remarry, but I didn't want to be reliant on Sully anymore, so I made sure to opt into the benefit when I started my new job.

I didn't want any of my decisions, including whether I remarry in the future, to be dictated by this man.

I shake my head. Right now, I can't focus on any of that. The idea of being with someone else, let alone marrying someone else, is ludicrous. It's hard to remember how I ever thought I could move on from Sully. Obviously even then I was lying to myself. That was proven by my recklessness the night I had unprotected sex with my husband back in September.

A flash of that night hits me, and my core clenches in response. I clamp my thighs together, mentally berating myself, hoping like hell Sully can't sense that little spike in desire.

"Sloane Murphy." The nurse's call couldn't have come at a better time.

I stand and shuffle across the room with Sully on my heels. Once she's left us in the exam room with instructions for me to change, awkwardness creeps in. For a moment, Sully and I stare at one another. It's nothing like the way we interacted during my first pregnancy. Back then, I wouldn't have thought twice about undressing in front of him. Hell, more than once, I tried to convince him to get me off before the doctor appeared. Back then, we were fearless. Head-over-heels in love. Disasters for one another.

For most of our time together, there wasn't a moment when I wondered if my husband was attracted to me. I liked undressing in front of him. Even after T.J. was born and my body had changed. Because Sully always made it clear how much he loved every inch of me.

He thumbs over his shoulder and clears his throat. "I could give you privacy if you'd like."

We're so painfully considerate of one another's feelings now. So aware and careful. It's like a punch to the stomach. I can't imagine keeping up the act for the rest of the pregnancy. We're sharing a damn bedroom, for fuck's sake.

I shrug. "Or you could sit and relax." I hold back the *and enjoy the show*, though I think my lifted brows say the words for me.

Throat bobbing, he nods. "Yeah, okay." He settles in the chair beside the exam table, but when he looks up again, I swear to God the fire in his eyes is hot enough to incinerate my clothes and do the work for me. If there was ever a question about whether my husband is still attracted to me, I have my answer now.

I shimmy my dress up my thighs and remove my stockings first. When I straighten, Sully is holding out a hand to take them. I drape them over his palm, and when our hands brush, his touch echoes through my body. I have to force myself to breathe evenly as he folds them and then sets them on his thigh.

I'm frozen in place, watching him, until he looks up, and when his eyes meet mine, they simmer with heat and expectation. Like he knew I was waiting for his attention before I continued to undress.

I turn away from him, my voice raspy as I ask, "Can you unzip me?"

"Come here." His command makes my knees go weak.

I shuffle backward until I think I'm close enough. Sully must disagree, because he pushes his chair forward, causing it to scrape loudly in the small room. He drapes my hair over one shoulder, then slides the zipper down slowly.

Once he's stopped, I swear I feel the ghost of a kiss against my lower back. Not a physical touch. More like he breathes me in. His lips so close I can almost feel their dampness.

I push the sleeve off one shoulder and then the other, but before the dress can fall to the floor, he catches it and holds out a hand, a silent offer to steady me while I step out of it. I shuffle around to face him so I can take the garment, inadvertently lining my breasts up with his face.

His tongue slips out, moistening his lips. "Are you cold?" he murmurs, his focus fixed on the pointed nipples beneath the lace of my bra.

Did I intentionally pick out a matching set? Maybe. Did I go with black and sexy on purpose? I'll never admit it.

"I think we both know I'm not," I breathe out.

Then, because I like the way he's looking at me, because I'm feeling bold under his lust-filled gaze, I thumb the waistband of my lace panties and push them down. Sully's thighs are spread wide, and he makes no effort to hide his erection. "Christ," he mutters, rubbing a palm over his mouth as he drinks me in, lingering on the spot between my legs. He digs his fingers into the fabric of his trousers, as if it takes effort to keep them there.

I can't help but push him just a little more.

"I need help with the bra," I tell him as I turn.

He stops me, his hands firm on my bare hips now. I swear to God, we moan in unison at the contact. "I can get it from here."

My heart lodges itself in my throat.

Shit. Shit, shit, shit. I'm such an idiot. Until now, I hadn't considered how it would feel to be naked in his arms again. I've been so focused on teasing him, on putting on a damn show, that I forgot how *he* affects *me*.

And he's running with it. As if reminding me that I'm his wife, ensuring I understand just how comfortable he is in this situation, he runs both hands up my waist and slides them around my back so he can unclip my bra. As he does so, he tips his chin up, giving me a front-row seat to his reaction when my bra falls, exposing my heavy breasts. My nipples practically bow to meet his lips, and the way his blue eyes darken with longing has a needy cry creeping up my throat.

Not a single inch of him is actually touching me now. Not his lips, not his hands, and certainly not his tongue. And yet I feel him all over.

The rap of knuckles against the door startles me. With shaky hands, I reach for the gown the nurse left out for me. Then I hustle to the examination table.

Flustered doesn't begin to describe how I feel as Sully calls to the doctor to let her know I'm ready. As I will my heart to settle, I worry she can smell the arousal in the air. Shit. Can she feel the sexual tension still threatening to suffocate me?

"How are you feeling?" she asks casually, oblivious to what she interrupted. As she settles on the stool beside the table, she scans my chart on her tablet. Even if my first pregnancy had been a cakewalk, my age alone would make me high risk. Add the preeclampsia I suffered, which resulted in over a month on bed rest, and an emergent delivery to the mix, and it's hard not to be cautious.

"I feel good," I say strongly, as if I can will the sensation to stick with me through the next six months. I'm a stubborn person. If there was even the slightest chance I could control the uncontrollable, I'd figure out how. My goal is to get to full term, but with my history, it's unlikely.

"Any dizziness or weakness in your extremities?"

I hold out my hands and wiggle my fingers. "All good."

She smiles. "Good. Your blood work looks great, so all we have left is to see how baby is measuring." She rolls away and brings the sonogram machine closer. "Dad, do you want to stand on the other side of Mom so you can see better?"

Sully glances at me, seeking approval, and my heart trips over itself. This shouldn't be so hard. I wanted another baby for so long. I want to enjoy this with him. I hold out my hand, and he breaks into the biggest smile I've seen from him in years. He sets my clothes on the chair and rounds the table, taking my offered hand in both of his and squeezing. As if it's second nature, he leans down and presses a kiss to my forehead.

It's so devastatingly sweet. Achingly tender.

Before I can lose myself in the moment, before I can spiral about what this all means, the doctor says, "It's going to be cold."

Then she slides the transducer over my belly, and a loud static noise fills the space. She presses down, and the black screen is replaced with the image of our baby. Though, I saw my little gummy bear the last time I was here, today the baby's features are more prominent. Arms and legs, still so small but fully formed, and the most beautiful whooshing sound, strong and steady.

Sully hisses above me, snagging my attention. And damn am I glad I looked. He's never looked more handsome than he does now, with his lips tipped up and the skin around his eyes crinkled, creating the most delicious creases, as if putting an emphasis on his joy.

He bows his head and catches my eyes, seeking out my reaction just as I sought out his. His eyes are a brilliant blue when they meet mine. This color is one I only see when he's emotional, and by the way his eyes fill with tears, there's no denying just how powerfully this moment has hit him.

"You did good, sweetheart. So *fucking* good," he rasps as he looks at our baby again.

My heart expands in my chest, like his words have filled me with helium. I was nervous about this part. For so long, Sully didn't want another baby, and though he's told me he's happy about this pregnancy, a niggling doubt has clung to me since the day I told him. This reaction is all I need to be certain that he hasn't just been humoring me. He really does want this.

When the doctor assures us that the baby looks perfectly healthy, I cling to her words, knowing I'll be rolling them around in my head often over the next few months. She reminds us of the symptoms of preeclampsia, and we discuss precautions. As she hands me a towel to swipe away the goop on my belly, she says, "Did you want to know the sex? We have the results in your blood work."

I glance at Sully, my mind going blank, and in return, he gives me a soft smile. "I'd really like to include T.J. when we find out. Is that okay with you?"

Tears well in my eyes so quickly that I have to look away before they spill. I nod, unable to get the words out.

"Then we'll wait," the doctor says cheerfully. "Schedule your anatomy scan on your way out, and we'll see you in four weeks."

I smile gratefully. "That sounds perfect."

The day itself is perfect, in fact.

That is until Sully and I enter the apartment in Jersey again and find ourselves engulfed in chaos.

He steps in front of me, as if he needs to shield me from the mayhem. "What in the bloody hell are you doing?"

CHAPTER 18
Sloane

"**I**sn't it perfect?" Cal's shout is strained, since he's balancing what is easily a twelve-foot tree while Lo stands back and yells *to the left, to the right.*

Yeah, there's no way to center that damn tree. Not when it literally touches the ceiling. We either need to cut a hole up there or trim the top.

Considering I get more than enough of Madame E as it is, I don't think cutting a hole in her floor is the way to go.

I cringe. "I don't know if I'd call it perfect."

Sully, who's still standing between me and all the commotion, shouts, "Why in bloody hell would you buy a tree that big!"

Cal straightens and huffs, like he's affronted by the question. "It's Murphy's first Christmas with us."

In his effort to explain, he releases the tree, and it tilts to one side. Luckily, it's wedged against the crown molding, so it doesn't fall over completely.

"Now look what you did," Sully grumbles.

Lo yells, "More to the right!"

"Where's Brian?" I ask. "And the kids?"

Lo shifts her focus from the tree to me. "They went to walk Fuzzy. How was the doctor?"

I smile at Sully. "It was good. Baby is measuring right on time."

Cal grins widely at us. "I can't wait to be an uncle again. When are you telling T.J.?"

"Telling me what?"

We spin around to find T. J. and Murphy with Brian and his monstrosity of a cat behind them.

Rather than step into the room, the cat cowers, backing away from the tree, and darts behind the man he's imprinted on.

"What the hell did you do?" Brian yells. He steps forward, only to tumble to the floor because the cat's leash is wrapped around his legs.

"Shit." I rush to help him up while Sully tries to unhook Fuzzy from his leash. "Maybe try rolling left."

He goes right.

"Your other left."

He goes right again.

"Brian," I grit out. "Work with me here."

"Dammit," T.J. and Murphy say, mimicking Brian's voice. They dissolve into fits of giggles and fall into a heap.

The cat, thinking he's being called, prances around them.

I yank on the leash, figuring I might have an easier time, but I think it gets caught on Brian's zipper, and he yowls, grabbing his crotch.

"Dammit!" he grits out.

The cat lunges for him, landing on his chest with enough force to knock the wind from him. His back paws, unfortunately, hit Brian right where the sun doesn't shine.

The howl he lets loose sends shivers down my spine.

"I'll get ice," Lo calls.

"Why doesn't Fuzzy ever snuggle me like that?" Cal pouts.

Sully blows out a breath. "Maybe we should take T.J. out to tell him the big news."

I nod. "Good idea."

"Can I get ice cream?" T.J. asks before we've even entered the restaurant across the street. He's been begging us to tell him *the big news* since we got Brian untangled.

Bringing T.J. to the Grasshopper to tell him feels right. There's a sense of kismet here. This is where we had dinner the night our baby bear was made, so telling T.J. about him or her here feels like coming full circle.

Our future may still be uncertain, but Sully and I are a team. We have to be. So I'm thankful we can do this together.

"Let's sit, then we can order ice cream," Sully tells him.

Before he can finish the sentence, T.J. is asking for change so he can play Pac-Man.

So much for his dire need to know our secret.

We let him go, figuring it's best if he works off some of the energy before we force him to sit and talk. At least he'll have ice cream to entertain him when he comes back.

"So what are we telling him?" I ask once the server has dropped off his ice cream.

Sully shrugs. "That he's going to be a big brother?"

I nod, though suddenly I'm not sure that's the angle I want to go with. But what's the alternative? "Good, good. That's exactly how we should present it. Good idea."

Brows lowering, Sully assesses me for a second. Then, with a shake of his head, he calls T.J. over.

He's right. It's important for us to focus on our son and his role as a big brother. That will make it easier to steer clear of questions about our family dynamic. A week ago, I would have been dead set on sticking to that. Now, though, the idea leaves me feeling a little crushed.

Maybe because I've gotten so used to being in the apartment with the little family that Sully, Cal, and Brian have created because of Terry's trust. It's nice having people around. It leaves little time for me to feel lonely.

What'll happen when it's time to leave?

My stomach twists painfully at the thought.

Will Sully and I share custody? Two apartments. Mine unbearably quiet on the nights Sully has the kids. And spending days away from an infant? I don't know that I can handle it, yet it would be unfair to keep Sully from his child.

Shaking free of my spiraling thoughts, I force myself to focus on the matter at hand.

"We have some exciting news," Sully starts as T.J. shovels ice cream into his mouth.

"Yes, you're going to be a big brother. Isn't that exciting?" I ask with a smile.

T.J. freezes with another spoonful of ice cream in the air, his eyes locked on me, his expression flat. "You're having a baby?"

Dread washes over me like a wave. Shoot. I hadn't considered that he might not want to be a big brother. What if he freaks out? Maybe we shouldn't have done this in such a public place. It wouldn't be out of the realm of possibility for him to toss his ice cream across the table.

"Yes," Sully chimes in. "Your mother is having a baby, which means you get to be a big brother. Isn't that exciting?"

"Where will the baby live?" T.J. asks, still pensive. The question is almost accusing. Far too knowing.

And dammit, my stomach is in knots.

"With us," Sully responds easily.

T.J.'s whole body relaxes and he breaks into a smile. "Cool." With that, he shoves another bite of ice cream into his mouth.

It occurs to me then that our son is far more in tune with what's going on than I realized.

And it kills me that he even has to be concerned about it. I may be questioning what will happen in the future, but I never want my son to have to worry about that. I hate that it's even a thought. More than anything, I want this time to be joyful for him.

"Is it a boy?" T.J. asks.

"We don't know, bud. We thought we'd wait to find out with you at Mum's next doctor's appointment."

With another nod, he stabs his spoon into the bowl in front of him. As usual, he's determined to eat quickly so he can play again.

"If it is a boy, he'll be your little brother, just like Cal is my little brother," Sully says with a grin.

"Can I go play again?" he asks, holding up his empty bowl.

We nod, and he's gone.

I sigh as he trips over his feet but rights himself without falling. "That went okay, I think."

Sully nods, his attention set on our little boy. "I should have kept him around and talked up the idea of a sister too. Hopefully he'll be happy either way," he says under his breath.

"I'm just happy he won't be alone like me," I quip.

Sully stiffens and frowns at me. "You're not alone."

I try to smile, try to make it easier on him. Brush off the off handed remark like it's nothing, but Sully's frown doesn't fade. He studies me like he knows how scared I am of the future. Like he understands that I can barely breathe when I think of a future without him in it. "Sweetheart," his voice is a whisper as he reaches across the table to squeeze my hand. "You've got all of us. No matter what happens between you and me, *we're* family."

My heart free-falls in my chest. His tone is stern, but it's sincere, his words the honest truth. And they're exactly what I needed to hear.

CHAPTER 19
Sully

Across the massive dining table, Brian stares vacantly, the melancholy expression out of place, especially because it's Christmas Eve.

"You good?"

He lifts one shoulder and lets it fall. The colored lights from the tree make his face look blue, which seems to fit his mood. "I don't know. Just feels weird."

"What?" I need clarification. He could be talking about the enormous tree or the massive cat that's practically on his lap or the smell of whatever Cal burned that's still lingering in the air.

"Dad moved up to Boston with Dylan, and with everything going on, I couldn't make the trip up. It's weird, not being with my family on Christmas."

Six months ago, Frank Machon relocated so he could be closer to Brian's sister and her kids. And I'm a jackass for not even considering that Brian might be lonely.

I've always assumed that Brian knows that, as far as the Murphys are concerned, he's family. We've been friends for twenty years, and my dad hired him straight out of law school. There's no way he'll ever shake us.

"You've got us," I remind him, putting my thoughts into words. If I learned anything from my problems with Sloane, it's that I have to tell people how I feel, not just assume they know.

He purses his lips, and for a second, I think he'll argue. Instead, he nods once. "I know. But now that you and Cal have your own families..." He shrugs. "I'm not sure I belong."

"Belong where?" Cal asks from behind me.

Brian looks at Cal, his eyes widening.

Oh bullocks. What has my idiot of a brother done now? With a grunt, I turn and assess him. Immediately, a sound halfway between a scoff and a laugh leaves my lips.

"Isn't it great?" Cal twists, shaking his arse, flaunting his ridiculous pajamas. They're a god-awful green color and looks similar to what one of Santa's elves would wear. The bottoms even have an arse flap.

And his name.

Daddy Cal.

I shake my head. God only knows whether he chose the name because of his relationship with his son or if that's a nickname courtesy of Lo.

"It even has a hat." Cal adjusts the pointed stocking cap on his head, jingling the white ball on the tip.

Brian snorts, and I can't help but laugh.

Bloody hell, my brother looks ridiculous.

"They're perfect, Uncle Cal." T.J. barrels into the living room, dragging his cousin behind him.

The sight of the boys in matching pajamas—both with their names stamped on their own arse flaps—makes it hard not to smile.

T.J. bounces up and down beside my brother.

"Aren't these so cool, Dad?"

I nod. My little lad looks adorable in anything. Even outlandish pajama sets.

He beams up at Cal, his hands clasped in front of him. "See? I told you he'd wear them too."

My lungs seize up. *What now?*

Cal grins, his chest puffed out. "Uncle Brian, too, I hope. We're a family, so it's not Christmas unless we're wearing matching pj's."

Murphy, who looks slightly less enthusiastic, steps up and sets two clear packages on the table. "Apparently, we all have to be elves. Lo and Aunt Sloane are changing into theirs too."

In almost any other situation, I'd flat-out refuse to take part in my brother's nonsense. But it's Christmas. I want it to be perfect for both T.J. and Sloane. If T. J. wants us to wear matching pajamas, then I'm in.

"We'll put them on," I assure my son.

"You know what would be fun?" T. J.'s eyes dance in a way that concerns me. Like there's a good chance he's about to scale the side of the building like Spider-Man. Again.

"What? I need to know so we can have all the fun." Cal claps a little too loudly. Since Murphy showed up unexpectedly a few months ago, it's been my brother's mission to make sure his son is happy. And having the best Christmas is important. I understand his obsession more than I ever thought I could.

"It's fun that Santa will come," Murphy assures his dad.

Cal's expression darkens. Last week, when Murphy told us that Santa always skips his house, I thought my brother was going to book a flight to LA so he could curse Murphy's mum out in person. Maybe ring her neck too.

Lo talked him down, and now Cal is focused on ensuring this Christmas is over-the-top enough to make up for the six lackluster years Murphy lived before meeting his father. My brother may irritate the piss out of me most days, but I have nothing but respect for how he handled unexpectedly becoming a father to a six-year-old.

I would not have been as easygoing had I discovered I had a child only when he was left at our office with nothing more than a backpack and a note. My brother never went on the attack, though. He just became the father Murphy needs. And that's a feat for a reformed man-child. He's matured decades in the handful of months that Murphy's been here.

"I think it would be fun if Murphy and I could have a sleepover in his room," T.J. announces. "Right, Murphy?"

Murphy eyes his dad. "If it's okay..."

"Anything you want," my brother promises.

"Yes!" T.J. pumps a fist and bounces closer to his cousin. Then he whisper-shouts, "We can stay up and catch Santa together."

"What?" Cal's spine goes ramrod straight.

I chuckle. T.J.'s tried to catch Santa for the last two years, but there's no way he won't pass out before midnight. "You two go brush your teeth. Then we'll read *The Night Before Christmas* and get cookies out."

"And everyone gets to open one present," T.J. reminds us, as if we could possibly have forgotten that. All day he's been talking about whose present he'll open.

"I still think you should open mine." Cal rocks back on his heels, smirking.

"Or..." T.J. drags the word out. "Maybe we should open one from *each person.*" He tilts his head and breaks into his most winning smile. The little bugger never quits. We've shot down the suggestion three times already today.

"T.J.," I warn.

He giggles. "Okay. Only one present tonight."

I point to the hall. "Teeth."

With a nod, he turns to his cousin. "Let's go. We can make a big bed out of blankets on your floor." He darts toward Murphy's room with Murphy a few steps behind him. Once the boys disappear, I stand up.

"They can't catch Santa." Cal's panicked comment is directed at me.

I chuckle. "Don't worry. They'll be asleep in an hour. Come on." I pick up both sets of pajamas off the table and toss one to Brian.

He swipes the bag out of the air and stands, knocking the cat's head off his legs. The cat lets out a *how dare you?* hiss in response.

"Chill." Brian frowns at the giant feline.

With a twitch of his nose, he leaps onto the table.

"Aw, over here, Fuzzy," Cal coos.

Nose in the air, the cat ignores him, instead gracefully jumping to the floor and padding toward Brian's bedroom.

"Dammit." Brian glowers as Fuzzy disappears through the open doorway.

"Don't worry, he'll come back for the Christmas treats I got him." Cal rushes to the tree and picks up a bag adorned with a kitten in a full Santa suit. "We'll do presents once you wankers have changed."

Brian groans. "You really expect me to wear this?"

"The whole family needs to match," I say. "And that includes you."

Cal nods, fiddling with the gift bag. "Yes, and we elves have a lot of work to do after the kids go to bed. We have to put the bikes together and hang the stockings and wrap the rest of the gifts."

Brian shakes his head. "Sounds like Christmas at Dylan's."

"Exactly." I skirt around him. "This is what Christmas with family looks like, and we're family," I remind him.

I knock on my closed bedroom door, and when Sloane says, "Come in," I twist the knob and duck inside.

The view before me stops me in my tracks.

"Do not laugh at me," she warns, running her hands down her sides to smooth out the red shirt. The fitted pajamas give me the perfect view of the small bump on my wife's lower stomach. The knowledge that our child is growing safely inside her makes my chest swell.

"I know I look ridiculous."

"No, sweetheart." I take a tentative step forward. "You could never look ridiculous. You look radiant."

Fighting the urge to reach out to her, I clench my hands at my sides.

As if she noticed the movement, she shuffles closer and gently grasps my wrist. Then, with her eyes locked on mine, she places my palm against her lower stomach.

Her warmth soaks into me, waking up every dormant part of me. I haven't felt this alive in months. Maybe years. Emotion welling up inside me, I lower my focus to where we're touching.

"You can't feel anything yet." Her voice is low, raspy.

Nodding, I swallow down the lump in my throat. That'll come later. Right now, touching her, feeling the swell that is our baby, is enough.

She wets her lips, searching my face, the look in her eyes one I haven't seen in months. It's pure desire. She looks like she wants me to kiss her. Hell, she looks like she needs it.

A weight I've been carrying for way too long lifts, making it easier to breathe. My wife still wants me.

I angle in a fraction, and she tilts her chin up and inches closer to me. My pulse kicks up, thumping in my ears. Six inches. That's all the space left between us. Her lips part, her breath warm on my face. The need to kiss her, to once again feel her mouth against mine, pounds through me.

The door flies open with a bang, sending my heart lurching, and we jump apart.

"Mom, Dad. Hurry up!" T.J. calls from the doorway.

When I glance back at Sloane, all the heat in her eyes has tempered.

"I'll let you get dressed." She steps away.

I nod, swallowing back a rush of disappointment. When the door clicks shut behind her, though, the lightness of that moment stays with me. Things between us are changing, and from the look of it, they're moving in the right direction.

A smile tugs at my lips as I step out of my trousers and into the awful green pajama bottoms. The expression is quickly replaced by a grimace when, even with my boxer briefs still in place, I feel a breeze where the bloody flap is.

Twisted at the waist, I glare at my arse. Or try to, at least.

"*Daddy Sully.*"

I spin at the sound of Sloane's voice.

She drinks me in, slowly inspecting my bare chest and stomach, then lingering on my cock, which twitches under her gaze.

Once again, her eyes heat. "*Daddy Sully.*"

The breathless words go straight to my groin, and the tight cotton does nothing to hide the reaction.

She smirks, clearly enjoying this interaction as much as I am.

"Did you get the hat?" another voice calls. *Lo.*

Sloane startles, her eyes darting away. "Yeah. One sec." She steps in and swipes the green hat off the bed. And with one more look of longing, she steps away.

Bloody hell. I want to chase her. I want to toss her over my shoulder and bring her straight back to bed. The fierce need to run my tongue along every inch of her skin steals my breath. The temptation to pin her down and fuck her so good she's screaming my name overwhelms me.

I'm halfway to the door before good sense reins me in again. Yes, I desperately want my wife's body, but I want her heart more. And I don't have it. Not yet.

Tonight, my focus needs to remain on making this Christmas everything Sloane and T.J. deserve.

With two deep breaths to get my cock calmed the fuck down, I toss the ugly green shirt over my head.

My excitement distracts me as I head back to the lounge, and I forget to duck in the doorway, instead slamming into the frame.

"Dammit." I press a hand to the aching spot.

The cat appears, thinking I've summoned him, and a giant paw bats at my trousers.

"No," I warn, darting out of the way. His nails are enormous; there's no way the cheap material of my pajamas would stand up against them.

"Fuzzy." Cal shakes the bag of treats he stashed in the gift bag.

The beast turns and darts toward him, his body nothing but a gray blur.

Cal tucks the treat bag behind his back and says, "Sit."

I huff. Why Cal still thinks he can train the cat is beyond me. The damn thing doesn't listen to a word he says. Hell, he barely follows any of Brian's commands.

Unsurprisingly, the cat bats at my brother.

"No, Fuzzy. Sit," Cal commands.

But the cat has no patience for his nonsense. He simply stalks around him and swipes at the bag dangling in front of Cal's ass. As he does, his claw catches on the cheap material of the elf suit.

Then he's yowling and Cal is yelping, and when Fuzzy yanks his paw back, he takes the flap down with him.

"Oh my god," Lo cries as Cal's bare arse comes into view.

Both boys fall into hysterical laughter, holding their bellies.

Quickly, I avert my eyes. "Why aren't you wearing underwear?"

"Jesus," Brian snaps. "No one wants to see your hairy ass."

"I do not have a hairy arse." Cal reaches for the flap that's now dangling behind him. "Tell them, Lo!" He spins the other way, still grasping for the material.

She, Sloane, and both boys are laughing so hard they're crying.

"Let me," Lo forces out between giggles. She scurries over to Cal and quickly buttons the flap back into place.

When the boys finally tire of laughing, T.J. tips his head and surveys Brian.

"You don't have kids," he says, pointing to the *Daddy Brian* stitched on my best friend's arse.

Lo giggles. "We all know he's Dammit's daddy."

Brian drops his head back and groans. "For the love of God, I didn't ask for a cat. He's not mine."

"Don't say that," Cal hisses, frantically scanning the room. "He'll hear you."

The cat has disappeared, along with the whole bag of treats. He's probably living it up in Brian's room.

"No, he will not," Brian grumbles. "Let's open presents so I can get the image of Cal's hairy ass out of my head."

Both boys break into fits of giggles again.

"I don't have a hairy butt," Cal whines.

"You have a perfect butt." Lo rubs her boyfriend's back. "I love your butt."

T.J. guffaws. "You love his poopy butt? That's so weird."

"Presents." Sloane claps, changing the subject before he segues into a conversation about poop.

"Why don't we give Mum hers first?" I suggest to my son. It's a miracle his excitement hasn't caused him to ruin the surprise. He was so proud of himself when he found the pink lava lamp.

Sloane's genuine smile as she opens it fills me with confidence. Yeah, she'll like the rest of her gifts too.

After the boys open presents from Brian—a Lego Santa sled and Christmas tree—Murphy gives Lo a set of illustrated *Percy Jackson* coffee table books.

It's too late for the boys to tear into their Legos, so we send them into the kitchen to get the cookies for Santa, then settle in to read *The Night Before Christmas*.

Cal pulls Lo onto his lap in the oversized chair while Brian and Sloane join me on the couch.

T.J. and Murphy wiggle their way between us, and I tuck them into my sides while I read.

When I get to the last line, one of many I have memorized from years of practice, I look at Sloane.

I stumble over the words, my breath threatening to escape me. Because her gaze is filled with a tenderness I haven't seen in far too long. And fuck, I've missed it.

In this moment, it seems possible that my wife might actually like me. And it feels like a turning point. Like this moment could change everything.

CHAPTER 20
Sloane

"Tonight was a good night," Lo says as she snatches torn wrapping paper from the floor.

Brian, trash bag in hand, nods, wearing a small smile.

The expression makes me pause. It's been so long since I saw him smile. Truly, even though we're living in the same space, it's been a while since we've spent any real time together.

I've never been the kind of person who has a whole lot of friends. In law school, Brian was one of the precious few I was close to, and not long after Lo came to work with us, she became another. It feels good to relax with the two of them and not feel awkward.

Because awkward is a mild descriptor for the interactions Brian and I have had over the last few months. When I filed for divorce, Brian suddenly became my adversary, working on Sully's side while ironing out the settlement. Naturally, that made me push him even farther away. Now, with a little time, I can see he was doing the best he could in a very difficult situation.

But when we first separated, I just assumed Sully would keep Cal and Brian, and I'd get Lo. It was better that way. The last thing I wanted was to put our friends in the middle of our issues. When the rest of them were forced to move to Jersey, and Lo was forced to work in a small office with my husband, I thought I'd lose her too.

I'm relieved that I haven't lost any of them.

"You seeing anyone?" I ask, cupping the mug of tea Sully made for me.

Brian chuckles. "You been talking to Sully and Cal?"

I eye Lo and shake my head. "No, why?"

He waves me off. "They have it in their heads that I need to meet someone."

"My Sully is telling you that you need a woman?" I can't hide the shock in my voice. I can't even picture Sully entertaining that type of conversation, let alone engaging in it.

"*Your Sully?*" Lo teases.

With a roll of my eyes, I sip my tea and study Brian. "So have you?"

Lo scoffs as she pads to the kitchen. "He'd have to actually talk to women in order to meet one, right?"

I hum in agreement, inhaling the earthy scent of the steam rising from my mug.

"I don't have time," Brian grouses. "Besides, how the hell would I explain this living situation to a date?"

Eyes widening, I gasp. "Oh, Brian is a naughty boy. I was just talking about going out to dinner, not—" I put my tea on the coffee table, then make a circle with one hand and poke my index finger through the middle of it. "Fucking," I mouth.

Brian covers his eyes. "I forgot how crass you can be."

From the kitchen, Lo calls, "This is my favorite version of her."

I grin. "So?"

Cal's ginormous cat wanders into the room and rubs his head against Brian's knee.

"Oh," he says. "Looks like the cat needs a walk."

I laugh. "Oh, now you call him the cat and not Dammit?"

"He's a damn good cat." With a wink, he stands and heads for the door.

"Might want to change before you go outside," I call.

He stumbles, then whips around, covering his ass with both hands, and backs out of the room so we can't see his flap.

I burst into laughter. The pajamas are ridiculous. Lo joins in from where she's wiping down the kitchen counter, and the two of us lose it completely. We're just coming down from it when he reappears in jeans and a jacket, the cat following him out the door.

Catching my breath, I lean back against the couch and survey the enormous Christmas tree. It took ten strands of multicolored lights to illuminate it properly. It's ridiculous. And kind of perfect.

As Lo returns to the living room, Sully and Cal reappear, still wearing their matching pajamas.

Lo lights up as she takes Cal in, stretching her arms dramatically. "Well, I'm super tired. I think I'll go to bed."

Cal mimics her. "I'm knackered." He yawns loudly, tapping his hand against his mouth.

I roll my eyes. "We know you guys just want to get freaky. You don't have to lie on our account."

Beaming back at me, Lo strides toward the hallway. "Okay, see you in the morning."

As she passes Cal, he sweeps her off her feet and throws her over his shoulder, making her squeal.

Dammit, they're adorable.

"Are you tired?" Sully stands across the living room, the look on his face one of yearning. Or maybe that's the Christmas tree lights making my imagination run wild.

"Not really." I pat the cushion beside me. "Want to sit with me?"

He hums. "This was always your favorite part."

"What was?" I ask. He's right, but I didn't think he'd ever noticed.

He eases onto the couch and leans back, draping an arm along the back so it's almost around me, but not quite. Then he gives me his full attention. "The Christmas lights after everyone goes to bed."

My eyes fall shut and I sigh. It feels good to be seen, to be understood. And this is a reminder that there was a time when he paid attention to my every move. When I wasn't just an afterthought. "Yup."

"Want to know my favorite part?"

Surprised by his question, I shift so I'm facing him. I truly don't know what he likes about Christmas. Honestly, I never thought he cared for the holiday enough to have a favorite part. And he's never gone out of his way to open up to me about this, along with so, so many other topics.

Typically, on Christmas Eve, we'd sit like this, in comfortable silence, me watching the lights, him probably falling asleep.

Tonight, though, the moment feels more profound.

"Decorating."

I let out a surprised laugh and eye him. "No way. You hate the mess."

He shakes his head, his eyes dancing, like he's delighted that he's shocked me. "I love it. It started our first year of law school. Do you remember that ridiculous tree Brian brought home?"

A giggle escapes me. "Oh my god. I forgot about the Charlie Brown tree." I peer at the big one, grinning. "Not sure which one is worse."

"Back then, I don't think you could have found a tree you hated more than that one."

"It was a twig with a Columbia scarf wrapped around it and one lone ornament that made the whole thing tip sideways. It was offensive." I purchased a single string of lights, hoping it would help, but the tree was beyond saving. Sully and Brian hosted a Christmas party —really, just beer and chips because we were students, even if our parents had plenty of money—and in my mind, that meant they should have a nice tree.

Sully's lips twitch. "You put on Christmas music because you said it was a crime to decorate without it. Then you danced around our living room, laughing and smiling, lighting up my pathetically depressing life."

I frown, studying him more closely. I don't remember Sully ever being anything even close to pathetically depressed.

"And remember the year we moved in together after we took the bar? That Christmas, you covered every surface in twinkling lights."

I smile as I remember that day. "You were so worried the fire marshal would show up. You checked the outlets ten times before we left for the firm's Christmas party."

Sully nods, a wistful expression on his face. "I knew we'd be out late that night. Didn't want to come home to embers."

I bite my lip. "We danced all night."

"That's not all we did," he murmurs, his fingers playing with the ends of my hair.

"Nope, after doing one too many shots at the bar, you snagged the bottle of whiskey the bartender left out, then dragged me through the hotel kitchen and into a closet so you could have your way with me."

His eyes fall to my lips. "I needed you right then. Couldn't wait."

I laugh at his honesty and then give him a dose of my own. "I miss that. That feeling. When we couldn't keep our hands off one another." Emotion wells up inside me, making my words garbled. "When you couldn't look away from me." I bury my face in my shoulder, hiding from his scrutiny.

Sully palms my cheek, gently forcing my head up. "I can't look away from you now."

I give him a sad smile. "This is different. I'm pregnant. We're—" I shake my head, leaning into his palm and inhaling deeply.

Even now, after all we've been through, he still smells like home. His touch still feels like home. Yet here we are, two people who once loved each other so much and now find it difficult to even have a full conversation.

He holds my gaze as he cradles my cheek. "We're still us, sweetheart. You're still the love of my life, and I'll do anything to prove that to you."

The truth in those words bleeds out of him. They wrap around me like a heavy blanket. Warming me. Thawing my frozen heart.

Could it be this easy? Could I *choose* to believe him? To trust us? To try?

"I never gave you your present," I say, my voice barely audible. I can't take my eyes off him.

Sully shakes his head. "Having you here, pregnant with my child, even just talking to me, is the best present you could ever give me." He brushes his thumb against my cheek.

I let out a long sigh. God, I need so much more than that little touch. I need so much more than these small moments. And if I don't act, I'll never know whether I can have them.

I place my hand over his and brush my lips against his palm. "But what if I want to give you more? What if I *need* to give you more?"

His eyes flare, the blue of his irises igniting. "A thousand todays with you wouldn't be enough, sweetheart."

The familiar words settle around me. A promise. A vow.

Breath catching, I nod. "Then let's make today something to remember."

As I lean across the couch, my husband's expression turns to one of surprise, but when I press my lips to his, he doesn't hesitate to kiss me back.

CHAPTER 21
Sully

I have a second to consider whether she's ready. A mere heartbeat to determine whether this is lust or a rekindling of our love. If I was asked to assess what my wife was thinking, whether she was ready and maybe whether I was, I'd say that the same look she wore the day I asked her to be my wife is the one she's wearing now as I lean in for this kiss.

It's hope. It's need. It's uncontrolled want.

Want for a future that lasts beyond just a few minutes. Want for pleasure that can't be fulfilled through mere touch.

I don't question whether we're ready. In this moment, I know what my wife needs because our souls are finally aligned. Maybe it makes me selfish, but I absorb that feeling. I sink into it, slide down, and get comfortable. The deep ache that burrowed within my every nerve, that made simply existing painful when she was no longer mine, is soothed the moment her lips touch mine.

It's not enough for her, though. Tiny fingers dig into my pajama top, and she tugs me closer. Her warm breath tickles my lips as she lets out the softest of sighs.

"I missed you." The words are quick, muttered against my lips.

"God, I fucking missed you," she says again, like the sheer act of saying them is healing.

"Sweetheart." I cup her cheeks and breathe her in, needing to ground myself just as much as she does. She's my anecdote. The calm to my restless heart. I stare into her eyes and promise: "I'm not going anywhere."

Like the words aren't enough, she climbs onto my lap and wraps her arms around my neck. The quick intake of breath leaves me smiling. My wife just smelled me. Inhaled me.

She presses her lips to my neck, and the smile slips as my body shudders and a moan escapes me.

"I'm not going anywhere," I say again.

Sloane shifts on my lap, and the slight movement, the friction, feels decadent.

"Fuck," I rasp.

Stilling, she looks into my eyes, her lips parting. Then she does it again, rolling her hips forward.

Fuck. I grunt in satisfaction. In frustration. In *need.* "*Sloane.*"

She does it again.

Her blue eyes are dreamy in the glow of the Christmas lights. She's a vision. The most beautiful thing I've ever set my sights on. And she wants me.

That knowledge encourages me to slide my hands across her arse and squeeze. Still holding her tight, I lean up and take her lips in another kiss. This one is longer. Slower. Our tongues mingle, and I loosen my grip and let my hands roam. I relish the ability to touch her. I reacquaint myself with the feel of her warmth on top of me, beneath my fingers, and against my tongue.

I delight in the sounds she makes and the way she tastes.

I remember every little thing, as if I could have forgotten. How did I lie in bed next to this woman, have a life with this woman, and not do this every moment she asked? How could I have let her doubt that she was the very air I sought, the joy I lived for, and the pleasure I needed?

Whimpering, she plucks at my waistband.

"Wait," I mutter, grasping her wrist.

Her eyes fly open and she breaks into a mischievous grin. "You worried I'll ruin your pajamas?"

I can't help but smile. It's been so fucking long since my wife and I fooled around. But it's been even longer since we smiled during it. Since we laughed with one another.

That knowledge has me grasping her hands and holding them still, afraid I'll fuck this all up. "We should take this slow, sweetheart. Kissing you is enough."

Sloane huffs. "But what if it's not enough for me? What if I need this? What if I tell you—" She inhales sharply, surveying my face, a war raging behind her eyes, like she's trying to decide just how honest she wants to be.

"Tell me. You can tell me anything," I plead with her. I'm truly not above begging.

"As much as I missed you," she admits, her voice going soft. "I've missed me even more." She rolls her tongue over her lip. "I need to feel like me again. I need to know that you aren't just doing this—" She huffs like she's annoyed that she doesn't know how to properly express herself.

I squeeze her wrists quickly and then release them, giving her complete control.

When she settles her palms against my chest, likely feeling my pounding heart, a thrill shoots through me. Maybe it's my nerves that give her strength. Or maybe it's the way I look at her. I hope she can see just how badly I yearn for her. That she can sense the complete and utter desire I have for her every thought.

"I need to know it's not just because I'm pregnant. I need to feel like us again. I don't want to just do this for the kids. Yes, I'm glad you want to be a better daddy, but I also need you to be a better partner. *My partner.* My husband. Be my husband, Sully. Show me I'm yours."

"You are mine," I growl as an innate understanding of precisely what my wife needs takes over. I lift her into my arms, feeling like fucking Hercules. Like I can do anything.

She squeals as I carry her toward the bedroom. Maybe it's not our bedroom, not like the one at home, and maybe we've been sharing it with our child, but tonight it's ours. Tonight it's just her and me, and it's time I remind her that until my dying breath, no matter what the circumstance, her and me is what I want it to be.

"This outfit is ridiculous," she says as she tugs on the bloody elf costume I was roped into wearing.

I settle her on the bed and pull the ugly top over my head. As I toss it, I stride for the door to lock it. There are too many people in this house, and I have no interest in being interrupted tonight.

"Don't plan on wearing it for long." I turn back and, smirking, slide the ridiculous pants down and fist my hard cock.

"Yes," she hisses, her eyes zeroed in on my dick.

That look alone is enough to make it pulse and my spine tingle.

She kicks at the covers and pushes herself back, like she's settling in for the little show I'm providing. She gave me one hell of a performance last week in the doctor's office. Mine isn't nearly as sexy, but I take my time, drag it out.

"Get over here." Her voice is needy, desperate.

God damn, I love that she's the one begging for once. I'll gladly beg, and I'll put in the work to get her back, but it's good to know she's just as desperate for this. Just as desperate for me.

With intention, I walk toward her, slowly stroking my length, holding myself in an excruciating limbo. I want to live in this moment. In this point in time when Sloane looks at me like I'm the answer to her every wish. Like nothing else in this world could satisfy her.

It's the way she's looked at me since we were stupid, naïve twenty-two-year-old law school students. Even then, she made me want to be better. She's always made me want to be better. To deserve her. To earn her. Tonight is no different.

I prop my knee on the bed beside her, only to wobble when the pregnancy pillow is in my way. I growl, annoyed that she even needs it. When she was pregnant with T.J., that thing spent more time on the floor than anywhere else. Back then, all my wife needed at night was my body. All she craved was me.

"I'm taking back my spot," I say as I push it over.

Eyes flashing, she kicks it to the floor. "I hate that thing."

I pause, studying her. "What?"

Face lowering a fraction, like she's avoiding eye contact, she says, "I never liked it. Not when I was pregnant with T.J. and not this time. But I haven't had you." She shrugs, finally dragging her eyes up to meet mine.

"Sloane Marie Murphy, you always have me. I just wanted you to be comfortable, and I knew that you weren't comfortable with me. I thought—" It's tempting to look away, but I make myself hold her gaze, lose myself in the blue eyes I'll spend my last seconds on earth chasing. "I thought you didn't want me in your bed. That you didn't need me anymore."

Sloane lets out a breathy laugh, taking me by surprise. "God, if we just talked, where would we be? If we just said what we meant rather than putting words into one another's mouths..." She grins at me. "No more, Sully. No more distance, please."

Every nerve in my body lets out a sigh. I feel it to my toes. Even my heart seems to relax. I lean down, caging her between my arms. "No more distance," I murmur, my lips a breath from hers. "From now on, we talk."

She takes me in, her eyes dancing over my face. I can't help but think she's memorizing everything about this moment just like I am. "Less talking right now, though."

"Yes, less talking," I rasp. Finally, I take her mouth. I kiss my wife the way I've been wanting to for months. The way I've craved for years. I take back my space in her bed and hope that I'm taking up residence again in her heart.

She presses her warm hand to my chest, though the touch is tentative.

Eager for more, I growl into her mouth. "Stop being so careful with me. You own me, sweetheart. Act like it."

Her eyes widen in surprise, and then a delicious smile finds her lips. "Okay, then."

Almost instantly, both of her hands are on my chest, electricity zapping through me at the contact. I take her lips again, and as she explores, another groan slips out of me.

Finally, she begins to act like the wife I remember. That I so desperately wanted for all these months. The one whose touch burned me. She brands me with her hands against my skin, warming every delicious inch, and when she goes even lower, I engage my core muscles and break the kiss, my forehead pressed to hers, so I can watch her finally take my cock in her fist.

The first touch is so shocking, I hiss through my teeth. "Oh fuck."

Sloane hums in delight, squeezing my dick tighter, like she's reacquainting herself with me.

"Oh god." She's the one who whimpers this time. My wife fucking whimpers at the mere feel of my length in her hands.

I can't help but pump into her fist, and in response, she gasps and focuses on my face again.

"I want to feel that down my throat."

I leak into her hands. My wife has always loved sucking my cock. And she's fucking phenomenal at it.

But I can't remember the last time she begged for it.

I'm so keyed up by her touch, by the thought of her tongue, that I thrust into her hand again. "Tonight's about you."

She licks her lips, eyes down, lusting after my cock. "Exactly. Now give me what I want."

I drop my head to her shoulder as my dick literally weeps in her hands. Begging for me to give her what she needs. Relieved that it's still me. "Need you naked first," I say with a kiss to her neck.

Forcing myself up onto my knees, I give her room to wiggle out of her pajamas. She doesn't go slow, and she doesn't try to give me a show, but still, the moment her smooth skin is bared to me, my heart races.

"Bloody hell, Sloane, you're beautiful." I cage her in again and suck a nipple into my mouth, drawing a keening cry from her. I play with the sharp peaks, giving them equal attention.

"Oh god, I think I could come from just that," she babbles, thrusting her hips up into my knee.

"Not a chance," I tell her as I climb up her body. "You come around my cock."

She knows what I want. I want her lips around my shaft when she comes. She loves it like this. She loves when I settle my knees on either side of her head and feed her my cock. When I fuck her mouth nice and slow until she's ready to take me down her throat. She loves to moan around my dick while she plays with her clit. And I love to clean up the mess she makes the moment she shatters.

It happens quickly. She wasn't lying. When she detonates, moaning around my shaft, I have to squeeze my arse cheeks to keep from coming with her. As her delicious tongue dances around my crown, I clench my eyes shut. I only give myself a second to savor it before pulling back and working my way down her body. She widens her thighs for me, but I palm them and spread them farther, then take one long, slow lick, relishing the taste of my wife's orgasm.

"Fucking perfect." I press a kiss to her clit, and when she squirms beneath me, I suction my mouth over her clit and suck. I tease her with my tongue, back and forth, back and forth while she humps my face, babbling about how badly she wants me to finger her pussy. Or her arse. She likes both.

I haven't gotten my fill of watching her writhe, though. Or the begging. First to kiss me, then to touch me, and now for my cock. Heart thundering, I growl into her flesh. I'm lost to the blood pulsing through my veins, the word *mine* on repeat in my head.

"This pussy is mine," I tell her as I finally give her a finger.

She spasms, moaning and fisting the sheets and bucking up into me.

"That's it, sweetheart. Give me another one. Come all over my fingers." I give her another one, and she cries out at the intrusion. "Fuck, Sloane, you are so bloody tight. You're going to strangle my cock."

She nods violently. "Yes, that, please now."

With a shake of my head, I position my mouth over her clit and suck again. Fucking hell, I want it too. I'm desperate to slide home again, to bury myself in my wife, but she needs to come again first.

I drag my thumb through her pussy, collecting her arousal, then drift down her perineum and over her arsehole. "Gonna take this again too."

She cries out again. My wife loves anal.

I push in and play, fucking chuffed that I've now had all my wife's holes. With my lips sealed over that bundle of nerves, I finger her pussy and thumb her arse until she's a wreck, squirting into my mouth and crying out my name.

Only when I've wrung every last delicious drop of her orgasm from her do I climb up and press my mouth to hers, making sure she can taste what I've done to her.

"Mine," I snarl into her mouth.

She claws at me and wraps one leg around me, trying to force me to fuck her.

"Then show me," she pants. "Be my husband, Sully. Fuck me." Her words are desperate now. Exactly like I need them.

And when I sink into her, just that first inch, finally feeling the tight heat that I'll never not crave, I kiss her in the exact same way. Desperate to hold on to this moment. Desperate to hold on to her. The only woman I've ever loved. And the only one I ever will.

CHAPTER 22
Sloane

The gentle hum of breath slipping past my husband's lips is a balm to my soul. So familiar and yet so foreign. I haven't awoken to that sound, or to his face buried in my hair, in far too long.

I'm naked, my skin pressed to his, not because I stripped out of my clothes, but because I fell asleep almost immediately after he wrung the third orgasm from my body.

With his arm wrapped around me, he holds me tight to his bare chest. The sweetest and most excruciatingly familiar detail of all is the way his fingers are intertwined with mine. Yes, for years we were one of those weird couples who held hands while we slept. At least as the night began. My sleep stripping often meant we didn't stay that way for too long. But the moment Sully stirred, he'd twine our fingers and press a kiss to my shoulder.

God, we used to be so sweet.

It takes effort not to get ahead of myself. I'd forgotten about this gentle, devoted side my husband possesses. There was a time when he'd work so late that I'd be asleep long before he got home, and he'd be up with the sun and back to the office long before my eyes even opened.

Better Daddy

Though he's literally wrapped around me, I can't help but miss him with a ferocity that makes it hard to breathe. I slip my hand from his as I ease out of bed, and once I've found my robe, I rush out of the room. I need space. I need air. I need to get a grip on the emotions crashing over me like a rogue wave.

Shit, shit, shit. I stand outside the door, sawing in harsh breaths and blowing them out again. Only when I no longer feel like I'm suffocating do I remember that it's Christmas morning. That thought is followed by a sinking sensation, because we forgot to come out and put the presents under the tree. I scurry down the hall, hoping like hell the boys aren't awake yet. It's quiet, but that only means there's a 50 percent chance that T.J. is sleeping. It's just as likely that he's getting into mischief. As I skid into the living room, I pull up short, struck by the sight before me.

Beneath the enormous tree sit piles of beautifully wrapped gifts. Stockings embroidered with the boys' names are propped up close by, along with a pair of bicycles, one green and one blue.

Tears fill my eyes, making the scene blur. I'd like to blame my stupid hormones for the reaction, but it's so much more than that. It's genuine affection and joy, because Sully and Cal are both coming into fatherhood in a way that has my heart squeezing tight.

I may have run from my feelings moments ago, but I won't any longer. Sully is trying. I need to let him.

According to the clock on the stove, it's just after five. Knowing T.J., he'll be up soon, so I might as well get my day started.

As soon as I step into the bathroom, I notice something is different. My stall is glowing.

Intrigued, I pad closer, my slippers scuffing the tile floor. When I pull back the curtain, I gasp. The entire back wall is covered in Christmas lights. Maybe more so than the tree in the living room.

I snort. Or maybe it's a sob. The sensation rushes up my throat as tears spill down my cheeks. With my hand cupped to my mouth, I take in each detail. The pink lava lamp T.J. and Sully gave me last night is lit up, sitting in the corner, on top of a tufted white cushion.

Beside it is a creamy chenille rocking chair with one of those stools that sway along with it. The cold blue tiles are now hidden beneath a pink rug the exact shade of the curtain.

It's still a handicap bathroom stall in a shithole apartment, but somehow, it's magical.

"Merry Christmas," Sully says from behind me, his voice thick with sleep.

I don't even startle at his presence. Subconsciously, I knew he'd be there.

"It's not Paris," he says as he slips his arms around my waist and presses a gentle kiss to my shoulder. "But we'll get there, sweetheart. I promise you, we'll get there."

This time, the sound that escapes me is definitely a sob. I spin around and wrap my arms around his neck, burrowing into him, my cheek pressed against his steady heart. "I missed you." Another sob racks my body.

Sully drops his head forehead to my crown and inhales deeply, like he's committing this moment to memory. When I pull back and peer up at him, his pupils are blown wide, and his face is a mask of emotion.

How the hell did I miss this before? His devotion is written all over him. It's devastatingly obvious. I feel naked, stripped to my core, as I search each line of his face. Maybe what I once recognized as signs that he was falling out of love with me were really just the instances when he was getting it wrong. Fucking up. Making mistakes. Because it's clear as day now, as memory after memory assaults me, that even as he was working too much, sitting silently at the dinner table, texting just to say hi less and less, that he never forgot me. He merely forgot to let me know he still cared.

Rather than drive that point home, rather than insist he's been here all along, Sully drops his forehead to mine. "I will claw my way back to you if that's what it takes. Please, sweetheart, just tell me you'll let me try."

The tear that slides down my husband's cheek is what breaks me completely. Shatters every wall. Obliterates all my excuses.

"How?" is all I manage to get out.

Straightening, he clears his throat, like he's getting ready to sell his pitch. "We date."

"We date." I try the words on for size. They feel all wrong. I don't want to date my husband. Dating is foreign. It's for people who don't know one another. And yet, do we?

We did, once upon a time, but over the years, we've gotten so much wrong. So maybe we didn't know one another as well as I thought.

"I don't want to confuse T.J." He was my primary concern when I filed for divorce, and that hasn't changed.

Sully nods. "I agree."

"Okay," I say. It's a breathy sigh, but it's resolute and maybe hopeful.

"Okay?" Sully's expression slowly morphs into a genuine grin. "Really?"

I nod. "I want to try. Do we, like, check in with each other about how we're feeling, in case you change your mind?"

An emotion I can't decipher crosses his face, further proving just how much I have to learn about my husband.

"Let's take it a day at a time," he says. "We're not going to fix us overnight. I may be ready to jump back into this marriage with both feet, but you're right to be hesitant. I was—" He huffs out an aggravated breath. "I was a bloody wanker to you for too long. Don't let me off the hook easy, okay? I can do better and I want to earn you."

I rub my thumbs against his jaw, enamored. The earnest self-reflection is a surprise. Though after the way he's behaved for the last couple of months, picking me up from work, listening, giving me space when I need it, the dedication is not surprising. And his sheer will to get this right leaves me filled with hope.

"You weren't the only one who made mistakes," I say. "I should have spoken up sooner. I should have—"

He presses a finger to my lips. "Shh, sweetheart. Let me own this. You can tell me all about your faults later."

A surprised giggle escapes me. "I don't have any faults, baby."

Eyes warming, he pecks my lips. "I've bloody missed that name." He angles in for another kiss, this one longer, messier, and licks into my mouth like he can't get enough. And with his hands on my ass, he lifts me and turns toward the door.

I pull back. "Where are you taking me?"

"To our bed, sweetheart. I'm taking my wife to our bed so I can do some more apologizing."

I sigh against his mouth, because there's nothing I want more.

We wake sometime later to giggles and loud whispers. "Shh, maybe if we're quiet, they won't know we peeked."

Amusement rushes over me, mixed with a hint of frustration. That's totally T.J.

"Um, no thanks. My dad will freak out if he misses my reaction to our first Christmas."

I bring a hand to my mouth. God, Murphy is the sweetest. I don't think there's another six-year-old in existence who possesses the kind of empathy he does. And he's not wrong. By reining T. J. in, he's ensuring none of us have to deal with a nuclear-level meltdown from Cal. If he misses a single second of this first holiday with his son, we'll never hear the end of it.

Unfortunately, T.J. is just as good at having epic meltdowns. "Come on, it's just one present."

I nudge Sully. He better get out there before this blows up.

Like he's thinking the same thing, he presses a quick kiss to my cheek and climbs out of bed. "I've got this. I'll start a cup of tea for you. Come out whenever you're ready."

He tiptoes out into the hall, closing the door behind him, and a moment later, I hear Murphy's door creak open and Sully whisper-shout, "Caught you!"

Both boys squeal, but Sully shushes them.

I sink back into the bed and squeal myself. The last twenty-four hours have been nothing short of joy-filled. I press my hands to my cheeks. They're tight from all the smiling I've done and they're warm to the touch, the rosiness more than a simple feeling. It's emotion spilling out of my pores.

"But *Dad*, Santa left the presents and he didn't say we had to wait for everyone," T. J. whines.

Laughing, I get out of bed and pull on the matching pajamas Cal forced upon us all. If the adults don't get out there soon, I can't be held liable for what my son might do.

A few minutes later, I find Lo in the kitchen pouring a cup of coffee. Brian, the good sport that he is, is wearing his pajamas too as he sips from his own mug.

"Where are the guys?" I ask them.

Lo motions to Murphy's bedroom. "Cal went to wake them up. Can you believe they slept in so late?"

I hide my smile. If she knows the boys were preparing to peck, she may tell Cal, and it's too early for that kind of drama. "Is Sully with him?"

Lo nods. "Did he sleep in the bunk bed last night?"

Thanking my lucky stars that I'd already schooled my expression, I turn to the kettle and make an *uh-huh* sound. It's not really a lie. It was more of a noncommittal response. If she wants to interpret it as a yes, then that's on her.

Lo shuffles closer, humming right back at me, her attention raking over me like she's trying to read my damn mind.

Fortunately, I'm saved from an interrogation when the door to Murphy's room swings open and Sully backs out, camera in hand, recording the boys as they rush to the living room to discover what *Santa* left them.

"Make sure you're using the wide angle so you get everything," Cal instructs over Sully's shoulder.

My husband twists away, keeping his focus on the screen. "I've got this. Just go enjoy the bloody moment."

Without argument, Cal skirts him, his face lit up with glee.

"Look, Dad," Murphy yells. "I got a bike!"

T.J.'s already ripping into a present. I don't bother telling him to stop. He'll only be a kid for so long. He might as well enjoy it.

We take our drinks to the couch while Cal pulls out his phone and puts on a Christmas music playlist.

Brian turns on the television and finds a loop of a crackling yule log on one of the streaming services. "Not exactly like home, but it's not so bad," he says when he settles on the couch.

After the boys have torn into a few presents, we slow them down and convince them to let us all take turns. When Cal hands me a card, I eye him with suspicion. It's hard to know what the ridiculous man might pick out. But when I open it, I squeal. "You mean I can buy *whatever I want* at Banana Republic?" It's not a gift card. Oh no, it's so much better. It's a single sheet of paper, and Cal has written *One-hour shopping spree with Cal at Banana Republic.* He's done similar things in the past, and we always turn the shopping sprees into entire days out.

Cal may be the biggest man-child I know, but he's incredibly fun to be around and has the biggest heart. It warms me that he thought to do it again. Sully isn't the only person I've missed.

"Yes. Now tell me you've forgiven me for calling you an incubator." Cal pouts dramatically.

Sully's eyes go wide with panic, and his whole body goes rigid. Like he's worried this comment will cause me to shift back into the angry wife I've been for so long.

He was right when he said we can't fix our relationship overnight, but I know without a doubt that my husband wants me for more than my baby-incubating abilities now, so he doesn't have to worry.

"Yes, Cal, I'll forgive you for that, but only if you throw in a stop for blue slushies."

He grins, his blue eyes sparkling. "Consider it done, Sloaney."

It takes over an hour to get through all the gifts, and while Lo and I make breakfast, the guys spread out on the floor and help the boys put toys together.

Near the couch, Sully and T.J. sit side by side, looking adorable in their matching pajamas, chatting in a way that's still surprising to me, even though I've seen them do it often over the last few months. When Sully was still living in the penthouse with us, it seemed as though he barely had time to do more than ruffle his son's hair in passing. Now, he tilts in close and asks, "How was your sleepover in Murphy's room?"

T.J. shrugs. "It'd be better if we had beds."

"I didn't mind," Murphy says.

"That's because your bed is too small," Lo calls over. "Cal, we really need to get him a bigger one."

"You know," Sully starts in a tone a lot like the one he used when he pitched the whole dating idea to me.

What's my husband up to now?

"There are three mattresses in our room."

"Yeah, but there are three of you," Brian points out.

"Right, but if Murphy needs a mattress," Sully says, "it's only right that we make sure he's taken care of. Since he's my nephew and all."

I snort. Lo does too. Clearly, I'm not the only one who sees right through his little plan.

"We could move the bunk beds. Then the boys could each have their own bed, but they could share a room. That'd be fun, wouldn't it?" He arches a brow and peers down at our son.

"We could share a bedroom!" T.J. high-fives Murphy, though an instant later, his face falls. "But where would you sleep, Dad?"

Sully glances at me and smiles. "I'm sure your mother and I could figure something out."

Lo nudges me with an elbow. "Didn't sleep together last night, my ass," she hisses.

I ignore her.

"What do you say, sweetheart?" Sully calls. "Do you think we can make it work?"

Sully's good, I'll give him that. And if T.J. and I weren't sleeping in the same room, I could wear one set of pajamas to bed rather than sweltering in layers.

"Yeah, I think that could work," I agree.

"Yes!" Murphy and T.J. yell in unison.

"This is going to be awesome," T.J. adds.

Pouting, Cal asks, "But what will we do with the race car bed?"

"I'm sure I can find a family in need," Lo comforts him.

Under his breath, Brian says, "Yup, one with a toddler."

Once breakfast is ready, we sit at the table, and each of us talks about which present we loved most.

When we've finished, T.J. drops his fork and frowns at me, his little mind working. Finally, he eyes Sully. "Did you get Mom anything?"

I cough out a laugh. This boy may be bouncing off the walls most of the time, but he can be so sweet and thoughtful. "Yes, your father gave me a beautiful gift this morning."

Brian scowls and Cal's eyes light up.

"Not like that, you fools," I mutter. "It's in the bathroom."

T.J.'s head tilts. "Dad got you a toilet?"

I giggle. "No. He decorated my stall."

My little guy's face morphs into a look of absolute revulsion. "I don't ever want to grow up. Parent gifts are weird."

Laughter fills the air, the sound making me feel lighter than I have in a long time.

The rest of the day continues like that. Little imperfect moments that will become lasting memories. I cherish every second of it, constantly aware of how close I came to missing out on all of this, to giving it all up.

Better Daddy

As I settle on the couch with my family that night to watch *Elf*, I vow to do everything I can to keep it from happening again.

CHAPTER 23
Sully

"I hate it when Mommy has to work late." T.J. flops back onto the pillows of the bed Sloane and I now share.

Our bed. That thought brings a smile to my face. Typically, I'd agree with my son. If she'd listen, I'd convince her that there's no reason to ever work late. Especially with Will. It's bloody awful that she's with that man every day. However, she's not at the office tonight. No, she's waiting for me at our flat in the city.

"Mum's job is important, bud." The bed creaks as I settle on the edge.

"And you're going to an important work meeting." He rolls his blue eyes and blows out a breath that ruffles his hair. "It's not fair that I can't come with you."

I will always treasure the time the three of us spent together over the holidays, but tonight, I finally have a chance to take Sloane on our second *first date*.

Sloane took the week between Christmas and New Year's off so she could be home with T.J. during his winter break. And since she is still firmly in the *we aren't telling anyone we're back together* camp, it made more sense to wait until she was back in the office, when we both had reasonable excuses to be in the city, to have our night out.

The wait has been pure torture, but it's given me ample time to make tonight perfect. It's taken several phone calls, but it's official: our night out will be a recreation of our first date. It will be filled with the same kind of magic we felt the first time I was given the honor of having Sloane on my arm.

Back then, I took two weeks to plan the date. Brian made fun of me daily as I tossed out ideas. We'd already slept together at that point, but I wanted it to be special. Memorable.

I planned a horse-drawn carriage ride through Central Park on the night of the full moon, when the sky was at its brightest, certain she'd be blown away. But I was the one who ended up under her spell. We talked for hours, the conversation easy, her eyes dancing the whole time.

Somehow, over the years, that spark was snuffed out, and I let the world around me cause too many distractions. Tonight, I'm determined to find my way back to our old ways, to remind her of what we could have again.

"You get to hang out with Uncle Brian," I remind him with a single raised brow. "And he picked up new Lego sets for you and Murphy. I figured you'd be begging me to leave you alone so you fellas could get busy building."

He rolls his lips tight, just like his mother does when she is fighting a smile. "Fine."

"Come on." I stand and slip my jacket on over the white button-down, then lead T.J. out of the room.

As we enter the common area, the door opens and Brian stomps in with the cat behind him.

"At least it hit forty today. It's a nice change. Not freezing my fingers off." He lets the massive cat off his leash, and it takes off toward his room. "Dammit," he mutters, glaring at the feline's back.

At this point, it would take a lot of stress off Brian if he'd give in to the relationship he and the beast have found themselves in.

"Is it snowing yet?" I ask, trying to redirect his attention.

Brian scoffs. "Did you miss the part where I said it's forty degrees? It's too warm for snow tonight." He slips his coat off and hangs it on a hook behind the door.

"Knockity, knock, knock." Madame E opens the door and steps in without being invited. "Where are my favorite yoga partners?"

Maybe it should shock me that my brother joins her for yoga twice a week, but honestly, after the last year, nothing surprises me.

"We're right here." Lo skip-hops into the room with a rolled-up yoga mat strapped to her back. "We've been antsy all day. Yoga Jess said we're going to work on our crow pose today. Cal's been practicing."

Cal appears, tucking Lo into his side and whispering in her ear.

Instantly, her cheeks turn pink and she ducks her head. Jesus, I don't want to know what the fuck that's about.

"Anyway," Brian mutters.

Cal looks up, giving me a once-over. "Better grab your rain jacket."

No. I refuse to believe it will rain. "It's supposed to snow."

"Nah." Lo shakes her head. "A warm front came through this afternoon. Instead of the ice and slush, we're supposed to get a few inches of rain."

Teeth gritted, I zero in on Madame E. "Tell them it's going to snow."

She purses her lips as she studies me. "Do not fret, Sullivan. It's going to be a perfect night."

I let out a long breath. That's all I need to hear. If she says it'll be perfect, then it won't rain. Because a perfect night in Central Park requires a light snowfall. I even have a blanket in the car to tuck around us. I can already picture Sloane's soft smile as the white flakes settle in her dark hair.

"Perfect might be a bit much for a night with Storm," Brian jokes.

Oh. That's right. They think I'm meeting a very demanding client. A few years ago, his ex falsely accused him of abuse against their then two-year-old. It took over a year and multiple court appearances, but eventually, the record was cleared, and he was given custody of their daughter. Recently, the ex has started up the claims again, and it takes a lot of coddling to keep him from giving in and retaliating.

"He won't care about the rain." Lo shrugs. "He'd meet you during a cat-5 hurricane if he thought it was important."

That last part is very true. He's a devoted parent.

"Yeah, yeah." I wave them off and head down the hall to say good night to my son.

"Night, T.J."

He jumps off the bottom bunk and throws his arms around me. "You promise you'll be here if I wake up in the middle of the night? And you promise we'll get donuts in the morning?"

I nod and hug him tight. One of the unfortunate side effects of our separation is the constant need for reassurance that he now requires. It breaks my bloody heart to hear the concern in his voice when he's worried I won't be around.

He finally releases me and goes back to his bed. "Love you, bud," I say as I step into the hall.

On the drive to the city, I ignore the temperature reading on the dash. So what if it's forty-two? Now that it's dark, the temperature will surely drop. And Madame E said it would be a perfect night, so it will not rain.

The fates want Sloane and me to work out. Even Madame E knows it. They wouldn't let rain ruin our night.

The nerves that swirl in my gut as I take the elevator up to our old flat are unfamiliar. Coming home, to the penthouse we shared for years, to Sloane and T. J., used to be the most peaceful part of my day. I want to get back to that, and tonight, I'm taking one more step in that direction. Showing my wife how special she is, how much she means to me, is my sole focus.

I made meticulous plans, even booking the same company I used twenty years ago for the horse-drawn carriage ride. Then I made reservations at her favorite restaurant.

As the elevator reaches our floor, I shift the bouquet in my hand,

and when the doors open into the small hallway, I stride straight for the door. I have a key, but rather than use it, I knock.

Sloane opens the door moments later, beaming. "I love the gray suit on you." I know. It's the entire reason I wore it. "Am I underdressed?" With a small frown, she glances down at her black pants and the blue cashmere sweater that molds to her body like a second skin.

I can't help but focus on the small bump where our baby is growing, my hand itching to touch her. At sixteen weeks, she is starting to really show.

It probably isn't my smartest move, but I give in and settle my palm over her lower abdomen.

"You're perfect," I whisper. With my other hand, I hold up the flowers. "For you."

Her eyes go soft as she takes them and brings them to her nose. When she lowers the bouquet, I angle in and press my lips to hers.

She sighs into my mouth, and my heart stutters.

Yes, this is going to be perfect.

Though as we stand outside the building ten minutes later, I'm doubting that sentiment *and* Madame E. How in the bloody hell has it gotten warmer since I left Jersey? And when did all the clouds appear? Like this, not even the full moon is visible, let alone the stars.

It's strangely quiet as a man on a bike stops in front of us. Attached to the bike is a small, half-covered cart with a neon sign that says *Love.*

"What is that?" Sloane says.

Oh, for fuck's sake. My stomach pitches and sweat breaks out at my temples.

When I called about the horses, the bloke I talked to mentioned that the rides were different now. Though he didn't tell me just how different, and I didn't ask. I just told him that it was fine, as long as the concept was similar.

Bollocks, I really should have asked, because the small seat behind the bike is barely big enough for me, let alone both of us and my blanket.

"I believe that's our ride. It'll take us around the park." Or not. I can't imagine the little man on the bike can actually pull the two of us around.

"Do you think this is a good idea?" Sloane asks, not looking away from the ridiculous bicycle-carriage contraption. "It's supposed to pour."

"No," I assure her quickly, my chest pinching. "I have it on good authority that it will not."

She looks up at the heavy cloud cover and shrugs. "If you say so."

The man on the bike is bathed in an eerie pink glow when he says, "Mr. Murphy? Hop in. We should get going if we want to beat the rain."

"It's not going to rain," I grumble, though I'm feeling less sure of myself as the clouds grow darker above us.

He cocks his head, his face cast in strange pink-hued shadows. "Whatever you need to tell yourself."

I help Sloane into the carriage, if it could be called such a thing, then climb in and squeeze myself next to her. The foot of space between the bench and the front of the carriage means my feet barely fit, and my knees are wedged just below my chin. But with a long breath out, I force away the irritation gathering in my chest and tuck Sloane into my side.

"This is cozy." I smile, though it feels more like a grimace.

Sloane rolls her lips, just like T.J. did an hour ago, and hums.

The man starts to pedal, standing up and using all his body weight to get the cart moving, and we move through the street.

As we turn the block onto the avenue, he spins back to us. I want to tell him to watch the damn road, but I don't want Sloane to glare, so I keep my mouth shut.

"Normally," he says, "we play music, but my sound system is on the fritz." He gives us a small shrug.

That figures.

"The good news is I love to sing." Before I can assure him we're fine listening to the sounds of the city, he breaks into the ballad "Fools Rush In."

Bloody hell. When he hits the melody, I can't help but wince. So much for the perfect night.

I turn to apologize to my wife, only to find her pressing her lips together with enough force to make them go white. Her eyes are dancing and her cheeks are pink as she works hard to fight a laugh.

"It sounds like Dammit this morning when Brian went down to the office without him." Her giggle washes away the anger clawing up my throat, making me laugh instead. She's right.

"Not sure I can take this for much longer," I say as the guy hits another high note.

Sloane leans into me, burying her face in my chest and falling into a true fit of laughter. "God, I missed having fun with you," she admits once she's collected herself.

I pull her tighter to me because, damn, I miss us too.

"Remember karaoke nights during law school? You used to love listening to all the people getting up there to sing, especially the bad ones," she teases me.

That's not all I remember about karaoke, but I nod, because the other memory will cause me to pitch a boner right now, and I'm not sure any of my extremities can move in this cramped space.

"I don't think Brian ever recovered from your impersonation of Britney Spears," I tease her.

"He's such a baby," she says with a roll of her eyes, likely remembering how she tried to drag him up on stage and when he wouldn't join, she brought the mic over to the table, sat on my lap, and serenaded him. To this day, Brian shudders at the mention of karaoke.

She gives me a wistful smile. "I'd love to do that again."

Fucking hell, I'd give anything to give her a night full of bad music and laughs. The need to make that happen for her is as strong as the need to hold her.

"We did get him up on stage that one time, though," she points out.

Above us, a raindrop hits the top of the car with a *tink*. It's followed by another, then a third, but I ignore it, focusing on my wife.

"Only because he was bloody pissed."

She smirks. "Drunk, Sully. You've spent more than twenty years in the US. We say drunk."

I chuckle. The woman has always given me shite, and I wouldn't want it any other way.

The patter of the rain on the roof gets a little steadier, but even as the legs of my trousers get wet, I don't mind.

"Fine," I say. "He was *drunk*. And so were you, after seven Jäger bombs."

She shakes her head. "It was redheaded sluts."

"Bloody lies." I scoff.

"No way. I hate Jäger bombs, so you let me pick." She flashes me a smile that instantly convinces me that she's right.

Come to think of it, that's probably how she got me to toss back those rank shots she chose that night.

"So," she goes on, "we drank redheaded sluts."

"Maybe." I kiss her forehead, knowing she's one hundred percent right. I know well enough that if she had wanted the drink, I would have let her order without protest. I'd give her anything, back then and now.

As we turn into Central Park, the rain turns from a steady drizzle to a mighty pounding. My legs are soaked, and since we continue to move forward, the rain now hits my chest and shoulders.

Beside me, Sloane shivers, so I pull her in closer.

When the man on the bike finishes his fourth song, he stops and turns around. "I know you paid for the full park tour, but are you sure you want me to continue on, sir?"

I glance at my wife, at her damp hair and her wobbling bottom lip. Though she's being a good sport, she's soaked and no doubt miserable.

"Take us to the restaurant." My heart sinks as I make the decision. So much for my perfect night.

"Sully." Sloane burrows closer, her teeth chattering.

I'm a fucking plonker. What was I thinking, bringing her out like this?

"We can't go anywhere like this," she says. "Let's just go home."

Fucking fuck. She's right.

Tamping down my frustration, I calmly tell the man to head back to our penthouse. As we ride in silence, her words hit me, and my mood lifts. She wants to go home. *Our home.* Not her place. Home.

By the time he pulls to a stop in front of our building, the rain is coming down so hard, I can barely make out his words when he tells us to have a good night.

I rush to open the door for Sloane, but she's already beyond soaked. Her hair clings to the side of her face as water runs down her cheeks, and her entire body trembles.

"Go on up. Take a warm shower. I'll find us something to eat," I promise.

Though I expect my independent, sassy wife to protest, to swear she wants to help, she goes without a fight.

I dart back out into the rain, headed for the Quick Mart across the street. For a few minutes, I wander, unsure of what to pick up. But when my eyes land on the yellow and white package, an idea strikes. When Sloane was pregnant with T.J., she craved BLTs constantly. So with any luck, the simple meal will be a hit.

I'm standing at the stove in my sweats, almost finished with the bacon, when she comes out of the bedroom.

"I've missed this view," she calls over the soft music I turned on.

I glance over my shoulder, and my heart lifts a little. She's dressed in yoga pants and a tank top, looking flushed and warm. Turning back, I flick on the burner for her teakettle.

"Me or bacon?" I ask with a smirk, head turned so I can see her.

"Definitely the bacon." She's teasing and I bloody love it. When she steps up behind me, wrapping her arms around my bare torso, and presses her lips to my back, my heart skips. The moment is almost too good.

I swear I'm floating a foot off the ground as I pull the last two pieces of bacon off the pan and set them on the paper towel with the rest. Then, ensuring the burner is off, I spin and pull her into my arms.

The music changes to "Someone Like You" by Van Morrison, the tune instantly bringing memories to mind, and I sway with her in my arms. I swear the sigh that leaves her lips comes straight from her soul.

I brush my lips against the top of her head. It's been years since we danced in the kitchen. I can't for the life of me remember why I didn't pull her into my arms more often. But I know without a doubt that from this day forward, I'll make a point to do it more often.

"It's bubbling," she mumbles.

My brows furrow. "A bubbly dance?" I whisper, remembering Madame E's prediction.

Sloane laughs, having absolutely no idea what I'm talking about and her breath teases my bare skin, causing goose bumps to erupt. "No, the water. Give it a second, and it'll whistle."

"Oh." I release her, holding her forearms to ensure she's steady. "Go get comfy on the sofa. I'll bring your tea and sandwich."

I shut off the teakettle just as it lets out a whistle and pour the boiling water into her mug. While the tea steeps, I add the bacon to the sandwiches I prepped with mayo, lettuce, and tomato.

It takes two trips, and when I sit beside her on the couch, she's picking up her BLT.

"Mmm." She moans at her first bite. "This might be the best thing I've eaten in days."

I shake my head, cringing. "Clearly I've starved you tonight."

"Not at all. I just forgot how good your BLTs are. They were my favorite when I was pregnant with T.J."

"I remember." I take a bite of my own sandwich.

For the next few minutes, we sit side by side, eating in silence. It's not awkward, and there's no tension in the air. It's the best kind of quiet.

"Tonight was the best," Sloane says as she sets her empty plate on the table in front of us.

I scoff. "You mean a mess."

She shakes her head, wiping her mouth with her napkin. "No. I mean everything went wrong, but we got to be together, laughing and snuggling." Her eyes sparkle with a hint of emotion that hits me straight in the chest. "That's all I ever want. I don't need fancy. I don't need perfect." Her eyes glitter with emotion. "I just need time with you."

"Me too." As I study her, I make a silent promise. She'll never want for my attention again. Every day, I will carve out time for us.

I slide a little closer on the cushion and bring my mouth to hers. Her lips are warm and soft, her presence alone creating a haze around me, one where only the two of us exist. I cup her cheek and angle her head slightly up, seeking permission with my tongue. When she lets me in, I close my eyes and worship her mouth, owning every inch of it. The need to lay her back and dominate her body is all-encompassing. Somehow, I resist the urge, instead slowing the kiss, then pecking her lips one last time. If I get her naked, I'll never want to leave this flat, and as tempting as it is, that's not how tonight is going to play out.

"How about we get cleaned up and head home?"

She pulls back, her brows rising in surprise.

"As much as I'd love to crawl into bed here, I promised T.J. I'd be home tonight and that we'd go for donuts again tomorrow," I explain. "So I'd love to get you home and into our bed there."

My wife smiles at me. "I'd love that too."

CHAPTER 24
Sloane

Alone for the first time tonight, I find myself humming along to the music playing from my phone. The smile on my face won't go away, even as I brush my teeth and get ready for bed.

Tonight was good. *So good.* Every day, I sink deeper into whatever it is that Sully and I are doing.

Dating, maybe? Am I really dating my husband?

My lips twitch, and my smile grows. With my toothbrush in my mouth, I look ridiculous, like a damn schoolgirl with a crush. But I can't shake this giddy feeling.

I totally have a crush on my husband.

Just thinking of his face tonight when the rain came down against the plastic shell of our cart makes my heart pitter-patter. As we rode toward Central Park, the sheer panic etched into his expression made it evident just how hard he was trying. Six months ago, getting Sully to take ten minutes to have dinner with me felt like a chore, but now he's going out of his way, even when it's uncomfortable, to spend time with me and make it meaningful.

I appreciate it. And I'm working hard not to focus on the past. I'm determined to let it all go, to believe that he can change. Maybe this separation was what we needed. Not a permanent parting, just a reality check. A taste of what it would be like if we continued failing one another.

Once I've rinsed out my mouth, I survey myself for another second. Our relationship wasn't the only thing that needed work. Somewhere along the way, I lost myself. I became a person I didn't recognize. A person, quite frankly, I didn't like very much.

When "I Can't Get No Satisfaction" by the Rolling Stones starts, I pick it up and, toes tingling, I bounce around in my little happy place. Eyes closed, head tossed back, I dance, laughing at myself and with myself. This is another thing I missed. Me.

I stop, planting my feet a little wider, because all the spinning made me a little dizzy, and unlock my phone so I can text Sully. He'd get a kick out of me dancing in the bathroom. Before I can pull up his contact, the curtain to my stall rustles.

Excited that he came to find me, I spin, wearing a huge smile, ready to pull him in to dance with me. Instead of my six-foot-something husband, I find Lo, wearing pajamas, her head tilted to the side, like she's trying to figure me out. "Didn't know Sloane's had dance parties on Wednesday nights," she teases.

I snort. "Sloane's is full of surprises."

Lo nods. "Sure is."

I turn the music down and focus on my friend. "What's up?"

She shakes her head, her red hair swaying, then pins me with a suspicious look. "Nothing. How was your *work meeting* tonight?"

Oops. Clearly I was too optimistic when I convinced myself our friends would believe that Sully and I had meetings on the same night. I'm not ready to explain whatever this is, though.

"It was fine. You know how work is." I turn back to the mirror and pick up my face cream, distracting myself in the hope that Lo won't try to read my expression.

"Hmm, yeah. So weird that you and Sully both had meetings so late. Especially because Sully hasn't had a single dinner meeting since we moved to Jersey. Matter of fact, I can't remember you ever having one either."

I just shrug.

"Speaking of work…" Lo's tone is more serious now, rather than teasing, drawing my gaze to her in the mirror. "I wanted to get your opinion on a case."

I spin and lean against the sink, waiting for her to continue. "Okay?"

"Did I tell you Cal and I have been going to yoga?"

I let out a surprised laugh. "Seriously?" Forget about the case she mentioned. Just picturing my ridiculously tall brother-in-law twisting himself up to impress his girlfriend makes me giddy. Cal is the sweetest kind of guy, and he's head over heels for Lo. I'm glad they have each other. But still, the image makes me giggle.

Lo's entire face lights up like she knows exactly what I'm thinking. "He's so annoyingly good at it. Like seriously, the man has this insane balance, and his form is so stupidly perfect. I want to knock him over every time he sticks his ass up in the air and winks at me while he nails downward dog."

She blows out a breath and rolls her eyes.

"All the women in class are obsessed with him. I always thought I had decent balance, but he's so damn good it's annoying." Arms crossed now, she frowns.

I laugh harder. I can envision the entire thing. "God, I'd pay to see that. When are you going again?"

"Funny you should ask," she says, a twinkle in her eye.

"Oh god," I mutter, bracing my hands on the sink on either side of me.

"Come on. It'd be a fun double date."

I turn back to the mirror, snagging my hairbrush. "I don't know what you're talking about."

"Fine," she says. "You can pretend you're not secretly dating your husband if you promise to meet with this client."

"I'm not interested in taking on a disaster client you don't want. Work is hard enough."

"She's not a disaster. She's lovely." Lo steps a little closer, her green slippers clashing with the pink rug. "She's a single mom of two beautiful little girls whose ex has no interest in being a father. She's stuck in Jersey"—she shudders just saying the word; Lo has always hated Jersey, though she's settled in nicely now that she's with Cal—"because this is where they were married. She has family in Vermont, and she'd have help and support there, but her ex refuses to sign off on it."

A long, defeated sigh leaves me. "And let me guess: Brian won't take the case because, like me, he knows it's pointless? No judge is going to grant her request to relocate to another state, Lo. You know that as well as I do."

She nibbles on her lip. "Can't you just meet with her? Brian's caseload is ridiculous. He doesn't have the time. But I think if he did and he understood the details, he'd find a winning argument."

God, I hate letting anyone down. And I can't imagine what it would be like if Sully wasn't involved in T. J.'s life. Even at our absolute worst, we always put our son first.

"Has anything been filed?" I ask.

"No." Lo's eyes light up with hope. Dammit. "She works multiple jobs to support her kids, and the ex-husband jets around the country with his girlfriend. He never shows up for parenting time, and she's struggling with childcare and work. She needs help, Sloane." My best friend's eyes are pleading. "You know I wouldn't ask your firm to help if we had the time to help her."

I sigh. I hate how much they all dislike my firm. It's so petty. I'm not interested in Will Higgins. I never was. But he's always been a good friend to me.

"I'd probably have to convince Will. If they haven't filed the motion, it would take a few months and—" Of its own accord, my hand drifts to my stomach, as if covering my abdomen will protect baby bear from hearing the next part. "If I end up on bed rest or anything happens…"

Lo nods. "Of course, that totally makes sense. And if you trust Will, then I can too."

The confidence in her tone surprises me so much that I almost forget about my impending freak-out over any pregnancy complications. Almost. But there's no stopping the way my mood has dipped at the possibility. There's no coming back from this swirling discomfort, so I promise Lo I'll meet with her friend and head to bed.

Sully is already under the covers, scrolling on his phone. But when I step inside, he locks the screen and drinks me in.

I'm not wearing anything special. Just a simple Def Leppard shirt that used to be his and leggings. We both know they'll come off, even if nothing happens tonight, since I rarely wake up with clothes on.

Do I want something to happen tonight?

I nibble on my lip. Before Lo mentioned the pregnancy and I started my spiral, I did. Truly, as I survey my husband right now—his broad, bare chest, forever my soft place to land, my solace—I want nothing more than to go to him. To be comforted by him. But since Christmas, it's been only kisses and longing looks.

"What's wrong?" he asks, his tone filled with concern.

I blink back to the present and shrug. "Just having a bit of a moment."

Lips pursed, he zeroes in on me. "Do you want to be alone?"

I shake my head. I don't know much, but I do know that.

His whole body relaxes, and he holds out one arm. "Come here, sweetheart."

I rush toward him, and before I've even plopped onto the bed beside him, he's pulling me to his chest and stroking my hair.

The sigh of relief that escapes me is instantaneous.

"Talk to me, Sloane. What's going on? If this is about us, I can handle it."

My heart pinches and twists inside my chest. The desperation in his tone, the dedication to getting this right, brings tears to my eyes.

But his steady heartbeat instantly soothes my fears, allowing me to relax against him.

"I'm nervous." I breathe out the words, and instantly, I'm flooded with relief. "I'm nervous about the pregnancy, about us, about work. I feel bad that I'm not shouting from the rooftops about this pregnancy. I hate that while this should be a happy time, I'm filled with all kinds of mixed emotions. It's not fair to our child." I glance around the room. It's less crowded without the bunk beds, but it's still not a big space. "Where are we even going to put a baby? And what if I have to go on bed rest?" My nerves pick up, making my breaths come quicker again. "What if I can't work? What if I lose myself again? I don't want to go backward, Sully. Things are good, but—" I blink back tears. "I can't go back to who we were."

I know the words are probably hard to hear, but I needed to say them. When I'm met with silence, I'm nervous that maybe I shouldn't have. We had such a good date, and now I'm ruining it by dredging up the past. But when I finally get the courage to look up, he's smiling at me.

"Why are you smiling?" I murmur. My whole body relaxes against him. If he's smiling, then it can't be that bad, right?

My husband's grin only grows wider. "Because you're talking to me. And for so long, I ached for your words."

That—I shake my head. That can't be true. "Really?" I ask, frowning up at him.

He nods. "There wasn't a thing I didn't miss about us while we were apart. But that one, feeling like you'd completely frozen me out —deservedly so—broke me in a way I wasn't sure I'd ever recover from. Trust me when I say I'm not smiling because I think your emotions are silly. It's the opposite, in fact. They're completely valid. This place *is* a dump." His eyes warm as he studies my face. "And I'm scared too. I'm scared that you'll realize you're better off without me. That you'll go back to New York and I'll lose out on this chance to have my family back." His focus drifts to my stomach, and with a pained sigh, he closes his eyes. "And I'm scared that something will happen to you and our baby. I'm scared all the bloody time, Sloane. You are my world, and it guts me that I almost lost sight of that."

I swallow a nervous breath. For so long this is what I wanted. This right here: my husband opening up to me, holding me.

With another soft smile, he rubs his thumb against my cheek. "Despite all that, I can't help but be happy. Because though I may not be able to fix everything, I have a better chance if you're talking to me. So please, I beg you, keep talking. Keep telling me what I can do to make you happy. It's all I want in this life. To be what you and T.J. and this baby need." He cups my stomach and rubs soothing circles.

I shift so my mouth is there for the taking, and Sully doesn't hesitate to give me exactly what I need.

Maybe it is this simple. Maybe he's right. We just try. Nothing in life is guaranteed, and planning for every potential situation is exhausting. But opening up to him, talking to him, and knowing it's exactly what he wants from me? That is the opposite of exhausting. It's liberating.

His tongue gently prods against my lips, and then his hand is on my jaw, holding me steady as he takes and takes, deepening the kiss.

"Oh god," I murmur, dizzy with want for this man.

He tilts my head and presses open-mouthed kisses to my neck and my jaw and then my mouth again. "Tell me, wife. Tell me everything you want."

I claw at his chest, unable to verbalize exactly what I'm craving. All I know is I want him. All of him.

Sully drags me over his body until I'm straddling him. Then he rolls his hips, ensuring that I feel every inch of his hard length between my thighs.

"Oh shit," I rasp.

"Is that what you want?" he teases, a small smile on his lips.

"I want—" I mutter, delirious with need, grinding against him. "I want you to—"

He thrusts upward, and the tip of his cock teases my clit.

"Yes, that," I babble.

He lets out a dark chuckle. "I'll need you to be more specific."

My husband holds me still and stares up at me, waiting.

As much as I want him to take the lead, to make the decisions, his desire to know exactly what I want is utterly sexy.

His plea wasn't solely related to being open about my concerns. He wants to know every little thought that runs through my head. That knowledge is beyond intoxicating. It's empowering.

After years of feeling powerless, of feeling like nothing I could do would be enough to interest him, this is exactly what I needed to hear.

"I want you to undress me."

The moment the words leave my lips, my husband's eyes dance with delight. "Yeah?"

I nod, and he slips his fingers beneath my T-shirt. That tiny contact alone has me sucking in a breath. He fans his fingers out over my ribcage, his touch warm and strong, and pushes the fabric up slowly, only stopping when his thumbs brush the underside of my breasts.

Every inch of my skin is extra sensitive because of the pregnancy, but my breasts are on another level. Just the hint of his warmth there has me preening, desperate for more. Rather than giving me what I need, he pauses, his blueish-gray eyes watching me, waiting, the tips of his fingers hovering just a millimeter away.

"Touch me." The words are a whimper as I roll my hips. Though my clit brushes the tip of his cock again, sending a bolt of electricity through me, it's still not enough.

"I thought I was to undress you," he murmurs quietly as he finally drags the shirt over my head. Without taking his eyes off me, he tosses it to the floor. Then he places his hands against my thighs, his expression full of mirth. "Is this where you want me to touch you?"

"My nipples, please," I whine.

"See why it's so important to use your words properly?" His chiding tone is sinfully sexy, making the warmth in my core go molten. He plucks one of my nipples and rolls it, pulling a long moan from me.

"Your tongue," I beg.

"Where do you want my tongue?" he asks dryly, and god, does the sound of his voice set my blood heating.

"On my nipple."

Sully grins wickedly. It's such a beautiful sight. He sits up, wrapping an arm around me, and rolls his tongue over my nipple. Then he kisses across my chest and gives the opposite one the same treatment. He repeats this move, alternating between my breasts and making me crazy with want.

Tingles dance up my spine and through my extremities. "I think I could come from this alone."

"Oh yeah?" He bites down on one peak, and I bow back, a loud moan escaping me. Holy shit, maybe I really will come like this. Especially with the way he's gently rocking beneath me. I'm not even sure he realizes he's doing it. He's as turned on as I am, creating the most delicious friction while he licks and sucks.

"God, Sully," I mumble. "You feel so good."

He twirls his tongue around my nipple again and hums, the sound reverberating against my skin. "You're fucking delicious, sweetheart. I love having you in my lap, moaning for me."

"Take my panties off. I want to feel your cock."

He pulls back and grins. "I'd love to."

It takes a little—probably un-sexy—maneuvering, but after a few wiggles and grunts, the panties are gone, as are his boxers. Finally, it's just us in the dark, peaceful room, me on his lap again, his warm length hard between my thighs. I crane forward and kiss my husband. It's second nature, a move so familiar and easy. Yet my heart rate ratchets up as I do, because this man drives me completely wild. He always has. Letting go of my inhibitions like this with him again is the sweetest kind of relief.

"Now what do you want?" he asks, his eyes blazing with need, not only for my body but for my thoughts.

"I need you to fuck me." The words come easily and without question. "I need you to remind me that I'm yours and you're not going anywhere."

He squeezes my thigh, his face softening. "You are mine, sweetheart. And I'll only ever be yours. Now put me inside you, and don't you dare take your eyes off us for one moment."

I brace myself on my knees and do as he says, gripping him at his base and guiding him inside me. And I don't look away for even a moment as he reminds me of exactly who we are to one another. As he brings me a peace I haven't known in a very long time. As we both shatter in ecstasy, again and again.

CHAPTER 25

Sully

"**W**e need you to find a person we can both have sex with."

I blink at the women in front of me. The couple walked in ten minutes ago, explaining that there was a complication with their divorce. I've heard so many absurd things from clients over the years. Enough that by now, I'm mostly immune to the crazy shit that comes out of my clients' mouths. Yet here I am, at a loss for words as I replay the conversation in my head.

In the fifteen-plus years that I've been practicing, I can't say I've ever been asked to arrange for a client to have an affair.

I must be wrong about what they want.

I clear my throat. "I'm sorry. Can you repeat that?"

"We want to get divorced under the grounds of infidelity."

I nod automatically, though my mind still spins. Typically, when a client comes in and mentions infidelity, they're either spitting mad or sobbing, not smiling and batting their lashes at me and their spouse.

I glance from one woman to the other, confounded by how calm they are.

"We aren't comfortable lying about infidelity on the certification," one woman says. "We'd feel more comfortable using it if it were true."

"Right," I agree. Because perjury is never a good idea.

The other woman leans forward. "But we've realized that our marriage isn't working, and we want to separate on good terms."

Another nod. I'm still with them at this point.

"So we need you to find a man we can both sleep with."

My lips turn down without my permission. They lost me again.

The one on the left puts a hand on the desk and rushes through an explanation. "We wouldn't be jealous, because neither of us would enjoy it. And if we slept with the same person, then we'd each understand the other's experience." Her expression brightens. "And then we wouldn't have to lie."

I blink down at the yellow legal pad in front of me. I've taken no notes because I don't have the first clue what I'd jot down. *Find a male prostitute?* Bloody hell. I take a breath. As I exhale, an idea comes to me.

I push to my feet, my chair rolling back several inches. "This sounds like something our paralegal can assist you with. It's more of a support staff thing."

"Of course," the one on the right agrees.

"Great." I rush out of my office and close the door behind me. This isn't the time for the walkie-talkie Jersey intercom system. I need to get out of that room. "Lo!"

She peeks her head out of her office.

"These two need your help with a..." How do I phrase this? "Situation?"

She narrows her green eyes at me as she steps out into the hall completely. "I swear to God, Sully, if they're crying—"

"No." I shake my head.

Tears have always made me uncomfortable. For my wife, I'm willing to endure them. I can take any emotion she throws at me, but with anyone else, I run at the sight of moist eyes. And when I run, Lo is the one who has to step in and handle the issue. On multiple occasions, she's threatened to toss me out a window. At least while we're in Jersey, our office is on the first floor.

I plaster on a smile. "I promise it's not tears."

She exhales loudly, the tight line of her lips telling me she's still suspicious. Bloody hell, she has no idea. But she stomps to my office. The moment she steps inside, I dart out of the building.

Yes, I'm avoiding Lo's impending wrath, but I also need to run an errand before Sloane gets home. Today has been a quiet day, and Lo and I are the only people in the office, so now is the perfect time. Even my nosy brother is in the city picking the boys up from school.

I stride quickly around the side of the building, heading for my car. The box is tucked carefully in the trunk, but I've got to get it across the street without being spotted by Lo.

Package in hand, I slam the lid and spin. The sight that greets me makes me jump a foot off the ground.

"Sullivan." Madame E's jet-black hair waves gently in the cold breeze, that white streak as unnerving as ever. "Up to no good?" She laughs, her purple eyes scrutinizing me with an intensity that makes me shiver. "Hmm, maybe the opposite. Though it's important to know that the burn of fire and action might seem easy, it's not always the answer."

I run my hand over my face, deciphering—unsuccessfully—her words. She got the incubator right, and she even knew Sloane and I would dance in the kitchen with the teakettle bubbling nearby. But fire? I haven't made any plans that utilize a fireplace or a firepit or even candles.

Clutching the box tighter, I take a step toward her. "Can I ask a follow-up question?"

She chuckles and floats toward her Mini Cooper. "You boys need to remember that I only see what I see." With that, she climbs inside and peels out of the parking lot, cutting off a car on the road. The blare of its horn is ear-piercing, making me wince.

I shake my head. One day she's going to crash.

Once she's out of sight, I scan the parking lot, ensuring I'm alone.

Then I stride across the street to the Grasshopper. Inside, I make a beeline for the bartender, ignoring the way the hostess side-eyes me.

"Is the owner here?" I ask as I set the massive box on the bar top.

"What's up?" The guy, who looks to be in his twenties, tosses a rag over his shoulder and rests his forearms on the lacquered surface between us.

I give the box a tap. "I'm hoping to convince him to host a karaoke night this Saturday. I've got the machine here and will gladly pay for any other equipment you don't already have on hand."

He rubs at his jaw, giving me a thoughtful look. "This has winning back a woman written all over it."

I'd say he's perceptive, but when is any wild idea a man comes up with not because of a woman? We're always either chasing after or running from them.

"Help a bloke out?" I ask.

He straightens, lifting his chin. "I'll see what I can do." With a chuckle, he turns and pushes through a door I assume leads to the kitchen.

"Did you really buy that thing to impress your girl?" the man two stools down asks. He picks up a mug of dark beer and sips it, watching me over the rim.

I nod simply. "I'd do pretty much anything to make my wife happy."

He snorts. "Newlyweds."

Not even close. "Married over fifteen years."

The door behind the bar swings open before the man, whose eyes have gone wide, can respond, and the bartender steps out. "You've got yourself a deal..."

"Sully." I hold out a hand to the man who just made my day. If it were up to me, I'd pass on listening to strangers sing crappy songs all night, but what makes my wife happy makes me happy.

"Deal." He shakes my hand. "Saturday, it is. Gunner said he'll get a sign out tomorrow and will post about it on the bar's socials tonight."

"Perfect." I step back and stick my hands in the pockets of my trousers. "Thanks."

I hustle back across the street, preparing myself for Lo's wrath. The front door to the office hasn't even closed behind me when Lo hisses my name. "*Sully.*" Bollocks. She looks really pissed. She's leaning against the folding table where Amy works with her arms crossed like she's been waiting for me to walk back in so she can pounce.

"Lo." I dip my chin, going for casual.

"Since when does my job entail being a pimp?"

"What?" My stomach sinks. "That's not what I'm asking you to do. Bloody hell." Though I guess I didn't make that clear before I bolted out of here.

She taps the toe of her ridiculously expensive shoe against the ugly gold carpet.

"What did you tell them?" I ask as I move slowly toward the stairwell that leads to the apartment.

"That I would love to find someone for them to sleep with since, apparently, cheating is the only grounds for divorce their parents will accept. Because clearly, the only sane answer to this problem is for them both to cheat." Sarcasm drips from her lips.

"Well done, then. Jolly good." I pull the door open and escape.

"*Sully,*" she shrieks after me.

I allow her to yell, and nod along that of course I'm a ridiculous sod and absolutely she's deserving of a new pair of fancy shoes. Honestly, I'd give the woman anything she wants. There's not a thing that can't kill my good mood knowing how excited my wife will be when she realizes she's getting her karaoke night.

CHAPTER 26
Sloane

I cannot be late again. And this Uber driver is far more cautious than any I've ever encountered. If he doesn't pick up the pace, I'll be better off hopping out and walking the ten blocks to the courthouse.

"Think it'd be faster to take a side street?" I ask him, eyeing the gridlock all around us.

The man shrugs, keeping both hands on the steering wheel. "If we can get to one."

Slumping back against the seat, I close my eyes. Dammit. There's no way I'll make it to the mediation on time. I set my shoulders and type out a quick text to Will, letting him know I'll be there as soon as I can.

My phone rings almost immediately, and when I see my boss's name, I take a deep breath and answer. "I'm so sorry."

"It's fine, seriously. Take your time. I've got this."

I had a glucose test this morning, which I warned Will about weeks ago. While I'm thankful that he isn't berating me for being late, the way he's so quick to handle it without me stings. As if my presence during this mediation is completely unnecessary. He's assigned me to help with just about every one of his cases, yet he doesn't seem to *need* me on any of them.

"How did the appointment go?"

Shrugging as if he can see me, I sink farther into my seat, closing my eyes. "I'll have the results in a week or so."

"Don't stress. Go back to the office. I can fill you in on the mediation over dinner."

My eyes fly open. "Over *what*?"

"Dinner," he says firmly. "The judge is walking in, so I have to go. I'll be back by four thirty. We can go then."

"Um..." My chest tightens. Dinner tonight? I can't. My husband and I have a date night planned. One I was really excited about, too, because it included three hours with him. Naked. In our penthouse, without any of our roommates or our son.

But I can't very well tell my boss that. And I can't weasel my way out of it after I've blown off mediation today. Shoot.

I swallow back my disappointment and say, "Sure, sounds great. See you then."

After I've ended the call, I drop my head against the seat again. Sully is going to be so disappointed.

My phone rings in my hand, and I sit upright, assuming it's Will again. But when I see my mother's name on the screen, I silence it. I've successfully avoided her calls for months, and I've dodged invitations to get together because I'm not ready to let her know about the pregnancy. She didn't react well when I told her about the divorce, so there's no way this won't really bring out her judgmental side.

When the screen goes dark, I unlock the device and call Sully. I might as well break the news now. He's not going to be happy that I'm canceling, but what else can I do?

A woman should know when she's being taken on a date. In my opinion, that's a prerequisite. If a man wants to take a woman out and show her a good time, he'd better make his interest obvious. He'd better reserve the table in the corner of a dimly lit restaurant. He'd better look at her in a way that makes it clear he's interested.

But none of that should happen when said woman is out to dinner with her boss.

A boss she isn't dating, at least. I've dated the boss before. I married the boss, and I enjoyed the hell out of it for a few years.

But I did not consent to a date with my current boss, and there's no denying this is a date.

"Do you like the soup?" Will brushes his hand against mine like he's trying to get my attention.

Newsflash: we're the only two people in this corner. Who the hell else would I *think* he's talking to?

I pull back at his touch and pick up my water. As I sip, I run through what the hell is happening and what to do about it. "It's fine. I actually wanted to talk to you about a new case."

Will smiles. "Tomorrow. Tonight, let's focus on us."

My stomach rolls.

Us?

Shit, shit, shit.

See? I knew this was a damn date.

I examine Will, trying to remind myself that he's my friend. That when my life was spiraling, he offered me a lifeline, a job. At the time, it was what I needed more than anything.

But focusing on that doesn't temper the annoyance flaring to life inside me. How dare he put me in this awkward position? The audacity of this man.

Or am I the one to blame here? Have I led him on?

I've truly never even been attracted to Will. He's nice enough, and he's not bad-looking, but no one held a candle to Sully in law school, and to this day, no man has ever caught my attention the way Sully has. Truth be told, my husband has owned me, whether we were together or not, for almost twenty years, and I can't imagine that ever changing. Each and every day, he works to be better for me and for T.J. He's putting in the effort. Because of that, every day it's harder to remember why we separated in the first place.

"Us?" I say, finally finding my words.

Will grasps my free hand. His palm is slightly moist and the sensation makes my stomach roll. "Yes, us, Sloane. We've had no time together since Christmas, and I'd really like to change that. We went almost seven years without contact. It's been too long."

The man is delusional. Clearly. I pull back my hand. "Because I had a child and was working mostly on trusts. Of course we didn't see each other. I was never in court."

Will leans back in his chair, acting as if he's readjusting himself rather than recovering after I pulled away. "I know. And I missed you. I'm really glad you're back in my life."

A sense of utter bafflement consumes me. "You know I'm pregnant, right?"

After his question about my glucose test, there's no doubt he does. But with the way this conversation is going, I worry he's had a personality transplant, so maybe this new version of him isn't aware.

Will nods. "Yes, and I also know you were unhappy in your marriage, which is why you're getting divorced."

The boldness of his statement nearly knocks the wind out of me. "It's not that simple."

He frowns, like he's grappling with what I'm saying. Good. It feels like this is the first time tonight he's actually listened to me.

When he speaks again, his tone is sincere, once again throwing me for a loop. "I know, but the feelings I had for you during law school and for years after are back with a vengeance. I tried, Sloane. I tried to forget how I felt when you chose Sully back then, but fuck, you have no idea how goddamn irresistible you are. Do you know how many times I saw you in court and wished things were different?" He straightens his jacket and leans forward, his voice going soft. "Sully is an idiot. He fumbled. He fucked up his chance with you.

Now you're here with me, and I'm not going to let the opportunity pass me by. So I'm just asking"—he shakes his head—"no, I'm begging. Please give me a shot."

I gape at him, my mind spinning, my lungs starved for oxygen. Is this man seriously pleading with me?

All those years ago, I knew he felt some sort of way about me, but I figured it had more to do with fucking over Sully than fawning over me. I never meant to lead him on, and if I did? Shit, I feel terrible. Also, Sully is going to lose his mind. This is so, so bad.

"I don't know what to say," I whisper.

He shrugs. "I don't need an answer right now. I know this is a lot. I just—" He glances down at the table and then looks back at me. "You have a decision to make. You need to decide whether you're with Murphy and Machon or if you're ready to become a true member of the Higgins firm."

A wave of unease makes my stomach flip. "Is this about choosing between you and Sully, or choosing between your firm and his?"

"Aren't they one and the same?" he asks, his tone flippant.

I bristle, straightening in my seat. "Is that why you hired me? Because you wanted to date me?"

Will sighs, as if he's annoyed by the question. Or maybe because he thinks the answer is obvious. Too bad, because I'm not getting it. "Yes." He huffs, lacing his fingers on the table. "You're a forty-year-old associate, Sloane. People our age are partners by now. Even your husband didn't make you a partner."

I wince, that one hurts.

Will doesn't seem to notice, or if he does he doesn't care, he just prattles on with my list of deficiencies. "You haven't practiced in years, and you come in covered in coffee stains and late for every appointment. You haven't made it to one court appearance on time since you started. Any other associate would be gone by now."

My heart plummets, my mouth too dry to respond.

As if he wants to soften the blow, he puts his hand on mine again. "But I want to be your partner, your teammate. If it's you and me, I've got you. But if it's not me, I can only cover for you for so long." His eyes harden, and suddenly, I understand why Sully always describes them as beady. "So you have a decision to make. Are we giving this a shot, or are you going back to your husband?"

Shocked, I disentangle myself from his hold. Is he telling me I won't have a job if I don't date him?

CHAPTER 27
Sully

I press down on the top of the pen, and it responds with a satisfying click. Then I do it again. Lo is speaking, but I can't focus. Even if what she's saying might be important. Hell, I know it's important. Lo doesn't waste our time, and I'm a wanker for wasting hers.

But all I can think about is my wife.

I'm still peeved that her work meeting got in the way of our date.

It's ironic, yes, considering I was always the one canceling dates for work. I understood before, but the full sensation of the sting Sloane felt so often really hit me with her canceling on me.

I made reservations for dinner at a small French bistro where the menus are printed in French and the servers speak it fluently. My goal was to show her that I still remember the trip to Paris we always dreamed about. I paid a ridiculous sum to reserve the entire restaurant for the night. When she canceled, I wanted to track her down, toss her over my shoulder, and drag her to the slice of heaven I'd curated for us.

I didn't of course. I reminded myself that her job is important. Her needs and wants are important. I want her to feel fulfilled. So I sent Cal and Lo to dinner in our place and spent the evening playing

Minecraft with T.J. and Murphy. I tried to be fun, but mostly, I was disappointed. The pain only grew when Sloane came home, because although she curled into my chest and burrowed into me like she was trying to escape the outside world, she hardly said a word.

I blamed the silence on exhaustion, since she didn't get home until almost eleven, but in the two days since, she's been just as quiet, and my unease has grown.

The wanker that I am, I was certain we'd moved past that. When she opened up to me about her worries regarding the pregnancy, about our future, it seemed as though we were back on track. Yet I suddenly feel as though I'm walking on a tightrope. Like each step I make has the potential for disaster.

"Sully." Lo smacks a stack of papers against my desk.

"Yes," I agree automatically as I blink back into the moment. It's a safe answer, because honestly, Lo is almost always right.

She scowls. "What is going on with you? Cal's usually the one who gets lost in his own world."

I shake my head. "Sorry."

"If you tell me you were thinking about which color slushie you want for lunch, I will lose it."

"No." I chuckle. "I'm just worried about Sloane."

Her eyes soften. "I know her last pregnancy was hard, but she seems to be doing well this time."

For the past few months, I've consciously put concerns about Sloane's pregnancy out of my mind. Yes, she suffered from preeclampsia the first time around and ended up on bed rest. Yes, her blood pressure spiked so high it became dangerous to her own health. But that doesn't mean it will happen again, and there's no sense in worrying about the unknown.

The fear that gripped me when there was a chance I could lose my wife, especially after her placenta ruptured and she was rushed in for an emergency C-section, kept me from being eager to have another baby. However, I could never regret the surprise blessing we've been given. This little peanut is special not only because they're a physical representation of our love, but because this tiny being has given me hope that our family will be okay. Hope I'd almost given up on.

I nod, not wanting to talk about how terrifying the risks are any more than I want to share my worries about Sloane's silence. "What were you saying?"

"Will you sign this complaint? That way we can get these two women divorced." She flings the pages at me.

I frown at the names that come into focus. "Did you find someone for them to sleep with?"

Lo glares daggers at me.

Bloody hell. That was not the right thing to say.

"Of course you didn't." I rough a hand down my face. "What am I saying?"

She doesn't take her green eyes off me until I'm squirming in my chair. Damn, this woman is something. I don't understand how my brother doesn't shrink into the floor in front of her when she looks at him like that. And she does. Often. He's full of utter nonsense.

"*Lola.*"

Her eyes soften slightly at the sound of Cal's voice. Ah, yes. That's why he's still alive—she loves him.

"Lo-la," he chants again, appearing at the door to my office. "You'll never guess who came for a holiday."

"Who?" Lo's red hair falls over her shoulder as she tips her head.

"Mum!" Cal is wearing a smile, but his eyes are screaming *help me! Help me!* as he drags the tall, thin, dark-haired woman who raised us into view.

I know the feeling. There's nothing more terrifying than a visit from dear old Mum.

Her blue eyes light up upon seeing me, but before we can greet each other, Lo turns and steps between us.

"Ms. Murphy. What a surprise." Lo's tone is formal, like she's talking to a client and not her boyfriend's mother.

It makes sense. Lo and our father were close. She was practically a daughter to him, and Mum and Dad's relationship was bloody awful from about the time Cal was born until the day Dad died.

"My dear." My mother gives her a tight smile.

My brother's eyes flash with a foreign kind of anger. Cal is the definition of happy-go-lucky. If he's peeved off, then our mother better be very careful. He might be the friendliest of blokes most of the time, but if she says one unflattering thing about Lo, I have no doubt she'll be booted from the office in the blink of an eye.

Mum assesses Lo, her expression pinched. "You look lovely." Without waiting for a response, she rounds the desk, headed for me.

But I'm frozen in horror. Fuck, fuck, fuck. Nothing annoys Sloane more than my mother's tendency to show up unannounced.

The surprise aspect of her visits is especially maddening, considering that she lives across the pond. One would think she might drop us a line before she hops an international flight, but they'd be wrong.

Sloane and I have made incredible strides over the last few months, but suddenly, the ground beneath us feels shaky again, and this little surprise might be enough to lead us to an epic disaster.

"Mother." I force myself to my feet and greet her with a kiss on the cheek. "To what do we owe the pleasure?"

She smacks my chest. "Don't be so stiff, Sully. I came to see my family."

That's hard to believe. Though we lived with her in England when we were children, she had very little time for us. Nor did she have much interest unless it was to tell us how awful our father was. She always had time for that.

Her eyes drift over my shoulder. "Plus, I must meet the woman who finally captured my little boy's heart."

"I'm thirty-two," Cal grumbles from the doorway.

Lo giggles. "But only five at heart."

My brother shakes his head, but his expression lights up.

"We really must go out for tea, Lola." Mum turns back to me. "Sloane too. She's so good at making reservations. She can take care of that, right?"

"No." The single word is sharp and forceful. For years, I was too busy to deal with my mother's demands, so I pawned off the tedious parts on Sloane. And yes, the choice to do it was made easier by the dislike I hold for the woman who likes to pretend she raised me.

But those days are over. I kick myself each time I think of the bullshit I piled on Sloane's plate. Fuck, I was a selfish bugger. "She's busy now that she's back at work."

"What about this weekend? Surely she has *some* free time." Lips pursed, Mum crosses her arms over her mint-green sweater.

Yeah, she's pissed off. But she can bloody well be upset. Better her than my wife.

"We have plans."

Sloane might not know yet, but her karaoke weekend is approaching.

"Plans, huh?" Lo cocks a brow. The damn woman has been decoding my every statement, trying to suss out the state of my relationship with her best friend. "What kind of plans?"

The kind that are none of your business.

That's what I want to say. In reality, I need her on board. Cal too. Though I hate to admit it, my brother is the life of every party, and Sloane could use more fun. I want her smiling all night.

"I told Cal." I look toward my brother, whom I mentioned the plan to, knowing I could count on him to help me make it happen. "Remember? We're going to karaoke this weekend."

Cal snorts. "Yeah, I've never seen Brian so excited to babysit."

My poor best friend spent way too much time at that bar with us after Sloane discovered they had twice-a-week karaoke nights.

My mother frowns. "What an awful idea."

"That's okay. You don't have to join us," I say. Bloody hell, she better not join us. If she did, it'd surely ruin Sloane's weekend. "We'll do karaoke without you. If you'd like to spend some time with your grandkids though, I'd be happy to arrange something on Sunday."

My mother scoffs. Of course she has no interest in seeing the boys. She has no time for anyone who can't spoil her. Bollocks. Even though I already knew that, somehow it hits me all over again. Just like when I was a boy and she had no time for me.

"Sully, I raised you better than this."

"That's just the thing," I say, finally seeing the truth of it all. "You didn't. I get it, Mum. Parenting is hard. Maybe I didn't fully understand how hard until I was faced with doing it on my own. But that's still no excuse. I never should have expected my wife to do it all. I refuse to be like you. I refuse to make my kids an afterthought or a chore to attend to. My wife taught me that. So yes, this weekend, I am taking her to karaoke. Then I'm going to spend time with my son and my nephew. If you'd like to spend some time with your grandkids—or you know meet Murphy—you can schedule a time that works for all of us, but Sloane won't be making the tea times or hotel reservations."

My mother's shocked expression makes it abundantly clear that I've not gotten through to her. Hell, she probably didn't hear a word after no. But I've spent the majority of my life trying to appease the wrong people: my father, my mother, clients. I won't do it anymore. My wife and my children come first.

I'll be better. For all of them.

"Should I call you a car?" Cal offers.

My chest inflates with pride, because bloody hell, I'm glad he's got my back.

My mother gapes at him and then huffs. "I instructed my driver to stay. I didn't believe you were really living here. But I see you're both just as delusional as your father was. When you wish to apologize to me, you can find me at the Ritz."

I snort. Fat chance that will be happening.

Lo pulls her lips together to stifle a giggle and averts her gaze as my mother storms out.

We're all still stunned silent when Brian peers into my office, wide-eyed. "Bloody hell, did that really just happen?"

His teasing makes my body relax completely.

"You're a real wanker," I say with a chuckle. Then I turn my attention to Cal. "Thank you for that."

My little brother shakes his head. "Without you, I'd have been completely alone growing up. You should know by now that I'll always have your back."

Emotion clogs my throat and I avert my gaze. It's hard to think about our childhood. It's hard to picture the little boys we used to be. Because that's truly what we were when Mum regularly ignored us. When she told us time and again that it was our fault that our father cheated. That motherhood had robbed her of the lifestyle she wanted.

Is that how Sloane felt all these years? It hurts to think I ever treated her the way my father treated my mother.

Regardless, Sloane never failed to show up for our son. Never failed to bring light to his childhood.

"We're going to make this weekend the best ever," I tell Lo. "God, I've been a bloody wanker to my wife, haven't I?"

Lo shrugs. "You're trying now."

I nod. I am. "She'll like the karaoke, right?"

"What?"

My eyes snap up to the door. I didn't hear Sloane come in, and I wanted it to be a surprise. Immediately it occurs to me that she might just have run into my mother, and if she did, I can only imagine how badly it went.

Shit.

CHAPTER 28
Sloane

"Did you say karaoke?"

Brian steps up behind me as I stand in Sully's office doorway.

Excitement zips through me, and a smile blooms on my face. It's the first I've mustered since Will laid down his ultimatum three days ago. I've internalized the emotions that have plagued me since that night because I worry that if Sully knows, it'll set us back, and we've made so much progress.

The moment he found out I went to work for Higgins, Smith, and Dodge, he told me that Will had only hired me to get in my pants. It crushed me that he believed I wasn't worth more than that. But with time, I realized that, though his words were harsh, he was concerned about me and for me. And now I know he was right.

And worse, Will is right too. I am exactly what he said I am: a forty-year-old mother who has no business as an associate. I'm not good at my job. Hell, I'm not sure I'm even a good mom. I'm definitely not a good wife. For years, I've blamed Sully for the way our marriage crumbled around us, when I was equally at fault. And now, I'm keeping secrets from him. I've asked for so much from him, and his only request in return is that I talk to him. And I can't even do that. I'm lying by omission.

But how can I not? I don't have the first clue what to say. I need a game plan before I get Sully's feelings involved. I want to be with my husband. I want to try. The end. There's nothing else to consider. However, I don't know what to do about my career. Do I just give up? Lose my identity again? I'm five months pregnant. I can't just start at a new firm. If I leave Higgins, Smith, and Dodge now, it'll be at least another year before I can even think about working again.

The thought alone is debilitating.

For so long, I wanted to try for another child. I wanted to expand our family, but when it didn't happen, I came to terms with it. And when T.J. started school, I adjusted my point of view and chose to embrace the chance to focus on myself. Now all of that has been thrown into question again.

I hate it. Is it really too much to ask to have a good relationship with my husband, to have happy, healthy kids, and a career? Why does achieving one mean losing the other?

And then there's the financial aspect. Not working means I'm solely reliant on Sully again. The thought guts me. It's exactly how I felt at the end of our marriage, especially when he offered a hefty amount of spousal support.

It was like a sucker punch, the inference that he was certain I needed him. Like he believed that even after our marriage was over, I could only keep my head above water because of him.

"*Yes*," Lo screeches, dragging me out of my head. "Do you follow the Grasshopper on Instagram? They announced that tomorrow is karaoke night."

"You didn't see Mum outside?" Cal asks at the same time Lo speaks.

"I really wish you didn't have to miss karaoke, Brian," Lo says. "I've heard your skills are unmatched."

I can't focus on her teasing or Brian's reaction, though, because I'm having a completely different conversation in my head again.

Sully's mother is in town? Shit. When did she get here? And where is she right this moment? And what does she think of Sully and me and the baby? Does she even know? Is he going to tell her?

My husband calls my name, and my heart stutters to a stop. I'm sure the war playing out in my head is written all over my face.

"Your mother is here?" I repeat. I don't want to dislike his mother, but she's worse than my own. At least I know my mother has always cared. Maybe she cares because she wants to mold me into her protégé—or at least she used to wish she could, now I'm sure she'd settle for just an upstanding attorney who shows up to court on time —but Sully's mother ignored both Cal and Sully when they were children, and she's no better with T.J.

Honestly, I'm shocked she made the trip and not looking forward to seeing her again at all. She was one part of the divorce I didn't mind.

Sully stalks toward me, his expression panicked. "I didn't know she was coming," he says quickly.

"Where is she now?" I look over my shoulder around the hallway, hoping she's not in one of the other offices.

"We sent her back to her hotel," Sully explains. "I didn't want her to ambush you."

The fact that he even thought about my reaction is surprising. For so long, she would show up, and he'd send a simple text. *Could you make reservations and make up the guest bedroom? My mum's in town.*

Despite the dread that washes over me when I think about facing his mother, it almost feels like the universe has stepped in to show me how different Sully really is.

A test to see how much we've changed.

He's passing with flying colors. But am I?

I have a choice to make. I can pack up and stay at the penthouse until she's gone. Let Sully handle his mother.

Or I could lean into the mess we've created and the two of us could find a way forward together. I could show his mother—and everyone else, for that matter—that we're figuring it out. That we're trying. That we're a family, no matter what happens. And, more importantly, that we're determined to put our children first, which is something she and Terry never did.

Determined to get this right, I take the final steps toward my husband and wrap my arms around his shoulders, making a statement without saying a word. And if the surprised smile that hits his lips is any indication, he's thrilled by this turn of events.

"Are you okay?"

His brows tug together. "Of course I'm okay. I just want you to be okay. She always stressed you out, and I won't let anything stress you out. I told her she's not welcome here unless she can be kind to you. And you're not making reservations for her. Also, she didn't even ask about Murphy. She's never even met him and it was like he was an afterthought."

"Sully." I don't even know what to say. His mother was always selfish and awful but that's a new low.

Truth is, I never brought up how arduous my interactions with his mother were. I kept it to myself, always proud that his mother and I never fought. In reality, that was a mistake. It meant that I stewed. As much as I thought I fought my husband, I probably didn't fight enough. Instead, I gave up. That's why we stopped speaking long before the marriage ended. God, my stomach tumbles at that realization.

Sully's eyes say it all. They're filled with desperation. He needs to know that I believe him. That's he changed. "I don't want to be like her, Sloane. I want to get this right."

He's nothing like his mother, and the fact that he's even worried about it, is proof enough that he's changed.

Unable to help but smile, I inch closer. When I'm hit with his familiar scent, the people around us fade away. "Then let's make sure we give it our all." I scan his face, making sure he understands what I'm saying. "If that's what you want, I mean."

Sully's voice is raspy when he responds. "I've never wanted anything more, sweetheart. Is that what *you* want?"

Popping up on my toes, I let my lips brush over his and murmur, "That's exactly what I want."

"Are we going to talk about that kiss?" Lo asks from the rocker in the corner of *Sloane's*.

I spit into the sink and rinse my mouth, then turn and give her a smile, but I don't respond.

Her brows lift to her hairline. "Oh, is that how it's gonna be?"

"I'm not ready to talk about it," I say as I drop my toothbrush into its holder. "I don't exactly know what's going on yet, but I think maybe I'm dating my husband?"

Squealing, she points at my face. "Oh my god, you're blushing."

I bite down on my bottom lip. "I really like him, Lo."

She snorts, the sound echoing off the tile walls. "I'd hope so. You married him."

I don't know how to properly explain it, but I'm giddy every time I think of my husband and what we're doing. It's like I've reverted back to the Sloane from law school. The emotions are so reminiscent of those that overwhelmed me when Sully and I started dating. Only this time, I don't have to wonder whether he's in it for the long haul. I know he is because he keeps telling me he is.

So now I've found myself in a unique situation where I know he's safe and these feelings are real, but we're still exploring and learning new things about one another. It's exactly what I need to move forward. Of course Sully figured that out, probably before I did, and is giving it to me.

"I, for one, am very excited for karaoke. And even more excited to watch Sully woo you some more." Lo tucks her legs beneath her and presses her lips together, like she's gearing up to say something.

Internally, I cringe. I don't want a warning about being careful. Careful is the last thing I feel like being right now. In fact, I want to be reckless, and I want my husband to be a little reckless with me. We married young and went straight to work, slipping into our roles as proper adults, doing all the things that were expected of us, and look where that got us. Now, I want to throw caution to the wind and chase the fire burning inside me, between us. I'm desperate to discover what type of explosions we can create. Our lives could use a bit of a shift.

"Have you had the chance to talk to Will about Yoga Jess?"

My heart sinks.

That's what she was gearing up to say.

I hate to let her down, but I haven't spoken to Will since our dinner. I can't. Not until I figure out what the hell to do about my job. But how do I explain that to her without telling her about his ultimatum? Her reaction will be a lot like Sully's, I imagine, and once again, I question whether I'm ready for that shitstorm.

Then again, she's my best friend, and keeping this all bottled up isn't getting me anywhere.

So, heart in my throat, I ease into it. "I haven't, actually."

She tilts her head in surprise. "Oh, I thought you wanted to help."

"It's not that I don't," I say quickly. Then, before I can back down, I admit the truth. "I'm just not sure how much help I can be."

Mouth tugged in a frown, she straightens in her seat. "Why?"

"I'm really fucking up at work," I admit with a sigh. "Like daily. Between this pregnancy and being so out of the game after so many years off, I feel lost."

"It's probably just your nerves," she says. "Or maybe it's because everyone at that firm is so awful."

I sigh, my chest deflating.

One shoulder lifted, she says, "Tell me I'm wrong."

"You're wrong." My words lack the intensity that would come with them if I really believed them, though, and she knows it. "Never mind. I'll talk to Will."

Her eyes narrow as she scrutinizes me, seeing far more than I'd like her to. "What aren't you telling me?"

My heart stumbles. This is it. My opening. So I go for it. "The other night at dinner," I say, lowering my gaze to the pink rug between us, "it wasn't a work meeting."

She frowns. "Then what was it?"

"A surprise date?" I say, though the statement sounds more like a question.

"A surprise *what*?" Her eyes bulge. "How does someone surprise date another person?"

"Exactly." I throw my hands up. "That's what I'm saying." Feeling vindicated, I lean forward. "But it was clearly a date. And while we were there, Will laid out exactly what he wants from me. What, you ask, might that be? Well, it isn't that he wants me to work on more cases with him. That's for sure."

Lo snorts. "Let me guess: he wants you naked, spread out on his desk."

I look away, cringing. Defeat overrides the anger brewing in me when she puts it that way. "I guess."

"Oh my god," she shouts. "That ass. What did you say? What did Sully say? *Jesus*." With a hand to her chest, she sucks in a breath. "To be a fly on the wall when he knocks Will out."

I still can't look at her, so I study the lava lamp and the way the blobs continue to morph.

"*No*," she hisses. "Sloane, look at me."

With my face screwed up, I obey, bracing for her to yell.

"Please tell me you told him to stick it where the sun doesn't shine."

"He's my boss," I protest weakly, my eyes stinging.

"Yeah, and your boss has no right to talk to you that way."

This time I'm the one who snorts. "Right, because I'm sure your boss doesn't talk to you like that."

She tips her head back and huffs. "Cal and Will are on opposite ends of the creep spectrum, trust me. Cal's comments are wanted. Are Will's?" Nose scrunched, she gives me a questioning look.

I shake my head. Though I'm at a loss for how to handle this situation, I can say with certainty that never in my life would I have welcomed the comments Will made that night. "I just want Sully." I wring my hands, nerves skittering through me. "More than I've ever wanted him, if I'm honest. And I want my job. And our family. Is that too much to ask? Why do I have to choose?"

Lo stands and pulls me into a hug, sighing. "You shouldn't have to, babe. You absolutely shouldn't have to."

"I just want the chance to explore what Sully and I could have. Is that so wrong?"

"No. But eventually..." she hedges.

I nod. She doesn't have to finish the statement. Eventually, I'll have to make a change. Because no matter how unfair it is, it's obvious I can't have *that* job and my husband too.

CHAPTER 29
Sully

"You honestly think I don't know your son by now?" Brian looks down at the list I gave him.

Maybe I'm being over-the-top, but I can't risk ruining Sloane's night, and a surprise from my unpredictable son could very easily do that.

"I know you do, but even I wouldn't have expected him to try to eat the leaves of Cal's fern to see if they tasted like lettuce." I sigh. "Plus, lately, he's taken to climbing the counters and jumping off."

Brian chuckles. "That kid definitely takes after his uncle. The only other person I know who's eaten a leaf *just because* is Cal."

I run a hand over my face. "We're screwed. My brother has been a bloody pain in the arse most of his life. Is that what I'm in for?" And we're about to add another one to the mix.

He drops his hand to my shoulder with a heavy thud. "I couldn't think of two people more equipped for the challenge."

The smile he gives me could be described as encouraging, I suppose, but it's foreign on my typically salty friend's face. That can't be a good thing. Brian doesn't bullshit me, ever.

"Wow, I didn't realize I was that utterly fucked." I shake my head.

"Nah." He backs away, propping himself up against the ugly Formica countertop. "I'm just happy to see you and Sloane working things out. Together, you can handle anything life throws at you."

"You think?" I've been clinging to that hope. With Sloane, I can do anything. Raise a hellion, have another little one, be happy. All of it.

He nods and tosses the list I gave him onto the counter. "I hated watching you two fall apart. I wish I could have stopped it somehow. I may be an outsider looking in, but…" He shrugs.

"It was always the three of us," I correct, my chest pinching. "You brought her into my life, and half of our memories include you."

His smile builds slowly. "I'm forever the third wheel."

The statement hits too close to one he made a couple of weeks ago.

"Never seemed like it to us." I take a breath and gear myself up for what I need to say. I hate this kind of *none of my business* statement.

Historically, Sloane has taken on the heart-to-heart conversations with Brian when they were needed. But I'm here, and if he wants to talk, then I want him to know I'll listen. Fuck. I rough a hand through my hair. I wish I was better at this shit.

"Do you ever think about giving a relationship a shot?"

For the almost twenty years I've known Brian, he's never been involved in a situation that even remotely looked like a relationship. He's not a monk. I know that. But bringing a woman home for the night isn't the same as opening up his heart.

For a few beats, he gives me a blank look, like his mind has checked out. I consider backtracking. Telling him to forget that I asked. I really should leave this shit to Sloane.

Finally, he sighs and blinks back to the moment. "If you lost Sloane, would you try again?"

I don't even need to think about that. "Nope."

My whole adult life, there's only ever been one woman for me.

Losing her for good is my worst nightmare. But if that happened, I'd still love her with my whole heart.

He gives me a clipped nod. "When you lose the right one, no one else could ever be enough."

His eyes are haunted, the ghost of his past rearing its ugly head. He was head-over-heels in love during his undergrad. It was before he and I met, so I never got the full story.

Maybe I should have tried harder. We were roommates through the entirety of law school. I had the time.

My father put me up in a flat close to Columbia, and for the first couple of weeks, I lived alone. Brian and I became fast friends. Though in the beginning, we did little more than meet to study. He was too busy commuting from his father's house in Brooklyn for much else. His younger sister was raising a baby on her own, and he helped her as much as he could. But quickly, the drive to Columbia five days a week got to be too much, so I offered to let him move into my spare room. He took me up on it, and although he still went home a couple of times a week to help, the time saved by not commuting allowed him to become the overachiever he is today.

"You ever look her up?" He's mentioned her name before, but I'm fucking awful at remembering shit like that. Julie maybe. If Cal were listening in, he'd know.

Slowly, he shakes his head. "Nah. She's probably home in Vermont, married with four kids, and happy as hell. She should be." His words are rough at the end, his throat bobbing.

"You should try. You never know." After the shit Sloane and I have been through, I fully believe that.

"Try what?" Lo bops into the kitchen, eyeing me, then Brian. "You thinking about asking someone out?" The excitement radiating from her is so painfully obvious that I can't help but chuckle. "You *are*," she accuses. "I need the tea."

"Dammit," Brian mutters.

The cat, who's been lounging on the floor beside him, lifts his head, as if he's been summoned.

"What did the cat do now?" Sloane appears behind Lo.

"Nothing." Brian glowers down at the massive feline. "Go back to sleep."

The cat doesn't seem bothered by Brian's attitude. In fact, he purrs and rubs against his black trousers, leaving a trail of light gray hair on the dark material.

"Now look at what you did," Brian chides.

Sloane breaks into giggles, the sound lighting me up from the inside out.

"I'm so excited for karaoke." Lo ignores Brian, probably because she's used to his attitude.

"Me too," Sloane agrees.

"That's it. We need to party hardy with a singy blingy." Cal clambers up from the living room floor, where he's been playing with the boys, and rushes into the kitchen.

"What?" Lo frowns.

"Murphy needs a full-out over-the-top karaoke party."

My brother has become obsessed with throwing the world's greatest birthday party for his son.

I can't blame him, really. He's missed out on six of them already. Though he will absolutely go overboard. Knowing Murphy, who's reserved and pretty easy to please, he'd be thrilled just to spend the day with his dad, but there is no telling Cal that.

Brian shakes his head, roughly batting at the cat hair on the leg of his trousers. "No, he doesn't. Kids don't have karaoke parties."

Cal frowns, his hands on his hips. "I need a good idea."

"You'll come up with one, baby." Lo wraps an arm around my brother's waist.

"You know who won't be invited though," Cal says, expression hard.

Lo sighs. "I know, your mother."

I don't think I've ever seen my brother as angry at our mother as he was when he read her text this morning. She said she was heading to Arizona for some facial treatments. She never made an effort to meet his son. Never asked about T.J. either. I've made my peace with it but I know he's still struggling.

She expect us to apologize but it's not happening. I have a feeling we won't be hearing from her for a while. Or at least until the next time she decides to randomly show up and expect us to cater to her.

"Are you all leaving or what?" Brian huffs.

I wince. Fuck. I hate that he's annoyed. And I hate even more that, though he'd never admit it, it's because he's alone, while Cal and I are with our girls. He feels like the odd man out because he's missing his other half.

But I don't have a clue how to fix that for him. And right now, I'm still focused on ensuring that I won't lose the love of my life. With any luck, in the near future, Sloane and I can find a way to help him.

"Come on, sweetheart," I whisper into her ear.

Brian's attitude aside, tonight is going to be perfect.

CHAPTER 30
Sloane

The cold February air steals my breath from my lungs. Shit, it's colder in Jersey than the city, I swear.

Sully wraps an arm around my shoulders and pulls me into his side. "Will be a quick walk."

It is, as it's only across the street, but if it meant we could stay like this, then I'd consider pulling him down the block and taking the long way.

Yup, I have a full-fledged crush on my husband. With each day that passes, I crave these little moments with him more. We've yet to talk to T.J. about our relationship because we're both concerned about getting his hopes up, so inside the apartment, we mostly keep our hands to ourselves.

But now that Lo, Cal and Brian know, we don't have to censor ourselves constantly, and that knowledge makes it hard to contain my excitement.

From the look of things, the bar is busy tonight. Cars line both sides of the street, and even from outside, I can hear the din of chatter and music. When Sully pulls the heavy oak door open for me, I'm assaulted by the smell of stale beer, whiskey, and fried food.

It's glorious. There's nothing I love more than a dive bar, and the

Grasshopper is one of the best I've found. It reminds me of the one across from Sully and Brian's apartment in law school. The place where I first discovered my love of karaoke.

My mother has always been the kind of woman who would rather die than set foot in a place where her heels would literally stick to the floor. Despite that, or maybe because of that, I fell in love with the atmosphere instantly.

The first time we discovered karaoke night at that bar, we were celebrating Sully's recent success on an exam.

At the time, Sully and I were just friends, though I had a massive crush on him. So did every girl in our class, yet he never gave any of them the time of day. I would have done anything to get that boy to see me as more than a friend, so I used his love for rock music—a shared affinity—to make my big move.

Up until that night, I'd felt like the third wheel. The guys were best friends, and I figured that, like most people, they invited me into their friend group because of who my mother was. Everyone talked about wanting to work for a judge during the summer because it looked good on applications. So the vast majority of our classmates thought it beneficial to be friendly with me.

Because of that I wasn't unpopular, but none of my friendships at that point felt genuine.

Sully and Brian never asked about my mother. They never talked about summer internships either. Sully was a bit of a slacker, skating by on his charm and putting in the bare minimum. Brian was a good influence on him. Honestly though, it was our study sessions that pushed Sully to do so well on that exam. He broke the class curve and was high on it.

While he ordered drinks for us, I excused myself, telling him I needed to use the restroom. Then, while his back was turned, I went up to the karaoke guy, requested a song and rushed off the the bathroom to apply the reddest of lipsticks and fix my hair. When I returned, Sully stood at the bar, our drinks in hand, and I put my plan into action. I'll never forget the way his face lit up when the emcee called my name.

Despite my nerves, I sashayed up there, hips swaying, and took the mic. I sang my heart out, getting almost every word wrong. It was terrible. So terrible that everyone in the bar was clapping and laughing at my horrible rendition of "Pour Some Sugar On Me."

But Sully's reaction made it all worth it. He watched me with a hunger that lit up my nerve endings. It's the same way he looks at me now, though tonight there's a slight smirk touching his lips, like he's remembering that night too.

By the time I replaced the mic all those years ago, Sully was stalking toward me, and when we were face to face, he pulled me into his chest.

"That was awful," he murmured, a huge smile on his face. "Bloody fucking awful."

"Hey." I reeled back, smacking him.

He only pulled me in tighter, his focus dropping to my mouth. "And the hottest thing I've ever seen."

Electricity pulsed between us as we stared at one another. One that couldn't be ignored. So when he leaned forward and murmured, "I'd like to kiss you," I made the move first, pressing my mouth to his.

Instantly, we were consumed, the chemistry between us igniting like fireworks. We weren't soft with one another; we were hungry. I devoured him, all remnants of the shy, reserved daughter my mother had raised completely gone.

And then I fucked him in the barroom closet.

Maybe it wasn't the most romantic of encounters, but the memory still makes my heart race to this day.

We couldn't wait another minute. We didn't discuss what it meant, whether it was a one-time thing, but we didn't need to. Because despite the hard way he took me, Sully told me exactly how he felt as he sank inside me.

"I've been wanting this for months. You're a bloody dream."

Unlike the boys I'd been with in the past, he knew exactly how to pleasure me. There was no fumbling to find my clit, and he wrapped his hand around my throat and held on tight. I'd never even read about that kind of thing in a book, but in that moment, the move felt exactly right. He manhandled me and kissed me softly at the same time.

When we returned to the table, Brian barked out a laugh at the red lipstick that stained our faces. Maybe I should have been embarrassed, and maybe I would have been, but Brian's next words wiped any doubt from my mind.

"Congrats, Sul. You finally got the girl."

Months later, I asked Brian what he meant by that.

He shook his head, a big smile on his face. *"If you can't see that Sully's been crazy about you since day one, I don't know what to tell ya."*

I look at my husband now, catching him watching me, clocking my reaction to the scene in front of us, and hear Brian's words all over again.

"Ah, if it isn't the man of the hour." The bartender rounds the bar and holds a hand out to Sully. "Everyone's loving the karaoke idea. There's a table up front reserved for you, just like you requested."

Sully shakes his hand and then follows him toward the makeshift stage.

The bar is more crowded than normal, but from our prime spot, we get to witness everyone's embarrassing renditions of their favorite songs.

The karaoke machine is smallish. It's nothing like the equipment bars in New York would set up for nights like this. But after the bartender's comment when we came in, I'm certain it's Sully's doing. He probably ordered the damn thing online.

His thoughtfulness leaves me slightly dizzy and filled with lust.

With the crowd they're garnering, it might be beneficial for the bar to invest in a nicer sound system to keep this up. If they did, I'd be here every week. At least until our time in Jersey is over.

I may be getting bigger by the day and I may not be able to drink, but this is my kind of entertainment.

"So who's singing first?" Lo eyes each one of us, practically bouncing in her seat. I think she might be as excited as I am.

"I've always wanted to sing one of those boy band songs," Cal says. "Like 'I Want It to Be Me.'"

Lo frowns, her brow furrowing. "That doesn't sound right."

He hums a sort of familiar tune and holds out both hands, doing a motion that looks like it's part of the chicken dance. Or, on second thought, maybe it's *NSYNC's "Bye Bye Bye" dance.

"Oh!" I clap, sitting straighter. "He combined *It's Gonna Be Me* and *I Want You Back*. They're by two different bands, Cal."

"Which one is the bouncing up and down with the hands song?"

"That'd be *Bye Bye Bye*," Lo tells him before hopping up and darting to the karaoke signup sheet.

"You going to sing with him?" I ask Sully.

With a smirk, he tugs my chair closer, only stopping when I'm wedged between his legs. He drapes an arm around me and places his free hand over mine on the table. "You know how I like to sing at karaoke."

God, and I do. Always like this. His lips pressed to my ear, the words a rasp between us.

I lean into him. And into the memories this action conjures. Memories that span almost two decades.

The guy manning the machine cues up a song and takes the mic himself. Then, with a nod to Sully, he breaks into a rendition of "All the Way" by Frank Sinatra.

Goose bumps erupt across my arms, and my heart flutters. It's the song we danced to on the night we got married. When we got home from our little reception and realized we hadn't danced once, Sully held me close and twirled me around the kitchen slowly, singing it in my ear.

I'd forgotten about that. How is that possible? Though my heart aches at that realization, it quickly lifts when it hits me that Sully didn't.

The dive bar and everyone in it fade away, and I'm taken back to that little apartment in the West End. Our parents hated it, which only made us love it more. As I look into my husband's eyes, I find a kaleidoscope of memories reflected there. Lazy Saturdays in bed. Late nights with a bottle of wine between us. Urgent, needy kisses. Achy limbs and swollen lips. Sweaty bodies pressed together against the couch, or the counter, or the wall.

My nipples are hard as he dips in close and mumbles the words of the song against my heated skin.

"Sully," I whisper. I'm slick with want and so, so needy. Turning, I bring my lips to his so he's now singing the lyrics against my mouth.

His eyes light up, his expression knowing. I don't have to tell him what I want. He already knows. Just like all those years ago, my husband can read my every cue.

"Does my wife need something?" he asks quietly, dropping a hand to my knee.

My body bows into his and I whimper. "You. Now. Please."

With a grin, he pulls back. "Lead the way."

We stand together, somewhat abruptly, doing a terrible job of sneaking out.

I'm already eyeing the back hallway when I reach for Sully's hand and drag him with me.

"Let's go across the street to the office," Sully says when I open a closet door, only to be hit with a smell that almost makes me gag.

"No, need you now." Not bad enough to get it on in there, though that doesn't deter me from my mission.

We may be older, and we may be parents, but we're still those two people who couldn't wait another minute, so the second I find an empty closet that doesn't stink, I pull my husband inside and push him up against the door. As I slam my mouth to his, it's like the last little puzzle piece clicking into place. The ferocity with which we kiss and the strength of his fingers as they dig into my hips remind me that this man is the only person I've ever wanted in this way.

It's like coming home. Like clicking the lock and finally feeling safe after a long, stressful day.

I sink into this kiss and revel in the feeling of us.

When Sully whispers, "Turn around, I need to fuck my wife right bloody now," his voice gruff, I know he's finally snapped too.

For months, he's let me lead. He's checked in. But he's done asking me what I want. He's giving us both what we need. And god, this may be the hottest moment of my life.

As I spin, he undoes his belt, the buckle clinking. The sound is followed by the familiar trill of his zipper lowering. He presses his hot body against mine and hikes up my dress before pulling down my underwear. Then, in one long thrust, he enters me.

Legs shaking, I palm the wall to keep myself upright. Every time Sully enters me, it feels like the first time. His presence is all-encompassing, his body attuned to mine. It's not just his size; it's the way he takes me. *All of me.*

Wrapping an arm around my front, he palms one breast. As he tweaks my nipple through the material of my dress, he snakes his other hand along my hip and puts pressure where I need him most. He rolls my clit between his fingers as he thrusts, all the while whispering dirty promises in my ear.

"You're my fucking wife," he grits out. "My dirty girl loves to get fucked in public. You like how my cock feels dragging through you, don't you? That's right, squeeze me. Right fucking there. Bloody hell, I'm losing my fucking mind. I need you to come. I'm not gonna last."

Stars dance behind my eyelids and blood whooshes in my ears as my own orgasm barrels down on me.

"You like that. You want me to come in this hot pussy. Want me to fill you up again and again."

That's all it takes to send me over the edge.

As I tumble, a shuddering, sweaty mess, he mumbles, "Yes, sweetheart. Fuck, you're so perfect, squeezing my cock like that. God, I love you."

I drop my head back against his chest as we both come down, our breaths loud in the confined space. I commit this moment to memory, set on remembering every detail so I can replay it later.

Sully kisses my cheek, and when I arch back to look at him, he presses his mouth to mine. "Are you okay?"

I laugh against his lips. "Bloody perfect."

"You're bloody perfect," he says, burying his face in my hair. "But this cupboard is empty. There's nothing here to clean you up with."

I waggle my brows. "Looks like I'll be walking around tonight as a marked woman."

Cursing, he pulls out of me. Then he helps me right my underwear and tugs my dress over my ass.

I wrap my arms around his middle and hug him tight. "Thank you for tonight."

A content sigh escapes him. "A thousand todays would never be enough."

I close my eyes and rest my head against his steady heart. Because he's right.

But I'm excited to have as many of them with this man as I can get.

CHAPTER 31
Sully

Blue or pink.

On the bed, two shirts are laid out. One blue, one pink.

Today is the day we find out whether we're having a little girl or another little man. My crazy-arse brother was set on having T-shirts made, one sporting *Team Blue* and the other *Team Pink*.

I would have gone along with it, but Sloane didn't love the idea of wearing a T-shirt, so instead I had buttons made and told everyone to wear their team color. Hopefully everyone in this bloody flat did. I'm still debating between the powder blue and the pale pink polo.

I had the doctor write the baby's gender on two slips of paper and seal them in envelopes, then I took one to the bakery down the road and had them make a cupcake filled with either blue or pink frosting, depending on the single word on that piece of paper, for T. J. to snack on during the ultrasound. With any luck, it'll save us from having to explain the whole lack of a penis in front of an ultrasound tech. Knowing T.J., he will have many questions, and there will be no filter.

Until this week, I never imagined I could be as over-the-top as my brother, but here I am. I took the second envelope to the florist and ordered a massive bouquet of either blue flowers or pink and arranged to have it delivered to Sloane this afternoon.

It might be a lot, but I just want everything to be perfect for today. Including the health of the baby and my wife. I refuse to even think about preeclampsia or losing her. Not when this pregnancy had been going so well.

As I eye the shirts again, a phrase I've been hearing a lot floats through my head. *Don't doubt a mother's intuition.* Sloane is sure this is a baby boy. So sure that she has already started a list of potential boy names starting with *T*. Regardless of gender, we're sticking with a *T* name to go with T.J. Since Sloane and I both have *S* names, it's fitting. Can't say I love Tristan, but it's currently her favorite.

My eyes drift back to the pink polo. I cannot erase the image of a dark-haired little girl with Sloane's blue eyes and smile from my mind. So, I might be wrong, but I'm going pink.

I slip the polo over my head and wander out to the kitchen, trying not to second-guess my choice. The last thing I want is for Sloane to think I don't trust her.

Cal's eyes narrow at me the second he sees my shirt. "Blue." He points to his navy pants, blue dress shirt and blue striped tie. "Blue," he repeats, pointing to the two buttons he's pinned to his chest, one on each side of his tie. "Even Fuzzy understands." He nods toward his cat, who's batting at himself, trying to dislodge the massive blue bow someone—*probably Cal*—put around his neck.

I sigh. We had a conversation about the risks of going against Sloane's intuition. I'm not against Sloane in any way. She's probably right, and I will be thrilled with another son. But I can't help the way my heart tugs at the thought of a baby girl.

Frowning, he flings a hand toward his girlfriend. "She got the memo."

Lo scoffs. "I think it's a girl, but I don't do pink. So." She gestures to her dress. "Navy it is."

Brian hardly looks up from his laptop, where he's probably

reading the *Wall Street Journal* like he does every morning as he leans to the left, showing off his team blue button and matching tie.

Before I can respond, T.J. races out of his room in a Superman T-shirt. "Team Blue!" he announces with a fist pump. "Baby brother, here I come."

"Murph." Cal frowns, craning his neck.

When I get a look at my nephew, the betrayal in my brother's tone makes sense. Murphy is sporting a skateboarding shirt with a sunset painted in oranges and pinks.

"Well." He rocks back on his little feet and tucks his hands into the pockets of his pants, looking so much like his dad. "I know you said not to upset Aunt Sloane, but I think she's wrong." His forehead scrunches a bit. "Plus." He squints at my son, who is running around the room, arms spread wide like he's an airplane, chasing Dammit. "I think one T.J. is enough for this family."

Brian chokes on a cough; I can't help but smile.

A throat clears softly, then my wife appears at the end of the hall. Her bright blue sweater matches her eyes and her face is glowing, making her look even more beautiful than she normally does.

"Pink, huh?" She steps up and wraps an arm around my waist.

"I'm not itching for a row. I swear—" I stammer.

She lifts a finger to my lips, silencing me. "I might be feeling boy," she whispers, a soft smile twitching at her lips. "But I hope you're right."

"Just to make it interesting," Cal pipes in. "Let's make a bet. Losing team cleans the—"

Lo growls.

Cal whips toward her. "Losing males. Not you," he promises with his token pretty boy smirk. When she rolls her eyes, he turns back to me. "The losing males clean the bathroom for a month."

Sloane's answering giggle sells me on the idea instantly. "Sure," I agree. "But if we don't go now, we'll be late."

"You'll text as soon as you know, right?" Lo reminds my wife.

"Come on, T.J." I snag the bakery box off the counter and herd my family out of the flat.

"If I put this here, you'll hold it right, bud?" I ask as I set the small box on the seat next to him.

"We can strap it in." T.J. pulls the belt around the little box, causing the cardboard to crush a little.

I wince, but I bite my tongue. The damage won't change the taste, and that's all that matters. That and the gender reveal part.

"Yoo-hoo!" Madame E calls. "So excited for the big day!"

I turn and give her a small wave. "We are."

She stops in front of me and surveys my button. "I always knew you were an intuitive one, Sullivan. While the rest of your crew walks around sporting all that team blue silliness, you and I clearly know it's a baby girl."

Sloane freezes halfway into the front seat and darts a look at Madame E. "What?"

No, no, no. I see it on Sloane's face. If Madame E confirms it, then she'll believe her. And I have a plan.

"No—"

Before I can shut her down, our resident psychic predicts the future. "Yes, a little baby girl. I've been seeing her for a while now. And I love the name. Tia H—"

"Don't." I cut her off, looking desperately to my wife, whose lips are pursed like she's fighting a smile.

"Oh, yes," Madame E responds, her voice fading as she moves to her tiny car. "Maybe you haven't picked it yet, and oh, how fun the surprise will be."

Bloody hell. *Now* she realizes we might want a surprise?

I turn back to Sloane, who's fully seated in the passenger seat, giggling, and close her door.

"Did she say it's a girl?" T.J. asks his mum, his voice loud enough to be heard outside the car. "Does that mean we don't have to go to this boring doctor thing?" he asks as I climb in.

"What?" I ask.

Sloane shrugs. "We know it's a girl now."

I suck in a breath. "We bloody well don't. We aren't just taking her word for it." Yes, the woman might make clever guesses from time to time, but I'm not taking her word when it comes to such a big detail.

"I'm not eating a pink cupcake." T.J. huffs. "Pink is gross."

Great. I rub a hand down my face. There goes my perfect day.

"We're still going, Sully." Sloane pats my leg. "This is also an anatomy scan."

"We don't know—" I stop myself. It's pointless. I can see in my wife's eyes that she already knows. Frankly, who the hell am I to doubt Madame E? She's annoyingly accurate.

The appointment turns into a chore rather than an exciting experience. T. J. fidgets through the scan, and we tossed the cupcakes—yes, plural; in case Sloane had a craving for something sweet—on the way in, because according to our son, no one eats pink cupcakes.

Although the tech confirms that we're having a healthy baby girl, the blood pressure reading the nurse said aloud as she documented put a damper on my excitement. It's still well within a healthy range, but it's higher than the last time we were here. The doctor might not be worried, but that doesn't stop my own concern for the love of my life.

"Can we go to Extreme Energy?" T.J. asks on our way out.

"Might not be a bad idea. Burn off some of his energy?" Sloane suggests.

The indoor playground with the ninja warrior course is on the way home and does wonders for wearing him out. So I begrudgingly agree. This way, at least one of us will be happy.

We're hardly in the door before T.J. is scampering up the rope nets hanging above the ball pit. Less enthusiastically, Sloane and I make our way to a table and I help her sit.

"I'm sorry today didn't go the way you wanted." Sloane rubs her round tummy as she watches the throng of kids playing in front of us. "Your efforts didn't go unnoticed, and I'm still excited."

"Sloane." I place my hand over hers. "I wanted today to be special. I wanted you to know how much you and our family mean to me. But that doesn't mean I'm not over the moon about our little girl."

That image from this morning reappears, and a lump lodges itself in my throat.

"A little girl with your eyes, and your sense of humor and your smile."

Sloane's eyes glisten with unshed tears. "As long as she has your heart."

I give her hand a squeeze.

"I do like the name Tia," she muses.

"Tia Hope." I nod. "Because this little girl is the reason I finally have hope. Hope for myself. Hope for us. Hope for our future."

With a dip of her chin, she sinks her teeth into her bottom lip. "Tia Hope Murphy."

She leans toward me but just as our lips meet, our son screams. "Help me, Daddy!"

I yank back and scan the room. When I don't find him immediately, I jump out of the chair and rush toward the climbing area.

"I'm up here!" he announces from somewhere above me.

I tip my head up toward the top of the structure but I don't see him. Frantically, I look a bit higher on the poles that hold the ropes.

"No, I'm up here," T. J. repeats.

I look higher into the rafters and find him sitting far above the nets, on what looks like an AC vent.

"How in the bloody hell..." I scan the room, finding the yellow ladder-like structures that lead up to metal scaffolding that probably holds the entire climbing gym together. Above that are the rafters and the vents. My son, who never thinks anything through, clearly just kept climbing.

I shake my head.

"I'll get the little Superman," I assure Sloane.

"Of course you will. You're Super Daddy," she says.

"Not super but trying," I remind her.

"Better Daddy."

Her words bring back that lump in my throat. That's what I'm desperate to be. Better for her. Better for our kids.

Since I'm quite a bit larger than my six-year-old, it takes time and maneuvering to fit myself up through the ropes and rafters to get to him. It takes twice as long to get down with him clinging to me like a baby monkey. Add in the traffic getting back over the bridge into Jersey, and it's dinnertime by the time we make it back to the flat.

"Where have you all been?" Cal asks the second we're through the door.

"We were at Extreme Energy," T. J. explains, conveniently leaving out his adventure into the rafters.

"That's it." Cal snaps his fingers. "It's the perfect place for Murphy's party. Come celebrate Murphy turning seven with the best climby timey ever!"

Sloane groans, though the sound is cut off when she notices the massive bouquet of pink flowers on the Ping-Pong table.

"They came for you a few hours ago. Along with a card." Lo plucks it out of the bouquet. "I swear, even I swooned."

I scowl. I didn't mean for her to see it.

"I don't know whether these will be blue or pink yet," she reads, "but I know he or she will be perfect because they are ours. I hope you enjoyed our special day. A thousand todays would never be enough. Love Sully."

Sloane takes the card out of Lo's hand and tucks it against her chest. Maybe today didn't turn out the way I wanted, but seeing the smile on Sloane's face makes it feel perfect anyway.

CHAPTER 32
Sloane

Giggling, I lean back in my office chair. Cal has already been dropping hints about knocking Lo up, and she doesn't find them amusing. My smile falters when I spot Will in my doorway, watching me.

Unease washes over me as I set my phone on my desk. "Hey." I try keeping my tone casual. "What can I do for you?"

He doesn't make a move to enter. "I thought maybe we could grab lunch. Go over what we talked about two weeks ago."

It's wild how quickly time has passed since he laid out his intentions. It's even more odd that I've been able to mostly forget about that dinner since karaoke night.

Ignorance has been bliss.

Sully and his many dates have kept me busy. Last night, we took T.J. and Murphy to a diner so Cal and Lo could have a kid-free evening. Sully and I shared a vanilla milkshake and French fries while the boys played Pac-Man. It was oddly reminiscent of the night we made our baby girl. Though this time I didn't shoot daggers at him. Instead, we discussed plans for a vacation he'd been thinking we should take before the baby arrives. Our last one as a family of three.

He suggested Disney, and I almost walloped him. After making sure T.J. was nowhere in sight, I agreed to Florida. Warm weather and my husband in swim trunks? Sign me up.

Just thinking of the water sluicing down his hard chest has me licking my lips.

"Sloane?"

I blink, and Will's frame materializes in front of me again—not my very hot, very naked husband. I jolt forward as realization dawns, banging my knee against my desk. "Sorry, yes. What were you saying?"

He chuckles, like my forgetfulness is adorable and finally steps inside. "I was saying I'd like to take you to lunch." He dips his head a little, and his tone goes raspy. "On a date."

I shake my head immediately, like Sully is standing beside me, palms pressed to my cheeks, moving my head from side to side. Then, in solidarity with my husband's spirit, I grasp my stomach, reminding the man that I'm not only married, but I'm pregnant.

"I'm happy to meet with you to go over cases, but I'd prefer to do that in the office."

He raises his brows, almost like he's surprised that I'd say no. "That's how you want to play this?"

"I'm married, Will. And I intend to stay that way."

With a shake of his head, he slips his hands into his pockets. "He's going to disappoint you again."

My chest pinches with a sense of fear that he might be right, but I close my eyes, fighting against the sensation. I'm choosing to trust my husband, but that doesn't mean I'm doing it blindly. What we're doing requires making choices daily, and I'm aware that it won't always be as easy as today is. "If you have nothing else to discuss..." I say through gritted teeth.

With a disappointed sigh, he turns and stalks toward the door. "There's a mediation statement due on the Simpson case first thing tomorrow," he says over his shoulder. "I'd like it on my desk by six p.m."

As he disappears, I'm left with my jaw hanging open. I've never even heard of the Simpson case. *That dick.* It's one thing to expect me to get my own work done in a timely manner, but by doing this, he's going out of his way to set me up for failure.

Tears burn at the backs of my eyes, but I take deep breaths, staving them off. There's no sense in getting emotional. If I have any chance of completing the work on time, I'd better get a hold of that file now.

I send Julius off to find it, and when he returns with two Redwelds in his arms, he looks completely confused. "When does this statement need to be complete?"

He hands me one file and drops the second one on the corner of my desk.

I sigh. "Will wants it on his desk by six."

"Tonight?" His voice is high-pitched, like he's been kicked between the thighs.

"Yeah, he's being difficult, but this isn't too bad. I'll look through the case notes first and get the associate who worked on it to fill me in on the important stuff."

He shakes his head. "This is just the case notes. This divorce has been going on for five years. There are three drawers full of financials alone. It has its own cabinet."

My stomach sinks as I slump in my chair. Will really is setting things up so he can let me go, just like I imagined he would if I turned him down.

Shit.

"What did you do to piss him off?" Julius asks.

I blow out a breath. "Turned down his advances."

"What. The. Fuck?" he says, every word dripping with dramatic flair.

I nod slowly, my mind whirling. I always thought Will and I were friends. I thought Sully's disdain of him was unwarranted and that the guy was mostly harmless.

Boy, did I underestimate him.

"He's going to fire me. I've been a disaster since I found out about the baby. He said he could let that slide if I agreed to give us a go, but if not—" I settle my hands on my stomach again, like I can protect Tia from hearing any of this.

Julius paces the office. "First of all, fuck him."

I nod.

"Second, they can't fire you because you're pregnant."

"No, but they can fire me for not doing my job." Will found a workaround. And I'll have to deal with the consequences.

My assistant whips around and paces back. "No, I mean they can't fire you *because* you're pregnant. It's a lawsuit waiting to happen. Document it, baby. March down to Will's daddy's office and tell him that you're pregnant. Tell him what that weasel of a son is trying to do. *Document it.*"

For as much as I don't believe pregnancy should be used as a weapon, that goes both ways. And if I'm going down, I might as well go down swinging.

I push my chair back and stand. "You're right."

With a grin, he pulls on his lapels. "Of course I'm right. And when you eventually leave this firm in the dust, make sure you take me with you, baby mama."

Snorting, I pat him on the shoulder and head for the door. "Then you'd have to work with baby daddy, and I know you aren't a fan of his nickname for you."

Julius grins. "Eh, baby daddy is hot when he goes all smoldery and calls me Caesar. I could dig it."

I'm still smiling when I hit Will Sr.'s door.

But as the implication of those last comments hits me, it slides off my face. I may have joked about returning to Sully's firm, and I know they'd take me in a heartbeat, but I'm not quite ready to give up on a career set apart from that safety net. So I straighten my shoulders and prepare to fight for my right to make that choice.

I don't want to go back to Murphy and Machon by default. If I do eventually return, I want it to be because they really want me there. Because I really want to be there myself. Right now, I'm not sure that's the case.

Working on our marriage is vital, and I don't know that jumping back into working together would be helpful.

I knock, and when I'm greeted by a loud *"Come in,"* I push the door open.

Will Sr.'s office reminds me a lot of Terry's old one. Actually, the man himself reminds me of Terry. He's larger-than-life, which is probably a necessity if one wants to run a firm that bills tens of millions of dollars a year. Though Terry extremely handsome and charming, whereas, Will Sr. has a round face, barely any gray hair left on his head, and a protruding gut.

He smiles and stands when he sees me. "Sloane, to what do I owe the pleasure?"

I sit in the chair across from him and get to the point. "I actually wanted to discuss my role at the firm now that I'm pregnant. I understand that you only hired me because of Will—"

"Who said that?" He leans forward, wearing a baffled frown. "When I heard from your mother that you were looking for a job, I told Will to reach out. I wanted to bring you on because of your trust knowledge. Especially the special needs trusts. As you know, few people are dedicated to the niche, and we have many clients who need consults. It's a growing market and not many understand the nuances. But Will told me you wanted to focus on litigation. Either way, I was happy to bring you on. I knew you'd be a great fit no matter where we put you."

My heart stutters to a stop. *What?* My mother was the one shopping jobs for me? I truly thought Will's timing was kismet.

To find out my mother put them up to it is less than appealing. But I'm more than thrilled that Will Sr. was interested in my skills, and not my relationship with his son.

"I had no idea," I admit.

Sighing, he leans forward. "My son has been interested in you for quite a long time, though I've always believed him to be respectful. If he's done anything to make you uncomfortable—"

I shake my head. I don't want to get into that right now. "Is the trust position still available?"

He sits back, surprised. "Yes. There are still very few people who know much about that area of the law."

"I'm a little rusty," I admit. "But I would love to get up to speed and help."

Will Sr. smiles. "I'd love that as well."

I nod, relief rushing through me. "Thank you, Mr. Higgins."

"Congrats on the baby. Nothing is more important than family. I hope you and Sully enjoy this special time."

I walk out of his office in a daze. Did I really just get everything I wanted?

CHAPTER 33

Sully

Bassinet, mini crib, co-sleeper. There are so many options even for our small space.

The idea of having Tia in the bed with us makes me a bit on edge, especially with Sloane's sleep-undressing habits, so I'm leaning more toward a bassinet. Though I worry she'll outgrow it too quickly. So maybe a mini crib is best.

"What do you think?"

Brian's voice pulls me from my thoughts. Blinking, I look from my computer screen. Right. We're in the middle of a meeting.

Cal kicks his feet up on the conference room table and tosses his mini basketball into the air, clearly leaving me to answer.

Unfortunately, I don't know what the question was so I go with the one that would work in just about any situation.

"I trust you." At least it's the truth.

Brian bows his head, closes his eyes, and sighs.

Lo giggles. "*Someone seems distracted,*" she sings. "Let's try again. The question was, should you or Cal take on the Sonesta matter."

Without warning, the orange ball that raises my blood pressure upon sight bounces off my head.

"Pay attention," Cal teases.

"Oh." I rub my forehead. "Sorry. I was considering the best type of baby furniture for our room. Sloane's been so busy at work, so I figured I'd handle it on my own. Thought I'd surprise her. But what the bloody hell do I know about baby furniture?"

With T.J., Sloane made all the choices, and I just nodded and accepted each one.

Lo's face softens as she reaches for my laptop. "Let me see." She tips her head to the side and pulls her hair over her shoulder as she studies the options I have pulled up. "Ooh. I love this one. The white would be so cute with pink bedding."

"White lace itches."

At the sound of Madame E's voice, we all straighten.

"Amy!" Brian calls. "You're supposed to let us know when guests come in." He fiddles with the walkie-talkie beside him, ensuring it's turned on, and grumbles, "We're in the middle of a partner meeting."

The walkie-talkie crackles before Amy's voice comes on the other end. "Meeting? What meeting? I just transferred a call from the court to Sully. He's not in his office?"

Bloody hell. I rub a hand over my face.

"No, Amy." Brian grits out. "We told you we're having a partner's meeting and you were to hold our calls."

"Huh. Don't remember that. That's so weird." I can picture the shoulder shrug that came with the words.

Lo growls.

Madame E waves her hands. "You're missing a partner, and if you don't act quickly, someone else will make her theirs."

"Oh, is that a riddle?" Cal drops his feet and straightens. Then he nails me in the head with the ball again.

"Bollocks." I heave forward to snatch it and give him a taste of his own medicine, but the bugger is faster and scoops it up before I can.

"Pay attention," he tells me. "Madame E, is that a riddle?"

She sighs wearily. "They aren't riddles, Callahan. They're my visions."

"Yup, visions of the future," Lo tilts her head. "So this is about Sloane, I'm guessing."

Unease hits me as I turn to Madame E again. "Say it again. Who is going to make Sloane theirs?"

Brian shakes his head. "She means we need to make her a partner, right?"

With a smile, Madame E spins and strides out. "I only see what I see."

Lo squints at the now-empty doorway. "Did she come in here just to say that?"

My brother, who's already leaned back in his chair with his feet on the table again, tosses the ball back into the air over his head. "Bet it was about Sloane and Will."

My spine snaps straight. My arch nemesis's name and my wife's should never be uttered in the same sentence.

"No," Lo says evenly. "I don't think that's a thing. Sloaney was pissed after their date last week."

My heart lurches, and I lunge forward; the chair beneath me catches on the hideous carpet as it scoots back. "Their what?"

All the color drains from Lo's face. "She never told you."

I push myself out of my chair, and on shaky legs, head for the door. No, my wife did not tell me that she went on a date with Will Fucking Higgins. And last week? Last week I was fucking her in a barroom closet. I've held her every night this week. We took our son out to celebrate when we found out our baby is a girl. We picked a name for our child. And my wife never bothered to mention that she was dating someone else.

My brother grabs me by the arm before I can reach the conference room door and yanks me back. "Don't do it."

"Don't do what?" I grit out.

"Don't go storming into her office and boss her around. If you go in there demanding she can't date anyone but you, it will only end badly." He holds my gaze, his expression full of compassion and understanding.

Fuck. I blow out a breath and pull at my hair. "What do I do, then?"

"Exactly what you were doing. Continue showing her that you're the better option. Go to the store. Get the flat ready for the baby. Be there for her. Don't dictate her life."

"She doesn't want to be with him," Lo says softly, joining me by the door. "She wants to be with you."

My body revolts at the idea of not demanding answers, but bloody hell, they're right.

I slump into my office chair. Just as my arse hits the cushion, my mobile chimes in my pocket.

Sloane: Hi, you don't have to pick me up tonight. I've got another late-night dinner with a client, so I'll just stay in the city.

My heart plummets.

"What?" Lo asks, peering down at my mobile.

I don't even bother hiding the screen. No, I let the device clatter to the table.

She hisses in a breath. "It's not what you think. I'm sure of it."

But even she doesn't sound sure.

Still, I do what my brother says.

> Me: Okay, sweetheart. If you need anything, just let me know.

CHAPTER 34
Sloane

The silence in the penthouse is eerie.

Sure, having my own bathroom with an actual tub is nice. As is the freedom to pull off my bra when I walk in the door. But I guess I've gotten used to all the noise. I miss the sound of the boys playing Legos after dinner. And one of my favorite parts of the day is settling on the couch with Lo, me with a cup of tea and her with a glass of red wine. Also, Ping-Pong has become strangely entertaining. Mostly because Cal can't resist hitting Sully in the head with the ball repeatedly. As chaotic as the small apartment is, I miss it more than I imagined I could. Even if I'm only away for tonight.

All day, I warred with myself over whether I should stay here or go home. My heart urged me to go home, but I needed the peace the penthouse offers so I could study up on the three new cases Will Sr. had given me.

Before filing for divorce, that's what I did at Murphy and Machon. Easing into estate law after maternity leave was simple since the work was mostly handled outside of court. I could do it after T.J. went to bed so long as Sully could manage T.J. when I had to meet with clients.

Truthfully, Lo was the one to watch him because Sully's career was always more important. He had more going on. He was a partner. He had court.

To a degree, I understood. Even if I hadn't, there was no changing Sully's ways.

At least the old Sully's. The new Sully? He's surprised me with his patience and care and thoughtfulness every day. He's surprised me by putting me and our son before his work time and again.

And for the time being, T.J. is in school, giving Sully and me equal opportunity to invest in our careers. We'll have to figure something out after Tia is born, though.

Rubbing my belly, I lie back in bed and talk to our girl. I can't wait to meet her. Can't wait to see what she looks like. Who she looks like.

After a moment, I force myself to focus again on the computer screen in front of me. Or I try to. It's late, and the words are all blurring together. I've been working for far too long, but every time I remember how eager Mr. Higgins was to move me to trust law, a zing of energy courses through me, giving me the motivation I need to make it a little farther.

Just as that boost of energy begins to wane, my stomach flutters and I freeze. Chin tipped, I stare at my rounded belly and will her to do it again. Tia's been very lazy, unlike her brother, who I could feel doing gymnastics in there at fifteen weeks. Maybe that means she'll be a more laid-back child.

God, one could wish.

When that magical bubbly dance reappears, I splay my hand over my stomach and drop my head back, laughing. God, that feels good. I've spent most of this pregnancy worrying about what could go wrong. Yet this moment feels nothing but right.

I pick up my phone, wishing I were home so I could share this moment with Sully.

Home. Did I really just call the apartment in Jersey home?

My heart stumbles a little at the thought.

And even more so when I realize the answer. Home is wherever Sully and T.J. are. And right now, they're in Jersey.

> Me: Hey, call me after you get T. J. to bed. I just felt Tia move…and I miss you.

The dots don't even dance on the screen before a message appears.

> Sully: On my way.

> Me: Sully, it's late. It would be silly to drive all this way. I'll see you tomorrow. I was just missing you and wanted you to know it.

I've barely set the phone down when there's a knock on the door. *What the hell?*

I set the computer on the bed and pad to the entryway, and I'm only a little surprised when Sully's face greets me on the other side of the peephole. I throw the door open quickly, excitement coursing through me. In a sweater and a pair of jeans, he looks utterly delicious. But it's the smile on his face that makes my stomach flip.

"Has she done it again?" he asks as he sets a brown bag on the table in the foyer.

"Not yet, but what are you doing here?" I ask as he wraps his arms around me.

The feel of him pressed up against me sends emotions flooding my system. The smell of him, the hardness of his chest, and the comforting warmth emanating from him pummel into me, overwhelming me in the best of ways.

He dips his head into my shoulder and breathes me in. With a kiss to my neck, he murmurs, "I missed you too much."

I peek up at him. "T.J.?"

"Was excited for spaghetti night with Cal. They put butcher paper down on the table and dropped the spaghetti and sauce and meatballs directly onto it. They were eating with their hands when I left." He scowls.

Laughter bubbles out of me. "Oh my god, that must have driven you crazy."

He chuckles. "Yes, sweetheart." With one arm still banded around me, he snags the paper bag and leads me inside.

"No wonder you came to the city for dinner." I chance a glance at him quickly to see his reaction, because something tells me that wasn't what he was doing.

He rolls his eyes. "Right. No wonder."

"So whatcha got there?" I ask, pointing to the bag.

He gives me a sexy as hell smirk. "Cheesecake from Paulo's."

Mouth watering, I reach for the bag. "Seriously?"

He laughs. "Kitchen or bed?"

"Totally eating in bed."

"I'll grab the utensils. You go pick a movie," he tells me, heading for the kitchen.

I practically skip into our bedroom, grinning like a fool, only to pull up short at the sight of my computer.

With only a second's hesitation, I shut it and move it to the night-stand. My excitement over Sully's surprise far eclipses any excitement I had over the new job.

When Sully walks in, I'm cozy under the covers, propped up by a mountain of pillows, with the to-go container set between our spots.

"What did you pick?" Sully eyes the TV with an easy expression.

He doesn't care what I put on. He rarely stays awake for an entire movie. If he's not planning to stay in the city tonight, he'll have to, I guess, but my goal, I've already decided, is to lure him into spending the night here.

"*Top Gun*," I tell him.

He grins. "Your favorite."

I shake my head. It's not, but I've never admitted to the lie. Years ago, he and Brian watched it all the time, and since I just wanted to hang out with him, I told them it was my favorite.

Not only was I desperate for time with him, even before we were dating, but anything was better than sitting in my apartment by myself. I grew up in a quiet home where my parents emphasized studying over friendships. In law school, most people I met were the same way, but Sully was more relaxed, and over time, he convinced Brian to let up a little too. Rather than studying at the library, they would invite me back to their apartment, where we'd break up study sessions with drinks and movies and joking around. We still aced exams because Brian and I were overachievers, and despite Sully's skate-by mentality, he was really freaking sharp.

I smile at the memory. We used to have so much fun. During our first few years at the firm, we'd work hard and party even harder at night. What we were doing now didn't resemble that kind of partying, but we'd reverted back to that in a way now that we were all in Jersey. Our nights were full of Ping-Pong tournaments and dance parties and anything else ridiculous Cal came up with. And the rest of the crew still worked hard together all day before drifting upstairs for the night. My stomach twists a little at the thought. Though I love our evenings, I'm missing out on all that time with them during the workday now that I'm stuck working for Will.

Ugh.

Sully steps up to the edge of the bed, his eyes narrowed on me. "What's wrong? Is the smell of the cheesecake bothering you?"

Slumping, I shake my head. "No. It smells delicious."

"Then why the frowny-upside-downy?" He waggles his brows.

I snort out a laugh. "Did you just do a Cal-ism?"

"I'll do anything to make you smile." He hands me a spoon and then settles beside me. "Now tell me what the frown was about."

I've been hesitant to tell Sully about Will's ultimatum, afraid I'd let his opinions cloud my decision. But I realize now I should have been honest from the beginning. I promised I'd talk to him, yet I've been keeping things bottled up again.

So I tell him everything. How Will tricked me into a date. How he basically blackmailed me, hinting at my job being in jeopardy if I didn't date him. And how, when I finally told him I wasn't interested, he gave me an impossible assignment, knowing I'd fail.

"I'll kill him," Sully grits out when I go quiet. Despite how red in the face he is, not once did he interrupt me or lash out while I explained.

"I'm sorry I didn't tell you sooner."

He rolls his teeth over his bottom lip, his gaze darting away. "Is it because you were considering it?" he finally asks, his voice low.

My heart cracks in two at the uncertainty there. As tears prick at the backs of my eyes, I pull his hand into my lap and shift so I'm facing him completely. With my other hand on his cheek, I duck, waiting for him to look at me. "Not even for a second."

Sully leans into my touch, his eyes closing.

"You have to know there's only ever been you when it comes to my heart." I press his hand to my chest so he can feel the rhythm that only he's ever inspired. It's a few beats faster than resting because I'm always more excitable around him. Sometimes because he's pissing me off, but more often, it's because he's sweeping me off my feet.

He searches my face, his eyes bouncing between mine, like he's looking for the lie.

He won't find one. I just smile at him. "After I told him I wasn't interested, I went to speak to his father, and get this—my mother was the one who got me the job, not Will."

Sully blows out a breath, and when he shakes his head, I drop my hand from his cheek. "Why?"

I shrug. "I don't know. She wasn't happy when she found out about the divorce. My guess is she figured I'd need a job."

Sully's jaw ticks, but he doesn't respond. He and I will never see eye to eye on that subject. Maybe he would have been happy to bankroll my entire life, even after we divorced, but I never would have been okay accepting his money. I worked hard for my law degree, and whether we separated or not, I wanted my career. It was time I found myself again.

"Will Sr. offered me a position in trusts and estates. That's why I stayed in the city tonight. I want to brush up on the cases he assigned me. I'm anxious to start on them and be done with Will for good."

Rather than the relief I expect to see on Sully's face, there's nothing but anger.

"They can't take you out of litigation," he says, his tone low and rough, "just because his slimy kid didn't get what he wants."

I grasp his wrist and smooth my thumb over the inside of it. "I love trusts. It's actually what I like handling the most. I think the idea of litigating was exciting because it was badass. My whole life, that's what I've been told real lawyers do."

My mother's voice and opinions have always been loud in my head, but over the years, I've discovered that I can't dedicate my life to making others happy. I need to make myself happy first. Fill my own cup and all that.

Sully scoffs. "Sloane, you've always been incredible. My father always sang your praises when it came to our trusts and estates."

I let out a long breath. "My mother had me so convinced that the whole lot of you were mommy tracking me, and I let it get into my head. I resented you for it."

Sully's eyes go wide. "What?" Now he's the one grasping my hands. "We knew you were incredible with those clients. And your brain, sweetheart? The things you'd come up with? Brilliant. Brian may be good at estates, but he's nothing like you when it comes to creating relationships with the clients. You and Cal were our front line."

I bite my lip and pick at the comforter. Sully has never said any of this before. I never realized how much they appreciated my work. "Really?"

He nods. "Really."

Feeling more grounded in my decision, I nod. "I'm excited to do it again. Excited for a position that I think will be a better fit than litigation."

"I'm happy if you're happy," he says, his eyes roving over me.

"Know what would make me really happy right now?"

He breaks into a cheeky grin. "Eating your cheesecake?"

"No."

"Definitely that. But also, will you stay with me tonight? Watch this movie with me? Hold me? Just be with me?"

Sully's face lights up. "Nothing would make me happier, sweetheart."

"I think there's a pair of your sweats in the drawer." I tilt to one side and roll myself to my feet in the most unsexy of ways. Crouching, I pull the sweats from the drawer, and just as I stand, Tia does another little dance. "Sully!"

He's at my side in the space of a heartbeat. "What's wrong?"

I snag his hand and guide it to the side of my belly where she's moving. "There's our girl."

Dropping to his knees, Sully lifts my shirt and cradles my belly with both hands, before pressing his mouth to my skin. "Hello, love. It's your daddy."

When she moves again, he lets out a delighted chuckle and his eyes find mine. They shine with hope and so much love. God, is there a lot of love. And in that moment, I know that I don't just have a crush on my husband. It's official: I'm full-blown in love with him.

CHAPTER 35
Sully

I set my alarm for four a.m. so I can be home for when T.J. wakes up but my eyes open at three, my mind still a bloody mess from the night before. On the one hand, I'm thrilled my wife finally told me what was bothering her. Thrilled that she called me and told me she missed me. Thrilled that she asked me to stay in her bed.

But there's this rage bubbling at the seams that I can't seem to quiet.

It's not necessarily directed at Sloane because I understand where she was coming from. Though, I don't love the lies.

Really, I'm angry with myself though. Angry that I put us all into this position to begin with. Angry that another man even had the option to take my wife out on a date because I'd left her available for the taking.

And fucking ravaged that a man put her in that position. That Will Fucking Higgins had the audacity to dangle her career like a fucking carrot in exchange for a relationship with her. It makes me sick how any man could do that. But to have it done to Sloane. I'm seeing bloody crimson.

"Sully." My wife's sweet voice calms me for a moment. I know she isn't awake, she's just talking in her sleep. I have to fold my lips in

to keep from laughing as she jackknifes up and pulls at her tank top. It's the only garment left on her after two bouts of sleep walking resulted in her losing first her pants—which she folded and placed back in the drawer without once actually waking up—and then her panties, which she flung across the room.

The room is dark save for the sliver of moonlight peeking through the curtains, but it's just enough to douse my wife in a beautiful glow as the tank top disappears and her full breasts come into view.

Bloody hell my wife is perfect.

My chest tightens as I think how I almost lost this. Almost lost her.

Sloane doesn't lie back down immediately, she stretches her arms and yawns.

Normally, I don't wake her, but I get slightly nervous when she shifts that she'll fall off the bed, so I wrap an arm around her bare thigh and squeeze. "Sweetheart, come lie back down."

Her eyes seem to focus at the sound of my voice and she blinks twice before shaking her head. "Did I sleep walk?"

I smile up at her. "Almost."

She glances down and finds herself completely nude, then her expression seems to morph into one of delighted surprise. When she raises her eyes, I know exactly what she's thinking. With a suggestive curve of her lips, she beckons me closer. "Almost indeed."

"Do you need something, wife?" I ask, my voice coming out gruff from a hazy need that takes over every other emotion in my brain.

Sloane shifts onto her knees. "You know what I need."

I tighten my fists to keep from reaching for her. Then I slide my palms behind my head. "I'm not sure you've earned it."

Sloane's brows lift in challenge.

Truth is, I'm not sure I can be gentle right now which makes me scared to touch my wife. I want to ravage her. Remind her that she's my wife and no one else's. I want to imprint myself on every inch of her body, mark her, make sure she, and everyone else, knows that she's mine.

"Do you need me to beg?" she husks.

My cock swells, scratching against my boxers, and I blow out a breath as I give a single nod.

Sloane's lips curve up wickedly. "You know I love begging."

I chuckle, because, yes, I do know that. So while this could be considered a punishment to some, with my wife, it's just another way to show her I love her.

That she drives me fucking batty. That I need her in a visceral way that can never be fully explained.

Sloane's slides a hand over her shoulder, down her neck and between her breasts in a seductive show. When she reaches her nipple, she tweaks it and cries out from that simple touch.

My groan is deep. "I love how responsive your tits are when you're pregnant. Your nipples pebble up so fast, just begging for my mouth to play with them."

She licks her lips. "I need that."

I shake my head. She must do a better job at begging than that.

"Just one little lick?" She pleads, crawling toward me, her heavy breasts swaying with her movement. She settles right beside me and then leans over, pressing her tits to my lips.

I'd have to be dead not to lick them. My mouth waters and I give in to my own desire, sucking one of her pebbled nipples into my mouth and then rolling the hard peak between my teeth. Sloane hisses in surprise. "Fuck, yes, don't stop."

I do exactly that though. I pull back to the sounds of her whimpers, knowing she's probably already soaking our bed.

"Please Sully." Her plea is breathy this time as her hand slips between her thighs.

I watch her reach for her clit and then make the split second decision to stop her, grabbing her wrist and holding it there. "No."

I shake my head as the anger resurfaces again. As the need builds, bubbling to the surface. "No, sweetheart. You don't get to touch this pussy because this pussy is mine."

Sloane nods. "It is."

Possessiveness surges in my chest. "Hands on your thighs and don't move," I tell her.

When Sloane settles back and places her palms flat against her legs, I shift so that I can pull down my boxers. My cock springs up, hard and angry. Need courses through me and my jaw flexes as I force myself not to reach for myself to relieve some of the building tension.

My mouth waters as I return my focus to my beautiful wife. She's sitting patiently, watching me, awaiting instruction. I could stare at her like this for hours. The slope of her long neck, the swell of her perfect tits.

But what I really need is the taste of her cunt on my tongue before I slip inside her and fuck her hard and deep, reminding her that she's mine.

"Now sit on my face and don't you dare fucking come," I warn. "This is for me."

Sloane scrambles to straddle me, not hesitating even once to give me what I want. The first hit is ridiculous, she tastes so good I lap at her like she's a delicacy. As I suspected, she's soaked, her pussy swollen and needy. In doesn't take long for Sloane to forget my rules and grind against my face, seeking her own pleasure, but before her pussy starts to quiver between my lips, I dig my hands into her thighs and hold her still. "Not yet," I grind out. I'm just as desperate to taste her orgasm. To feel her pussy flutter around my cock.

"Please Sully," she whines, trying to ride my face.

"Please what?"

"Make me come. Fuck me. Please." She scrambles down my body and tries rolling her hot pussy over my aching length. We both groan the moment she does it, and my tease of a wife knows she's going to get what she wants.

Trying to gain control, I flip us, and push her thighs wide so I can settle between them, making sure not to put too much of my weight on top of her body. I reach for her roaming hands, pinning her wrists above her head, and hover my mouth above her lips. "Patience, wife, I think I need to teach you a lesson first. Remind you that you're *my wife* and no one else's."

She's practically panting now, thrusting up and trying to take control. "I'm sorry, I swear you're the only one I've ever wanted. The only one I ever will."

A warmth floods me at her words.

"Say it again," I taunt, brushing my lips against hers. Even now as I attempt to punish her, I hover above her, protecting both her and our baby.

"You're the only one I want. The only one I need. Please Sully, fuck me." She thrusts up again, rolling her soaked pussy against my thick cock.

The groan that leave my lips echoes between us. "You're so fucking ready." I shift, adjusting my cock into position, then reach between us, so that I can slide my crown in a slow circle against her oversensitive clit. Teasing her. Taunting her.

It's just as much of a tease for me though. My cock is weeping to get inside her.

When she can't take it anymore, she bucks up, crazed, and I slip inside. Her hot cunt hugs my cock tightly, squeezing me, and steals then breath from my lungs. "Oh fuck sweetheart, you're so good. Your pussy is gripping my cock so bloody tight."

Her pussy quivers around me, and I thrust, once, twice, dragging my cock all the way out and then burrowing deep inside her again. Fuck, I can't get deep enough. I want to live inside this woman. Spend my life buried deep within her. "Come on sweetheart, be a good little wife and squeeze me. Come on your husband's cock."

Her head thrashes back and forth and my spine tingles as I hit the spot deep inside her that makes her pulse around me. "Just like that," I growl.

"Yes! Sully! Fuck, right there," she cries as she explodes, pulsing around me. I continue to thrust, milking every ounce of her and my pleasure until I come on a long moan, with my wife's name on my tongue.

I fall to my side, making sure not to crush her, and then pull her into my chest. "Fuck I love you," I murmur, emotion rolling over me in waves.

Sloane burrows into my chest, hugging me tightly. I know she feels it too. I know she loves me too. But fuck, I just wish she'd say it. I'm desperate to hear her say it.

Tugging her hair gently back, I force her gaze to mine. "You're mine Sloane Murphy. My wife. Don't ever go on a date with another man again."

Sloane's eyes soften and she crawls up my chest until she's the one hovering above my lips. "I'm yours, Sully. I'm completely yours."

CHAPTER 36
Sloane

"Yes," I sigh in ecstasy, then tug on my husband's dark hair, holding him in place. This is the best way to be woken up. As I grind up against his face, I use my free hand to tweak my nipple, causing a spark to shoot straight to my core.

He moans in response, like he's enjoying this as much as I am. I'm beginning to think he does, because he's woken me up like this every day this week. Since the night he surprised me in our penthouse things have been nothing short of perfect. I think it's the honesty, and the knowledge that we're both all in, that has taken our relationship to a completely new level.

A different kind of warmth spreads through me. Everything is different with him this time. The intense desire that always exists in Sully's presence is still there, but now I feel cherished. Every touch of his hand, every brush of his lips, is laced with so much more.

He flicks his tongue just the way I like it, then drags his thumb through my arousal and presses inside my ass. I sigh in bliss. I've been so turned on lately, and nothing satiates it. "Gonna fuck this," he says, eyeing me over my small bump.

I thrash beneath him, desperate. "Promises, promises."

With a chuckle, he goes back to playing. When I hit my peak, he drags the sensation out, heightening the pleasure so acutely that I have to smother myself with a pillow to keep from waking the whole house.

I'm still coming down, my breaths still ragged, when he's crawling over me and reaching for the lube in the nightstand drawer. He eyes me as he holds it up, making sure I'm still game.

"You're going to have to cover my mouth," I tell him in answer. If I could barely keep myself quiet when he was simply going down on me, there's no way I'll stay quiet if he fucks my ass.

His eyes go hazy. "Deal." Looming over me, he presses a kiss to my lips. It's meant to be quick, but we get lost in it, tongues tangling, teeth clashing, sucking on lips, and moaning loudly.

Eventually, I fall back, breathless, and he sits up on his knees and uncaps the lube. His cock is so hard it looks angry as it juts between us. "I'm going to—"

The door flies open, hitting the wall, and Cal appears.

My husband falls on top of me, covering me. "What the fuck?"

"My eyes!" Cal screams. "My bloody eyes!"

"Your eyes are bleeding?" T. J. asks from what I'm hoping is a few steps down the hall.

I snort into my husband's shoulder.

He grunts in response. "This isn't funny."

I fold my lips in to stifle my laughter, but another giggle escapes. "I'm sorry, but it really is."

"Why don't we go for a walk?" Lo suggests.

"But his eyes are bleeding. Shouldn't we help him?"

The concern in T.J.'s voice sends me over the edge, and I completely lose it, laughing uncontrollably.

It takes Sully a beat, but eventually he laughs too.

Now that the moment has been interrupted, I'm reminded of the plans I have for today. And they don't include hiding out in this bed for even a minute longer. Poor Sully doesn't know it yet, but he's definitely leaving Jersey with blue balls.

Several hours later, my husband is back to smiling. "I can't believe you pulled this off." He scans the entrance to the stadium like he's memorizing every single detail.

Over the last few months, he's planned date after date, and he's gone out of his way to show me, in big ways and small, that he cares.

Today, I want him to experience a little bit of that magic himself. Also, today is the day I plan to tell him that I really want to give us a shot. That I'm in love with him. And I want to tell T.J. that his parents are back together. I'm ready to stop hiding from the world.

I want to be his wife again. Officially. And I want to do it in an epic way.

"Cal called in a favor for me, since the Metros are playing the Revs today."

The owner of the Boston Revs, Beckett Langfield, is a client of the firm, so I asked Cal if he could get tickets. He did one better, and I'm buzzing with excitement to show Sully the suite. It's the perfect way to propose an end to our separation and the beginning of a new chapter.

My husband's face is lit up like T.J.'s when we take him for donuts. "Remind me to tell Cal he's my favorite brother."

Amusement threads its way through me. "Noted."

With a spin, he dips closer, giving me his full attention. "And you're my favorite wife."

I grin. *That* is why I did this. I pop up on my toes and kiss him. "And you're about to get very lucky, Sullivan Murphy, because we have a suite all to ourselves. How does a baseball game and a blow job sound?"

Even Sully's eyes smile. "Perfect fucking wife."

We make it upstairs, and his joy only grows when he discovers that the suite is stocked with Strongbow, his favorite English beer, and Thatcher's Gold, a cider.

I've also made sure to order the Italian sausages the stadium is known for.

As we settle in our seats, I swear my husband is happier than I've seen him in years. "This is incredible, sweetheart. I really appreciate it."

Cheeks heating, I set a hand on my stomach. "You've done such a good job of taking care of Tia and me, so I wanted to do something special for you."

He stretches out his legs, getting comfortable but also inspiring me to make good on my promise. The man has been more than patient. I won't make him wait any longer.

I've just grabbed a pillow and am about to settle between my husband's thighs when the door to the suite swings open and loud voices reverberate off the walls.

"Sully, my mate!" Beckett Langfield appears with his wife, Liv, by his side.

She offers a quick wave as I scramble up and fiddle with one ear, hoping like hell they believe I was retrieving an earring.

"There it is," I say, my voice high-pitched.

Wide-eyed, Sully looks from me to his client and back again. With his blood all settled in his groin, it takes him a minute to catch up. I kick the pillow out from beneath his chair, praying our guests don't notice.

Unfortunately, Liv is definitely hiding a smile and avoiding eye contact.

Dammit. Me and my hussy hormones really walked us into this one.

Sully stands and adjusts himself discreetly before turning to greet them.

"When Cal mentioned you'd be at the game, I figured a night away with my wife and good friends would hit the spot." Beckett smiles like he'd love nothing more than to spend the day with us.

While I appreciate his graciousness, I really wish we were going to be alone.

"Yes," Liv chimes in. "But if you two would like a few hours alone, we're happy to go sit in the Miller family's suite." She nudges her husband pointedly.

"And miss out on catching up with Sully?" Beckett, clearly oblivious, gives his wife an incredulous look. "I made reservations for the four of us tonight. Wait until you try the steak at this place. Melts like butter."

Liv mouths an "I'm sorry" as Beckett yammers on. It's another hour before Liv convinces Beckett to take a walk with her and we're alone again.

When the door clicks shut behind them, Sully drops his head back and sighs. "Bloody Beckett."

All I can do is laugh. This day has gone completely off the rails, but it has been fun.

"Fuck, I love the sound of your laugh," he says, his blue eyes vibrant thanks to the sun shining down over the stadium and the joy that radiates off him.

And I love you.

I almost say it. I *want* to say it. I'm pretty sure my husband can see how much I want to say it. It's right there on the tip of my tongue, but the words won't budge.

The moment passes, and he blinks.

Dammit.

What is wrong with me? Why didn't I just say it? I'm happy. My husband's happy. I know what I want, and yet, still my tongue feels heavy in my mouth as the words just don't come.

What's it going to take to convince my heart that this feeling isn't just temporary?

CHAPTER 37

Sully

Seven months. My wife is seven bloody months pregnant, and in an hour we're headed to the doctor. If Sloane were forced to deliver, Tia's chances of survival have just gone up immensely.

A hint of relief comes with that knowledge, but mostly, I'm hoping she keeps cooking for many, many more weeks. Sloane had the date circled on her planner, so my plan has been to take her out to lunch at the boathouse, where we held our spur-of-the-moment post-marriage dinner all those years ago, to celebrate. And luck seems to be on my side, since the air has finally begun to turn warm and the April sky is a dull blue rather than gray.

"Psst." Lo peeks her head around the corner out of Murphy's bedroom.

I turn and glance her way giving her a silent what?

"You haven't seen Cal right?" Her eyes dart frantically around and then she pulls the little clear cup of water from behind her back. A bright blue little beta sits about halfway up the cup.

"Another one didn't make it?" I whisper.

Lo sighs. "Bubbles number eight just bit the dust. One to go."

Madame E had told Lo months ago Cal would go through nine of these little guys before one finally stuck. So Lo and Murphy had bought backups and kept them in Murphy's closet.

"Do you find it crazy that you can keep all these fish alive in the cups for months, while my brother can't manage to keep the one in the tank from going belly up?"

"Shhhhh." Lo hisses and she rushes toward Cal's door.

"Lola!" My brother's voice has Lo visibly cringing, but she spins with a bright smile on her face. "What are you doing?"

"Taking bubbles for a walk." She beams.

But my brother frowns as his eyes drop to a new Bubbles who is slightly less bright blue than the last two. I wonder if he is finally going to realize that she has been secretly replacing his fish for months.

"You cannot walk a fish like that."

Although to most people that sounds reasonable, it's bloody ridiculous coming from my brother who has a firm belief in walking down the street with his entire fish tank letting the neighbors stare.

Lo's eyes widen. "Umm." She looks from the fish to me and back again.

My brother scoffs. "Bubbles can't make it in that little guppy cuppy."

I don't bother to fight the laugh. Guppy cuppy. "If you had any idea..."

Lo glares at me quickly before shifting her attention back to her boyfriend. "You're right. I'll put him back."

"That big tank is heavy for you." Cal reaches for the cup. "I'll take it."

"No!" Lo clutches the fish to her chest. "I mean." She thrusts it at me. "Sully will do it." I barely catch the cup before she grabs my brother's neck and spins him to face her. "Because I need a kiss. Like now."

Behind his back she waves me toward the tank and I finally realize that she hasn't disposed of bubbles number eight yet.

My clueless brother smirks. "Whatever Lola wants..." And he

presses his lips to hers. I try not to groan as I step past the couple into their bedroom.

It takes less than a minute to get the live Bubbles into the tank and the dead bubbles into the cup. I know better than to question if Lo has Cal distracted and I'm proven right when I step out of the doorway and only see Murphy.

"Lo said I'm on fish duty." Murphy holds out his hand and I give him the cup. He glances at the fish floating upside down. "Do you really think Dad's only going to kill one more of these?" His lips purse as his gaze lifts to me.

I fight the smile as I realize I couldn't ask for a better nephew. He's the perfect balance of his dad.

I clasp his shoulder. "I do wonder but I struggle to doubt Madame E."

"Me too." He nods and then turns, heading to the toilet to dispose of his father's fish.

I'm barely into the main room when Cal yelps.

"Ow!" The cupboard door snaps back and clearly it must have caught his fingers. "Evil snappy trappies."

Just as I step into the kitchen, Lo goes up on her tippy toes, shaking her head, and slides the baby-proofing clip off for him. "How many times do I have to show you how to do this?"

She looks at me and when I give her a quick nod, her body relaxes. Not only did my brother hit the jackpot in the kid department but Lo couldn't be more perfect for the nutter.

"No baby yet. Sully is just Cal-proofing," Brian mutters as he pulls the creamer from the fridge.

"Yeah, Tia isn't even born yet." Cal glares at me. "And it'll be years before she's tall enough to even reach up here. She"—he points to his short girlfriend—"can barely reach."

Eyes narrowing, she slams the cupboard shut. "Fine. You get it, then." Backing up, she crosses her arms and waits for Cal to figure it out.

He stares at it, tongue in cheek and lifts the clip. When it slaps back and closes on his finger, he screeches. "This cannot be safe!"

With a grunt, Brian leans around Cal and unlocks the cabinet. "Lift and squeeze," he grumbles.

Cal holds out a hand for the cup, but rather than hand it over, he passes it to Lo. It's hard to remember that living with this group annoyed me at first. Now, I wouldn't trade it.

Behind me, my wife giggles. "It's probably unnecessary," she says as she saunters in and heads for the same cabinet.

I snag her wrist and pull her back to my chest before pressing a kiss to her lips. "Good morning, beautiful."

Yeah. I wouldn't trade this for the bloody world.

She rolls her eyes, but she's smiling. "I woke up with you."

I smile. "And it was a very good morning."

She snorts, though when I lean down and press my hand to her belly, the sound is cut short.

"Good morning, love." I drop a kiss to her now-rounded stomach and savor the ability to do so. I don't take any of it for granted anymore. Not my wife's presence here or my son's love for bedtime stories. We'll only be a family of three for a little longer, so we've been having extra donut days and little adventures to places where T.J. can't climb up the rafters and scare the shite out of me.

Sloane and I have also focused on date nights. The baseball game Sloane surprised me with was one of the best. After dinner with Beckett and Liv Langfield, Sloane and I spent the night in the city. When we woke up, she showed me the baby furniture she'd been considering for the penthouse. Since, as she said, *we'll eventually end up back here.*

The way she said it, like we'll all return together when it's time, made it the greatest morning in a long bloody time.

The weekend ended perfectly that afternoon, when Cal, Lo, and Brian brought the boys to the city and the seven of us played a round of pickup in the park.

Life feels perfect. Happy. Right. And it's all because of the woman smiling down at me while I give her belly one more kiss.

That serene sensation dissipates quickly, though, at the doctor's office later that morning.

"Your blood pressure isn't where I'd like it to be," the doctor starts.

I grasp my wife's hand and squeeze. "What does that mean?"

"If we were only dealing with elevated blood pressure, I'd say maybe nothing, but there's also protein in your urine. And your amniotic fluid is on the low side." She studies her computer screen and sighs. "I'm not putting you on bed rest yet..."

Sloane lets out a relieved breath.

I don't feel nearly as relaxed. "But should we?"

Sloane whips her head in my direction. I'm sure she's glaring, but I remain focused on the doctor. The older woman settles her focus on my wife. "Not yet. But I want you to take it easy. No running around to court—"

"I don't go to court," Sloane interjects.

The doctor nods. "Desk work. Feet up at night. I want to see you next week so we can monitor this closely."

Sloane shakes free of my hold and nods several times, like she's working to convince herself that this is her reality. "Right. Of course."

"But Sloane..." The doctor's tone makes my hackles rise. "If you feel the slightest bit off, dizzy, nauseous, light-headed, I want you to call the office immediately. With your history, I don't want to take any chances."

With her history.

Though I outwardly keep it together, my mind spins. My wife needs me to be strong. But fuck, this is exactly what I've been worried about all these years. Doing this again. Risking her again.

I'm gathering my thoughts, readying to launch into a thousand questions, ready to try to covertly push the doctor to encourage Sloane into going on bed rest, when my wife grabs her purse with a trembling hand.

All the bluster escapes me. She doesn't need me to freak out. She needs me to be calm. So I thank the doctor, take the card she offers, where she's jotted her personal mobile number should we need it, and guide my wife out to the car.

When I go to take a left out of the parking lot, Sloane speaks up. "Where are you going?"

"Home."

"Sully, I have to go to the office."

My stomach rolls. "Maybe just rest today?"

Her face is ashen, her eyes wide with terror, but she shakes her head. "I'm not on bed rest yet. Please, Sully. I need to work for as long as I can."

I nod, the movement jerky, forced. The last thing I want is to leave my wife in the city. So after dropping her off, I head to the New York office of Murphy and Machon. I'll work from here until she's ready to go home.

Somehow, I make it through the day without pulling my hair out. Though I do spend the majority of the afternoon googling every possible symptom Sloane could present with and every suggestion for ways to help keep Tia on the inside for as long as possible.

By the time I pick her up, I'm spiraling again.

To keep myself from blurting every one of those suggestions and going over the list of reasons why I think she should quit her job— which will only raise my wife's blood pressure—I turn on music.

Sloane slumps against her seat and closes her eyes, mumbling along with "Don't Stop Believin'," every word wrong, as usual. As I head through the Lincoln Tunnel, my heart squeezes impossibly tight. I love this woman so goddamn much. When we finally pull up to the building in Jersey, she's sound asleep. I, on the other hand, am wound tighter than a bowstring, my knuckles white on the steering wheel.

I guide her inside and lead her straight to bed. Minutes after I've helped her change and tucked her in, she's out cold.

Only then do I rush out of the flat and stomp up the steps to

Madame E's place. It's early. Not even dinnertime, but even if it were two a.m., I'd have no qualms about bothering her. The woman inserted herself in our lives, so she only has herself to blame. Now I can't do a goddamn thing without wondering what Madame E knows.

The door swings open with a flourish, and she appears, totally at ease and dressed in one of her typical flowing dresses with a gold belt that jangles around her waist. "Good evening, Sullivan. Sebastian and I have been expecting you." She waves behind her to the ghost she alleges lives in our building.

I sneer. I can't help it. I'm too out of sorts to even hide my disdain for the ridiculousness she brings to every interaction.

Am I really asking a woman who believes in ghosts for advice on my wife's medical condition?

Then I remember the way Sloane's hands trembled this afternoon in the doctor's office and shake off any hesitation. "Tell me my wife and baby will be okay."

Madame E's expression softens. "Why don't you come in? I'll put a pot of tea on and we can chat."

"What do you know?" I plead. I can't just sit around. I need to *do* something.

The older woman frowns. "Sully, I only—"

"If you say you only see what you see, I'm going to lose it."

She shakes her head like she's at a loss, but footsteps on the stairs behind me catch our attention before she can respond.

Fuck. If I turn around and there's no one there, I really will get on the Madame E and Sebastian are real train. I turn around, and when my brother and Brian approach the landing, I breathe out a relieved breath. They're peering up at me with worried expressions, like they've heard our entire interaction.

"Good evening, gentlemen. Do you want to come in for tea?" Madame E offers.

Brian shakes his head. "Another time. Come on, Sul. Let's let Madame E enjoy her evening."

I nod woodenly, suddenly feeling foolish, and follow them downstairs. It isn't until the door to our flat is shut behind us that I even take a breath.

"Want a beer?" Brian asks as he heads toward the fridge.

I survey the living room. "Where's Lo?"

"Reading to the boys." Cal picks up a table tennis ball and tosses it in the air. "Want to tell us why you're such a broody dudey?"

Brian returns with three beers, tops all off, and hands one to me. I tip it back and drink half of it in one go. Not because I need the drink, but because I need the time to collect my thoughts. It's hard to explain this sensation inside my chest, the way I feel like if I don't hold on tight to what I have and make the exact right moves, I'll lose everything.

They wait me out, though Cal continues to toss the ball in the air.

I finally lean forward and snatch it.

To my surprise, he doesn't stop me and he doesn't complain. Bollocks. He must be really worried about me.

"The doctor said her amniotic fluid is on the low side and her blood pressure is higher than she'd like."

Cal's eyes widen, but Brian simply nods, the calm in every storm.

"Does that mean bed rest?" Cal asks, all teasing and walkie-talkie jokes long forgotten.

"She doesn't want that," I grumble.

"The doctor or Sloane? If it's Sloane, we can talk to her. Lo can talk to her." My brother stands like he's about to interrupt story time.

I yank him back down. "The doctor. She said Sloane needs to take it easy, but she doesn't need bed rest. Not yet."

"But you don't like that answer," Brian infers.

I pick at the label on my beer bottle, pulling it back and exposing the dark glass. "No. There's no reason for her to work. So why take the chance?" I shake my head. Fuck. Sloane would hate that answer. "I can't lose her."

"You won't. She's going to be fine," Brian assures me.

"We'll make sure of it," Cal promises.

Head down, I pull at my hair. "I'm scared."

That uncontrollable emotion consumes me even after our conversation is over and through T.J.'s bedtime routine. It eats at me as I settle beside Sloane two hours later. As I curl up beside her, studying her without touching her, not wanting to wake her.

"I can feel you watching me," she mumbles, not opening her eyes.

I press a kiss to her cheek. She looks gorgeous, all rumpled from sleep. "Sorry. Go to bed."

With a soft hum, she wraps an arm around me and snuggles in closer. "I'm going to be okay, Sully."

My eyes fall shut and my heart splinters. Of course, she knows I'm freaking out. She's probably known for hours. "I'm sorry if I worried you. I know you'll be fine. I'll make sure of it."

She angles back, her eyes locked on mine in the mostly dark room. "I know."

My throat clogs with emotion. "You do?"

Her lips tip up in a small smile. "Yeah, I know you'll make sure we have the best doctors and I know you'll be at my side every step of the way."

"You really believe it?"

For months, I've worked hard to prove myself. To make up for all my wrongs. To know that she sees how I've changed steals all the air from my lungs.

Sloane brushes her mouth over my cheek. "Yes, Sully, I believe it." She sets her hands against my heart. "I never once doubted that you would protect me. It was the emotional stuff that you were not so good at."

"I'm trying," I say. It guts me that I wasn't better all along.

"I know. And that's all we can do. Both of us. *Try*."

I bury my face in her neck. "I love you so damn much, Sloane. All I want in this life is you and our kids to be happy and healthy."

Eyes glazing over with tears, she takes a deep breath. "I love you too. And I am. Happy and hopefully healthy."

My heart skips at her words. Words that at one point I didn't think I'd ever hear again from her lips. Words I've been hoping to hear again but have been worried I don't deserve. My wife loves me. My wife, who I am utterly besotted with, who will always own my heart, still loves me.

I fall back against the bed with a smile on my face and laugh. The day's stress—hell, the year's stress—washes away the moment Sloane breaks into a fit of giggles.

Then we're reaching for one another, quickly discarding our clothes. Our bodies melt together as we tell each other we love one another again, this time without words.

CHAPTER 38
Sloane

Me: I think we should throw a party.

Lo: Oh, a baby shower! Yes! You've finally agreed!

Cal: I've already got the perfect theme.

Me: NO! I meant like a real party. A fun one. Maybe invite some women.

Lo: Sounds like a baby shower.

Cal: Balloon animals! Think about it. Fuzzy could be the model for it. A million giant cats floating through the air.

Lo: I've literally got chills.

Cal: It's awesome, right?

Lo: No, baby. No, it is not.

Me: Could the two of you focus? I'm talking about a cocktail party. Brian won't go out to meet women, so let's bring the women to him.

Lo: Oh my god. She's in love.

Cal: Who?

Lo: Sloane! She's in love, and now she
wants Brian to be in love too.

Me: You are so annoying.

Cal: Don't worry. Your secret is safe with us.
We won't tell him.

Sully: I'm literally in this chat.

Snorting, I shake my head and smile down at the phone. Just the sight of Sully's name on the screen makes me damn giddy. What is that?

Maybe it's love. Because Lo is right. I'm in love with my husband.

I try to cover my face so no one walking by my office sees my dopey smile, but really, why should I hide it? So what if I'm happy? Isn't that a good thing?

And I am. God, am I happy. The past month has been a fever dream. Despite my nerves surrounding the potential of ending up on bed rest, I wasn't lying when I told Sully I knew we'd be okay. My doctor has been keeping a close eye on my labs and insisting I come in weekly, and I'm doing everything I can to keep my blood pressure down—including heading home at a normal hour, putting my feet up, and focusing on the good in my life and not the stressors—and Sully's gone above and beyond to help with all of it.

Now that I've passed 34 weeks, I can breathe even easier. Going into labor soon wouldn't be ideal, and the idea of her ending up in the NICU is scary, but I have faith that we'll all be okay. Now if I can make it to nine months, that'd be stellar.

No matter when I deliver, we don't need a baby shower. Our room is barely big enough for Sully and me, and besides a bassinet and changing table, the baby doesn't need much for the first few months anyway. By the time she's old enough to sleep in a crib, we'll be back in New York City.

God, just the thought of moving back home with Sully, of returning to our home as a family of four, has my smile growing again.

Because I can see it. And I can see us being happy there.

Though I refuse to rush this time we have in Jersey. Surprisingly, I kind of enjoy it. I'll even go so far as to say that I'll miss it when we leave. Or maybe it's just my friends that I'll miss.

"What did baby daddy do now?" Julius asks as he saunters into my office, a wicked grin on his face.

I try to school my expression. "What are you talking about?"

He leans against my desk, studying me. "You're all smiley. Why are you all smiley?"

I roll my eyes and tap at my keyboard, ignoring him. "What's in your hand?" I point to the piece of paper he's holding tight between his fingers.

"I'll share mine if you share yours." This level of excitement from him makes me suspicious. Maybe it's dirt on Will. Maybe he's fumbled a case. It would serve him right after the stunt he pulled two months ago.

In the end, the Simpson matter resolved in our favor. Apparently, he'd done the mediation statement long before he assigned it to me. While I used to tolerate him, now I see him for what he really is: a weasel.

I've stayed away from him since then, and fortunately, since I was assigned to the estates division, he's stayed away as well.

I snatch the paper out of Julius's hand while he's distracted, still gloating, like he thinks he's getting one over on me. As I read the court order, though, my eyes narrow. "I've been appointed by the court to represent a child," I murmur.

It's a domestic violence matter. One that's arisen during a divorce. The child is developmentally disabled, so a special-needs trust will be required. That's where I come in.

This isn't how I typically find myself involved in these cases, so I'm immediately suspicious. "Where did this come from?"

"Your mother dropped it off on her way into Higgins's office ten minutes ago."

I groan. I should have known. This has my mother written all over it. What is she doing now?

Squinting, I look past him. "What are the chances I can make it to the elevator and out of the building without her knowing?"

Julius tilts his head. "Considering I told Higgins I'd send you in at ten, I'd say slim to none."

I pout. "Come on. You like me more than you like him."

"Until you take me away from this sad existence, baby mama, we're relying on his paychecks, so I assure you, I like him more."

I snort. "Et tu Brute."

He rolls his eyes. "Your husband says it better."

I wish I could laugh at his snark, but my mind is racing, working through scenarios that would get me out of this impromptu meeting with my mother and my boss.

I feel like I'm sixteen again. Which is ridiculous. I'm forty years old. My mother doesn't control me.

Though she does control half the district. And she garners the respect of every single person who does control me.

God, this is annoying.

My phone buzzes on my desk, and the sight of my husband's name momentarily lightens my mood.

> Sully: Lunch? I had a meeting in the New York office and don't feel like driving to Jersey, then coming back again.

I smile. The only reason he would have to come back again is to pick me up, which is completely unnecessary. But I know better than to argue.

> Me: It's only ten. I can't meet for a couple of hours. I can take a car service home tonight if you don't want to hang around.

Sully: I don't mind. I can get work done here
while I wait. I'll pick you up for lunch at 12.

Just knowing that I'll see him in two hours makes the idea of dealing with my mother a little less dreadful.

Though that dread is back in full force when I hear the familiar clickity clack of her heels. Her walk is distinct. She doesn't cower. No, she wants her victims to know that she's coming. I think making people nervous gives her a thrill.

But I refuse to give her that. Instead, I motion for Julius to go and turn my attention to my computer. When Julius announces over the intercom that she's here, I continue keeping my head down. "You can send her in."

Despite all my posturing, the moment my mother steps into my space, my head snaps up and my back straightens. My body is trained to peacock for this woman. "Hi, Mother."

It takes everything in me not to stand up. But if I have any hope of not discussing my pregnancy—a pregnancy I have yet to disclose because I'm not ready for her commentary—then I need to remain behind this desk. Hidden.

This is ridiculous. I'm *forty*, not sixteen. So what if I'm pregnant? So what if she's judgy about it? Her opinion shouldn't matter.

But I should have told her earlier. Shit. I should have dealt with this months ago. Though there's no time like the present, I suppose. I stand and cradle my stomach, making the bump, which is now well and popped, even more apparent.

My mother, whose middle name should be unflappable, registers my movement with nothing more than a raised brow. The reaction is so quick that if I weren't looking for it, I'd have missed it. But I didn't, and I take great satisfaction in the surprise. After the stunt she pulled with this job, I'm happy to return the favor. Also, I'm still trying to figure out what her angle is with this appointment in the domestic violence case.

"You look well." She doesn't even attempt to round the desk to greet me with a hug, and she doesn't make any mention of my obvious pregnancy.

I'd be disappointed if it weren't exactly what I expected.

When I was a little girl, there were no cuddles or bedtime stories. When she sent me to camps for the summer, educational ones, she didn't hold me tight and tell me she'd miss me. I'm not even sure she was home the day I left for college, and when I graduated, I received a perfunctory nod and a new car to take with me to law school.

My parents met all my needs physically, but they gave me little attention. Their way of parenting is the antithesis of mine, and I hope like hell Sully and I are doing a decent job with T.J.

"Thank you, Mother. You do too." And she does. Her hair—which is mostly gray since she'd never do something so frivolous as spend hours in a salon each month to keep up with coloring it—is pulled back in a low bun today. Her blue eyes, the same shade as mine, are still vibrant, and her skin, though aged, is still smooth because she rarely spends time in the sun. Her blue suit is simple, understated, and the large diamond on her left finger is the only outward sign of her wealth.

"My assistant just gave this to me. What's going on?" I hold up the paper, figuring I might as well dive right in.

She sits across from me, perching on the edge of the chair. "Will told me you've been taken off litigation."

Her tone is flat and unimpressed, which is not surprising in the least.

For once, I go with the God's honest truth. "I like estates, and now that I'm pregnant, keeping up with litigation files is a challenge."

My mother nods. "This case should help with that."

Confused, I stare at her. "How?"

"This will prove that you can do it all," she says like it should be obvious. "You'll be in court. You'll make a good impression. It's a win-win."

I grind my teeth together, though I can't exactly shoot down her theory. And I do like being in court.

She isn't wrong; the situation is pretty damn ideal, really. I just hate that she's the one giving it to me. Again.

"Why didn't you tell me you got me this job?" I ask pointedly.

"Why didn't you tell me you'd dismissed the divorce?"

My jaw ticks. She's too smart not to know the answer to that. She's already looked at the file. She knows it's still pending. A couple of months ago, Sully and I agreed to wait until after the baby is born to make any final decisions. Yes, we're both in this one hundred percent, but we've had plenty of other things on our minds, so we've stuck to the plan and haven't talked about the divorce proceedings at all.

But none of that is her business.

My mom huffs when she realizes I'm not going to give her a response. "I can only ask for so many favors, Sloane. You won't make partner here if you don't think outside the box. If you simply want to raise your babies and work on trusts, then it's probably best you go back to your husband's firm. It's bad enough that you've stopped litigating. At least there you were a partner."

Her words land, hitting me in a spot I don't think she even knew existed. One I was wholly unprepared for. "I was never actually a partner," I admit.

For the first time in my entire life, I think I actually shock my mother. She jolts backward. "What?"

I avert my gaze, peering out the window. "I wasn't a partner."

"What do you mean?"

I shrug, going for aloof, despite the way that fact has always bothered me. "The guys are full partners. I worked mostly from home after T. J. was born. I hoped that after he was in school..."

I don't finish my sentence. My mother isn't an idiot. She doesn't need me to explain how I naïvely believed that when T.J. went to kindergarten, I'd have time to focus on myself and my own goals again. I was the one at the top of our class in Columbia. I aced all the tests. When I joined Sully at his father's law firm, I had offers from just about every other large law firm in New York that was worth talking about. I had fast-track to partner written all over me. *I* was the prize.

Until I had a baby.

He wasn't an easy baby. He took more of my time and energy than I expected. Even after he went to kindergarten, someone had to do school drop-offs and pickups, and Sully never had time.

I was drowning, with a child who fought me every time I dropped him off, who would cry until I took him home with me. And on the days I could bribe him into going, I'd head to the office, only to be treated like I was there to catch up instead of work. Like I wasn't a lawyer there too. Not one of them saw me, least of all my husband.

I blink, forcing the thoughts from my head. I don't have it in me to go back to that time. Sully and I have worked through so much. Maybe we haven't touched on these parts yet, but that's probably because I've never mentioned how I felt about not being partner.

But we're good now. We're communicating. Every day, he goes above and beyond to show me that my career matters just as much as his. I'm not going to go borrowing trouble.

"I'm happy mother. I know this isn't the career you pictured for me—" My mother scoffs, but I hold up my hand, forcing her to hear me. "My child is happy. My life is full. And Sully and I will figure out how to move forward, together."

With a shake of her head, my mother stands. "I hope for your sake, you're right."

I hate that even after she leaves my office, her words stay with me.

CHAPTER 39

Sully

♥

Like a complete schmuck, I whistle all the way up to Sloane's floor. Happy doesn't even begin to describe how I feel lately. My wife loves me, my son hasn't climbed any structures and gotten stuck lately, and we're in the last quarter of the trust requirement.

In four months, we can move back into our penthouse in New York and I can return to my office here as well.

And now I get to have lunch with my gorgeous wife.

I step off the elevator, humming Frank Sinatra's "All the Way," and nod at every lawyer I pass. Many I recognize, though there are several new, young faces.

When I see Julius, I point at him. "Caesar, my mate!"

"Oh, baby daddy's in a better mood than baby mama." He arches a brow in warning. "Go easy on her."

I frown. What happened in the time between my text at ten and now?

If Will Higgins is responsible, I will actually break his nose. And I'll fucking relish it. At my wife's behest, I've said nothing since I found out about his disgusting ultimatum. It's better this way. Knocking his arse out would only cause more problems for Sloane.

But just imagining how good it would feel to wipe that smug look off his face makes my fingers twitch and my palms itch.

"Sully?" I snap to attention at the sound of my wife's voice. She's standing in the doorway, a sheet of paper in her hand.

Her dark hair is pulled back in a low ponytail, which is very unlike Sloane. She only wears it that way when she's nervous or angry. She gets overheated in those situations, and she hates the feeling of her hair sticking to her skin. She doesn't look red, though. She looks pale and tired, like she's seen a ghost.

I eat up the space between us quickly and wrap her in my arms. Though she's stiff at first, she softens quickly, letting out a long breath. "I'm really glad you're here."

"Always." I press a quick kiss to her forehead and guide her back into her office. Figuring she needs a few minutes to compose herself, I shut the door. "Want to tell me what's going on?"

She eyes the door, then her focus drifts down to the paper in her hand. She sighs. "My mother was here."

Ah, that makes far more sense. "Whatever she said, she's wrong," I tell her.

Sloane's mother has a way of making her feel inadequate, and she can do it in a matter of minutes. It's ridiculous, really. Sloane was a powerhouse in law school, and she created one hell of a career for herself before T.J. was born. And look at her now, back to rebuilding what she had to put on hold for so long. I'm unbelievably proud of her, and it baffles me that her mother isn't too.

Sloane lets out a dry, brittle laugh. The sound breaks my fucking heart. She's tired and dejected, and she looks so damn sad. "She had me appointed as guardian in this case, then said, and I quote, 'I can only ask for so many favors, Sloane. You won't make partner here if you don't think outside the box.'"

I frown. Why the fuck would she want to be partner here? I survey the room as if to emphasize my point. "Screw 'em. You don't need it. Do whatever you want."

Sloane shrugs. "It's not a bad case. The little boy was abused and needs a guardian ad litem to represent him in the divorce action." She thrusts the paper she's still clutching in my direction.

As I scan the case caption, my stomach sinks. "I'm on this case."

Eyes widening, she takes the document back from me. "You are?"

"Yes, I represent the mother. It's a bloody awful case."

"I'll have to read over the files."

I shake my head. "You absolutely shouldn't read over the files."

Brow furrowed, she shakes her head. "Why?"

Fuck, she really is wiped. If she were thinking clearly, it'd be as obvious to her as it is to me. So I spell it out for her. "Because you're going on maternity leave soon. This case won't be over by then, and when you come back to work for Murphy and Machon after maternity leave, we'll be conflicted out of the case if we're both on it."

Sloane steps back. "*For?*"

"Yes. When you come back to work for me, I won't be able to work on this case anymore," I explain slowly. Surely she understands the huge implications of all of this.

"*With*, Sully. When I come back to work *with* you."

I nod, though the anger in her tone confuses me. "Yes, same thing."

"No, it's not the same thing." Frustration practically oozes from her pores.

I don't understand why. Why would she want to stay here? Will has been bloody awful to her.

Now I'm frustrated. "Your mother is just trying to control you. Why are you allowing that?"

Sloane huffs. "She's just watching out for me."

"And I'm not?" I step back, heart in my throat and completely flummoxed. "You're not staying here, Sloane. I've played along with this game for long enough. After our baby is born, you're coming home." I snap my mouth shut, instantly realizing that I've fucked up. It's the damn incubator thing all over again. *Fuck.* "Wait." I reach out for her. "That's not what I meant."

She pulls back. "This *game?*" Her voice is shrill, her face now red in anger. "Is that all this is to you? A damn game?" She throws her arms out, the document rustling. "This is my *career*, Sully? My life. For years, my career has taken a back seat to yours. I gave up everything so you could advance. When is it my turn? Why do I have to be the one to give up this opportunity? Why can't you?"

"It's a domestic violence case." I rough a hand down my face. "Bloody hell, the woman needs my help."

"Oh, but the child doesn't need mine?"

"That's not what I meant, and you know it."

She whips around and paces across the room, each step a staccato beat against the floor, emphasizing her anger. "No, you just meant that if it comes down to who can be more helpful, the clear answer is that it's you. Your career comes first. Always. Your family. Your friends. Your firm. And I just work *for* you. In our marriage, at the firm, with our kids." She pulls up short and stares me down. "God, how could I have been foolish enough to think you'd changed?"

I pull at my hair. How the hell did this go so off the rails? "Sloane, no. I have changed, sweetheart—"

She holds up a hand. "Don't sweetheart me. I need—" She shakes her head. "I need space. I'm going to stay in New York tonight."

"Then I'm staying here too. I'm not leaving you like this."

Her eyes go hard, the blue the color of ice. "Go home to your firm, Sully. They can't possibly survive without you. But as you proved to me every time you chose it over me, I can survive just fine on my own."

CHAPTER 40
Sloane

My head is pounding. I barely slept last night. My mind was too busy running through our conversation—*no, our fight*—on repeat and working through what I could have done differently. Should I have agreed to turn down the appointment? Maybe.

Sully's work is so important. I've always believed that, and I've always been incredibly proud of him. Representing domestic violence victims, especially in divorce cases, is extremely taxing. It's noble work.

But why can't he see that what I do matters as well? Why does it always have to be one or the other? And why, when it is, am I always the other? The one who has to bend, who has to let go of goals and dreams.

But do you even want this?

The words are a mere whisper in the back of my head, coaxing me from my anger.

God, that's the hard part. I'm right to be angry, but do I even want the thing I'm fighting for?

What I want is for my husband to realize that my career matters too. What I want is for him to treat me like an equal. For years I gave up everything to support him and to raise T.J. I'm just asking for a little recognition. A little compromise. And partnership. In our marriage, and maybe at work too.

Maybe that's delusional after the way I stepped back for so long. But that doesn't stop his words from hurting, and it doesn't excuse the way he always fails to see my worth. He used to ask for my opinion. He'd ask for my help. Now I'm no one. Just another obligation. A person to take care of. I suppose it's better than not seeing me at all, but only marginally. I don't want to be another thing on his agenda. I want to be his equal.

I rub at my head, and the white squiggles behind my eyelids only get worse. I really need to lie down. This feels more like a migraine than a simple headache.

But I promised Lo I would meet with this Yoga Jess girl, and I refuse to let my best friend down. I can rest afterward.

The office is abuzz with activity when I walk in, which is no surprise. It's just a typical Wednesday in New York. No one else's lives have gone up in flames. Hell, is my life even in flames? That'd be exciting and new. Nothing about how I feel is new. The sensations rushing through me are far too familiar for my liking, since they've plagued me since T. J. was a baby. Now, though, they feel more jarring. Probably because I had convinced myself that Sully had changed. That he was different. That I was different. That *we* were different.

"Morning, Sloane." The greeting is echoed by person after person as I stride to my office. I nod to each one, though with every step I take, their voices grow more muffled. I need to get out of my head and focus on this meeting. I promised Lo.

"Baby mama!" Julius croons the moment I step into the entryway of our suite. Like every other day, his blond hair is slicked to the side, his jacket is perfectly pressed, and his navy pants stop at his ankle, leaving him looking like he should be heading out for a night on the town rather than stuck in this office.

"Good morning." Even to my own ears, my voice sounds despondent.

His smile falls. "What's wrong?"

I shake my head. "Is the new client here?"

He eyes me for another second, like he wants to pry. Instead, he nods and picks up a folder from his desk. "She's in the conference room. Want me to take your bag and bring you in a cup of tea?"

Coffee would be better, but tea will have to do. "Yes, thank you." I slip the bag down my arm, but as I hold it out, another wave of exhaustion hits me, making me stumble. This time the squiggles in front of me move rapidly, and I sway. As I reach for the desk to steady myself, Julius lunges for my arm. "I don't—" The rest of my words get stuck in my throat.

"Sloane," he says, his tone panicked. He grips both of my arms, holding me up, and shouts, "Someone call 911!"

Then it all goes dark.

CHAPTER 41
Sully

I didn't go home last night. After I called Cal and filled him in, he agreed to plan a fun night for Murphy and T.J. so I could stay in the city. Then I booked a room at a hotel near the penthouse so I'd be close if my wife needed me.

Needed me? I blow out a damn breath in frustration. Why in bloody hell would she need *me*? She's right. Time and again, I've failed her. Bloody hell, I'm the one who needs her.

She was right. She was right about everything.

Why should my career come first? My wants? My needs? Why is she the one who's always expected to bend? To compromise?

Is it because of the way my mother would speak about my father? Did her constant derision subconsciously make me think that my dad was right to work? To prioritize his career? The way she demonized it made me glorify it, perhaps. Because my mother was awful to us when we were boys.

I despised her, and the more terrible things she had to say about Terrance Murphy, the more I wanted to be like him.

Now I realize that I don't want to be either of them. Neither knew how to make a marriage work. Neither believed in compromise.

Though maybe my dad learned the value of it later in life. Maybe that's why he created this damn trust. He saw I was mucking it all up, so he did this to ensure we didn't make the same mistake he did. Yet here I am.

Because by picking my firm over my family, I did exactly what he did when he didn't put up a fight when Mum moved us to England all those years ago.

I need to do more than tell Sloane she's right. I need to make a change before I go to her. So I drive to Jersey the next morning, determined to get this right.

It's after ten a.m. by the time I get there. Cal is in the bathroom, getting changed, after having dropped off the boys at school, so I grab the walkie-talkie we keep in the flat and call down to Lo and Brian, asking them to meet us in the bathroom.

"*Sloane's* really does have better lighting," my brother says from my wife's little haven. He ducks lower, his eyes on the mirror as he styles his hair.

With a growl, I turn and face the wall. I can't focus on my brother's bloody hair right now.

"Sully?" Lo calls when she enters the flat.

"We're at *Sloane's*," Cal calls. He turns around and holds open the curtain, beckoning her to join us.

Brian follows close behind, a scowl on his face. "Why are we in here?"

I drag a hand down my face. "I'm moving back to New York."

"You're *what*?" Lo rears back.

"You heard me. I'm moving back to New York. Sloane thinks I put this firm first. That I constantly pick it over her. That I put my career before hers."

Lo tilts her head and shrugs like this isn't the first time she's heard this. Like she agrees. Brian and Cal both nod, like they see her point too. Like none of this surprises them.

Fuck. Every single one of them saw it? Fuck. Fuck. Fuck. Why was I the last to realize the real problem in my marriage? For months,

I've been thinking that if I paid attention to my wife, I could fix what I broke. But it's so much bigger than that.

"I'm done doing that. If that means the firm has to shut its doors, then so be it. We'll start over. I'm sorry, but—"

Brian holds up a hand. "Don't apologize for this. You've got a chance to be with the one person who makes you happy. You better fucking take it."

My heart clatters around wildly in my chest. As much as I appreciate the sentiment, I have no idea if I actually have a chance. But I have to try.

"We can start over in New York," Cal says.

Lo smiles. "Of course we can."

I blow out a breath. "Really? You're all on board? I was ready to throw down and force the issue."

Cal shakes his head. "Nothing matters more than family."

"Why do all the big conversations happen in the weirdest places?" Lo mutters as she takes in the small glowing stall we've crammed into.

Chuckling, Cal pulls her into his side. "I think that was Dad's whole point. That's why he set up this trust. To show us what really matters."

Brian smiles. "I think you're right. It's too bad I didn't write it better. Give us an out if we did the right thing."

Cal laughs, but I'm nowhere near feeling lighter. I have a hell of a lot more work to do today. I clap Brian on the back. "I've made peace with this. I can lose the firm, but I can't lose Sloane. I just want to fix my family. Be a better husband, a better daddy."

When my phone trills loudly from my pocket, I scramble for it, hoping it's Sloane. When the number for her office flashes on the screen, my whole body lights up. I'll tell her I'm coming to see her. And when I get there, I'll talk to her about the new firm. Get her input. We'll be partners. She'll be happy. I'll keep my wife. I'll keep my family.

"Sweetheart, I'm so sorry," I rush out.

"Sully, it's Julius. You need to get here quickly. It's Sloane. It's, uh...it's bad."

CHAPTER 42
Sloane

I hate hospitals. Most people do, because really what is there to love?

But I despise them. The smell, the sounds, the entire vibe? All of it sets me on edge.

But the hospital isn't the problem today. It's my stupidity. I'm here because I'm stubborn and I didn't listen to my body when it gave me so many warning signs.

Dammit. Hot tears lick down my cheeks as my doctor explains how my blood pressure has shot up and what our next steps are.

I hold my stomach, unwilling to let go of this precious life inside me, even for a second, and force myself to listen. I need to hear this.

Dammit, what is taking Julius so long? He's better at listening than I am.

When the door swings open and hits the back of the wall with a loud thud, I whip toward the sound.

What the hell is wrong with h—

My thoughts screech to a halt at the sight.

The tears make it difficult to make out the details, but there's no confusing my six-foot-four wall of a husband for my slim, young assistant. He's wearing a look of fear, the lines on his face taut and severe. "*Sweetheart.*"

The word breaks from his chest in a sob, and he's by my side in two strides, pressing his hands to my face, then my shoulders, then my stomach. He crumples, resting his head on my belly, his shoulders shaking. "I'm so sorry," he says between sobs.

I run soothing circles through his hair and shush him. "She's all right. She's fine. Tia's fine."

He turns his head, his red eyes meeting mine. "But are you?"

I manage to form a sad smile. "I'm still breathing."

Eyes shut again, he shudders.

Shit. Clearly my attempt at levity did not land the way I hoped.

"That's not—" He shakes his head. "That's not good enough."

I nod as tears crest my lashes again. He's right. This was too close. And it's my own damn fault. My own stubbornness is to blame.

"Mr. Murphy, as I was telling your wife, your baby is doing okay. As is she. For right now. But that was too close."

Sully straightens at the doctor's words and looks up at her like he's only now realizing that we aren't alone. Maybe he is. Maybe, when he got here, all he saw was me.

That sets off another fresh set of tears.

"For the moment, you and the baby are healthy enough for the pregnancy to continue. But only if you're on bed rest. Between the protein in your urine and the low level of amniotic fluid, an event like today could easily lead to an emergency C-section."

I shake my head. "I'll be good."

"We'll do whatever is necessary," Sully tells her.

The doctor gives us a detailed list of what she wants us to do. Mainly, I need to rest. Work is out of the question, but honestly that's the last thing I want to do.

After she's gone, my nerves take over and dread washes through me. Sully has every reason to be angry with me. I could have lost our child, all because of my stubborn pride.

A full minute after she's gone, he's still staring at the door, like he can't bear to look at me.

"I'm sorry," I whisper, the pain of this moment making it hard to breathe.

Seated beside me on the hospital bed, he spins, a severe frown pulling his eyebrows together. "What are you sorry for?"

I grip my stomach with both hands, unable to meet his gaze. "I could have lost her. It would have been all my fault."

"We could have lost *you*," Sully says, sounding tortured. "I could have lost you, and it would have been all *my* fault."

My heart stumbles. *What?*

"Sweetheart." Tone softening, he searches my face like he's trying to find the words to explain what's going on in his mind. "I'm so sorry. I've let you down again and again. I should have been with you. I should have—" He shakes his head. "No more. We're not doing this anymore. We're moving back to New York. You need rest. Quiet. You need a fucking regular bathroom and your bed."

I roll my eyes. "Sloane's is fine. And our bed in Jersey isn't that bad."

His jaw ticks and those blue eyes go stormy. "We're not going back to Jersey. Ever. You were right. I picked the firm again and again. Over you. Over the love of my life." He pulls at his hair and lets out a frustrated grunt. "I can't believe you stayed as long as you did. That you put up with it all."

"*Sully.*"

"I told the others this morning. Fuck the trust. Fuck the firm. You're all that matters."

I reach for my husband's hand, desperate to assure him, to calm him down. This is obviously the adrenaline talking. The fear. "Sully, I'm fine. You don't have to throw your whole life away. You heard the doctor; I'm going to be okay."

Sully straightens, looking affronted. "I'm not doing it because of this. I'm doing it because I choose you over everything. It might have taken me fucking forever to realize that I was taking you for granted, but you and our children are all that matter."

Shocked, I open my mouth, but only a choked sound comes out.

For so many months, T.J. and his cousin have spent every waking moment together. They've become best friends. And I've loved all the time I've spent with Lo and the guys. The Ping-Pong tournaments and games of pool after dinner. The bedtime stories. The ridiculous Christmas tree. The bathroom that morphed from my worst nightmare into my sanctuary. Karaoke nights and laughter.

All of it has changed my life for the better. And during our time there, I fell in love with my husband again.

If we move back to the city, then that's all gone. The firm. This special time. On top of all of that, if we move back, then every one of the people who has been by my side, supported me, helped me survive not only our separation but our reconciliation, will lose everything. I can't be the reason they lose their livelihoods.

With a heavy breath, I squeeze my husband's hand. "I choose you too."

Eyes wide, he opens his mouth, but before he can respond, I go on. I'm not done yet.

"You and our children and our family mean everything to me. Maybe I needed to hear you say that you would pick me, and I appreciate it more than I can express right now, but I don't want to lose the firm." As soon as the words are out, an assuredness washes over me, reinforcing my belief. "It's our family firm."

Sully's expression is understandably guarded. "What are you saying?"

It's time to jump. To leap and trust that we'll make it. For better or worse. The only way forward is for us to *try.* "I'm saying let's dismiss the divorce filing. I told you I wanted to do this, but I can't be half in, half out. So I'm in...if you'll have me."

All those severe lines disappear in an instant, and Sully lights up like a kid, making him look so much like T.J. "Are you kidding me? Of course I'll have you." He scoots in close and palms my cheek. "I love you." He murmurs the words against my lips.

"I love you too." I grasp his forearm, clinging to him. "And I'm so sorry it took me so long to get here, but I don't want to be anywhere else."

"So you're coming back to Murphy and Machon?"

"If you'll have me."

"Oh, sweetheart, it's *your* firm. Just like I am. Completely yours."

"I'm yours too."

He breaks into a glorious smile. "Bloody hell, I've never heard anything better."

Then my husband kisses me, and my world rights itself again.

CHAPTER 43

Sully

"Hey love," I whisper softly as I smile down at my tiny daughter. Ten finger and ten toes and the sweetest little face I have ever seen. Six pounds of perfection.

I press a kiss to the top of her forehead, the fresh scent of baby powder overtaking the harsh antiseptic of the hospital.

Tia's little eyes crack as she blinks up at me.

Tia Hope Murphy didn't give us quite the scare her brother had. After a few weeks of bed rest the doctors decided it was time for a c-section. The whole thing went as smooth as any c-section can go, and now my wife is resting in the bed beside me and our daughter is lying in my arms.

Happy can't possibly describe this feeling rushing through me.

Tia yawns and her eyes drift closed again so I glance over at my gorgeous wife, who's sleeping peacefully.

The peace is fleeting. Cal will be here with the boys any minute now.

"Mom! Dad!" With a knight helmet on his head and a sword in his hand, T.J. bursts inside the hospital room.

"Shhh." I nod toward his mum who is already stirring.

As soon as he spots us, T.J rushes forward. Quickly, I twist to keep the baby away from the plastic weapon.

"T.J.," Lo huffs as she, Cal and Murphy hurry in after him. "We aren't allowed to run."

My son shrugs and drops his sword on the empty chair before he moves toward Sloane again. "I was excited."

I reach out and catch T.J. with my free hand, stopping him from reaching his mum."Be careful. She has a hurt stomach."

T.J. frowns but he stays a step back, and I can see the concern on his little face.

"We're excited to see you too." Sloane clears her throat, attempting to get rid of the husk in her voice. "What's with the costume?" Her eyes move from T.J to Murphy. She shift and then winces as she moves to give T.J. a hug.

That's when I notice that all four of them are wearing matching pink t-shirts.

My son looks down at the shirt he's wearing which announces he's the *best big brother*. "Well Uncle Cal said we need to take care of the people that we care about and that sometimes that means doing things we hate." He scowls and grumbles, "Like wearing pink to claim our sister."

Cal beams. "I got you both shirts too. Best mommy and better daddy!"

I glance at the *best aunt*, *best uncle*, and *best cousin* shirts that the three of them are wearing and then glare at my brother. "Really, I don't get best daddy?"

Cal shrugs. "We all know *I'm* the best daddy. Don't worry though, we know you're trying."

A half scoff, half laugh breaks through my lips. My brother, the king of humility. Motioning to T.J., I say, "Take off the helmet and come see your sister."

"Oh, yeah, I forgot about the helmet," T.J. mutters as he pulls it off his head. "We took a horse ride through the park to come meet the princess."

"It was an adventure," Cal explains as he wraps an arm around Lo's shoulders. "The king and queen and their best knights took a horse drawn carriage just like in the old days."

Murphy glances up at his father. "It was awesome until the horse pooped and it smelled."

Sloane perks up. "Wait there were horses in the park?" She glances at me and my face settles into a frown.

"Yeah." Lo leans into my brother, a ghost of a smile on her lips. "We were planning to walk and fight some trees along the way. Ya know get some energy out. But, this guy—" she points over her shoulder—"took one look at the line of horses and changed plans."

Murphy shrugs. "So we didn't get energy out."

"But we had fun." Cal and T.J. say almost simultaneously.

"That's odd. I heard they didn't do those horse rides anymore," I mutter, standing up and offering my seat to T.J.

Lo giggles. "Oh, some companies say that to gullible schmucks to get them to ride the bikes instead."

Sloane snorts and her eyes find mine. "Schmucks, huh?"

For a second I think about apologizing but then I stop. "Ya know what? I think those bikes can make for a perfect date."

My wife's smile softens and I know without a doubt she's remembering our second first date. The pride of knowing my wife well enough to read her thoughts again warms my heart. We've come so far. And although I hate the pain we went through I can't say I'd change where we are now.

"Dad! I want to hold her!" T.J. whines, drawing my attention back to him.

I bend down, and help T.J. adjust his arms before gently placing a swaddled Tia into his arms. The second she settles against his chest, my heart explodes. I blink hard. Across from me my wife's eyes fill with tears.

A perfect moment.

T.J. blinks down at her. "Why doesn't she have arms?"

Lo snorts and I huff out a breath. "There inside the blanket buddy."

He shrugs. "Weird." Then he shifts closer. "I guess she's kind of cute," he says, and I think he's about to press his lips to her nose when she lets out a miniscule burp. T.J. rears back. "Ewwww. What was that?" He looks on horrified as she burps again and this time she spits up too. "Get it away from me," he cries.

I grab Tia back as gently as I can before T.J. throws her, but hardly have her settled in my arms before Lo swoops in with a burp cloth. "You have to share, Sully," she teases before taking my daughter and settling beside Sloane on the bed. The two women whisper back and forth as they stare down at our girl.

I catch my brother staring at Lo, a look of longing in his eyes. "Ready to add to the family, huh?" I tease.

He licks his lips nervously. "She wouldn't even marry me."

"After two weeks of dating. Like a reasonable person she said no. I bet now she might feel different."

He swallows but before he can say more the door behind us opens again and Brian appears wearing a pink shirt that labels him the *second best uncle.* Clearly, a Cal special. "I heard we have a cute addition for our awful apartment!" Brian jokes.

"No she pukes, that's not cute." T.J grumps before he sees the beverage carrier in Brian's hand. "Slushies!"

"Yup. One for the big brother. And the big cousin." He hands them out. "And one for the funny man." He passes one to Cal and my brother completely lights up, all thoughts of Lola's rejection to his ridiculous proposal months ago long gone.

Brian heads for Sloane, a tray of coffee in his other hand. "And for mommy," he says, pressing a kiss to her cheek. "A tray full of caffeine as requested."

"You're the best," Sloane mutters as she grabs one of the cups from the tray.

Brian sets the other tray down and then rubs his now empty hands together. "Now give me the little girl."

"Ya know," Cal says swallowing his blue sugar rush. "I think we need to schedule a session with Madame E."

I send him a side eye.

"No really." He lowers his voice. "Look at that guy. He's totally ready for a new shirt. Maybe he can be *tied for second best daddy*."

Even as I shake my head, I can't deny as I watch my best friend coo down at my daughter that I see what Cal means. Brian might not realize how ready he is for his own happily ever after, but it's obvious to the rest of us.

"I think we can make it happen," Cal sings.

I glare at him. "Butt out."

Cal laughs and shakes his head. He's totally not going to listen.

Our women glance over, wondering what Cal and I are arguing about. Meanwhile, Brian ignores us completely and the boys play quietly in the corner. I smile, loving this moment with our little family. It might not always be perfect, but I wouldn't change a thing.

CHAPTER 44
Sloane

"Aw, love. Don't cry."

I blink away the sleep from my eyes and take in the scene before me. God, this man is delicious. My husband is shirtless as he bounces around our tiny bedroom with the most beautiful little girl in his arms. Our daughter.

It's been a week since Tia entered our lives. Since then, Sully has handled every diaper, including a few blowouts, talking our little one through them with the gentlest tone.

Calling her *love* each and every time.

God, do I love him.

And our three best friends have been keeping T.J. occupied so he doesn't feel like he's being held captive in this room with us.

Terrance Murphy might have been on to something when he created that trust.

Tia lets out one of those cries that is too adorable not to smile over. Unfortunately, the sound triggers my boobs to swell, and a moment later, moisture leaks from them. "Bring her to me," I say, taking Sully by surprise.

"Morning, sweetheart. I was hoping you could get a few more minutes of sleep, but I think she's too hungry to wait."

I laugh lightly. "I got that."

Sully settles on the bed beside me and helps me adjust Tia. As soon as she gets comfortable, she latches on and quiets down quickly. The girl loves to eat.

Sully presses a kiss to my shoulder. "Did you get any sleep?"

I catalog the precious details of our gorgeous girl like I do every time she's in my arms. She's got a head of dark hair and creamy skin, with big blue eyes that are just like mine. Her nostrils are heart-shaped, which might be one of her most adorable attributes. Or maybe it's her little toes, which she curls up and twists when she gets hungry. Or her teeny, tiny hands that ball into fists.

I can't stop staring at her.

I bring my nose to her head and inhale, soaking up that newborn scent. If only someone could figure out how to bottle it, the world would be a happier place.

"I got a few hours," I tell him.

Sully's good about waking up with me when Tia cries, but he often dozes while I feed her, so I try to let him sleep until she cries again.

He's been involved in every moment for the last week, determined to prove to me that this isn't just a phase. He's a better daddy this time around. A better partner. And he's intent on staying that way.

"T.J. was asking if we could take him to the park today," Sully says, his eyes full of uncertainty.

Honestly, the fresh air sounds like a great idea. It would feel good to stretch out my legs and act like a human again.

I smile. "Sounds perfect. After I feed her, I'll put her down for a nap and take a shower. Then I can feed her again before we get in the car. With any luck, she won't fuss too much."

Sully presses a kiss to Tia's head. "My love would never."

I laugh. Right. The girl already has her daddy wrapped around her finger.

Three feedings—and diaper changes—later, we've finally

unloaded the carriage from the back of our new SUV, and T. J. is bouncing with unrestrained energy, ready to rush to the swings.

"Let's have lunch first," Sully tells him, carrying a cooler that he must have packed during one of Tia's many feedings. Thank God for that too, because now that I think about it, I'm starving.

"But I want to take a swan ride after lunch," T.J. says. It's something I've always wanted to try, but T.J. used to scream if we brought him anywhere near them, so I'm shocked that he's asking to go on one.

"Hey, bud. Let's eat first. Then you can pick what you want to do."

T.J. huffs like a bull and stomps his foot, but with one look from Sully, he straightens.

That reaction is just as shocking. Our strong-willed boy rarely listens that quickly.

Sully guides us to an area surrounded by large sycamore trees with enough shade to lay out a blanket. Once I'm seated, he scoops Tia out of her stroller and sets her in my lap. "I'll get the food set up, and then I'll take her so you can eat."

I keep my eyes on T.J. as he runs between trees, chasing after a chipmunk, so I don't notice that Sully's returned with our food until he clears his throat.

He's kneeling beside me, a little closer than I expect, when I turn toward the sound.

Kneeling... on one knee.

And between two fingers, he holds a gorgeous diamond ring.

My throat grows tight at the expression on his face. So hopeful and loving.

"*Sully.*" His name is a breath on my lips. An answered prayer.

He smiles. "Sweetheart, I have loved you for nearly two decades. We've been through it these past few years, and I can't begin to explain how grateful I am that you're giving me this second chance. You've given me two beautiful children and more love and happiness than I deserve."

Tears quickly form and flow down my cheeks. "You deserve all the happiness."

Angling in, he swipes at the tears.

I don't mind them one bit. These are tears of joy. We've earned them.

"The last time I did this, I was full of ideas. I thought I knew precisely what I was signing up for. Promising to love you for the rest of my life was as easy as promising to breathe."

Tia squirms, her face scrunching up, and lets out the tiniest wail.

Sully rubs her head softly, and when she settles, he takes a deep breath. "But the truth is, I didn't understand that loving you is only part of this promise. Because love is an action, not just a feeling."

I nod. God, he's got it all right.

"So today I'm not just promising to love you for the rest of our lives. I promise to show up. I promise to be present. I promise to hold you and talk to you and have fun with you." He smiles, and then, in a low whisper, like he's nervous Tia will understand, he adds, "And find random closets where I can fuck you."

I cough out a laugh. "Yes. Yes, to all of that."

He grins. "I haven't finished."

With a roll of my eyes, I huff, but I nod for him to continue.

"And I promise to be there for our children. I promise to make time for all of us. To put us first, always."

I give it a few beats before saying, "Are you finished now?"

Lips twitching, he shrugs. "Yes, sweetheart, I think I am. So, what do you say? Will you be my wife again?"

My answer is simple and truer than I could have imagined a few months ago. "A thousand todays would never be enough. Yes, Sully. Of course I'll be your wife again."

With a small whoop, he hovers close and presses his lips to mine. With this kiss, we promise to keep showing up. To keep trying. To keep loving one another. Knowing full well that it won't be easy, that life will get in the way, and that we'll have to work to keep our marriage going.

That marriage is a daily commitment. An action. A choice.

And I'll choose him every single day.

When he pulls back, he's smiling. "You hear that, love? Your mommy agreed to marry me again." He brushes his lips over her head. "Teej," he calls, turning around. "She said yes."

Excitement rushes through me. T.J. was in on the surprise? No wonder he listened to Sully so easily when he gave him that look.

When T. J. doesn't appear from behind the tree he was just running circles around, a niggle of worry works its way through me.

"T.J." Sully stands and scans our surroundings. "Did you see which way he went?"

I shake my head. "He was right behind that tree."

With a nod, he steps off the blanket. "I'll go look for him."

"Here, take the baby. I'll help."

He's back in a heartbeat, putting Tia in the stroller. Once he's helped me to my feet, we wander, calling for our son. As seconds bleed into minutes, panic grips me and my stomach twists more painfully. Each time we yell his name, more bystanders join in our search. I'm pulling my phone from my pocket to find a photo to show the people offering to help, on the verge of hyperventilating, when Sully grabs my arm and mutters, "Oh fuck."

He points to the middle of the lake, where our precocious son is sitting in a damn white swan boat. Crying.

"How the hell?"

Sully grasps my hand and puts it on the stroller handle, ensuring I've got it, and takes off. "Stay right there, bud. Dad's coming."

"I wanted the swan," T. J. cries, "but I don't like the water."

Right. The kid doesn't like heights, yet he scaled a building last fall. And he's afraid of water, so naturally, he'd jump into a swan boat. It'd be comical if it wasn't so scary.

My husband rushes toward the dock, and without hesitation, jumps in. He surfaces quickly, covered in mud, and stands, the water hitting him below his waist.

Only once he's dragged the damn swan boat to the dock and

pulled T. J. out of it—T. J. completely dry and my husband covered in muck—do I finally breathe.

My little guy launches himself into my arms, and I squeeze him tight. Unable to let him go, I eye Sully, trying not to laugh as he pulls mud leaves from his shoe.

"You better say thank you to your daddy."

T. J. turns around in my arms and faces him. "He's Super Daddy."

Sully smiles easily. "Better than the firefighters who rescued you?"

"The best," T. J. agrees.

He's right. Sully's not just a better daddy. He's the best daddy around. And he's mine.

EPILOGUE
Sully

There's nothing more beautiful than my wife nursing my daughter, her lips puffy from the kiss I just gave her, a hickey on her neck, and my ring on her finger.

"Stop staring at me," she grumbles without looking up. While I stare at her, she stares at the adorable seven-pound, eight-ounce bundle in her arms. I know her precise weight because we've been to the pediatrician every other day this week to weigh her since her reflux has made it difficult for her to gain weight.

"Impossible." I drop a kiss to her forehead and head for the door so I can stop by the bathroom to fix my tie in front of the mirror. "I'll take Tia down to the office before court so you can shower."

I've got a hearing I can't avoid, and Sloane swears she doesn't need me staring at the two of them all day. She insists she'll be fine, and if she's not, she's got the walkie-talkie, so she can contact the rest of the crew in the office.

In the living room, Lo and Brian are drinking coffee. Cal has already left to take the boys to school.

"Make sure you have those walkie-talkies on," I remind them.

With a sigh, Brian pulls one from his pocket and waves it in my direction.

"Test it out," I tell him.

"Oh, for fuck's sake," he grumbles. "You sound like Cal."

"Oh, sorry for being a caring father who wants to make sure his wife and baby have help should they need it."

Lo flattens her lips, trying not to laugh at me.

I motion to her. "You too. Where's yours?"

"Right here." She swipes it off the counter. "They're all set to the loudest setting, per your request, and I'll keep mine on the charger at my desk so there's no risk of it dying."

I nod. That's good. Very good. But...

Shit. "I should just stay here. Cal can handle it." I drop my tie onto the couch.

"No." This comes from the open door to the bedroom.

Sloane.

In her robe, with the sash cinched tight, no baby in sight, she glares at me. "I'm fine. I love you and I love how overprotective and caring you are, but..." She gives me a smile like she knows I won't like what she says next, so she's softening me up. "You're smothering me."

I walk toward her. With her dark hair messy, her eyes still a little swollen from lack of sleep, and her face flushed with annoyance, she's the most beautiful woman I've ever seen.

Settling my hands on her hips, I murmur, "I just love you so much."

Smiling, she presses a kiss to my jaw. "I love you too, baby, but you have to work."

I frown. She's not exactly wrong, Cal could never handle this divorce.

It's the two women who were insistent that they should cheat with the same person. Apparently, they found a willing participant.

Cal would find that way too fascinating, and though the basis isn't a lie, it's not exactly playing fully with the truth either.

"Oh, and don't forget you're meeting with Jess today," Sloane tilts to one side, eyeing Brian.

Lo claps. "Yes. This is going to be brilliant."

Her excitement throws me for a loop. Lo is typically all business. No-nonsense. She must really like her yoga instructor.

I swipe my tie from the couch and leave them to talk about the case while I head to the bathroom to finish getting ready. Then, while Sloane takes a shower, I take Tia down to the office so I can look over the divorce file before court. I don't even make it through one email before a familiar warmth coats my shoulder.

"Ah, my little love. Is your belly bothering you again?" I pat her back and grab one of the handful of burp cloths I brought with me. I dab at her mouth first, adjusting her so she's not resting in spit-up, then head toward the stairway so I can change.

Before I can make my way up, Madame E appears out of nowhere, and I go rigid. The woman still creeps me out, even if she's helped me a time or two.

"Things are about to get messy," she singsongs, her bracelets jangling along like a warning.

I scowl, motioning toward the spit-up on my shoulder. "That was an easy one, Madame E. You aren't even trying with your predictions today."

"I wasn't talking about you. I was talking about that." She points to the front of the office, where Cal and Lo are greeting a client.

I frown. Shit, did Cal pick up a slushie on his way back to the office? If he spills it on a client, I'll kill him.

Cal shifts, giving me a glimpse of the woman he and Lo are chatting with.

Stomach bottoming out, I grab the walkie-talkie out of my pocket. "Uh, Sloane, I'm gonna need you to get down here."

The speaker crackles to life. "Did she throw up again? Dammit. I'm sorry. I know you have court. I'll come get her."

"That's not the issue," I grumble, my eyes still on the blonde I'd recognize anywhere. Brian used her photo as a bookmark in every one of his textbooks during our first year of law school.

I press down on the speaker. "What's the name of the client Cal and Lo were trying to get you to work with? The one Brian is meeting today?"

"Um, Yoga Jess?" Sloane says, her tone tinged with confusion. "Why?"

"Because the woman I'm looking at isn't just Yoga Jess, sweetheart. It's *Brian's* Jess."

"Oh shit," my wife mutters.

Oh shit is right

Nodding, Madame E singsongs, "I told you things were about to get messy."

Want to find out what happens when Brian's ex-girlfriend hires him?
Read **Bonus Daddy** now!

Acknowledgments

First and foremost, I (Jenni) need to say a huge thank you to Brittanée Nicole, who took over this book when it was only three quarters of the way finished and brought it home for us. Without complaint she jumped in when I needed her and made Better Daddy the best book it could be. You are the best friend a girl could ask for.

Now we also have a ton of other people to thank.

Thank you Sara, for making the Dad Com release happen. Without you we could not do what we do. You also come through no matter what we throw at you. And lately you have had more than any other one person could do. But you are literally the best. We love you so much and appreciate you more than we could ever express.

This book would not have come together without the help of some truly amazing people. Thank you Daphne Elliot for taking on this group project again with us. We keep throwing these ideas at you and you jump in full swing with us. Thank you Tiffany, Sara,and Jess, who helped us make this happen. More importantly though, the sincerest of thanks to Tiffany for helping us navigate this multi-cast audio production. To our beta readers, this book would not be what it is without your help and feedback!

To our lovely editor Beth, thank you for loving these guys and their girls as much as us and making the book better as you always do. Thank you for being flexible with us and we know we really made you jump around with this one. But you didn't hesitate to step us and be there for us. We are so lucky to have you as part of out team.

To our incredible street teams who help promote our books day in and day out, every release gets better because of you! We are in awe of your friendship and support. A huge thank you to Elen for the gorgeous cover image and the drawings brought Sully and Sloane to life. And to Melissa for creating the gorgeous covers. Especially thank you for not giving up when we ask for another option and another. You are the best.

Thank you Alyssa and Jeff for making sure the book was polished with your amazing proofing.

Finally, none of this would be possible without you, our amazing readers. Thank you for all of your messages, your Tiktoks, your dms, your posts and your rants. There is nothing we love more than hearing from each of you how a character affected you, or how a storyline made you laugh. We love your reviews, your anecdotes, and the notes you send. Make sure you follow us on facebook, instagram, and Tiktok (and join our Patreon) to keep up to date with the rest of this hilarious bunch.

Also by Brittanée Nicole

Bristol Bay Romance

She Likes Piña Coladas

Kisses Sweet Like Wine

Over the Rainbow

Love and Tequila Make Her Crazy

A Very Merry Margarita Mix-Up

Boston Billionaires

Whiskey Lies

Loving Whiskey

Wishing for Champagne Kisses

Dirty Truths

Extra Dirty

Mother Faker

(Mother Faker is Book 1 of the Mom Com Series, but is also a lead in to the Revenge Games alongside Revenge Era. This book can be read as a Standalone, or after Revenge Era and before Pucking Revenge)

Revenge Games

Revenge Era

Pucking Revenge

A Major Puck Up

Boston Bolts Hockey

Hockey Boy

Trouble

War

Playboy

Standalone Romantic Suspense

Deadly Gossip

Irish

Monhegan Summers (Co-Written with Jenni Bara)

Summer People

Dad Coms (Co-Written with Jenni Bara)

Who's Your Daddy

Better Daddy

Also by Jenni Bara

Want more Boston Revs Baseball

Mother Maker - Cortney Miller

The Fall Out - Christian Damiano

Back Together Again - Mason Dumpty

The Fake Out - Emerson Knight

The Foul Out - Kyle Bosco

Finding Out - Coach Wilson

The Freak Out - Asher Price

Curious about the baseball boys from the NY Metros

NY Metros Baseball

More than the Game

More than a Story

Wishing for More

Monhegan Summers (Co-Written with Brittanée Nicole)

Summer People

Dad Coms (Co-Written with Brittanée Nicole)

Who's Your Daddy

Better Daddy